THE MORTAL TEMPEST

OTHER BOOKS BY ANNA DURAND

The Mortal Falls (Undercover Elementals, Book One)
The Mortal Fires (Undercover Elementals, Book Two)
The Janusite Trilogy (Undercover Elementals, Books 1-3)
Obsidian Hunger (Undercover Elementals, Book Four)
Unbidden Hunger (Undercover Elementals, Book Five)
Cyneric (Undercover Elementals, Book Seven)
Echo Power (Echo Power Trilogy, Book One)
Echo Dominion (Echo Power Trilogy, Book Two)
Echo Unbound (Echo Power Trilogy, Book Three)
Passion Never Dies: The Complete Reborn Series
Banished in the Highlands (A Hot Scots Prequel)
The Notorious Dr. MacT (A Hot Scots Prequel)
The British Bastard (A Hot Scots Prequel)
Dangerous in a Kilt (Hot Scots, Book One)
Wicked in a Kilt (Hot Scots, Book Two)
Scandalous in a Kilt (Hot Scots, Book Three)
The MacTaggart Brothers Trilogy (Hot Scots, Books 1-3)
Gift-Wrapped in a Kilt (Hot Scots, Book Four)
Notorious in a Kilt (Hot Scots, Book Five)
Insatiable in a Kilt (Hot Scots, Book Six)
Lethal in a Kilt (Hot Scots, Book Seven)
Irresistible in a Kilt (Hot Scots, Book Eight)
Devastating in a Kilt (Hot Scots, Book Nine)
Spellbound in a Kilt (Hot Scots, Book Ten)
Relentless in a Kilt (Hot Scots, Book Eleven)
Incendiary in a Kilt (Hot Scots, Book Twelve)
Wild in a Kilt (Hot Scots, Book Thirteen)
Lachlan in a Kilt (The Ballachulish Trilogy, Book One)
Aidan in a Kilt (The Ballachulish Trilogy, Book Two)
Rory in a Kilt (The Ballachulish Trilogy, Book Three)
Brit vs. Scot (A Hot Brits/Hot Scots/Au Naturel Crossover Book)
The American Wives Club (A Hot Brits/Hot Scots/Au Naturel Crossover Book)
A Novel Secret (A Hot Brits/Hot Scots/Au Naturel Crossover Book)
One Hot Chance (Hot Brits, Book One)
One Hot Roomie (Hot Brits, Book Two)
One Hot Crush (Hot Brits, Book Three)
The Dixon Brothers Trilogy (Hot Brits, Books 1-3)
One Hot Escape (Hot Brits, Book Four)
One Hot Rumor (Hot Brits, Book Five)
One Hot Christmas (Hot Brits, Book Six)
One Hot Scandal (Hot Brits, Book Seven)
One Hot Deal (Hot Brits, Book Eight)
One Hot Favor (Hot Brits, Book Nine)
Natural Obsession (Au Naturel Nights, Book One)
Natural Passion (Au Naturel Trilogy, Book One)
Natural Impulse (Au Naturel Trilogy, Book Two)
Natural Satisfaction (Au Naturel Trilogy, Book Three)
Fired Up (standalone romance)

THE MORTAL TEMPEST

Undercover Elementals, Book Three

ANNA DURAND

JACOBSVILLE BOOKS · MARIETTA, OHIO

THE MORTAL TEMPEST

Copyright © 2019 by Lisa A. Shiel
All rights reserved.

The characters and events in this book are fictional. No portion of this book may be copied, reproduced, or transmitted in any form or by any means, electronic or otherwise, including recording, photocopying, or inclusion in any information storage and retrieval system, without the express written permission of the publisher and author, except for brief excerpts quoted in published reviews.

ISBN: 978-1-934631-97-3 (paperback)
ISBN: 978-1-934631-98-0 (ebook)
Library of Congress Control Number: 2017959859

Manufactured in the United States.

Jacobsville Books
www.JacobsvilleBooks.com

Publisher's Cataloging-in-Publication Data
provided by Five Rainbows Cataloging Services

Names: Durand, Anna, author.
Title: The mortal tempest / Anna Durand.
Description: Marietta, OH : Jacobsville Books, 2019. | Series: Undercover elementals, bk. 3.
Identifiers: LCCN 2019940076 | ISBN 978-1-934631-97-3 (paperback) | ISBN 978-1-934631-98-0 (ebook)
Subjects: LCSH: Magic--Fiction. | Spirits--Fiction. | Fairies--Fiction. | Shapeshifting--Fiction. | Time travel--Fiction. | Paranormal romance stories. | Romance fiction. | BISAC: FICTION / Romance / Paranormal / General. | FICTION / Romance / Paranormal / Shifters. | GSAFD: Love stories. | Occult fiction. | Fantasy fiction.
Classification: LCC PS3604.U724 M69 2019 (print) | LCC PS3604.U724 (ebook) | DDC 813/.6--dc23.

$\mathcal{P}$ROLOGUE

"LINNNZEEEE," THE WIND WHISPERS AS IT TOUSLES MY HAIR AND TICKLES my skin. The wind has a voice and, I sense, a body that could rip me to shreds if it wanted. And it does want. Everything. The air stirred by unseen forces possesses a sentient energy. It sees. It hears. It knows, and it schemes.

The wind escalates, no longer a tepid breeze but a hot and seething mass of rippling, gnashing gusts. It speaks my name, transforming Lindsey into a snarling epithet.

A gust slams into me.

I stagger backward, my white dress trips me up, and I flail my arms out to buffer my fall. I just stop my head from cracking into a boulder.

A figure materializes in front of me where I lie prone on the ground.

The manlike being towers over me, a living statue hewn of copper, his eyes swirling with sickening shades of green. This is Skeiron, Greek god of the northwest wind, former king of the sylphs, an elemental being of immense power and dark intentions.

I destroyed him. He came back. I destroyed him again.

And he has come back again.

"Janusite," he growls, "your power will be mine. The wind assures it."

I scramble to my feet, whirl away from him, and try to run.

He seizes me around the waist, hoisting me off the ground. With his mouth pressed to my ear, he hisses, "You will be undone."

Another figure appears before me.

This is Notus, Greek god of the north wind, king of the sylphs before Skeiron, as dark and powerful as his successor.

He stalks up to me, grasps my chin, and forces me to look into his roiling eyes.

"You," he says, "have done your last deed. Let it all be undone."

Notus conjures a sword. His mouth twists into a sneer.
He thrusts the blade straight into my heart.
And I am…undone.

Chapter One

I STUDIED MYSELF IN THE FULL-LENGTH MIRROR, TURNING SIDE TO SIDE TO get the whole picture of my wedding dress, from the lace that covered the bodice and short sleeves and billowed over the flowing skirt to the pearl-like beads that dotted the lace. Shimmering green-and-gold earrings imbued with good-luck magic dangled from my ears. The teardrop earrings not only shimmered, the colors swirled faintly too.

Here in the confines of my old bedroom inside the Porter family motor home, I appraised my reflection in the mirror once again. The glass revealed my mom and Ennea observing me from behind. My dad and my ten-year-old brother waited in the main area near the front of the motor home.

Today I, Lindsey Astrid Porter, would marry an elemental being.

My mouth gaped on a big, noisy yawn.

"Didn't sleep well again?" my mother asked, eying me with concern. "Nightmares again?"

"Yeah, but it's no big deal. Wedding jitters, I'm sure." I gave a phony laugh, the best I could muster. "After everything I've seen and almost died for, bad dreams are to be expected."

Mom rubbed my arm. "You sure, sweetie?"

"Absolutely. I'm about to marry the love of my life, what's to worry about? This is a happy day, so let's forget about my stupid nightmares."

So what if a cold, viscous unease had been slithering through me all morning. It meant nothing. Every bride got nervous on her wedding day. Besides, I probably felt a chill due to the November weather. My groom had promised to use his sylph magic to warm things up in the vicinity of our ceremony, but I wasn't there yet.

I turned to the fae witch responsible for my accessories, holding up my wrist to show off the diamond-like bracelet that twinkled even in the dark.

"The jewelry is amazing," I told Ennea, the redheaded fae with creamy, freckled skin and a sweet, lovely face. She may have looked young, but the leprechauns, her tribe of fae, always turned out to be much older than they seemed. In the few months I'd known Ennea, I'd never asked her true age. Learning my fiancé, Nevan, was over five thousand years old had been all the shock I needed for a good while. To Ennea, I said, "Thank you for the earrings and the bracelet. They're gorgeous, and I need all the luck I can get."

"Enh, it's simple fortune magic," Ennea said in her Bronx-like accent. "Child's play."

She waved a dismissive hand and slapped my mother's arm by accident.

Mom grasped her arm like it really, really hurt, though her smirk gave away the game.

The witch's eyes flew wide. "Oh Cindy, did I hurt you?"

"No, sweetie, I'm joshing. You elemental beings need the occasional reminder we mortals aren't invincible."

I sighed. "Mom, could we skip the culture-clash lessons for today? I'm walking down the aisle in five minutes."

And my stomach was churning. My shoulders had bunched of their own accord, and my pulse quickened at the mere thought of what I'd be doing in a few minutes. Marrying an ancient warrior, a former human forged into an immortal sylph. As my thoughts drifted to Nevan, the anxiety trickled out of me and my shoulders relaxed. Marrying Nevan. Tall, impossibly muscular, bronze-skinned Nevan with the swirling, mesmeric eyes. His wild ebony hair. His lips. His smile. That loincloth. Mmm, and everything hidden beneath the scrap of tawny fabric.

"Cut that out," Ennea said, slapping *my* arm on purpose. "No mooning over your gorgeous sylph before the ceremony. Save it for after, when he whisks you away for an exotic honeymoon."

Ah yes, the honeymoon. Nevan wouldn't tell me where we were going, only that it was somewhere in the mortal realm. I would have plenty of time to drool over my new husband then.

Drool. Lick. Devour.

Ennea clipped me with the back of her hand again. "Focus, Lindsey. You look beautiful."

She fluffed the waves of my chestnut hair, which she had coiffed for me. The locks fell over my shoulders and framed my face. The makeup my mom had applied accentuated my pale-blue eyes. Nevan would love this. He'd never seen me spiffed up before.

In the mirror, I caught my mom dabbing at her eyes with a tissue. She sniffled. "Oh Lindsey, you're as pretty as an angel."

"Thanks, Mom." I got a little choked up too. "Don't make me cry, it'll smear my makeup."

Cindy Porter sucked in a breath and swiped at her eyes. "No more tears. It's time for smiles."

"Yes, it is." I straightened, smoothed my dress, and nodded. "I'm ready."

I whirled around, skirts flouncing, to face the door.

Ennea swung it open, and she and my mom stepped aside—as much as they could in the tin-can space.

Chin up, shoulders back, I marched out into the short, narrow hallway and straight through the living area past my dad and my brother. Ken Porter sprang up from the breakfast nook, banging into the table. My father, who loved to *ohmm* and take the lotus position, was gaping at me like he'd never seen me before. My ten-year-old brother, Ash, hopped up to stand on the curved bench seat of the nook. He clapped and cheered.

I winked at both of them.

My entourage trailed me out of the motor home, Mom and Ennea right behind me with Dad and Ash behind them. The rest of the wedding party awaited us at the ceremony site. We traipsed past the rock shop where I'd once been a lowly hourly employee and now served as a salaried assistant manager. The barn-red, corrugated-metal building squatted amid the woods of the Keweenaw Peninsula, the northernmost part of Michigan that housed many secret doorways to the Unseen realm. I led my little procession across the gravel parking lot, behind the shop, and through the garden populated with concrete statues of fantastical creatures like unicorns and trolls. The gravel path turned to dirt as we exited the garden and headed through the woods toward the waterfall.

Even from this distance, the waters rumbled.

We reached the healing vortex, marked by a not-so-subtle sign with white-painted letters proclaiming this the "HEALING VORTEX." Natural stone benches encircled the space. This spot did indeed possess regenerative magics, and it held sentimental value for me and Nevan, but this was not our destination. The further we traveled, the more the air warmed around us until it became as temperate as a Florida beach, thanks to Nevan's air-elemental powers. We stayed on the path until we reached the clearing beside the falls.

I froze, immobilized by the sight before me.

All the people who mattered most to me in the world gathered in this clearing, but I couldn't see Nevan yet. Maybe he'd hung back until I showed up. I glanced at each member of the wedding party in turn. Tris, Ennea's brother, stood alongside Brennus, the raven shapeshifter who now wore his humanoid form as a dark-skinned behemoth of a man with blue-tinged, shimmering skin and biceps the size of locomotives. Okay, that might've been a slight exaggeration. Tris seemed tiny next to Brennus. The leprechaun resembled a human teenager, with his rangy build and youthful face, but like his sister he was older than he seemed. With his peaches-and-cream skin and buzz-cut brown hair, he was a stark contrast to the shapeshifter. Brennus wore skintight shorts while Tris sported his usual ripped blue jeans, flannel shirt, and beat-up sneakers.

The leprechaun swiveled his bright-blue eyes to me and made the thumbs-up sign.

My mom and my brother joined Tris and Brennus.

A shadow among the trees shifted, and I glimpsed a familiar figure hiding there. A pang pierced my heart. The being formerly known as Travis Blackwell, sheriff of Mandan County, lingered in the shadows wanting to join the wedding party but afraid to do it. Travis had been my friend for years until he was forged into an elemental being—into a salamander, a type of incubus. Even two months after his transformation, he struggled to adjust to his new life.

It was my fault. All my fault.

"Wake up, Lindsey."

The voice of Ennea, my maid of honor, snapped me out of my jaunt down guilt-ridden memory lane. My boss, Stan Lagorio, hovered near the others. Though he'd come to terms with the existence of another world where magic reigned, he still preferred to avoid contact with that world and its denizens.

I looked toward the wooden railing that bounded the falls and the frothing pool beneath it. There, on the adjacent path, stood my friend and magical familiar, the incubus Max. He moved aside, and I saw Nevan.

My heart stuttered at the sight of him, like I hadn't seen him just yesterday and every day for the past three months. Tall and ripped, dressed in only his loincloth, he looked like the hottest Tarzan ever to grace the silver screen, except for his bronze-sheened skin and the molten ribbons of bronze, gold, and silver whorling in his amber eyes. When he caught sight of me, he smiled—a broad, ebullient smile that made me shiver with delight.

I was about to marry that sizzling-hot man.

My dad cupped my elbow in his hand and guided me toward Nevan and Max, his best man for the ceremony. Beside Nevan, our officiant waited. Bob, full name Bobanzhistilanovitz, was an oracle and a sort-of friend. He liked me and Nevan and had volunteered to conduct the ceremony when he heard we were tying the knot. The oracle wore his favorite attire—a finely tailored, navy-blue suit that hugged his slender body and went well with his short gray hair, which he always kept slicked back.

I took my position alongside Nevan with Ennea on the other side of me. Nevan and I faced each other, and he clasped my hands. His broad smile had softened into a gentler expression, loving and adoring. Tears stung my eyes again, threatening to flow, but I blinked them away. A dizzying mix of emotions swelled in my chest, and I focused on Nevan's face, on his warm hands holding mine.

"Welcome," Bob said in his odd accent, and his green eyes glittered with an internal fire. "We have gathered here for the handfasting ceremony of Nevan, king of the sylphs, and Lindsey Astrid Porter, the Janusite."

Why did he have to mention that? Sheesh, it wasn't very romantic to be called the Janusite at my wedding. I hoped he wouldn't recite the whole Janusite prophecy. So I had the powers of the Roman god Janus. Today, I was just a woman pledging her devotion and fidelity to the man she loved.

"These two individuals," Bob continued, "have expressed their heartfelt desire to join their lives and their souls, to become one in the most elemental sense. Can anyone give a reason why they should not be joined in this way?"

No one spoke.

A trace of a chill whispered through me, but I pushed aside the disquieting sensation and focused on Nevan, gazing into his whirlpool eyes. My breaths grew heavier as if the air had become thicker. I hadn't expected to feel this much, to be affected so deeply by a simple ceremony. Then again, we'd survived a hell of a lot to get here. I'd almost died, he'd almost died twice, and two worlds had nearly been destroyed.

My breaths grew more labored. I struggled to suck in air.

Nevan fought for breath too, his eyes widening.

This was more than excitement over the wedding. I glanced around and saw everyone, even Bob, gasping for air. My ears began to ring, and darkness encroached on my vision. My heart pounded as cold sweat broke out on my brow.

The ground trembled.

Nevan gripped my hands tighter.

A crack of thunder split the air, and the ground beneath us erupted.

Chapter Two

THE EARTH HEAVED UPWARD, CARRYING ME WITH IT. NEVAN'S HANDS were ripped from mine. The world became a blur of motion and dust clouds as the ground under my feet plummeted away from me and I sailed downward through empty space into a black abyss.

Hands seized my wrists.

I hung suspended in the blackness, choking on dust, my eyes squeezed shut to shield them from the debris raining down around me. The hands holding me hefted my body upward, out of the darkness. Weak light penetrated my closed lids.

A burst of sweet-smelling air gusted over me, dispelling the dust cloud. Only a sylph could summon clean air for me.

Without opening my eyes, I flung my arms around Nevan. "Thanks for the oxygen, honey."

He clutched me tight for a moment, then pushed me away to pat me down from head to toe. "Are you injured?"

His Irish brogue soothed me better than a swig of booze.

At last, I peeled my lids apart to gaze at him through a blur of grit-induced tears. "I'm fine. What about you?"

"Immortal, love. An earthquake can't hurt me."

Right. Only a weapon or poison endued with magic could take down an elemental. Since I'd just been attacked by the earth itself, I didn't feel stupid for forgetting the rules of the Unseen realm for a minute.

Nevan opened his palm. A wet washcloth appeared there.

Not as romantic as the day we'd met, on this very spot, when he'd conjured a perfect daylily for me. Not even as romantic as when he'd had my Bond Arms Mini derringer pistol endued for me. But as romantic gestures went, conjuring a washcloth to wipe me off after I nearly fell into the center of the earth ranked in the top ten.

He wiped my face, my neck, and the parts of my shoulders and chest exposed by my dress. The washcloth was filthy after that. He flicked the cloth, and it became moist and clean once more. While he cleansed my arms, I took stock of the devastation around us.

My parents and Ash looked dirty but otherwise okay. When I shouted to them, they replied they were unharmed. I shouted to Ennea and Tris too, even Brennus. All responded with affirmations they were all right. Stan stared into space, unblinking, his face ashen. When I called to him, he swung his gaze toward me.

"Somebody help Stan," I said. "He's in shock."

Max strode up to my boss and conferred with him in hushed tones.

Tris and Ennea meandered across the clearing, inspecting the damage.

Bob stood serenely in the same spot as before, his clothes spotless and his hair shipshape.

I waved my hand to snare his attention and asked, "You have any idea what that was?"

"The earth moved."

"Gee, Bob, thanks for the insight."

Nevan thrust a hand through my hair, his palm emitting a burst of air, and all the grime vanished. My hair was as shiny and bouncy as before the earthquake.

Earth buckling. Earth upthrust. Whatever.

"It felt like an attack," I said to no one in particular.

Nevan, his hand in my hair, went stiff. "Why would you say that?"

"Because we don't have earthquakes in the Keweenaw." I sighed and shook my head. "I mean, there's a fault that runs through the spine of the Keweenaw, but the earth doesn't suddenly shoot up under our feet. Until today. Our wedding day."

Nevan glanced down, scrutinizing the ground, then jerked his head up. "The earth shot up under *your* feet."

I sagged my shoulders and groaned. "Please tell me this is not the work of another lunatic bent on stealing my Janusite powers. That shtick is getting really old." I glanced at the hole in the ground that had almost swallowed me. "This isn't what my nightmares looked like."

Nevan went rigid and stopped blinking. "You had another bad dream?"

"Yes, but I'm sure it was wedding jitters. It couldn't have anything to do with this. I dreamed Skeiron and Notus came back to life and wanted to undo me, whatever that means."

"It cannot be a coincidence." He picked a tiny leaf off my dress and tossed it away. "You have suffered from terrible dreams for several days, and now a terrible event has occurred. There must be a connection."

"You're probably right, but I'd rather hug my denial a little longer."

"Lindsey, you are the one who called it an attack."

"I'm vacillating, okay? Stress does that to me."

Brennus lumbered up to us. "My lady, you should be escorted to a safer location."

"No dice," I said. "I'm not running away because of an itty-bitty earthquake."

"Itty-bitty?" Nevan said, a muscle jumping in his jaw. "A canyon opened up beneath your feet. Brennus is correct, you should be taken—"

"Not running away. You know me better than that."

He grumbled out a sigh. "Yes, I do."

"Yo, peeps!"

Tris's voice echoed through the woods.

I searched the area with my gaze but couldn't locate Tris or Ennea.

The snarky leprechaun trotted out of the trees and flapped his hand, urging us to follow him. "Hurry up! We found something…interesting."

"Why are you running instead of poofing?" I asked. Teleportation would've been faster.

"In case ya didn't notice, the landscape's kinda changed. Might accidentally 'poof' into a big hole. Besides, sometimes it's safer to do the legwork. Get the lay of the land, so to speak." He flapped his hand again. "Hurry it up, will ya?"

Nevan grasped my hand and led me toward Tris. We followed him down a narrow deer trail until he abruptly stopped. Ennea emerged from the trees, her face paler than usual.

Tris pointed to his right. "It's over there."

Brennus pushed past us, marching straight in the direction Tris had pointed.

I tried to follow, but Nevan pulled me against him, capturing me with his arm around my waist.

"Wait," he said. "Please, love, let Brennus survey the area first."

Nevan worried about me, and I loved him for that. But I suffered from a curiosity that often made me take off after strange beings or odd noises. This time, I let Nevan restrain me. To be restrained by his strong arm and his sexy body wasn't much of a sacrifice.

Brennus returned a moment later and announced, "There is a being. He is asking for you, my lady."

"Me?" I said like the dumbest person on the planet. Shock would do that to a girl. "This being is asking for me by name?"

The shapeshifter nodded.

"Did this creature," Nevan said, "seem threatening?"

"No," Brennus told him, "he is calm."

Nevan took my hand again, and we followed Brennus through the trees to a small clearing. The earth had cracked open here too as it had beneath my feet. We approached the chasm with caution, leaning forward to peer down into its depths. From six feet below, a man observed us.

A naked man.

He tilted his head back to eye us. When his focus landed on me, he snapped his spine straight. "Lindsey Astrid Porter."

I bit my lip. "Um…yes. Who are you?"

The man puffed up his chest, chin held high. "I am Janus. And I want my powers back."

Chapter Three

"Excuse me?" Like I would believe a naked man who appeared in a chasm ripped open by an earthquake just because he said he was the Roman god Janus. I wasn't that dumb. Sure, he had freaky gold eyes and golden-blond hair, but that didn't prove anything. He also boasted big muscles, another unhelpful observation. Hands on my hips, I squinted down at the man. "Janus was destroyed a long, long time ago. His powers got scattered to the Four Winds. Why on earth would I believe you are Janus? I don't suppose you've got some identification."

"Identification?" the naked man said, his brows scrunched.

Nevan hooked his arm around my waist. "Gods don't have driver's licenses."

Lips pinched, I looked up at him. "Don't tell me you're buying this 'I'm the god Janus' crap."

"Perhaps not." He grimaced. "Or perhaps yes."

"Thanks for the ever-so-helpful wishy-washiness." I flapped a hand toward the chasm and the being standing within it. "How do we find out if he's legit?"

Nevan shrugged.

To the stranger, I said, "Do something godlike."

He scowled at me. "Since my powers currently reside in you, I cannot do anything remotely godlike."

"Don't get snippy with the woman you're trying to convince to buy your story." I gnawed my lip, considering the problem for a moment. "There must be some way to figure this out. Where did you come from, anyway? And if you don't have powers, how did you cause an earthquake?"

"I did not," he said snippily, ignoring my advice. "Even as a god with all my powers intact, I could not control the earth. Gnomes are the only elementals tied to the earth in such a manner."

Nevan grudgingly nodded. "He is correct. Gnomes have the power, but they haven't left their home territory in ages. They have no interest in the mortal world or in conquering the elemental realm. After the sylph army defeated them roundly several thousand years ago, they retreated into their domain and have stayed there ever since. It's a bit of a mystery why they attacked us at all. Gnomes have never been militaristic before or since that solitary battle."

"We can't blame the gnomes. Check." I set my hands on my hips and drummed my fingers as I returned my attention to the man in the chasm. "So, you're claiming it's a coincidence the ground ripped apart right when you turned up—in the middle of a hole made by that earthquake."

"Perhaps it is a coincidence, or perhaps not." The supposed god huffed out a breath, screwing up his mouth. "Apparently, I will need your assistance to determine the answer."

"Where did you come from? How did you get here?"

"I have been imprisoned within the Temple of the Four Winds for many thousands of years." He glanced around, frowning at his surroundings. "I do not know how I came to be in this place, but I assume the Winds released me for a purpose." His gold eyes zeroed in on me, and he canted his head. "They sent me to you."

"Gimme a break." My heart stuttered despite my dismissive words. If he was Janus, he must've been released by the Four Winds, those guardians and avatars of power who had helped me and Nevan a couple months ago. I'd asked one of the Winds why I'd been chosen to receive Janus's powers. She had told me to ask Janus.

Well, here was my chance. Assuming I believed this guy's story.

Nevan piped up before I could. "Why do you believe Lindsey has your powers?"

His Godly Snippiness hissed a breath out his nostrils. "She is the Janusite, the prophesied mortal female who serves as the vessel for my powers until I can reclaim what is rightfully mine."

My turn to get snippy. "Vessel? I am not a bucket for you to dump your stupid powers into. And since the Four Winds gave me these magics, they are rightfully mine."

"You are the vessel. I will not leave what is mine within you, subject to the whims of a mortal who does not deserve to command such power."

"Maybe you're the one who needs to prove you deserve it." I narrowed my gaze on him. "Gee, didn't the other gods destroy you? Probably did it because you're such an arrogant twit."

Janus opened his mouth to speak, but a throat-clearing behind me stopped him. Both Nevan and I twisted our heads around to glance at Brennus.

The shapeshifter said, "My liege, may I suggest consulting the oracle."

Duh. I'd forgotten about Bob. He must've been here. Somewhere.

I threw my head back and hollered, "Bob! Get your butt over here."

The suit-clad oracle materialized beside me. "There's no need to shout for me. Only the leprechauns are too stubborn to pay attention to a subtler call."

"Sorry, but we have an urgent problem and need your insight." I pointed down at the naked stranger. "This guy claims to be the god Janus."

Bob gingerly stepped closer to the chasm's rim, leaning forward to peer down at our new friend. He squinted, turned his head this way and that, then straightened and backed up to stand beside me again. "He claims it because he is Janus."

"You're positive?"

He gave me a fatherly smile. "I'm an oracle, child. I don't lie about such things."

"But have you ever been wrong?"

Nevan's arm tensed around me. He was probably worried I would offend the super-powerful oracle, but I trusted Bob not to smite me just because I opted for a blunt approach.

"Hmm," Bob began, rubbing his beard, "I don't believe I've ever been wrong. There is a first time for everything, though."

"That's the best you've got."

"Nothing is a certainty, not even death. You should know that better than most."

Yeah, I'd been healed by a mystical vortex when my formerly dead ex-fiancé tried to murder me. Nevan had almost died twice and been resurrected twice, once by a vortex and once by me. Anyone who submitted to the forging, the supernatural transformation from human to elemental, must die for the process to begin. Even Bob had been run through with an endued sword, the only type of weapon that could kill an elemental, and he came back too.

Death wasn't a one-hundred-percent certainty.

Oh, sometimes I missed the days when I had been free to scoff at the supernatural. At least then I'd known anyone who died would stay dead.

I opened my mouth to ask Bob another question, but he poofed away.

Bob's assessment that this was Janus relied on his statement that he didn't "believe" he'd ever been wrong. He had also implied he could be wrong in the future. Or today. Right now. About the naked man scowling up at me from the bottom of a deep crack in the earth.

"There is another possibility," the man calling himself Janus said, seeming to have tempered his, uh, temper. "The Winds might have sent me to you because they sensed a great, dark power emerging. That power may have caused the earthquake."

Which probably meant the quake had been aimed at me. *Fabulous.*

"Okay, fine," I said, throwing my hands up in defeat. "For the time being, I will accept you might be the god Janus."

Nevan arched one brow at me.

"Yeah-yeah," I muttered to him. "I know, this could be a huge mistake. What if he's right about the earthquake? Some tips from the god whose powers I have could be helpful."

My almost-husband growled under his breath. "Ye do attract naked men, don't ye?"

"Not my fault naked men keep getting sent to me as gifts."

An evil sorcerer had sent me Max to serve as my familiar, and the salamander had arrived buck naked, his preferred state. Now, the Four Winds had apparently sent me Janus. What was the return policy on supernatural gifts?

Max I would never send packing. The cranky god in the chasm was another story.

I bowed my head and sighed. "Would somebody please conjure clothes for this guy?"

Nevan withdrew his arm from around me and flicked his wrist toward the chasm.

Janus jerked as a fluffy pink robe and pink bunny slippers materialized on his body. He glowered up at Nevan.

"Honey," I said, patting Nevan's chest. "Let's not tick off the god, 'kay?"

"If you insist." Nevan flicked his wrist again. "Will this do?"

Janus now sported a plain white toga. No footwear this time.

The god waved a hand toward Nevan but looked at me. "Would you mind ordering your servant to assist me in climbing out of this hole?"

"Servant?" Nevan said with an indignation that hiked up his chin and roiled in his eyes. "I am the king of the sylphs, you impotent god."

Well, at least Janus didn't have any powers with which to smack down Nevan.

I hollered over my shoulder, "Brennus, help the impotent god out of the hole in the ground. Pretty please."

Nevan flinched at my use of the dreaded P-word, but we were in the mortal realm. I could be as polite as I wanted without incurring any magical debts. I should be more careful, though, since I didn't want to wind up owing any nasty types. Max owed me his life, and that debt bound him to me even two months after it was incurred. It would bind us forever unless I absolved him. The stubborn incubus wouldn't let me free him, for reasons I didn't yet fully understand.

Brennus sauntered up to the chasm, knelt, and offered his hand to Janus. The god stretched his arm above his head to grasp Brennus's hand. Once he'd hoisted Janus out of the hole, Brennus retreated behind me and Nevan.

I smiled brightly at the shapeshifter. "Thank you."

He bowed from the waist. "As you command, my lady."

Nevan frowned at me. "Lindsey, you know better than to speak those words."

A flap of my hand dismissed his concerns. "Mortal world, sweetie. Chill out."

"Someone with immense power may have instigated an earthquake." He leaned in to nail me with a hard look. "How do you know the perpetrator didn't summon a bit of the Unseen realm into the mortal world to accomplish the task?"

Oh. He had a point. When I'd dragged Tris over to this side to heal Nevan, the leprechaun had needed to pull a smidgen of the Unseen into the mortal realm to do it. I might have possibly incurred an itty-bitty debt to Tris in the process, since pulling a sliver of the Unseen into the mortal world had the same effect as crossing the veil into the land of elementals where magic reigned. I'd learned a lot since then, but clearly not quite enough. In my defense, a god had appeared and demanded his powers back. I had some stress to deal with here.

"My bad," I said to Nevan. "Won't happen again."

Janus, who now loitered six feet in front of us, chuckled. "I had thought you commanded him, but it seems the sylph has ultimate control over his consort."

"Not a consort," I said, hands on my hips once again. "We were about to get married before you so rudely interrupted. And what do you mean you want your powers back? Nobody told me these things were returnable."

"There must be a way. Ask your oracle."

My oracle? I wasn't sure Bob would appreciate that assumption.

Nevan took hold of my arm. "I will speak to the Janusite alone."

The god folded his arms over his broad, incredibly muscular chest. "What am I to do? Hang about in this forest?"

"Yes."

And with that, Nevan towed me away from the god and into the trees. We could see Janus and Brennus from here, but they most likely couldn't hear our conversation. I leaned back against a tree.

Nevan bracketed me with his hands on the trunk. "You're believing what that…creature tells you?"

"Of course not. I'm suspicious and paranoid, remember?"

"Suspicious, yes, but not paranoid. We have good reason to be distrustful of what that being tells us. And how does he know your name?"

"I would've asked him, but you dragged me over here."

Keeping one hand on the tree, he lifted the other to cup my cheek. "I worry for you, love. Twice before we've battled beings determined to appropriate your powers. This creature may have the same goal in mind."

"You've told me before you trust my instincts."

"And I do."

I laid my hand over his on my cheek. "I think he might be Janus. Bob said it too, and I have a gut feeling about this."

Nevan's head sagged, and he groaned miserably. "I suppose I have no choice but to defer to your instincts." He raised his head, mouth crimped. "For the record, I do not like this situation one bit."

"I'm with you on that."

He lowered his body to the ground like he'd suddenly aged a million years, his legs stretched out in front of him. "The wedding must be delayed."

"Oh hell no." I dropped to my knees beside him. "We are not putting our lives on hold because another nebulous baddie decides to wreak havoc. I'm sure Bob is hanging around, my family is here, our friends are here, and we are not canceling the wedding."

"Lindsey—"

"No, you cannot *Lindsey* your way out of it." I plopped my tush onto his lap and linked my hands at his nape. "We are getting hitched. Today. No griping, no grumpy mumbling, no excuses."

Nevan smirked. "I know better than to argue with you when you've made a decision. You are extremely stubborn."

"So are you."

He wrapped his arms around my waist and tugged me closer. "The wedding does lead to the wedding night. I'm looking forward to stripping this dress from your body, my sweet mortal morsel, and nibbling on your delicious flesh all night long."

I slanted in, my mind set on kissing those luscious lips of his.

Brennus cleared his throat.

We both looked at the shapeshifter.

"The god grows anxious," Brennus said. He fixed his coal-dark eyes on me. "He insists upon speaking to you."

Nevan rose, taking me with him and setting me down on my feet.

"The god can bloody well wait," Nevan declared. "We have a wedding to finish."

"What shall I do with Janus?" Brennus asked.

"Keep him here. I do not want him disrupting the ceremony."

"Yes, my liege."

Brennus marched back into the clearing, planted his massive body in front of Janus, and barred his arms over his chest. He towered over the powerless god.

"What is this?" Janus said. "I demand to speak with the mortal vessel."

"My name is Lindsey, which you damn well know." I pointed a finger at him. "Stay there. I'll speak to you after we get married. If you cause any trouble, I will use your own frigging powers to knock you back on your ass. Got it?"

He compressed his lips, nostrils flaring.

"Do you understand?" I said sternly.

Janus huffed out a breath and spoke through clenched teeth. "I will remain here."

Nevan and I, hands joined, turned our backs on the god.

And that was how, ten minutes later, we wound up standing inside the healing vortex ten feet from the crack in the earth that had almost swallowed me while Bob performed the handfasting ceremony. I paid little attention to the oracle's words as he explained the meaning of the tradition and how it represented our love and the binding together of our hearts and lives. Nevan made an impatient noise, spurring Bob to pick up the pace. We had an irritated god waiting for us, and neither I nor Nevan wanted to risk another earthquake or who-knew-what disrupting the ceremony.

We exchanged rings, a nod to the traditions of my world, and then paid homage to the elemental world.

"It's time," Bob said, "for Lindsey and Nevan to bind their hearts, minds, and lives in eternal devotion."

Facing each other, Nevan and I crossed our hands—my right hand in his right hand, my left hand in his left hand. We gazed into each other's eyes, and suddenly, the weight of this moment struck me. My throat constricted. Tears pricked at my eyes. My chest tightened, and my lips trembled the tiniest bit. I was marrying Nevan. After a lifetime of feeling out of place in the world, in any world, I'd found my home with him.

Bob hovered his hand over ours and intoned words in another language.

Energy zinged through me, soft and gentle. I felt it echo between me and Nevan, looping from me into him and back again three times.

"It is done," Bob said, withdrawing his hand. He smiled at the crowd behind us. "Congratulations to the happy couple. You may kiss the bride, Your Majesty."

Nevan pulled me into his arms and kissed me.

Cheers erupted. Hands clapped. Someone whistled.

As our kiss ended, I caught Max's gaze just as he lowered his fingers from his mouth, his piercing whistle completed. He grinned and shrugged.

Everyone surged toward us. I got hugged by every single being in attendance, even Bob and Tris. My mom and Ennea hugged Nevan, but the guys all slapped him on the back.

A figure amid the trees snared my attention. My gut told me the identity of the lurker, and I trusted my instincts.

Nevan was surrounded by well-wishers.

I snared his gaze and mouthed, "Be right back." Then I sneaked away from the group and into the trees.

Travis hunched behind a wide pine tree peeking around it toward the clearing that housed the vortex. When he saw me approaching, he ducked behind the tree.

"It's okay," I said, stopping a dozen feet away. "You don't have to hide."

He swung around so half of his body became visible and peered out at me. "Shouldn't have come. Sorry. I just had to, uh...Never mind, I oughta go."

"Wait, please." I took a step toward him. "How are you?"

"Fine, I guess."

His Texas accent had lightened since the last time I'd seen him two months ago. Max had warned me Travis would change now that he'd become an elemental, an incubus like Max. The transformation happened gradually, though, and Travis might lose his twang altogether. His body had changed, for sure. Like Max, he sported deeply tanned skin glistening with copper. He'd gotten taller and far more muscular, and his hair had darkened from dirty blond into a rich ebony. His eyes flamed red with ribbons of yellow and orange lashing within the irises.

Unlike Max, Travis preferred to wear clothes. Today, he'd donned faded blue jeans and a white cotton shirt with all the buttons undone.

"Congratulations," Travis said. "I saw the ceremony. You and Nevan deserve to have a good life."

"Thanks." *What the hell should I say to him?* A few months ago, before his transformation, Travis had admitted he was in love with me. After the forging, his attraction to me had proved much harder to fight, which was why I hadn't seen him in so long. *Glad you're feeling better and please don't assault me* seemed like an inappropriate response, but I couldn't summon anything more useful.

Instead, I clutched the skirt of my dress in my hands.

He noticed and flinched. "Shouldn't be here. You're afraid of me, and you got every reason to be. I just wanted to…I don't know. Be here for the big moment, I guess."

"Max says you shouldn't cling to your old life."

Travis slithered out from behind the tree, keeping one side of his body glued to it. "I'm real sorry, Lindsey, about everything."

He was sorry? Max had forged him because I'd been grief stricken by his death at the hands of an evil shrew with endued weapons.

"I'm the one who should apologize. This happened to you because of me." I wrung my hands in the skirt of my dress, making the fabric swish and crinkle. "You died protecting me, and Max forged you for my sake. I'm so sorry, Travis."

"Don't do that. This ain't nobody's fault." He scratched his bare chest, exposed by his shirt. "I've realized most things are out of our control. We do the best we can, but sometimes it's not enough. I have to accept there's a higher power overseeing it all, and things will work out for the best in the end."

Higher power. The elementals talked about the Oversoul, the equivalent of God in the mortal realm. Maybe Max had introduced Travis to the concept.

"You really do seem better," I said. "I'm proud of you. The forging can twist a weak person into something awful, like what happened to Calder. You're strong and good, stronger than your brother was, and you will get through this. I believe that."

He shifted his hips like his groin pained him. "Maybe I am better, but I probably should stay away from you."

And of course, my gaze unconsciously snapped to his groin and the bulge growing and hardening in his pants. The sight of me got him way too excited.

"I think it's the dress," he said, understanding that I'd grasped his di-lemma. "You look real pretty in it."

His voice had gone rough and deep, and his gaze had zeroed in on my bo-som. The neckline of my dress revealed a hint of the inner slopes of my breasts.

I crossed my arms over them, my hands on my shoulders. "Well, I guess I should get back to the festivities."

And the impotent god currently fuming while a shapeshifter guarded him.

"Yeah, sure," Travis said.

His focus moved past me, and his eyes widened.

Travis stumbled backward to hide behind the tree again, leaning side-ways to peek around it while keeping the lower half of his body hidden.

"Yes," Nevan said from behind me, "you should return to the festivities, Lindsey."

I whirled to face my husband. "Hi, sweetie."

He shook his head, his lips kinked in a sardonic smile. "Can't leave ye alone for a moment, can I? You sneak off to speak with an incubus."

"At least Travis wears clothes."

"Yes, I'm exceedingly grateful for that."

I glanced back at Travis. "See you later."

He nodded and vanished.

Nevan backed me up to a tree, his body molded to mine, and murmured in a sultry voice, "I need to give my wife a proper kiss."

Chapter Four

W̲E DON'T HAVE TIME—" I MOANED AND MELTED WHEN HE TOOK POSSES-
sion of my mouth, sweeping his lips across mine, nipping and licking,
teasing me until I moaned again and opened my mouth in a silent plea for
more. He mashed his lips to mine, thrusting his tongue deep. Every swipe
of his flesh against mine pushed me to respond, heightened my desire, set
my whole body on fire. I lashed my arms around him and bent one knee,
tipping it to the side to spread my thighs in blatant invitation.

While he ravaged my mouth, Nevan struggled to lift my skirts. The vo-
luminous layers of lace and satin hindered him. With a growl, he tore his
mouth from mine to glare down at my dress. "I can't get under your bloody
skirts."

"Sorry." I skated my hands up his naked back. "We don't have time for
sex, anyway."

"Perhaps not." He gave up on my skirts and twined a lock of my hair
around his finger, then let it unfurl. "The first time I saw you, I had the
strangest sensation I'd seen you before. Known you before."

I gave him a teasing smile. "Was the first time you saw me in the shop,
when you disguised yourself with a glamour? Or the first time you saw me
when I actually saw you too?"

"The former." He curled that lock around his finger again, studying it. "I
could not explain why I felt I'd known you before. Perhaps it was merely fate
nudging me in the right direction, leading me to my soul mate." He released my
hair and touched my nose with one fingertip. "To you, my sweet mortal angel."

"You called me that after the first time you made love to me."

"Because you are an angel. The savior who resurrected my heart by showing me Skeiron had lied about cursing me to have no feelings."

"You would've figured it out eventually." I took hold of a lock of his hair,
coiling it around my finger the way he'd done with my hair. "You saved

me too. You encouraged me to stop holding back my passions and let go of my fears."

Nevan leaned in closer and gazed into my eyes so deeply my heart sped up from the intensity of emotion in his whirlpool eyes. "After my forging, I swore…My memories of that time are hazy, but I have vague recollections of an angelic being who tended to me."

"You never mentioned that before."

"I had long assumed it was a hallucination brought on by the trauma of the forging. There are several periods in my existence of which I have only hazy recollections. Even an immortal's mind cannot hold on to every memory." His eyes began to shimmer and swirl faster, their colors brightening. "When I called you my sweet mortal angel, on our first night together, I used those words because you saved me much the way that other angel had done so long ago. And just now, when we bound our souls with the handfasting, I had the oddest feeling I owe everything I have with you to that other angel."

"Why didn't you ever tell me about this other angel?"

"I seem to always forget about my first savior until something reminds me." He stared past my shoulder into a distance only he could see. "It's as if someone or something prevents me from regaining my memories of the time after my forging."

"We'd better shelve that mystery for the moment. A god is waiting for us."

Nevan palmed my breast through my dress. "I want to be alone with you. Let us deal with the other troublesome supernatural being in a swift manner."

I knew he was referring to Travis when he called Janus the "other troublesome supernatural being." Nevan might have developed a non-hostile relationship with the formerly human former sheriff, but he and Travis would never become besties.

Nevan moved back half a step.

"Don't worry," I said, skimming my hands over his chest. "We can quiz the god some more, then stash him in a motel for the night."

Laughter rumbled deep in Nevan's chest. "Stash a god in a motel? In the mortal realm?"

"Got a better idea? He has no powers, which means he can't do any real damage other than annoying the hell out of anybody he meets."

"A motel it is." Nevan smirked. "I shall enjoy this."

"Is it Janus you don't like or gods in general?"

He sniffed, his nose lifting. "Gods are, as a rule, arrogant and dismissive of any being they consider to be of lesser stature. And they believe everyone who is not a god is a lesser being."

"Well then, let's get this over with." I slung my arms around him. "Blip us to the clearing."

One corner of his mouth kicked up because he always thought my various terms for his preferred mode of travel were silly, but he did blip us away. I could've teleported myself, tapping into his powers like I had many times before, but I liked traveling with Nevan. He always wrapped his arms around me even though it wasn't strictly necessary. Holding my hand would've done the trick.

Janus sat on the ground near the big hole, knees bent, arms draped over them.

Brennus hulked near the god's feet, his arms locked over his chest and his stance wide.

"Finally," Janus snapped, springing to his feet.

Behind us, footfalls pounded and crunched on dead leaves. Nevan and I half turned toward the sound and spotted Max emerging from the woods.

"Couldn't miss this," the incubus said in his usual English accent. "I heard there's a god out here who claims to be Janus. As Lindsey's familiar, it's my job to be at her side during any exciting events."

"Right," I said, "you're doing your duty. Your appearance has nothing to do with the excitement you mentioned."

Max grinned and shrugged. "I do love a good ruckus."

Shaking my head, I sighed with affectionate exasperation. Max was a good friend and a powerful ally, but he could be goofy sometimes. His life debt to me might also have encouraged him to join the party. I didn't yet grasp all the implications of another being owing me a magically enforced debt. God, I wished he would let me absolve him.

Max's mouth tightened, and he shook his head minutely as if he knew what I'd been thinking. Well, I had developed a problem with my emotions showing on my face. The days of locking up my feelings inside a steel-reinforced mental vault had ended months ago when Nevan taught me to embrace all my passions.

I faced Janus. "Okay, Mr. God Not Almighty. I want to know how you know my n—"

A hurricane-force gale tore through the clearing.

My hair whipped my face, and I stumbled backward. I couldn't see through my own hair.

Beneath my feet, the earth shuddered.

I staggered sideways, off balance as the ground undulated faintly. As the earth settled down and the wind died, a current shot through me. Magic? I had no clue because I'd never felt anything like it before. Sharp like a blade. Diffuse like a toxic cloud. Electric, searing energy. I tried to blow the hair out of my face, but it kept lashing me. With both hands, I peeled my hair away so I could see again.

Nevan was gone. Brennus too.

I spun in a circle. "Nevan!"

Max and Janus were here, but my husband had vanished. Nevan would not have left me alone.

Cold realization tingled through me. I couldn't explain how or why, but I understood on a visceral level something had changed. The world had changed. The woods seemed darker, denser, and the chasm from which Janus had emerged was gone.

I bolted for the healing vortex, tearing through the woods with reckless speed, my heart pounding and my skin tingling with that bizarre energy I'd sensed a moment ago. Max raced after me, shouting for me to stop. I could not stop or slow down.

Everything felt *wrong*.

Gasping for breath, I broke through the trees into the clearing around the vortex.

The stone benches had disappeared.

Everyone—my family, my friends, Nevan, and even Bob—had vanished too.

A flaming blur rocketed toward me. Max slowed his speed as he caught up to me, his skin alive with rippling fire. The flames dwindled and snuffed out. He seized my arm. "What happened? I felt something."

"Me too."

Janus trotted out of the woods.

I whirled on him. "What the hell was that? Where is everyone?"

He lifted one shoulder. "The timeline has shifted. If you are worthy of my powers, you should have sensed it."

"Seriously? You're getting uppity with me right now?" Fueled by a panic-driven rage, I rushed at him and pounded my fists on his chest. "The timeline shifted? What the hell does that mean?"

"Someone has altered the past, and everyone you know has changed as a result."

No, no, no, it couldn't be.

I barreled down the deer trail that had somehow replaced the dirt path to the rock garden. My skirts flapped around my legs, tripping me up a couple times, but I flew through the woods without any clue about what the hell I thought I'd do if Janus was right. He couldn't be. I had to cling to that denial because the alternative was terrifying. I ran and ran, breaking out of the woods into the rock garden—or where it had been.

The rock garden was gone.

Stumbling over a tree root, I flailed my arms out to break my fall.

Max caught me around the waist and steadied me. He kept his hold on me while I surveyed the new reality. Weeds covered the area that had once held concrete statues of whimsical creatures. My mouth fell open as my focus tracked further ahead, beyond the missing rock garden to the vacant field where the rock shop had once hunkered.

A vacant field. Weeds. Saplings. No shop.

The highway remained, but it cut through empty land.

"Oh God," I gasped, shaking my head so hard my hair flapped. "No, it can't be..."

"It is," said the voice of the powerless god.

Max would not let go of me even when I shuffled around to face Janus. Maybe he was afraid I would disappear too or that he would. I had no doubts plastering himself to me would not stop whatever was happening if the force behind it wanted one or both of us gone.

The god stood stiff and stone-faced a dozen feet away.

My bottom lip quivered, but I managed to snarl, "Explain."

Janus raised his brows.

"Don't act like you have no clue what I'm talking about." I stabbed a finger toward him. "You said somebody changed the past. I demand you explain yourself. Did you do this?"

"No. Since my powers currently reside in you, I have no capacity to influence time." He tilted his head, studying me. "Perhaps you did this inadvertently."

"Me?" Sure, I'd once frozen time, but this…I couldn't be responsible. "Why would I want everyone to disappear?"

"Why would I?" Janus rubbed his jaw. "This must be related to the earthquake."

"I thought that was connected to your return."

"The Four Winds cannot cause earthquakes, and neither can I."

Panic made clear thinking difficult. I had to calm down, despite the fact my husband was gone and my family was gone and the shop was gone. What else had vanished? Were my loved ones dead? Erased from history? Christ, I couldn't think like that or I'd lose it.

What little of "it" I had left.

Max's arm around my waist steadied me in more ways than one. Knowing at least one person in my life hadn't vanished helped to calm me. I drew in deep, slow breaths until the shrieking panic settled into a background hum of unease.

Pushing away from Max, I stalked up to the god. "You said the Four Winds must've released you for a reason and that they must've sent you to me."

"For what reason, I have no conception."

"I thought gods knew everything."

"You are confusing gods with the Oversoul. I am not and have never been omniscient. Nor am I an oracle gifted with prescience."

His mention of an oracle gave me an idea.

"Bob!" I screamed.

He appeared right in front of me.

I started to speak, but he cut me off with a raised hand.

"Yes," he said, "the timeline has been altered. No, your loved ones are not dead or gone, though they may not be as they were the last time you saw them. Afraid I can't help with the what, who, or why of the time shift."

A single fact smacked me in the face, and I had no clue how I'd overlooked its glaring obviousness for so long. Being completely freaked out by time shifting around me had messed with my head.

I glanced around at the three beings who had not vanished. "Why do we remember everything? Time hasn't changed for us."

Janus stepped closer, almost parallel to Bob. "You and I are immune to timeline changes. My powers bind me to time itself, which means you are bound to it as well."

"You don't have your powers. How are you bound to time?"

He gave me a look that said I was a puny-minded mortal and he would deign to explain these concepts that clearly were above my mental capacity. "I have shared a connection with you from the moment you were born. The connection became stronger once you came into your powers—my powers. That is how I know your name, and that is how I remain immune to timeline alterations."

Connection? I wasn't sure I liked that idea, but I had bigger problems.

"What about Max?" I asked. "How is he immune?"

Janus shrugged.

Bob cleared his throat. "I can answer that one. The incubus owes you a life debt. I can sense these things, and his debt to you is powerful. More than owing you his life, he feels indebted in a far-reaching way that goes beyond you. The power of that guilt has become entangled with the life debt, making it immensely strong and binding him to you in a much deeper way than any life debt should. That's how he has stayed immune to the time shift."

I looked at Max, but he'd bowed his head, refusing to meet my gaze. Did he feel that way? Indebted to…who? What? I knew about the woman he'd loved during his mortal life in ancient Rome, and how he had chosen the forging rather than death. Later, he'd forged Aurelia instead of letting her die a natural death the way she'd wanted. She became a succubus and went insane. Max had to destroy her. Could that be the far-reaching debt Max believed he owed?

Later, I'd quiz him about that. After we settled this time-shift insanity.

"And you, Bob?" I asked. "How are you immune?"

He smiled, his eyes blazing with an eerie green fire. "I am an oracle, child. As I've told you before, I'm beyond all designations, even time itself."

Yeah, he'd mentioned that "beyond all designations" thing. He'd been run through with an endued sword and survived it. But sidestepping time? I couldn't comprehend how any of us had accomplished that feat.

Magic, Lindsey, remember?

Would I ever get used to this stuff? I'd accepted being the Janusite. I'd accepted that my formerly dead ex-fiancé—Calder Blackwell, whom I had shot seven times at close range—had come back as a monkey-thing from another realm of reality. Hell, I'd accepted that Nevan's formerly dead wife from his mortal life had been resurrected by a sorcerer. And oh, I couldn't forget the fact the sorcerer had been an amalgamation of the essences of the sylph kings Notus and Skeiron jumbled up with the essence of Calder Blackwell.

Yeah, suddenly time shifts didn't seem all that crazy.

Bob rubbed his temples. "I may be immune to the time shift, but it's giving me a monster of a headache. All those timelines twisting and snapping and merging…I need to head back to my lair. The magics will shield me."

"You can't leave yet," I said. "How do I fix this time-shift thing?"

"The Janusite is one with time."

I threw my hands up. "That's your great wisdom? I'm one with time? Jeez, Bob, couldn't you be less cryptic this one time?"

He laid a hand on my arm, his eyes quieting to a subdued green and filled with empathy. "I know you're worried about your husband. But remember one thing." He leaned in. "Whenever you are, it's always him."

Seriously? That's all he had to say. Jeez, I hated oracles.

No, I didn't really hate Bob. He must have rules he had to abide by, like everybody did, and I needed to accept that he was doing the best he could to help me.

Bob squeezed my arm. "I know it's not what you want to hear. My foresight is like a picture book, not an encyclopedia. I see images of the past, present, and future, but I cannot control what I see or how detailed it is or is not." He rubbed his forehead, wincing slightly. "The Janusite prophecy is the only foresight I've experienced that came to me in words and pictures. It was like a Hollywood epic from the golden days, but with you and Nevan instead of Elizabeth Taylor and Richard Burton."

"I hope that epic wasn't *Cleopatra*. They both died in the end."

"Have a little faith, child. Remember what I told you after the sorcerer incident." He glanced over his shoulder at Janus, then released my arm. "When he asks, tell him."

Bob poofed away.

I didn't get a chance to ask what he'd meant. When who asked what? Guessed I'd find out eventually.

What he'd told me after the sorcerer incident. Bob had instructed me to remember it. I hadn't seen Bob after his running-through by the nasty piece of work once known as Nevan's wife, not until after we'd dealt with the sorcerer. Bob had approached me and Nevan, telling us two things. First, that we would have children someday despite the fact a human-elemental pregnancy could kill me. Bob had assured us "a way would present itself." Second, Bob had said, "Trust in Janus."

Oh crap. He wanted me to work with the powerless god.

Bob popped back in right in front of me.

I yelped.

He held out his hands, palms up. "I almost forgot to give you my wedding gift. Lay your palms on mine."

"Why?"

"Trust me, Lindsey."

I laid my palms on his.

Energy jolted into me through my hands, spiraling out into my entire body, settling in my womb. What on earth?

Bob withdrew his hands. His mouth tightened in a self-satisfied smile. "That ought to do it."

"Do what?" I asked.

"I gave you a magical prophylactic." He glanced down at my lower belly. "You can do what you need to do without worrying about a dangerous hybrid pregnancy."

"What exactly do you think I'll need to be doing that involves sex?"

He chuckled. "Remember, child. Whenever you are, it's always him."

Bob winked out.

I was so goddamn sick of vague bullshit and unhelpful advice that made no sense.

Janus watched me with a curious expression.

Max stared at the ground, peeking up at me every few seconds.

Enough of this. I needed someone who didn't feel weirdly indebted to me and the universe and who hadn't demanded *his* powers back,

I threw my head back and screamed, "Nevan!"

Nothing.

"Ah," Max began, fidgeting and glancing at me sideways, "he must've been affected by the time shift. What makes you think he'll come when you call?"

"We have a connection, one nothing and nobody can break." I spun in a circle, shouting to the trees and the heavens. "Nevan! Get your half-naked self over here right this minute!"

Nevan poofed in at the edge of the grassy area behind Janus.

I bolted for Nevan, flung my arms around him, and with my feet off the ground, crushed my mouth to his.

He stayed motionless, not reacting to my kiss.

My pulse roared in my ears, my heart pounding like a crazed drummer.

Nevan latched his arms around me and ravished my mouth.

The kiss was ravenous, wild, full of tangling tongues and groping hands. I shoved my fingers into his hair. He dragged one hand down to my bottom and the other up to grasp my breast. Even while we devoured each other, I sensed something off about our kiss. Nevan was always passionate, but this seemed not quite right. Too rough. Too…impersonal.

I pushed away from his mouth, though his hands pinned me to his body. Scrutinizing his face, I found no answers there. "Nevan?"

"Yes. And you are?"

My heart plummeted straight through the earth and out into the vacuum of space. "It's me. Lindsey."

Nevan set me down, his hands lingering on my hips. "Pleasure to meet you, Lindsey."

Chapter Five

"WHY WOULD YOU KISS ME IF YOU HAVE NO IDEA WHO I AM?" I ASKED, my mind reeling from his reaction. Sure, I should've expected it given the time shift. Though my brain understood this, my heart refused to accept Nevan could ever forget me. I felt a little queasy, my skin growing colder every second and the chill seeping inside to freeze my blood. He didn't know me. My husband didn't know me.

My gaze flicked to his left hand. His wedding ring had disappeared along with his memories of us. I swallowed three times, but the constriction in my throat would not abate.

Nevan slid his hands up to my waist, his mouth curving into a seductive smile. "I never turn down a kiss from a beautiful, sensual woman."

"I'm your wife."

He chuckled. "I think you're barmy."

My husband thought I was crazy. My throat ached. Tears stung my eyes.

I staggered backward out of Nevan's reach and spun around to face away from him, swiping at the tears gathering in my eyes. Looking at him shot stabbing pains into my heart. But the heat of his body, his unique scent, the timbre of his voice, the weight of his hands on my hips...

Those things would undo me.

Even with my back to him, I could feel Nevan watching me.

Max grabbed my arm and hauled me further away from Janus and Nevan. He turned me toward him, searching my face. "Are you all right? I know that's a rubbish question, but—"

"I'll be fine. Well, as fine as possible under the circumstances." The only way I could get through this was if I believed we could reverse the time shift, so I held on to the idea with all the strength of a shipwrecked man who had only a half-deflated life raft to keep him afloat during a hurricane.

The sympathy on Max's face made my gut twist. "You hoped he would remember because of your connection with him."

"If you and Janus kept your memories, why shouldn't Nevan?" I made a disgusted noise at my own pathetic hopes. "He thinks I'm some crazy chick who threw herself at him."

Max gazed past me, his lips puckering as if he were expending a great deal of mental power on puzzling out a mystery.

The brainpower I had access to at the moment wasn't enough to let me figure out what had caught his attention—or to care about it. Minutes ago, I'd been married to the love of my life, getting ready for my honeymoon, happier than ever before. Suddenly, everything had been ripped away from me. The tears I'd fought so far threatened to break free and trickle down my cheeks.

I sniffled, determined to keep them at bay.

Cut that out, I admonished myself. *No crying, no giving up, keep fighting.*

Max threw his arms around me, crushing me to his body, and began moving his hands in circles on my back while murmuring soothing sounds. I tried to pull my head back, but he slapped a palm on the back of my head and mashed my face into his naked chest.

"What on earth are you doing?" I mumbled into his flesh.

He shoved me away, smirked, and gestured past my shoulder. "Have a look."

"You suck at consoling me. I almost suffocated."

The incubus grasped my shoulders and whirled me around to face Nevan. "Look at him."

Christ, that was the last thing I wanted to do. Since Max seemed oddly determined to make me look at Nevan, I did it.

My husband-not-husband was glaring at Max, his gaze narrowed. A muscle pulsed in his jaw as he ground his teeth. He had shot ramrod straight, every muscle bulging, the picture of sheer power and boiling anger.

I blinked rapidly, sure I must've been hallucinating.

"See?" Max hissed into my ear. "He's jealous because I had my hands all over you."

"There's got to be another reason for his behavior. He has no clue who I am, so why would he get jealous?"

"Have you considered the possibility he might remember? On some level deep down in his unconscious mind. You and Nevan have a bond like nothing I've ever seen. If anyone could overcome a time shift, it's you two."

Oh God, how I longed to believe that.

I shook my head weakly and muttered, "False hope won't do me any good."

With a huff, Max slung his arms around my waist, dragged me backward into his hard body, and nuzzled my throat.

Nevan lunged at us. He ducked around me to seize Max by the neck and fling him thirty feet across the vacant field.

Max whumped down with a grunt.

I should have been concerned with his well-being, but instead, I slowly turned to face Nevan.

His chest heaved with breaths that gusted out of him. His shoulders rose and fell too, in time with his exhalations. An expression of total confusion tightened his features.

"I'm all right," Max called. "Don't worry about me."

The sarcastic tone of his statement indicated he actually was okay, and a quick sideways glance assured me of it. On his feet again, he dusted himself off and strode toward us.

Nevan bowed his head, grasping the back of his neck.

I couldn't stop myself. I moved toward him, laying my hands on his bare chest. "Why did you do that?"

He dropped his hands but kept his head down. "I've no bloody idea. When that creature touched you in such an intimate way…" He shook his head. "I could not tolerate it."

A dangerous hope flickered inside me, weak but undeniable. This was what Max had intended to happen. Make Nevan jealous. Insanely jealous. Somehow that would prove his memories of me, of us, lurked somewhere deep inside him.

Max came up beside me. "I was right, wasn't I?"

I twisted my mouth into a peeved expression. "Maybe."

Nevan lifted his head. His focus landed on me but then swerved away. He swallowed hard enough to make his Adam's apple bounce.

He vanished.

"Wha—" I spun in a circle, my heart thrashing in my chest. "No, no, not another time shift."

"It was not a time shift," Janus said.

Max and I turned toward the god in unison.

He leaned back against a tree, arms crossed over his chest. "You would have felt another shift. He simply left the vicinity."

Relief flooded through me, sagging my shoulders, weakening my knees. I sucked in a deep breath to calm myself. Janus was right. I hadn't noticed any change in the time-space continuum as I had when the shift occurred. Nevan's reaction to me, to Max's feigned sexual interest in me, had disturbed him so much he fled. Maybe that indicated what Max had suggested, that Nevan's real memories hid somewhere in the recesses of his mind. I had no frigging clue. Max and Janus retained their memories because of their connections to me.

What else had changed?

I seized Max's arm. "My family."

"You can find them if you concentrate and take us to them."

"What if I don't share Nevan's powers anymore? It was our emotional bond that made it possible."

Max laid his hand over mine on his arm. "You still have a connection, Lindsey. His jealousy proves it. Trust in that bond."

I nodded, but another problem occurred to me. I spread my arms and pointed my fingers at my body and the wedding dress. "I can't go out in the world like this. Could you conjure me something more appropriate?"

"Thought you hated conjured clothing. You told me so." He switched to a high-pitched voice that was apparently supposed to represent the way I talked, complete with a half-assed attempt at an American accent. "Oh please, Max, don't give me clothes you snatched away from who-knows-where, it's ooky."

"Very funny," I said. "This is a special circumstance. I've been living with Nevan, so I'm guessing all my belongings have disappeared thanks to the time shift. I give you permission to conjure me appropriate clothing."

He executed an exaggerated bow. "As you wish, mistress."

My dress vanished at the instant new clothing materialized around me. At least he hadn't gotten rid of my dress and waited a few seconds before giving me new stuff just so he could get a peek at my nakedness.

I appreciated that for about a second—until I took in my new appearance.

A leather bustier hoisted up my full breasts, which did not need hoisting. A matching leather miniskirt barely covered my rump, and thigh-high leather boots with black fishnet stockings completed the ensemble. For accessories, I had a leather choker with silver studs, leather wrist cuffs with silver studs, and black nail polish. When I shook my head, something moved up there. I raised a hand tentatively to touch my hairdo. Max had whipped it into a messy bun secured with—what else—a silver stake. Seriously. It felt like the metal version of the wooden stakes vampire hunters used.

"Honestly, Max," I said. "I need to blend in, not frighten children while I get arrested for solicitation. What should I call myself? Lindsey the Mistress of Pain?"

Max shrugged one shoulder, struggling not to smile. "It seemed appropriate to me."

Janus, propped against the same tree as before, observed us with a fascinated expression. With arms crossed over his chest, he lifted one finger to wave it toward me. "If this is how mortal women attire themselves these days, I shall enjoy spending time in your world."

I stomped my foot, which made my overly hoisted boobs jiggle. "Shush. No one asked for your opinion." To Max, I said, "Conjure me normal clothes."

Sighing, Max flicked his wrist.

The tension eased out of me when I took in my new outfit. He had given me leather pants, snug but not too tight and with a flare at the bottom to accommodate the sturdy black ankle boots that covered my feet. The bustier had been replaced with a short-sleeve, pale-blue shirt the color of my eyes. The choker and wrist bands were gone. And my hair, thank heavens, had lost the silver stake. It hung loose around my shoulders.

"Thank you," I told Max.

Both he and Janus winced.

I rolled my eyes again. "We're in the mortal world. I can say 'thank you' if I want."

Max examined my attire, tapping his chin. After a moment, his face lit up. "I forgot the most important accessory."

Something prodded my hip.

I glanced down. A holster tucked inside my waistband housed my Bond Arms Mini derringer. My gun could hold two rounds, and Nevan had gotten both it and the ammo endued. I had no idea if the time shift had stamped out that magic, but at least I had a modicum of protection. Two .357 rounds slamming into an elemental's forehead would slow the villain down and give me a fighting chance.

"The ammunition has remained endued," Max said. "I can feel the magic. Not sure how it's possible, but I was able to conjure this even though your world has changed."

"It's magic. Let's not overanalyze it."

"Good point." He glanced at my waist where the gun was concealed. "I conjured your weapon because I knew you would feel more at ease with it on your hip."

"Aw," I said, pinching Max's cheeks, "you got my gun for me. That's so sweet."

Max scrunched up his face. "Lindsey, I've asked you not to say things like that when others are around."

I patted his cheeks. "Don't be so uptight. You're a total sweetie-pie, and anybody who's met you knows it."

The incubus groaned, utterly defeated.

Janus laughed. "You are far more entertaining than the mortals I met last time I was corporeal."

"Gee, I'm so flattered." I flashed Janus a sharp look and turned back to Max. "Time to track down my family."

"May I assist?" Max held out his hands, palms up.

"Sure."

I held out my hands, palms down, hovering them a hair's breadth from his skin.

Currents of magic crackled between my skin and his where our hands almost touched. He was gifting me with magical energy to amp up my powers in the hopes our united strength would prove enough to enhance whatever latent connection I might share with the new version of Nevan. With any luck, it would allow me to tap into his powers to poof and whatnot. The energy permeated my skin, traveling down every nerve and blood vessel, penetrating through the physical to the heart of my being. My skin tingled, from my scalp down to my toes. The magic energized me, physically, emotionally, supernaturally.

I sucked in a breath, let it out gradually, and shut my eyes to concentrate on the image of my parents and my baby brother.

We whisked through the abysmal tunnel so fast I hardly felt the stinging pain of traveling the elemental way. I kept my eyes shut as we popped out into the real world. Sunlight radiated through my eyelids. I peeled them apart, squinting at the brightness of the world around us.

Max released my hand and moved away from me.

I surveyed the surroundings. A lawn of brown grass encompassed a small brick house with a detached garage. Beyond the lawn lay woods populated with leafless trees much shorter and thinner than the ones in Michigan. My parents lived in Kentucky, which also had tall trees.

This was not Kentucky.

"Where are we?" Max asked.

"Not sure."

I walked toward the house, suffering a weird sensation of wrongness that prickled the hairs on my arms.

The front door swung open, and my mom rushed outside. She sprinted for me, flinging her arms around me to haul me into a bear hug.

"Lindsey, honey," she said, "we were so worried. Where have you been? You weren't in your bed this morning when I came to wake you for breakfast."

My bed? Here? Where the heck was here, anyway?

"I..." Had no idea what to say to my mother. She let me go, and I mumbled, "Sorry I worried you."

Mom squinted at my clothing. "What are you wearing?"

"Uh...something new I picked up recently."

Her gaze drifted past me, her brows knitting together. "Who's your friend?"

I twisted my head around and noted Max had assumed his semi-human glamour. He wore gray slacks and a white shirt as well as black loafers. His swirling, glowing eyes had dimmed and calmed to a reasonable facsimile of human eyes, and his skin had a deep tan but no coppery sheen.

"Um, this is Max." They had met before, many times, but she had no memory of it. "Are Dad and Ash okay?"

"Sure. Why wouldn't they be?"

"No reason."

Mom lodged her hands on her hips. "Where have you been, Lindsey?"

"Uh..."

"It's my fault," Max said. "My car broke down, and I needed a lift. Lindsey was kind enough to pick me up."

My mother glanced around, her eyes going squinty. "Where's your car, Lindsey? The garage door is shut, but it seems like you came from the other direction. Almost like you walked out of the woods."

I was spared from floundering for an explanation when someone else raced out of the house to halt near me and my mother. A cold as deep as the vacuum of space froze my blood. I couldn't blink, couldn't speak, couldn't comprehend what I saw. Who I saw.

The man before me ran a hand through his sandy hair, his lustrous brown eyes searching my face. "Where you been, sweetness? We were worried sick."

I tried to summon words, but my voice emerged as a reedy croak.

Calder Blackwell pulled me into his arms.

Chapter Six

My arms hung slack at my sides. My body stayed stiff. The only sounds I could make were little choked gasps. My ex-fiancé—the man I'd shot seven times and thought I'd killed, the man who'd been transformed into one of the monkey-men known as kerkopes—was currently hugging me. He looked like he had before all the madness started. He looked like the man I'd agreed to marry, the man I'd thought I loved.

Calder let go and grasped my shoulders. "Lindsey, what's the matter?"

"N-nothing." *So convincing.*

His gaze roved my body, his forehead crinkled. "What are ya wearing, sweetness? Never seen this outfit before."

"Well, I, uh, thought I'd try something different."

"You don't seem like yourself." He picked up my left hand, caressing my knuckles, and his fingertips bumped the dual bands around my third finger. His mouth popped open as he stared at my diamond ring and gold wedding band. "What the—This ain't the engagement ring I gave you last month."

Last month? In the timeline I remembered, we'd gotten engaged more than three years ago.

Calder shuffled backward, baffled.

Another man rushed out of the house toward us.

Travis Blackwell stopped beside his brother. "What's going on? And what in tarnation are you wearing, Lindsey?"

In my timeline, Travis had been a cop in Texas before he followed me to Michigan after Calder's apparent demise. Travis had become sheriff of Mandan County, died protecting me, and had been transformed into an incubus.

Just when I'd gotten used to the new Travis, I was confronted with the old one. Or the newer one. Or…whatever.

My dad and Ash tumbled out of the house.

I did not have time to sort this out. My family was okay, that was enough for the moment. I ran to Max, grabbed his hand, and whisked us back to the field where we'd left Janus.

He hadn't moved one inch. "Was your family not what you expected?"

"You could say that." I rubbed my forehead. "This is giving me a headache. We need to reverse the time shift."

"And find out who did it and why," Max said.

"First, we fix it. Then, we take down the villain." I rounded on Janus. "How do we fix this?"

"With my powers, which you have."

"I don't have time for your bruised ego. I repeat, how do we fix this?"

He pushed away from the tree, pacing a ten-foot span of earth. "First, we must ascertain at what point in the past the timeline was altered."

"And we do that how?"

"You must do it. I do not have the power." He held up a hand before I could grouse. "This is not a complaint brought on by my bruised ego. It is a statement of fact."

"Okay. How do I do that?"

He stopped pacing, studying me with an unsettling intensity. "You seem to operate under the assumption you and time are separate entities."

"Time isn't an entity." I drew my head back. "Is it?"

"Not precisely, but it does behave as a living thing might. Wound it, and it will protect itself from further injuries. If the party responsible for the shift attempts another one, it will be more difficult to enact. This gives you a window of opportunity."

"To do what?"

"Connect with time."

I couldn't help the panicked laugh that snorted out of me. "That's crazy. Even if I could do that, what if I go back in time to fix things and run into myself? Physicists say that's a bad thing. A paradox."

He sighed heavily. "Mortals have limited understanding of such matters. You are not *in* the timeline, Lindsey. You are *of* the timeline."

Sure, that made perfect sense—in the world of total insanity.

I felt my lips tighten into a pucker. "Thought I was the mortal vessel, just a place to stash your powers until you, the imperious god, returned to claim them."

Janus flitted his gaze around the area, from the trees to the sky and down to the ground, then cleared his throat and looked at me. "It does not matter what I think. You command the powers, and only you can undo what has been done."

With all my heart and soul, I wished Nevan was here. My Nevan. The one who loved and cherished me and would do anything for me, as I would for him. The Nevan in this timeline had run away. I had no choice but to trust in Janus like Bob had suggested.

But that cold, slithery sensation inside me would not go away. I glanced at Max, who shrugged.

I scrunched my lips, zeroing in on Janus. "When you first showed up, you demanded your powers back. Now you're advising me on how to use them. How do I know you're not tricking me into giving back your powers?"

"Because I am not." He walked straight up to me, forcing me to bend my head back to meet his gaze. "Listen to me. I do want my powers back, but whatever is transpiring here overrides our personal desires. We must work together to prevent irreparable damage to the timeline. Temporal shifts are delicate and dangerous magics. Even I have enacted only one shift, and that was at the command of Jupiter. I had no choice but to obey my king."

"You have power over time, but you've never used it?"

"I have used it to travel into the past and future strictly to observe. Toying with the natural progression of events could wreak unspeakable consequences." He paused as if considering the issue. "This shift was relatively minor. We have a chance to undo it and prevent irreparable damage, but we must act swiftly. You must act swiftly."

Janus shambled to the nearest tree and leaned his side against it like he had the weight of a thousand worlds bearing down on him.

And I couldn't help wondering what consequences his one and only attempt at time manipulation had wrought. That was a question for after we undid this shift.

"I don't know how to do this," I said. "Connect with time? Sheesh. I froze time once, but that might've been a fluke."

Janus jerked away from the tree. "You froze time?"

"Uh, yeah." I shrugged. "There was a wacko sorcerer who absorbed the essences of Skeiron, Notus, and my ex-fiancé, Calder. Anyway, he had so much power none of us, not even my elemental friends, could stop him. I had to trick him into doing what I wanted. I figured the only way I could get the upper hand was if I sort of moved laterally instead of blipping from place to place. That's how I froze time. And my plan worked. The sorcerer is gone."

"I see." Janus stared at me like I'd grown a forest of red, spiky horns on my head. "I am beginning to understand you are no ordinary mortal."

Max chuckled. "You're just now figuring that out? Some god you are."

"You, salamander, should be grateful I am not one of the vengeful gods who easily takes offense."

"You have no powers. Maybe you, tosser, ought to be grateful I don't crush you to bits for disrespecting the Janusite."

"Ugh," I said. "Enough machismo. How do I connect with time?"

Janus stared hard at Max for a moment, but the incubus remained unperturbed. At last, the god spoke to me. "You must feel the connection. If you had a familiar—"

"She does," Max snapped.

The god gave Max an assessing glance, then sniffed his lifted nose. "A salamander as your familiar? I would have expected more from the mortal imbued with my powers."

At least he'd stopped calling me "the mortal vessel."

Max flattened his lips and tensed his whole body as if preparing to attack.

I shook my head at him, holding up a warning finger.

He growled softly but stopped preparing for battle with the god.

"Get over here, Max," I said. "I need my familiar's help."

My familiar trudged to me and held out his hands, palms up. I hovered mine over them with a minute space between our palms. We took a simultaneous breath and exhaled it slowly, our gazes locked. The magic crackled between our hands, sweeping up my arms in a tingling wave of energy, branching out into the rest of me until I felt like my whole body had fallen asleep and woken up with an electrical surge.

I shut my eyes and let all thoughts vacate my mind, focusing on the sensation of the tingling magic, blocking out everything else. The sounds of the woods dwindled into a silence. The whispers of Max's breaths and my own receded into silence. Everything receded from my consciousness, and I floated in a nothingness so vast I couldn't comprehend its dimensions. It had none, I supposed. This vacant space knew no bounds.

Time, time, where are you?

My single thought became a sing-song litany I repeated in my mind over and over, letting the emptiness take me wherever it wanted. For this was a river, the slow-moving and incomprehensible flow of…time.

I'd made it. I had connected with time.

The current of it propelled me forward, but I needed to go against the flow. Where was the event that had rewritten the entire timeline? When was it?

Show me the wound. Let me heal it.

The flow shifted course, curving and arching backward until it connected with itself again somewhere upriver from where I'd started. This place had no light, no landmarks, nothing to guide me except the sensation of movement, always movement. How could I find the time-altering event? I needed to jump into the point where the change had occurred and reverse it. Somehow.

That part I hadn't figured out yet.

I dived toward the point where the river merged with itself at the closing point in the loop. My fingers, not really fingers except in my mind, stretched out to touch the intersection. Almost there. A little further. *Stretch, stretch, reach for it, almost there.*

Just as I latched onto it, a massive burst of power slammed into me.

I careened out of the void, my eyes popped open, and I tumbled backward to land with my feet above my head and my butt in the air.

"Shit!" I rolled onto my side and accepted Max's help in getting up. I shook my whole body, needing to shed the remnants of whatever had ejected me from the time stream. I glared at Janus. "Connect with time. No problem. Thanks for the brilliant advice."

He lifted one brow. "What happened? Did you undo the change?"

"No. I tried, but something shoved me out with one swift kick of its ginormous, steel-toed, ethereal boot."

Max's lips kinked in a slight smile, but Janus simply stared at me.

Nice to know I could confound a god. It gave me a little glow inside.

"If I am of the timeline," I said, "why couldn't I get in there to fix things? Everything seemed okay, but then the cosmic boot punted me out."

Janus canted his head. "What were you doing when you were ejected?"

"Trying to connect with time. I sensed where, or rather when, the change had happened, and I was heading straight for that moment when—whack!"

I smacked my palms together to emphasize the point.

Janus's lips parted as if he meant to speak, but he sealed them again.

Max waved a hand toward the god. "I don't think he understands your terminology. Try speaking to him like he was a child." Max sidled up to Janus and spoke in a baby-talk voice. "Lindsey tried to make friends with time, but it got mad and wouldn't play with her."

I threw my head back and groaned. "Max, honestly. You are not helping."

Janus shot a haughty glare at Max before smoothing out his expression when he looked at me. "Your familiar is very protective of you. It is highly unusual, in my vast experience, and could become a problem."

Naturally, he emphasized the word vast to make sure we lesser beings understood our place.

Oh, I was getting really tired of his imperious attitude.

I jabbed a finger in the air in Max's direction. "I command you to stop harassing Janus. Understood?"

"Yes, mistress." Max sighed and scratched his neck. "If you insist."

"I do." His life debt to me ensured he would obey. I hated using magic in this way, but I couldn't have Max and Janus bickering while I tried to fix whatever some crazy-ass weirdo had done to the timeline.

Nevan, I really need you now.

A big, strong body materialized behind me, flush with my backside. Arms encircled my waist, tugging me more firmly into the hard muscles pressed against me. The heat and scent of him surrounded me.

"Nevan," I breathed, and leaned into his body.

Way, way in the back of my mind I realized this was the altered version of him, not my husband. Rationality insisted I move away from him. *Screw rationality.* I relaxed into him, resting my palms on his forearms, loving the feel of his hands clasped over my belly.

He dipped his head to murmur in my ear, "I tried to stay away, but something inexplicable draws me back to you."

Inexplicable. Because he had no idea who I was.

Oh, but he felt so good around me.

"I wanted you all to myself," he rumbled into my ear. "Do ye mind, darlin'?"

Mind what? That's when I realized I had my eyes closed. I opened them.

We weren't in the field near where the rock shop had once stood. Max and Janus were nowhere in sight. Nevan had whisked me away to a clearing in the woods. Where, I had no clue.

He nuzzled my throat. "Well, darlin', do ye mind?"

"That you brought me here? No." I should've pushed away from him, but I really, really did not want to do it. My body ached all over from whatever force had kicked me out of the time stream, and his presence soothed me. "Why did you come back?"

"I couldn't stay away. You intrigue me." His hands drifted up my belly. "I suffer from an intense need to claim your body."

He'd come back for sex. I should've been offended by that, I supposed, but I'd sunk too deep into the bliss of his presence to give a fig about anything. Maybe I should have sex with him. Forget the world, forget the wounded timeline, forget everything except the pleasure he could give me.

Those big hands of his drifted higher to cup my breasts, and he whispered to me in the sultry voice that always melted me. "I may not know you, but that's never stopped me before."

Suddenly, the wrongness of this hit me.

I smacked his thigh. "Hey! Get your hands off my tits. Do you fondle every strange woman you meet?"

"No, only the ones who claim to be my wife."

Wriggling out of his embrace, I rounded on him. "That happens a lot more often than you might think."

Yeah, I remembered the moment when his formerly dead wife had flounced out of the woods to proclaim she wanted her husband back. Like I'd ever lie down for that one.

I couldn't lie down for this battle either. I had to get back to Janus and Max and figure out how to repair the timeline.

Nevan snared me with one brawny arm and hauled me into his body. "I have no idea what you want, why you claim to know me, but as long as you're here…" He caught my bottom lip with his teeth, releasing it slowly. "Might as well enjoy the pleasure of each other's company."

My body responded like it always did—softening, warming, tingling in all the right places.

"I can't have sex with you," I said. "Not until you can tell me my name. My full name. First, middle, and last."

He palmed my ass with one hand. "Tell me your name, then, and I'll gladly repeat it."

"That's cheating." I wrestled free of him. "I'm sorry, Nevan. I cannot have sex with you until you say my name."

This time, I didn't need Max's help. I zipped myself back to the field, tapping into Nevan's powers much more easily than before. And yeah, I longed to believe that meant our bond endured and was growing stronger. Because maybe, just maybe, that would mean his memories were trying to resurface. I could not afford to cling to such a slender thread of hope. It would distract me, and distractions could be fatal.

Max gave me a closed-mouth, knowing smile. "Nevan swept you away for a quickie?"

"No." Well, that had been his intention, but I'd rebuffed him. Eventually. "Getting back to the matter at hand, do we have any idea what pushed me out of the time stream?"

Two supernatural beings shrugged and shook their heads.

"Come on," I said. "That's all you've got? Zippo?"

Janus cleared his throat. "I do not know what or who is behind the time shift, but to create one would require immense power the likes of which none have seen. The perpetrator would need to tap into the darkest magics."

"Oh jeez, I'm so tired of villains who tap into the darkest magics. Why can't you people destroy the world with giant bombs like normal lunatics do?"

Janus gave me that confounded look again.

"Forget it," I said. "How do I get past this immense magic that's locked me out of the time stream?"

"I do not know," the god said.

Max raised a hand like a kid in school. "Anyone care to hear my idea?"

"Go on," I said.

"When you're in there, freeze time."

I stared blankly at him for a couple seconds until I grasped his meaning. "When I'm reaching for that moment when time was altered, I should freeze time to stop that immense force from attacking me."

"Exactly."

"Max, you are so smart."

He puffed up a little. "Just doing my job as your familiar."

"It's a brilliant idea." I bit my lip. "Though I suspect I could get seriously hurt if this doesn't work."

Janus spoke up. "You must weigh the risks and benefits and decide which is more worthwhile."

I didn't need to think about it. "It's worth the risk."

"Then do it."

Without waiting for Max to assist me, I shut my eyes and soared out of myself into the sightless abyss of the time stream. Why didn't I need Max's magic to enhance mine, a small part of me wondered. I knew the answer without mulling the question.

Nevan. Somehow, my encounter with him had bolstered my spirits and my magics.

I followed the stream as it looped back around to the moment where I needed to be. That mysterious dark force stretched out its tendrils toward me, but I concentrated all my energy on the task I'd set for myself.

The flowing river of time stopped moving.

And the dark force froze too. I couldn't see it or feel it, but I sensed the change. Everything in the domain of time had ground to a halt.

Except me. Because I was *of* time, not in it.

I dived for that one point in time where everything had shifted. My body caught up to me with a whoosh that left me breathless for a few precious seconds. Smells and sounds of the woods tantalized my senses, and I dared to open my eyes.

Ten feet in front of me, frozen in time, Calder Blackwell lay prone on the ground at the edge of a small pool inside a clearing in the woods. A natural spring burbled up at its center. Deep scratches marred his face, his jacket was torn, and his hand had fallen into the water. The blood dripping from his fingertips hung suspended in the instant before it would have dropped into the water.

A cougar hunkered nearby, seeming on the verge of pouncing for the kill.

This was the moment when Calder had lain dying, and out of desperation, accepted an elemental's offer to be forged into an immortal creature. This was where everything had shifted.

I had to know why.

Chapter Seven

I WANDERED AROUND THE SCENE, TAKING IN EVERY DETAIL I COULD see. Calder had told me a cougar attacked him and it was the precipitating event that spurred him to accept an elemental's offer to make him immortal. Knowing the truth and witnessing it…two very different things. If I released my hold on time and let events unfold, I would watch Calder get ripped apart by a wild animal, then watch as he underwent the far more agonizing experience of the forging. It ripped apart the human body, transforming it into something new.

A memory barreled through me. Travis lying in a puddle of blood, dying. Me begging Nevan to forge Travis. Nevan had talked me through my grief, showing me it was selfish to do that to Travis without his consent. I was prepared to let my friend go, but Max had taken matters into his own hands. Linked to me by a powerful life debt, caring for me because we had become friends, Max did the one thing he'd sworn never to do again. He forged a mortal. He forged Travis.

But he'd done it for me.

Travis's forging had happened because I left my friends to fight alone while I took out the sorcerer. While I was gone, Ceara—Nevan's first wife and the sorcerer's accomplice, not to mention his lover—had attacked my friends. By the time I returned to them, it was too late. Ceara had slit Travis's throat right in front of me. Travis hadn't chosen his fate, but Calder had. He wanted the power and immortality granted to an elemental, and he hadn't cared if he became a monster in the process.

I tiptoed up to Calder where he lay facedown in the mud at the pool's edge. His eyes were open, evincing life. The cougar had been about to deal the final blow, the one that would end Calder's life, when I froze time. Could I watch this happen? I had no choice. I had to let him die and be transformed in order to repair the timeline. Something or someone had spared his life, triggering the time shift.

Calder Blackwell must die.

My gut twisted. I swallowed hard, my throat dry as sandpaper. Watch him die? Christ, why did the universe keep forcing me to be a spectator to death and destruction?

Tears stung in my eyes. I squeezed them shut, willing the tears to stop.

Rein it in, Lindsey. Do what you have to do.

I hadn't issued that mental command in months, not since Nevan stormed into my life and changed everything, changed me, changed the fates of two worlds with me. Rein it in? I hated resorting to my old ways, but I would never get through this unless I did just that.

Eyes wide open, I rose and marched to the edge of the trees, peering into the twilight shadows for any sign of the person or creature responsible for the time shift. Something had changed here, now, and Calder had not died. I walked the perimeter of the clearing, determined to spot the perpetrator, but I found nothing.

Wait. What was that?

I backtracked a few feet, squinting into the trees.

Between two closely spaced trees, something hovered. It looked like…a blur. A vaguely human-shaped blur in shades of beige and white. Everything else around me was as sharp as the best high-definition television, but the thing ten feet in front of me, suspended between two trees, seemed to have been moving so fast it froze as a blur. What on earth could move that fast?

Nothing of this earth could. Something or someone from another world might. I'd seen Max run as fast as any comic-book superhero, becoming a blur of flames.

A blur.

Could the hazy figure in the trees be an elemental?

Energy scraped at my psyche, and the world around me twitched. I couldn't describe it any other way. Everything moved slightly, then returned to its original position so swiftly I experienced it as a twitch of the world.

An instinct warned me of what was happening. The blur-being was fighting my time freeze.

I marshaled all the power I could but initiating the time freeze had consumed most of my magical energy. I took everything I had access to, every ounce of magic left inside me, and funneled it into strengthening the freeze. My head throbbed. My body ached like I'd done a three-hour workout at the gym. Not that I'd ever visited a gym. Cold sweat dribbled down my temples and the back of my neck. I squinted and gritted my teeth, concentrating everything I had on the task.

Blue energy sparkled around me.

The world jerked one way, then the other, and settled back into position.

Pain tore through my entire body. I gnashed my teeth, and an agonized sound burst out of me.

Time unfroze.

I staggered backward, gasping for air, phantom lights sparking in my vision.

The blur-being raced past me, bowling me over with a gust of hurricane strength.

Flat on my back, I struggled to catch my breath and gain my bearings. Everything spun around me, but it wasn't the world twitching again. Dizziness had seized me, and I could not summon the energy to get up. My muscles had turned to jelly.

"Linnnzeeee."

The raspy, breathy word originated to my right where I knew Calder lay dying. My hair had fallen over my face, though, blown there by the wind. I couldn't see a thing. With an effort that shot pains through my every nerve, I rolled onto my side.

The blur-being hovered beside Calder. Both he and the cougar remained frozen.

"Why are you doing this?" I asked, my voice strained.

The being blasted out another gale.

Calder and the cougar unfroze.

A skeletal finger stretched out from within the blur to point at the cougar.

The animal yelped and galloped away.

"Janusite," the blur-being said in that bizarre voice, part sigh, part growl. The "S" in Janusite became a drawn-out hiss. "You cannot stop me. Vengeance shall be mine."

The skeletal finger stabbed in my direction.

I careened across the clearing, rolling and rolling, rocks and twigs and other things I couldn't identify scraping and slashing at me. I shut my eyes and covered my head with my arms to shield my face. When at last I stopped spinning like a glass tube tossed down an oil-slicked incline, I realized I'd ended up on my back. Prying my lids apart, I saw the blue sky above me, darkening with every second it slid toward the impending night.

Scrambling to my feet, I bolted for the clearing.

Only to slam into a magical barrier.

I bounced off it, stumbling into a tree. When I regained my balance, I peered into the clearing.

The blur-being was nowhere in sight. Calder lay where he had before. His hand twitched. He moaned. With an agonized noise, rolled onto his back.

Movement drew my attention to the woods opposite where I stood. The blur-being hung suspended there.

Calder, hands shaking, dug his cell phone out of his pants pocket. He struggled to dial a number, succeeding after some nasty swearing. He held the phone to his ear, waiting for someone to pick up at the other end of the call.

"Yeah," he said, his voice quavering, "I need help. A cougar attacked me. Don't know where I am exactly." He listened intently. "GPS? Thank God, I don't know if I can walk."

Every cell phone had GPS built into it for just such a circumstance. First responders would track him down.

I had needed to stop this, to let Calder die in order to undo the time shift. Instead, I'd gotten blown away by a blurry creature with skeletal fingers.

My gaze flicked to the blur-being. It poofed away.

The magical barrier disintegrated.

Calder lifted his head, bleary-eyed and blood-stained. "Somebody there?"

I had no choice. To avoid any further damage to the timeline, I had to get out of here.

So I returned to the present, to Max and Janus.

And to Nevan, who was glowering at the other two like he itched to pummel them. He had his fists clenched at his sides and his every muscle tensed. His eyes burned and whorled with shades of black and crimson.

He was more than mad. He was infuriated.

"What is going on here?" I asked.

Max nodded toward Nevan. "The sylph is accusing us of keeping him away from you on purpose."

Jealousy again? My heart did a dopey flip-flop at the idea, but mostly I wanted to defuse the situation before Nevan did something rash like hurling Max or Janus across the nearest boundary. No elemental aside from Nevan could cross the invisible, magical boundaries around natural water features in the mortal world. Nevan got around the rule because of me, because of our deep connection and my Janusite powers, giving him the ability to go anywhere he wanted so long as I was somewhere in the mortal world at the time. For any other elementals, violating the boundary rule would result in their destruction, a process that disassembled their bodies molecule by molecule. I assumed Nevan had his immunity despite the changes in him, but I didn't care to test that theory.

The last thing I needed today was another display of misplaced machismo.

Nevan raised a fist, shaking it at Max.

I stomped up to Nevan. "Cut that out this instant."

He lowered his fist and turned toward me. "You vanished. Only an elemental being may travel that way, which means one of those two snatched you away from me."

"No, I did it myself."

"A mortal can't—"

"This one can."

He flashed a scowl at Max and Janus, but a tinge of desperation weakened its effect. "That is not possible."

"I tapped into your powers. You must've felt it."

Nevan's brows crinkled, and he grasped his head in both hands. "I felt…something. I do not understand any of this. No mortal could access my powers."

Max, of course, chose that moment to get snarky. "Bloody irritating, isn't it? You can commiserate with our friend the impotent god."

"Shush, Max," I said. "Could you and our new friend give me a minute alone with Nevan? Go over there or something."

I waved vaguely toward the other end of the field.

Janus balked. "I will not obey the commands of a mortal."

Max gave a melodramatic sigh, slapped his hand on Janus's shoulder, and said, "You'll want to obey this one. She's going to make out with Nevan, and trust me, that's not something you want to watch."

The god grunted, contorting his mouth, but then followed Max to the far end of the field.

I splayed my palms on Nevan's chest. "Take it easy, no one is taking me away from you. I'm yours. Even if you never remember what we had together, I will never leave you."

He relaxed visibly, exhaling a long breath. "If they did not take you, why did you abandon me?"

God, I wanted to throw my arms around him. Instead, I moved closer to gaze up at him with our bodies inches apart and my hands lingering on his chest. "I didn't abandon you. I had something to do, that's all. Didn't work out the way I'd hoped, but I had to try."

"What did you do?"

"I tried to undo the time shift."

His hands lighted on my hips, and his expression softened. "What went wrong?"

"Somebody else was there, some kind of blurry being with skeletal fingers. It knows what I can do, and somehow, it prevented me from correcting the timeline. That thing was outrageously powerful." I shivered a little thinking about it. "And that being said it wants revenge."

"Revenge for what?"

"I don't know."

Well, maybe I did if I could piece together the clues. The blur-being had rewritten the timeline by stopping Calder's forging. Of all the things the being could've done, why did it choose that event? As far as I knew, Calder hadn't done much of anything as an elemental other than trick Brennus the raven shifter into a bargain that enslaved him. Everything Calder had done after his forging served one purpose.

To get me back.

I'd refused the forging even when he had slashed my throat, prepared to die rather than become a monkey-thing like him. His so-called love had been nothing more than a need to control me.

Okay, but what did any of that have to do with altering time? I couldn't believe the blur-being wanted to spare Calder the pain of his transformation or spare me from the things Calder had done in an attempt to make me so desperate I'd choose the forging. Even his efforts to frame me for murder had not convinced me to become like him.

No, the blur-being had another agenda, but it must center on me.

Or maybe I was becoming narcissistic and thought every villain had it in for me. No, I'd been right those other times to believe somebody was out to get me. I trusted my instincts, and they warned the blur-being had a beef with me.

Great. What had I ever done to that hazy, crazy creature?

Think, Lindsey.

Something about the way my windy friend had called my name twanged a memory. I'd heard that voice before.

In my nightmares.

"Linnnnzeeee," the wind had called in my dreams. The last nightmare had involved Skeiron and Notus, but previous ones had been too vague and confusing for me to puzzle out their meaning. Maybe the blur-being had some connection to the sylphs. Nevan had control of the air and could even create thunderstorms. Of course, every sylph I'd ever met looked humanoid and had a solid, unblurry body. Besides, Notus and Skeiron were gone for good. The Four Winds had sent their essences packing and assured me no one and nothing could ever bring them back.

Okay, I'd stash the sylph connection in the mental box labeled "consider later, more evidence required."

Back to the me connection, then. What ripple effect had saving Calder effected? He was alive and human, apparently happy. So was Travis. Based on what I'd seen when I visited my family, my life had changed too. If I weren't immune to the time shift, I would've been living in Texas with my fiancé Calder, my good buddy Travis, and my family. What else, though? I never would've come to Michigan since I never would've needed to flee from Texas after Calder's disappearance and apparent death.

I would never have met Nevan, which meant I wasn't the Janusite—or at least, I would have no clue I was. The blur-being might have hoped to eradicate the Janusite.

There had to be more to it.

What about Nevan? The shift had altered him too.

My hands lingered on his chest, on his hot skin.

"You seem to be deep in thought," he said.

I chewed the inside of my bottom lip. "Who is the king of the sylphs?"

"Notus, of course. He has ruled over us for a very long time."

Another change. Skeiron had usurped Notus, and Nevan had ascended the throne after I took out Skeiron.

"What about Skeiron?" I asked.

"Notus destroyed him during the violent battle for the kingship three thousand years ago."

"So, um…" I tapped my fingers on his chest. "You have never been king."

He laughed softly. "Me? No, darlin', I have never been king of anything. After Skeiron's demise, I became the leader of the sylph army."

"If you're a general or whatever, why do you prance around in a loincloth?"

"Because I resigned from the army and requested to become the guardian of the falls." He nodded over his shoulder. "The waterfall here."

Requested? In my reality, Skeiron had forced Nevan into a bad bargain. Nevan had become bound to the falls, coerced into searching for the Janusite, all because he'd enjoyed a few rolls in the hay with Skeiron's daughter.

"Did you sleep with Skeiron's daughter?" I asked.

"Well, yes." Nevan smirked but then the expression melted away. "Skeiron never knew of it. How did you?"

"I know you, that's how. In my reality, you are king and both Skeiron and Notus are dead."

"That would be preferable. Notus has become quite depraved."

"Did you ask to be guardian of the falls to get away from him?"

"Partly." Nevan's gaze went distant. "I also had an overpowering urge to come here. I do not understand it." He nailed his gaze to me. "The need I felt then is similar to the need I feel now."

"What need?"

"To protect you and care for you." Though he kept his hands on my hips, he shifted uncomfortably. "To be with you, always. I did not like it when you vanished."

"I'm sorry about that." I glided my hands up to his neck. "I got scared, and I ran. That will never happen again."

"What frightened you?"

"You don't recognize me. After everything we've been through together, all the pain we've both endured to get to this day, our wedding day...I'm scared you'll never remember me, remember us."

He slid his hands up my back. "I may not recall the things you remember, but I can't stay away from you. Something pulls me back to you no matter how far I travel. I heard your call, but that shouldn't be. No mortal has the power to summon an elemental."

I'd screamed for Tris once upon a time, and he had come. But then, I'd already known him. He must've liked me even though he wouldn't admit it. He came when I called because he sensed I'd needed help to save Nevan's life.

Nevan came to me a little while ago because of our bond.

Maybe he didn't recognize it yet, maybe it was submerged under layers of time-shift confusion, but it had to be the truth.

"You came when I called," I said, "because we have a connection deeper and stronger than any magic, stronger even than time."

He stared at me for a moment, then nodded slowly. "Perhaps we do."

I'd settle for "perhaps." It meant he didn't think I was crazy, and that was a very good thing.

"Gah!"

The shout from across the field made both Nevan and me swing our attention in that direction. Janus was swatting at his shoulders and chest, twisting this way and that, spouting a slew of words in another language. Given his tone of voice, it sounded like he was swearing a blue streak.

I grabbed Nevan's hand. We rushed to the god.

Just as we reached him, a bright-red salamander leaped off Janus's shoulder and onto mine. The critter gazed up at me with large, dark eyes.

I pointed a finger at him. "Max, what did you do to Janus?"

He shrugged his tiny red shoulders. If a salamander had shoulders.

Max sprang off my shoulder onto the ground. In a burst of flames, he assumed his usual humanoid form, stark naked. Shaking himself like a dog, he said, "The impotent god was being imperious and bloody aggravating. A real wanker, that one. What else could I do?"

"Not tick off the god, that's what."

He grunted.

Janus clenched his jaw but said nothing.

"Still want your powers back?" I said. "Considering what happened to me in the time stream, I'm thinking I should hand over these powers and let you fix the time shift. You're the expert, right?"

I got a strange queasy feeling when I thought about relinquishing my magic, but then, it wasn't really mine. Never had been. I'd grown kind of attached to these powers I had never wanted.

Janus frowned. "I have no conception of how to transfer the powers back to me."

"Seriously? The first thing you said after popping up in an earthquake rift was 'give me back my powers,' but you have no clue how to do it."

"That is correct." His frown deepened. "I had assumed the Four Winds would enact the transfer upon my resurrection. They did not. Apparently, I am meant to assist you in some way before reacquiring my powers."

"Hmm." I wondered if maybe the Winds wanted him to learn a little humility first but decided to keep that theory to myself. "Anybody got another idea for how to reverse the time shift and stop the blur-being from creating any more of them?"

The group response came in the form of shrugs and noncommittal noises.

"Great," I said, throwing my arms up and letting them fall again, my hands slapping on my thighs. "I've got a god and two powerful elementals on my side, but nobody has a frigging clue how to handle this situation."

"You are the most powerful among us," Max said. "We're here to serve you."

"But I have to come up with a plan. Fantastic." I groaned out a sigh. "Last time we fought a big baddie, you guys helped with the planning. Besides, I doubt Mr. Prickly Godlike Being over there is here to serve me."

Janus sniffed. "I serve no one but Jupiter. And I am not a god*like* being, I am a god."

"Whatever." I rubbed my temples, head bowed, and tried to focus on the problem at hand. The blur-being was too powerful for me to fight alone. I jerked my head up. "I'll take Max and Nevan with me into the time stream. They can help fight the mystery villain, and together, we'll have enough power to undo the time shift."

"No," Janus said, looking at me like I was a total idiot. "You cannot take another entity into the time stream with you. Weapons are permitted, as long as they reside on your person."

"On my person? Jeez, I hope you don't mean it has to be surgically attached to my body."

"It does not. A sword in a scabbard attached to your belt will suffice."

Lifting my shirt a touch to expose my derringer in its holster, I said, "What about this weapon? I didn't have a chance to use it against the blur-being, too weirded out by seeing Calder in the moment before his forging."

Janus squinted at the handgun. "I am unfamiliar with that sort of weaponry, but it does reside on your person. So yes, it would survive the journey into the time stream."

"What if I wrap my body around Nevan's good and tight? Could he survive the journey then?"

Nevan perked up at the suggestion.

But Janus looked irritated at my ignorance. "He would remain a separate entity, not contained on your person."

I took another minute or so to mull what he'd said and how I might transport something useful into the time stream with me. I couldn't take Nevan or Max with me. They weren't "on my person" no matter how sluttily I pasted myself to one of them. Unless...

"What about this," I said. "Max can turn into a teeny-tiny lizard. If I tuck him in my pocket, would that qualify as on my person?"

Janus's brows cinched tight over his nose, and his mouth opened a smidge. He stayed like that for several seconds before he literally shrugged off his confusion and said, "I imagine it would qualify. Your familiar is bonded to you as a servant, a sort of weapon or implement. In his smaller form, if he were concealed in your pocket, he likely would survive the journey. However, having never attempted such a thing, I cannot guarantee it."

"Good enough."

Max's jaw went slack. "Excuse me? I'm to crawl into your pocket and pray the time stream doesn't annihilate me?"

Janus made an impatient noise. "It wouldn't annihilate you, tiny salamander. You would be forcibly ejected and might suffer physical injuries, which would heal."

"Oh." Max's expression brightened. "In that case, I'd love to tag along. But not in your pocket, Lindsey. I'll suffocate."

His smile mutated into a smirk as he zeroed in on my bosom.

I laid a hand between my breasts. "You want to ride in my bra?"

"There's no better way to travel than tucked between a woman's breasts."

Nevan bristled, snapping straight and stiff. "He will not."

"Cool down, Nevan," I said. "This is strictly business. Right, Max?"

"Of course," the incubus replied with a twinkle in his eyes.

Nevan narrowed his gaze on Max.

I laid a hand on Nevan's arm. "Relax. Max is an incubus. That means he's a big-time flirt, but it's just his nature. He has no interest in me except as a friend."

"Sad but true," Max agreed. "I spend a large amount of my time with a beautiful woman but never feel inclined to seduce her. It's bloody depressing."

Though he spoke the words in a light tone as if he were joking, I sensed something else beneath the surface. Max needed to feed on sexual energy to survive, which meant he needed to have sex on a regular basis to stay healthy and strong. Since he hung out with either Travis or me and Nevan most of the time, I wondered when he got a chance to get some.

He did have the faintest dark circles under his eyes.

Max squirmed under my scrutiny.

I waved for him to approach. "Shift into salamander form, and I'll slip you inside my bra."

Amid a flash of flames, Max shrank into his salamander form. I knelt to lay my hand, palm up, on the ground. He scampered onto my palm.

Rising, I took hold of my shirt's neckline and lifted it out, then let Max scamper off my hand and into the space created by my bra. He smiled up at me, his tiny lizard teeth exposed, and blinked his tiny lizard eyes once, slowly.

I let go of my shirt. Max was as "on my person" as anyone could get.

His long tail twitched, tickling my skin.

Shivering, I laughed.

Nevan glared at my bosom.

"Cut that out," I said to my bra where the roguish salamander resided. "Behave, Max."

I swore I heard an adorable, teeny-tiny sigh.

He settled down in his odd little nest.

"Okay," I said. "Here goes."

I shut my eyes and jumped into the time stream.

CHAPTER EIGHT

I EMERGED IN THE SAME MOMENT AS BEFORE, EVERYTHING FROZEN with Calder lying wounded at the pool's edge. A quick glance around showed me the blur-being hiding among the trees like the first time I'd been here.

Max skittered out of my bra, up to my shoulder, and leaped to the ground. At the instant he touched down, flames erupted. He resumed his humanlike form.

"Let's do this," I said, grabbing his hand. "We need more power."

The energy sizzled through his hand into mine, spiraling out into my entire body. The blue energy of my powers crackled and snapped around us both in a curtain of magic. With time frozen, would the blur-being remain immobilized? The being had enough power to travel through time and alter the past. Since she'd fought off my time freeze before, I couldn't count on it affecting the creature this time. We needed to hurry.

Max seemed to understand this without words. He funneled more energy into me, more than he ever had before, and the blue curtain shimmered and thickened into a semi-opaque haze alight with snapping sparks.

Now or never.

I raised my free hand and hurled magic at the blur-being.

The blast flung the entity backward, and it smacked into a tree with a wet cracking sound. The blurry cloud around the being dissipated in a puff, revealing the being that had hidden within it, but the entity was too far away for me to see anything more than dirty white robes.

No time to waste. I had to let Calder die.

I kept my one hand raised, spewing magic at the creature slumped on the ground, while Max channeled more and more energy into me. Somehow—I couldn't explain how, only that I sensed Max driving it—we became invisible. All of us. Me, Max, and the being currently prone on the ground across the clearing, further into the trees.

My gaze fell on Calder. Injured. Bleeding. Suffering. My stomach wrenched into tight knots, and I couldn't breathe.

He must die. I must watch it happen.

Oh God, Calder, I'm so sorry. I resisted the impulse to shut my eyes. If I had to do this, I must bear witness to it.

Holding on to Max's hand, surrounded by my blue magics, I released the time freeze.

A figure rose up out of the murky depths of the natural spring, water sluicing off its monkey-like, humanoid body. The being crouched over Calder. The creature—one of the kerkopes based on its wiry black hair and large, golden eyes—chanted in an alien language I had heard once before.

On the night Max forged Travis.

As Max had then, the monkey-thing chanted while he raised his hands, palms out, and shimmering orbs of bluish-white light popped up throughout the clearing, swarming around the elemental being and Calder. The lights flared brighter and brighter until I had to shield my eyes from the blinding brilliance.

Energy seared my skin, the backwash of the forging process.

Calder screamed with an agony and terror like nothing on earth.

On the night Max transformed Travis, I'd begged Nevan to tell me what the forging felt like. His words echoed in my mind now.

The forging will rend his limbs, his mind, every particle of his body and soul, crushing and melting them. A power beyond imagining will reshape his form, and he will be born anew through the scalding agony. He might wish for death with his last coherent thought before the pain and fire consume everything that made him human. Only his soul and his memories will remain.

Helpless to spare Calder, I covered my ears and squeezed my eyes shut. His screams penetrated into me anyway. Silence. I stood there for a moment, immobilized, my pulse racing. Somehow, I had held onto the magics keeping us invisible through the whole horrible event, but now, they crumbled away.

I opened my eyes and gazed into the clearing.

Calder and the monkey-thing were gone.

An inhuman shriek rattled my eardrums.

The formerly blurry being flew off the ground, through the trees, and straight across the clearing toward me. A burst of wind knocked me sideways into Max. He stumbled too, but just as we found our footing, the creature landed smack in front of me.

She landed.

And the earth shivered.

The female being stood half a foot taller than me, her waist-length, ghost-white hair tumbling over her shoulders in a tangled mess. Her skin was pale as death, her lips purple. Her fathomless black eyes glittered with red sparks. Perky little breasts seemed out of place on her emaciated body, covered by tattered and filthy robes that must've started out white. And those skeletal fingers…

The being raised one finger to point at me. The long, curved, and sharp-looking nail was black and resembled a bird's talon.

"Linnnzeeee," she said, her voice breathy and raspy like a roaring wind. "Lindsey Astrid Porter, Janusite and lover of the sylph king, hear this. You may have won this battle, but only because I had not expected your familiar to make it through the time stream. Next time, I will be prepared."

"What do you want?" I asked. "Why are you doing all of this?"

"Vengeance, my pretty," she said, stretching out that finger to slash the wickedly long nail in front of my nose. "Never again shall I suffer betrayal. You took them from me, and I will have them back whatever the cost. I shall avenge what you have done before it was done."

I tore the derringer out of my waistband and fired both rounds straight into her forehead.

Singed holes appeared where the rounds had struck her. She flinched, but no blood poured from the wounds. The creature jerked her head side to side with sharp cracking noises. The .357 slugs popped out of her forehead to plop onto the ground.

Endued bullets had no effect on her? How could I defeat an unkillable foe?

A gust of wind barreled into me. I tumbled into Max, we both got bowled over, and we wound up tangled on the ground. Max hissed in a breath, choking back a cry.

The woman-thing had vanished.

Chapter Nine

MAX AND I RETURNED TO THE FIELD MOMENTS AFTER THE WINDY Witch had smacked us down. With Calder's life path restored, his forging completed, everything should have gone back to normal. Well, as normal as my life had ever been. Maybe "back to the original timeline" was a better way to phrase it.

Except neither had happened.

We came back to the same empty, overgrown field. The rock shop had not reappeared. Before anyone could speak to me, I zipped away to the house in Texas where I'd found my family earlier—and found them there again. With Max's help, I'd figured out how to glamour myself invisible during Encounter Two with the Windy Witch. I stayed out of sight while I quickly reconnoitered the area around my parents' house. Peeking through the picture window in the living room, I spied my parents and Ash in the midst of a boisterous discussion with Travis. They were smiling and laughing, clearly exchanging jokes. I peered through every other window but saw no sign of Calder.

How could nothing have changed except for Calder? It made no sense. The Windy Witch had stopped Calder's forging in order to rewrite history, and his survival had set off a chain reaction that altered everything. Letting him die and undergo the forging should've reset the timeline.

Yet it hadn't.

I rushed back to the field. Janus and Nevan both gave me irritated looks.

Max slumped on the ground, propped against a tree with his legs outstretched. His coppery skin had taken on an ashen pallor beneath the supernatural coloring. Half-moon shadows darkened the skin under his eyes. He had his lids closed, his mouth open.

"Lindsey," Nevan began, but I cut him off with a flap of my hand.

I raced to my familiar, falling to my knees beside him. "Max?"

He peeled his lids open, revealing bloodshot eyes. "Not dead, if that's what you were thinking. I'm tired, but I will survive."

Biting down on my lip, I scanned his body but found no visible wounds. "You sure you're not injured? We got knocked on our asses back there."

"Used a lot of power too, more than I've used in centuries.'"

He held one hand around the fingers of the other hand as if hiding something.

I pried his hands apart.

The middle finger on his left hand was missing, broken off at the first knuckle, the flesh already sealed over the wound though a hint of blood stuck to the skin.

"What happened to your finger?" I demanded. "And why were you hiding it from me?"

He groaned. "It was crushed under my body when we got blown over. I tore off the damaged part."

"You what?" I couldn't help the shock in my voice. Who ripped off their own finger?

Max rubbed his eyes. "It will grow back faster than the broken bones would heal. I'm a salamander, Lindsey. You've seen me regrow body parts before."

Sure I had, but I'd never known him to snap off a damaged part. *Ech.*

His head lolled against the tree, though his eyes stayed mostly open.

I hadn't considered the toll our little escapade must've taken on him. I felt okay, but then, he'd been the one to bolster my magics with his own, giving more even than he had on the day we fought the sorcerer and Ceara. Plus, he had torn off his finger and needed more energy to regrow it.

I laid a hand on his forehead like I had any clue how to tell if he had a fever. Most elementals ran hotter than humans. I hadn't noticed it with Tris or Ennea, but Max and Nevan definitely had the hot-blooded thing going on in more ways than one.

"Max, I'm so sorry," I said. "Didn't think…It never occurred to me you'd be hurt by using so much magic. What can I do to help?"

"Nothing. Time is all I need."

"What about, um…" I didn't think I would ever get comfortable discussing this with Max, but I forced myself to do it anyway. "Do you need to feed?"

His lids had drifted shut again, but he cracked one open to peek at me. "Lindsey."

Great, now my familiar was Lindsey-ing me the way Nevan liked to do. Like he used to do.

I glanced over my shoulder at Nevan.

He watched me from a short distance away, his expression unreadable.

The back of my throat hurt. Somehow, without speaking to him, I recognized he had stayed the new Nevan rather than reverting to the man I'd vowed to share my life with earlier today.

I turned back to Max. "There's no reason to be embarrassed. When did you last feed?"

He screwed up his mouth and squirmed, avoiding eye contact. He opened his mouth as if to speak but shut it.

Yeah, he probably wanted to *Lindsey* me again.

A throat-clearing behind me drew my attention to Janus. The god loitered a few feet behind me, much closer than the discreet distance Nevan had chosen. Janus didn't seem to understand discretion or common courtesy. I supposed being a god could make a person arrogant after a while, assuming he hadn't started out that way.

Janus gave me a tight-lipped, squinty-eyed look. The message was clear: *Hurry the hell up and get back to paying attention to me.*

Oh yeah, he had definitely been born arrogant. Or created. Or however gods came into existence.

I flapped a hand in Janus's direction. "Shoo. I need a private moment with my familiar."

The god rolled his eyes and huffed, but finally backed away to stand near Nevan.

Focusing on Max again, I said, "When did you last—"

"It's been a while." He fidgeted some more and refused to meet my gaze. "Not since before I met you."

Before he met me? That had been over two months ago.

"How long can you last without feeding?" I asked.

"Once, I went six months without it. That was far too long." With his hands on the ground, he pushed up to sit straighter. "Being tired like this is a sign of malnutrition, but I'll recover without feeding. If I use up too much magical energy, or if I go too long without nourishment, things will…deteriorate rather swiftly."

"Deteriorate how?"

Face pinched, he finally looked at me. "The hunger will take over, and all my inhibitions will disintegrate. I'll have some control for a time, enough to keep from raping anyone, but if I don't feed within a few days of the hunger seizing me…"

He didn't need to finish that sentence. I could imagine. Witnessing Travis's struggles with his incubus urges had shown me a glimpse of what might happen. And Travis wasn't starving. He had his wits and his inhibitions intact. Without those things to keep him in check…

"The last time," Max said, "was after I had to destroy Aurelia. I—I couldn't stand to live with what I'd done to her. I wanted to die. As a newly forged elemental, I hadn't yet become aware of the full import of immortality. I'd gotten a handle on my urges, but I stupidly believed if I refused to feed, I would die." He gave a harsh, bitter laugh. "What a bleeding moron I was. I'd stayed in my lair for most of those months, waiting to die. When the hunger seized me, I went out to hunt for…prey. I attacked a sweet little leprechaun, but I managed to stop myself before I violated her. Word of my condition soon found its way into the Unseen realm's grapevine."

"Elementals gossip?"

"We're more like humans than you might think." He rubbed his jaw. "Thanks to the gossip, a certain goddess became aware of my plight. She sent two of her warriors to capture me and bring me to her temple. I was in no condition to hold back in any way, so I told her about Aurelia. She was sympathetic, or pretended to be, and she offered me something I couldn't refuse, particularly in the state I was in."

I wanted to ask questions but realized I needed to let him tell me in his own way. So, for the second time today, I ordered myself to rein it in.

"We became lovers," he said, his voice quieter, shame evident on his face. "The sexual energy she provided was intense and almost addictive. She has powers you can't even imagine, powers to seduce and give pleasure and make you never want to leave her. You don't want to know everything she talked me into doing, believe me. After a century or so, she finally went too far, and I found the willpower to leave her. She was not pleased to lose her favorite toy, and as it turns out, she has a tendency toward obsession. I've been hiding from her ever since."

My mouth refused to stay shut any longer. "Who was she?"

"Please, Lindsey, don't ask any more questions."

For him to use the P-word proved to me how much shame his time with the goddess had instilled in him. Whatever they'd gotten up to, he didn't want to tell me.

And I didn't need to know.

I flattened my palms on my thighs. "On a scale of 'just tired' to 'shacking up with a wacko goddess,' how bad off are you?"

"Midway between the two."

"Earlier you said you were just tired."

He scratched his arm, evading my gaze again. "This isn't something I ever wanted to discuss with you."

"I get that, but it's important. I need to know whether you'll be up to helping me or if I should send you home."

"Not going home. As long as you need me, I'll be here with you."

"That's sweet, Max, but I won't let you drain yourself to the point of, um, doing bad things without meaning to."

"I'll be right as rain after a little lie-down."

"Okay," I said, not believing him even a tiny bit, "you take a nap while I chat with Janus and Nevan."

Max's eyes slid shut. Within two seconds, he was snoring softly.

Jeez, I wished I could relax like that.

Had he relaxed in an instant, or had he passed out from exhaustion?

I considered taking his pulse, but I had no idea what normal was for a salamander. I had no clue about the vital signs of elementals in general. Even

Nevan's body, which I'd explored in every way imaginable, remained somewhat of a mystery to me. Besides, Max was snoring. He must be okay.

Reluctantly, I left Max to his "lie-down" and marched over to Janus and Nevan. I related what had gone down in the past, from the moment we'd entered the time stream until we'd reemerged in this field.

Nevan slipped an arm around my shoulders. "It must have been heartbreaking to allow your former lover to die and be transformed in such a way."

Even with weird timeline amnesia, Nevan's first impulse was to comfort me.

Janus, on the other hand, squinted at me with pursed lips.

I made a somewhat rude noise. "What's your problem now, Your Godly Snippiness?"

He arched one brow. "I am merely considering the facts you have related."

"And?"

"Describe this being to me in greater detail."

Seriously? I'd spent several minutes going through this in plenty-sufficient detail.

With sarcastic hand gestures to illustrate my words, I said, "She had wild, long hair that whipped around when she made the air go whoooosh. Her eyes were black. Her body was emaciated, her skin was pale, and her fingernails were long and curved like talons, sharp too. She wore white robes that looked like they'd gone through a meat grinder, and her voice was like a raspy wind. Endued bullets can't kill her. She kicked our asses. That enough detail for you this time?"

He rubbed his chin, staring at the ground. "And she wanted vengeance?"

"Yes, yes, and 'dammit, if you ask me again I'll bust your jaw' yes."

This god guy was driving me bonkers.

Nevan gave me a gentle squeeze. "You are concerned for your familiar, aren't you? That's why you have become…testy."

I glanced at Max, but he was still asleep. "Yeah, I guess so."

Maybe I should've apologized to Janus, but he'd done plenty to annoy me today. I didn't feel terribly inclined to say "sorry."

Janus at last lifted his gaze to me. "I believe you have met a harpy."

Chapter Ten

"A WHAT?" I ASKED. "YOU MEAN THOSE NASTY WOMEN WHO PUNISH men?"

"No," he said in a remarkably patient tone. "That is a mortal myth. The harpies are wind spirits."

"Well, that would explain her penchant for huffing and puffing. What else can you tell me about them?"

"Nothing. The harpies had only recently emerged when I was imprisoned in the Temple of the Four Winds."

After his buddies, the other gods, banded together to destroy him. I supposed his imprisonment would've hampered his knowledge of the Unseen realm, or any realm.

He made a pained face. "I am utterly ignorant of anything that transpired after my imprisonment."

I looked up at Nevan, who kept his arm around me. "Do you know anything about the harpies?"

"Nothing concrete, I'm afraid. I have never encountered a harpy." He gave a resigned sigh. "All I can offer is legends, little more than hearsay."

"I'll take it. Gossip away."

He ran his hand up and down my arm while he spoke. "They say the harpies started out as beautiful women, the female embodiments of the cardinal winds. As the counterparts of the male wind gods, the harpies inevitably became their lovers. All was well for a time, but eventually, jealousy took root. Their hatred for each other escalated into an all-out war. For centuries, they seemed content to fight with each other, always seeking vengeance for slights real or imagined out of blind envy. They stole each other's lovers. They plotted against each other. Some even obtained endued weapons in an effort to destroy their sisters."

"Did any of them die?"

"It's rumored a few did. They continued to procreate, though, spawning more wind spirits who took after their mothers, becoming depraved and fixated on vengeance for slights none of them could remember anymore."

"Awesome," I said, making a thumbs-up sign. "No wonder the Windy Witch I met was such a sweetie-pie. She's got a jones for vengeance, that's for sure. But I have no freaking clue what she thinks I've done to her."

"She claims you took someone from her. Correct?"

"Uh-huh. She said I took 'them,' but she didn't elaborate."

"Your familiar explained to me that you've 'taken out' several elementals."

I turned sideways to him, his arm staying around me, and let myself enjoy the heat of his body. This whole conversation, this whole day, had embedded a permanent chill in my bones. "I took down Skeiron. And the sorcerer. And Ceara."

Nevan stiffened. "Ceara?"

Oops. I'd forgotten he had no memory of his first wife's resurrection and the evil things she'd done.

"How do you know of my mortal wife?" he asked, clearly baffled.

"It's a really long story. The abridged version is a sorcerer brought her back from the dead, they became lovers and plotted to destroy you and me, they got nixed. The end."

He gaped at me like I'd spoken Japanese with a German accent.

"Never mind," I said, patting his chest. "What else can you tell me about the harpies?"

"Very little. The harpies are rarely seen, though any vicious storm is usually blamed on their actions."

"Harpies are the boogeymen of the Unseen realm."

"They are females, but in essence, your assessment is accurate."

I replayed my encounters with the Windy Witch in my mind. "Do harpies have earth powers? First, we had the big quake that split the ground open. Since then, whenever I see this witch the earth moves but less each time. It's like she's finding her footing, in terms of altering time."

Nevan regarded me for a few seconds as if considering what I'd said. "Harpies do not inherently possess that kind of power. If she has indeed acquired dark magics, perhaps those energies shake the earth whenever she attempts to use them. As she adjusts to her new powers, the earthquakes might indeed lessen in intensity, perhaps even stop completely."

Janus turned toward us, his expression grim. "If a harpy is responsible for the time shift, she must have acquired an immense amount of power, magics the likes—"

"The likes of which none have ever seen," I said. "Heard you the first time you gave me your vague explanation."

His nostrils flared on a huffing exhalation. "The point is that you and your familiar barely survived an encounter with the harpy. Even your combined magics were not enough."

"What can we do? How do we find and stop her?"

Janus's shoulders slumped. He gave a faint shake of his head.

"Okay," I said, "answer this for me. I undid the time shift. Why hasn't anything changed other than Calder dying? Everything should've gone back to the way it was before the shift."

He shook his head again, even more slowly.

A clueless god. Go figure.

"Lindsey," Nevan said, "are you certain nothing else changed?"

"Well, I took a peek at my family. Other than Calder not being there, things seemed like they were before Max and I fought the Windy Witch."

"Perhaps you should take a closer look."

"You want me to blip over to my parents' house."

The corner of his mouth kicked up. "Blip? What a charmingly unusual term for it. Yes, I believe you should do that."

"Will you come with me?"

He pulled his head back, chin tucked, and tipped his head to the side. "If you wish it."

"I do." Gesturing at his lack of clothing, save for the loincloth, I added, "But you'll need to glamour into a more mortal-friendly style."

Without letting go of me, Nevan effected a glamour pretty darn close to human, complete with jeans, a T-shirt, and sneakers.

I whisked us to my parents' house in Texas and shrugged out of his embrace. "Better act casual, like we're just friends. I don't want to freak them out."

"As you wish."

I knocked on the front door.

A moment later, the door swung open and my mom said, "Sweetie, why are you knocking? You live here." She squinted at Nevan. "Who's he?"

"My friend, Nevan."

The first time my mom had met Nevan, in the original timeline, she'd instantly adored him. Today, she studied him with suspicion.

Another person pushed past my mom.

Travis dragged me into his arms. "Lindsey, where ya been? Baby, I was worried sick when I woke up and you weren't beside me."

Beside him? In bed?

Shock paralyzed me, so much that I couldn't react when Travis kissed me like we were…a couple. In love. Married? *Oh no, please don't let that be.* I mean, I cared about Travis as a friend. But this was waaaaay too much.

He broke the kiss, keeping his hold on me, and turned his flinty gaze on Nevan. "Who the hell are you?"

"Nevan," the sylph said through clenched teeth.

His jealousy was back, and I knew I'd better get us out of here quick.

Travis lifted my left hand, fingering the engagement and wedding rings. "What the—We ain't even engaged yet. Where'd you get these rings?"

Christ, twice in one day I'd been asked the same question.

And for the second time, I dodged it. Squirming out of Travis's grasp, I snagged Nevan's hand and zipped us back to the field where Janus and Max waited. Janus was pacing while Max hadn't moved from his position slumped against the tree. Little snorts punctuated his whistling snores.

"Well?" Janus said.

"You were right, something changed." I rubbed my temples in a vain attempt to ward off a sprouting headache. "It makes no sense whatsoever. If Calder died and was forged like before, why am I married to his brother and living in Texas? I should've wound up fleeing the state after Travis accused me of murdering Calder." I grasped my head in my hands. "I should've wound up here, met Nevan, and…Gah! But the shop hasn't come back and Nevan doesn't remember me. I haven't felt another time shift, so what gives?"

My brain had begun to hurt. I needed a concrete explanation, but it seemed unlikely I'd get one. Both Nevan and Janus watched me like they expected answers to appear as a flashing neon sign on my forehead.

I asked Nevan, "Out of curiosity, who is the sylph king?"

"Notus, of course."

Okay, no change there.

Right then, Max roused from his nap. He yawned, stretched, and jumped to his feet. When he caught sight of me, frazzled beyond belief, he said, "What did I miss?"

"That was an awfully short nap," I said. "Are you sure you're rested up?"

"In rude health." He winked. "As always."

I explained what had gone on while he slept, then glanced at each male in turn. "Anybody got a clue here?"

Noncommittal noises and shrugs ensued.

Grr. I was getting awfully sick of that reaction. Elementals loved to think they were superior to mortals, and one of these guys was a freaking god, but they had no insight. Not even a half-assed guess.

"The earthquake started it all," I said. "Janus swears he didn't cause it and neither did the Four Winds. That leaves our gusty friend, the time-shifting harpy. Maybe when she made her first attempt, it failed—with earth-shattering results. She tried again, and it worked. Then Max and I reversed the shift, so she did something else."

Nevan cocked one hip and braced a hand on it. "Such as?"

Not a clue. I had to come up with something, so I took a few seconds to ponder the day's events. "Janus, you said time will protect itself if it's injured, like by a time shift."

"Yes," the god replied.

"The Windy Witch changed the past, stopping Calder from being forged. Max and I undid the change. What might happen if the harpy tried to make the same change a second time? Would time defend itself from another wound?"

"Perhaps." He angled his head left and right, examining me. "Are you suggesting that when she attempted to effect the same change again, time would not permit it? But you reported some circumstances had been altered."

"Yeah, but in a different way. Did you sense another shift?"

"No."

"Maybe trying to repeat the same change triggered a timeline defense mechanism, and things came out a little different. The shift wasn't complete, so we couldn't sense it."

Janus remained impassive for a moment, his gaze glued to me. When I was about ready to slap his face to snap him out of his standing coma, he finally spoke. "Your idea has a certain logic."

"Gee, thanks." I stuffed my hands in my pockets but changed my mind and folded my arms under my breasts instead. "We need to brainstorm ways to take down the Windy Witch."

"That is not her name," Janus said.

"Unless you know her name, I'm going to keep calling her the Windy Witch."

Janus stared at me blankly. "What is a brainstorm?"

"It's when we all think really hard and come up with ideas, then decide which ones are good and which totally suck."

He kept staring.

Nevan looped an arm around my waist, smiling at Janus. "Modern mortals have odd ways of speaking, and Lindsey enjoys inventing unusual terms for everything. You'll become accustomed to it."

Was he saying that because he remembered or because I'd called his favorite mode of travel "blipping"? I gazed up at him, admiring his profile and the confidence and sensuality he exuded without even trying.

He glanced down at me and winked.

Just like the old Nevan. My throat hurt for the umpteenth time today, and I swallowed. Every time he showed me a glimmer of the old Nevan, I got choked up. No wonder I hadn't come up with a solid plan for stopping the Windy Witch. The time shift and the changes it had instigated were keeping me on edge.

Exactly what the harpy wanted.

Max flapped a hand to gain my attention. Once he had it, he waved for me to approach.

I pulled away from Nevan, telling him, "Excuse me for a minute."

When I reached Max, he said, "You're distracted by the changes in Nevan."

Our Janusite-familiar connection seemed to give him insights about me I didn't want him to have. Then again, my distraction was probably plain for everyone to see.

"That's true," I admitted. "Can't help it."

"You need to help it. You need to get Nevan back to the way he should be so you can focus."

"I tried that. You were there, you know how it went down."

Max placed a hand on my arm. "I don't mean by undoing the time shift. You need to get Nevan back the Janusite way."

"If I could do that, don't you think I would have already?"

"Maybe I'm not being clear enough." He bent forward to level our gazes. "The good old rumpy-pumpy ought to do the trick."

"And that's supposed to be more clear?"

He bent even closer, our noses almost touching. "Shag him, Lindsey. It worked last time."

Well, at least I understood that term for sex. "Last time? Nevan has never before developed time-shift amnesia."

"But he did have his soul ripped from his body and tossed out in the cosmic bin. You saved him by having a good hump."

"Honestly, Max, stop throwing the dictionary of sex slang at me. My brain is already wiped out." I growled out a sigh and massaged my temples. "Besides, we didn't have sex until after I restored his soul. It was the soul stone that made it possible, and I don't have that anymore."

Oh, I had loved that little soul stone. The small, smooth rock imbued with a fragment of Nevan's soul had produced some unusual and titillating effects, besides fulfilling its purpose by letting me feel Nevan was alive and okay at any time as well as helping me to tap into his powers. Since I'd developed the ability to do that without the stone's assistance, and restoring his soul had drained the thing, I'd given up the soul stone. It lay in a drawer in my dresser in the underground home I shared with Nevan in the Unseen realm.

The soul stone was currently nothing more than a pretty rock.

Max straightened. "Sorry, I forgot about that."

"It's easy to get confused when we're constantly fighting supernatural baddies."

He patted my arm. "Couldn't hurt to try it. Give him a quick shag and see if it helps."

"Sure, I'll take him behind that bush over there."

"Yes, brilliant. Do that."

I wasn't about to take Max's advice and "shag" Nevan, but he did make a valid point. Unless I stopped fretting over Nevan, I wouldn't have the brainpower or the magical power to defeat the Windy Witch. I was always stronger with my husband beside me, but we needed our emotional bond intact for that to happen.

"All right," I said. "I'm going to try to jog his memory, but not with sex."

"Keep that option in your pocket. Trust me, an incubus knows the power of bloody great sex."

"Uh-huh." *Not going there—yet.* "Keep the nosy god out here, okay? Don't need an audience."

Max saluted. "Yes, mistress."

I marched up to Nevan, grabbed his hand, and towed him into the trees where neither Max nor Janus could see or hear us. Nevan seemed more amused than baffled by this turn of events, and he followed me without question. Once we'd traveled far enough to have some privacy but not so far I couldn't shout for help, I leaned back against a tree.

Nevan positioned himself in front of me, edging closer until he could brace one hand on the tree beside my head.

As always, his proximity made my skin tighten and tingle.

"You wanted me alone," he said, his voice a sultry purr. "What will you do with me now?"

He'd spoken those exact words on the night we'd first made love. After Skeiron had attacked us and I risked my life to get Nevan healed, I had needed to see all of him to make sure no wounds remained. Nevan had tossed fairy lights into the air where they hovered like supernatural versions of the sparklers kids played with on the Fourth of July. Then, he'd spoken those words.

Here I am, love. What will you do with me now?

I pulled in a shaky breath. Desire and anxiety shot currents of adrenaline through my veins, each vying for control of me. I had no time for an inner struggle, but my heart had other ideas.

Nevan fingered a lock of my hair, examining it while he twisted the lock around his finger, his head down. Without raising his head, without relinquishing my hair, he looked up at me through those dark, thick lashes. "You want me to be the man you knew."

I couldn't speak, couldn't move. Yes, I longed to have my husband back, but did I have the right to wipe away the man he was now? I'd brought him here so I could jog his memories of the original timeline, but that stupid anxiety kept haunting me.

He released my hair and bent his arm, bringing his face closer, his cheek alongside mine, almost touching me. He whispered in my ear, "Am I anything like the man you loved?"

Get a grip, Lindsey. Speak.

"Yes," I said, my voice breathless. "You are so much like him."

"Do you truly believe I can remember the previous timeline?"

"I do."

He nuzzled my neck and kissed his way up my throat to my ear. "I want to remember. I want to love you again."

A rock solidified in my throat. I gulped but couldn't get rid of it. My breaths came shallow temp and fast, my body melted against the tree, and without conscious thought I tipped my head back to arch my neck.

Nevan dragged his tongue up my throat to my jaw.

I shivered, overcome by the need to touch him, kiss him, hold him, make him remember everything we'd felt for each other and everything we'd done together.

He feathered soft little kisses over my skin, making his way from my jaw to the corner of my mouth. "Show me what we mean to each other."

Powerless to resist, I locked my arms around him and pulled his body into mine. Our mouths gravitated to each other, questing, craving, melding in a kiss of passion and desperation, our tongues lapping and scraping and delving deep. I moaned, and he wrapped his arms around me to haul me away from the tree, stumbling and grunting as he guided me down to grassy earth but never once severing our lip-lock. His hands roved my body, fondling, kneading, cupping my breasts and my ass.

I'd sworn I wouldn't have sex with Nevan until he spoke my full name, but in this moment...

Shagging him sounded like the way to go.

His hands whisked under my shirt. The sensation of his skin on mine drew a long, throaty moan out of me. Eyes closed, reveling in the kiss and his touch, I surrendered to the desperate need to feel him—on top of me, around me, inside me.

Right now.

The ground shuddered beneath us, but even an earthquake couldn't tear us away from each other or break through the blind hunger. He pushed up my bra. My breasts popped free into his waiting hands. The heat of his skin shot pleasure through me, but when he flicked his thumbs over my nipples, I whimpered into his mouth and latched my leg around his hip.

Another, stronger quake rattled the earth.

Even the crack of a tree breaking couldn't penetrate the haze of lust.

The weight of his body vanished. His mouth had abandoned mine, and his hands no longer explored my body.

My lids fluttered open. The brightness of the sun made me squint for a minute. While I waited for my vision to clear, I pushed up into a sitting position.

Nevan was gone.

An emptiness gaped inside me, a yawning hole where my connection with Nevan had once warmed and soothed me. Our bond was gone.

I scrambled to my feet. "Nevan!"

My cry echoed off the trees, as vacant as the void inside me.

"Nevan!" I screamed his name over and over, but every cry reverberated back to me through a giant nothingness. I spun in a circle, barely able to breathe, hands clenched into fists. The truth stabbed through me like a sword slicing out half of my soul.

Nevan had been erased from history.

I threw my head back and roared.

Chapter Eleven

A COLDNESS DEEPER THAN ANYTHING ON EARTH CONSUMED ME from the inside out. I began to tremble, my teeth chattering. This wasn't possible. No, it couldn't be true. Nevan must've had his memory altered again, and he wouldn't come when I called because the new time shift had further hampered our connection.

Dimly, I noted three facts. One, a large crack had split the ground ten feet from where I stood. Two, a large aspen had broken off and was lodged against neighboring trees, teetering on the verge of dragging the smaller ones to the ground. And three, a blur of flames was racing toward me through the woods. Though I noted these facts, I couldn't decipher their meaning.

The flames snuffed out as Max skidded to a halt in front of me, breathing hard. He grasped my upper arms. "Lindsey, are you all right?"

I shook my head weakly and spoke without knowing what I was saying. "Why didn't you poof here?"

"Too risky with the downed trees and such." Max glanced around, his jaw tightened, and he bent to meet my gaze. "Where's Nevan?"

I managed only one whispered word. "Gone."

"He's been erased," Max said.

Whether our bond had given him insight, or he simply saw the truth on my face, I didn't know. I nodded. He pulled me into his arms, holding me until I stopped shaking.

I stepped back and noticed Janus loitering behind Max. The god seemed strangely empathetic.

"Ah…" Max began, gesturing at my shirt. "You might want to…"

Glancing down, I realized though my shirt had fallen down to cover my breasts, my bra had stayed lodged above them. I turned my back to the men, fixed my bra, and faced them again. My heartbeat thudded in my ears as the deep-freeze inside me evaporated on a wave of hot, simmering anger. I balled my hands into fists, my shoulders bunching.

"I'm going to find that windy bitch," I said, "and rip her apart molecule by molecule with my bare hands."

Max scratched his neck. "I know you're angry and grieving but—"

"Not grieving. I'm going to undo this goddamn time shift and save him."

"Lindsey…" Max winced as if in anticipation of an outburst from me. "You couldn't fix the timeline before. Why do you think you can do it now?"

"The first time, I didn't have the right motivation." Despite Max's obvious fear I would freak out, I remained calm. My fists had relaxed, my shoulders too, and the simmering anger had cooled into an eerie composure that probably should've unnerved me. I didn't care. Let me be freaky-calm Lindsey. It was better than falling apart. "This time, I have the strongest motivation of all. She ripped my husband away from me, and that bitch is going to pay."

Janus sidled around Max to confront me. "Have you considered that this may be precisely what the harpy wanted? She claimed you took someone from her, and she has taken someone from you. She must have known this would anger you. Perhaps she wants you to strike out at her, so she might destroy you."

"I am not lashing out." I squared my shoulders, suffused with a grim resolve. "First, I undo whatever she did to the timeline. Second, I'll kick her bony ass back to the Big Bang."

"Your grief makes you irrational."

"This is not grief because Nevan is not dead." I aimed my steady gaze at the god. "Do I seem unhinged?"

"No," Max replied, "you're so bloody calm it's making my skin itch."

"You can help me, or you can wait here while I take care of this. Which is it?"

Max scrutinized me for a moment, scanning me up and down, his mouth tight. "If you're going into the time stream again, I'm going with you."

Janus sighed. "This is a mistake. In her condition—"

I surged forward to jab a finger into his chest. "You know nothing about my condition. Unless you have something constructive to say, keep your mouth shut."

Maybe I was a teeny bit irrational. My heart was overriding my common sense—like I'd ever had an abundance of that—and all I could think about was getting Nevan back.

Janus raised his hands in surrender and stepped back.

The fact I was scaring a god should have clued me in to the fallacy of this mission. I didn't care. I couldn't care. That blustery beast had stolen the only man I'd ever loved from me. If she wanted vengeance, I'd cram a potful of it down her raspy throat.

With a poof of flames, Max shrank into salamander form.

I tucked him inside my bra. He didn't even twitch his tail.

Janus gave me a strange look, something like fear. "I beg you to reconsider this action. Wait until you have calmed yourself before raging into a battle with a being who has defeated you twice."

A god was begging me?

Stop and think, Lindsey, before you screw up big time.

"Yes," Janus said, taking a tentative step toward me. "You see the danger. You realize this is not a wise path to take, and if you venture down it, you will lose more of the ones for whom you care so deeply. You risk losing yourself as well. Love between a mortal and an immortal leads to only pain and tragedy."

The rough tone of his voice implied deep emotion. I should have stopped to consider why he seemed so invested in convincing me not to do this. I should have stopped to think, period.

I couldn't.

"What are you saying?" I demanded. "Nevan and I are doomed anyway, so why bother saving him from the harpy's machinations? That's bullshit."

"This course of action is unwise." He paused, his face pinched. "I do not wish for you to die, Lindsey."

How bizarre that the man, the god, who had been nothing but a pain in the neck all day had suddenly become concerned for my safety. Had I misjudged him? Underneath all the godly arrogance, did he have an actual heart?

If Janus thought I was walking into a disaster…

Nevan wouldn't want me to do this.

The thought stopped me. My chest ached. I clutched my hands over my belly, feeling the rings on my left hand. "You're right. This isn't such a good idea."

A gale ripped through the woods.

The broken aspen, balanced against much slimmer trees, shifted.

Wind roared around us, swirling like a tornado.

And the aspen toppled straight toward me, dragging its brethren with it.

I staggered backward, tripped over the crack in the earth, and whumped down on my ass. The trees kept coming as if in slow motion, looming nearer and nearer. I scrambled backward like a crab. Max skittered up my chest, trying to climb out of my shirt, but my frantic movements sent him tumbling down into my bra.

Janus tumbled head over heels backward into the woods.

The aspen crashed down a dozen feet to my right. The tangle of skinnier trees smashed down on my legs. Agony tore through my left leg, and my hoarse cry reverberated through the woods.

The Windy Witch raced toward me, a blur of tattered robes and flying hair, surrounded by a mini tornado. She slowed when she reached the pile of trees that pinned my legs to the ground and stepped onto it. Even the weight of her emaciated body proved too much.

A new agony shot through me, and I let out a strangled scream.

Max scurried around inside my shirt, but he couldn't get past the slender branch that had landed at a diagonal across my chest.

The harpy grinned at me, exposing jagged teeth. She pointed at me with one taloned finger. "You took from me, so I took from you. How does it feel, Janusite?"

In spite of the pain, I mustered a nonchalant tone. "Fantastic. I couldn't wait to get rid of that annoying sylph. You did me a favor."

She hopped off the tangled trees to hunch beside me.

The shifting weight of the aspens had me choking back a cry.

"You lie," she hissed. "Your pain is great, though not as great as that which you inflicted on me."

"Who are you? Or should I just call you Windbag?"

"Perhaps you should know the name of the one who will destroy everything you care for and then destroy you." She tapped one talon on my nose. "I am Aello."

"Who is it you think I've taken from you?"

"*Daimones.*" She raked her talon down my throat, drawing a trickle of hot blood. "*Anemoi Thuellai.*"

Was she speaking Greek? I recognized the word *daimones*, though I couldn't remember what it meant.

Max scampered up my chest again, determined to get free.

The movement snared Aello's attention. She slipped her talon inside my shirt and tore it open.

With a tiny hiss, Max sprang off my chest.

Aello caught him in her hand, his little red head peeking out between her talons. She canted her head side to side, scrutinizing the creature in her grasp. "This is your familiar, a salamander. He was in human form when last I saw him."

Dread coiled in my gut, its tendrils snaking up into my chest.

The harpy turned her hand so I could see Max's tiny face. "You care for this one too, do you not? The bond between a magical being and her familiar is formidable."

Why didn't Max poof into human form?

As if she'd read my mind, Aello said, "Oh, he cannot shift while in my grasp. My magic prevents it."

"You're not the only one with powers."

"Perhaps not, but you are weak in comparison." She opened her hand, holding Max by the throat between two of her fingertips. Her talons curved under his small body, and his tail whipped against them. "I shall take another from you."

She slashed one of her talons.

Max's leg was severed from his body. It dropped to the ground.

He let out a squeal of pain and thrashed in her grip.

"I will take him limb by limb," Aello said. "Until nothing remains."

My pulse beat so fast it almost fluttered. Max could regrow limbs. I'd seen it before. He could do it again, he had to.

Aello moved her talon into position, preparing to slice off Max's other leg.

I ground my teeth, pouring all my energy into a single task—gathering enough power to stop this creature from hurting my friend. Blue magic exploded around me, sparkling, snapping, spreading outward toward the harpy. When it contacted her skin, she shrieked like a storm wind. Her fingers shot open, and Max tumbled to the ground.

A gale corkscrewed around us, shuddering the trees piled atop me.

I gritted my teeth against the pain, fighting for every breath.

Aello vanished.

Chapter Twelve

I GRIMACED AND GROUND MY TEETH WHILE JANUS HEFTED THE TREES OFF of me enough that I could roll out from under them. Pain stabbed through my left leg, but I kept rolling until I was clear of the trees. Gasping for breath, hurting in more places than I wanted to count, I lay sprawled on my back and struggled to understand…anything.

With a sharp bellow, Janus released the trees. They whumped down again.

He had no powers, and apparently, he had no super strength either.

A flash of red in my peripheral vision made me glance to my right.

Max, stuck in salamander form, lay motionless on the ground.

I sprang to a sitting position, determined to get up and run to him, but the pain in my leg seized my entire body. I cried out, my head spinning.

Janus crouched beside me, dead leaves clinging to his hair and his toga smeared with dirt. He examined my leg, probing gently with his fingers. Even his cautious examination hurt like hell and had me grinding my teeth again as breaths gusted out of my nostrils.

"I believe it is broken," he said. "In multiple places."

Wonderful. "Check on Max, please. He's not moving."

Janus nodded and scurried over to the tiny red form lying in the grass. He touched a fingertip to Max's little chest. "He is breathing. Perhaps you can force the shift and return him to human form. That will make it easier to deal with his injuries."

"Don't have the energy, magical or physical, to force anything." I glanced down at my leg. Something stuck out from it, poking into the fabric of my jeans. Something? I had a sick feeling I knew what it was. A broken bone. Nausea swelled in my gut, and my gorge rose into my throat, but I managed to croak, "The vortex."

Janus stared dumbly at me.

"The healing vortex," I squeezed out between my clenched teeth. "There was one behind the shop, when it existed. I have to assume the vortex hasn't gone away. Max and I need healing, fast, and that's the closest option. You'll need to carry me, I can't walk or teleport. And bring me Max."

For once, the god did not balk. He scooped Max into his palm and hurried back to me, then transferred the limp body of my familiar into my cupped hands.

Janus glanced around, clearly searching for something.

"What is it?" I asked, my voice scratchy.

"I will need to bind your broken bones with something sturdy to prevent further damage."

"No time. Get me to the vortex." I held my breath, wincing through a wave of dizzying pain. "Please."

He studied me with a tense expression, his Adam's apple jouncing as he swallowed hard. After a couple seconds, he slid his arms under me and lifted.

Agony. Searing. Wrenching. I cried out, battling against the impulse to clench my fingers because that would crush Max. "Hurry."

Janus raced through the woods, following my instructions for where to go. Sweat dribbled down his temples, and his breaths came fast and shallow. Sweat dribbled down my temples too, though I hadn't exerted myself the way he was doing. Mine was a cold sweat.

We reached the vortex, now nothing more than a patch of weeds, after a few excruciatingly long minutes. I fought to stay conscious despite the agony slicing through me with every step Janus took.

He carefully set me down in the weeds. "What should I do?"

"Wait and pray. That's all we can do."

I collapsed onto my back, Max cradled in my hands. *Please work, please.* Nothing happened.

When Tris had healed me and Nevan, on separate occasions, he had needed to consume a lot of copper to power up the vortex for the task. Nevan and I had been on the verge of death, though. I prayed the vortex had enough energy on its own to do this. I doubted Tris would answer my call if I screamed for him, since he would have no idea who I was.

A trickle of magic tickled my skin and fizzled out.

"Dammit," I whimpered.

Janus knelt beside me. "What is it?"

"I don't think the vortex is strong enough. We need a leprechaun."

"Call for one."

"Nobody knows me anymore. Would an elemental answer the call of an unknown mortal?"

"Try, Lindsey," he said with an intensity I hadn't heard from him before. "You are the Janusite. Infuse the call with your magic. It is a risk, letting a stranger know you have power. If you do not do this, you may die. Your leg may not heal properly and could become infected." He glanced at my hands. "And your friend is severely wounded."

I could do this. I had to—for Max, if not for myself.

Summoning all the magic left in me, which wasn't a hell of a lot, I screamed, "Triskaideka! Get your scrawny, obnoxious butt over her right this minute."

Nothing.

"Triskaideka!" I screamed so loud it mutated into a coughing fit.

I was about to holler again when the leprechaun appeared at my feet. His bright-blue eyes darted this way and that as he took in the scene, then he roved his gaze up and down my body. His lip curled. "Jeez, lady, you're a mess."

"Need your help."

"I don't do favors for no mortals."

"You sensed my magic. You had to. I'm no mere mortal." I tenderly shifted Max so he rested in my left palm and pushed up with my right hand, elevating my head and shoulders. "I have power, you want to know why, and the only way that happens is if you heal me and my familiar."

I spread my fingers to reveal the salamander in my hand.

Tris tucked his chin, staring at Max with his lip curled even more. "That's a frigging incubus, lady. I don't heal their kind."

I slammed my hand down on the dirt, gritting my teeth against the pain it triggered. "You will heal this one. There's a harpy screwing with the timeline. She's erased a powerful sylph from existence with a time shift. You could be next."

"Why should I believe you? Time shifts? Come on, that's crazy."

Janus surged to his feet and stalked up to Tris. "I am the god Janus. What Lindsey says is true, and you will do as she asks." He leaned in to tower over the much-smaller leprechaun, causing Tris to shrink back a smidgen. "Or you will suffer my wrath."

As much as I appreciated Janus's effort, I knew this was not the way to gain Tris's help.

The leprechaun rolled his eyes.

"How did I know your full name?" I said.

Tris darted his gaze to me, not blinking, lips parted.

"If I'm nothing but a worthless mortal," I said, "how do I know your name?"

"Well..." He focused on my feet. "I don't know."

"Because you and I have met, that's how." Another wave of pain and nausea hit me, and I collapsed onto my back. "In the original timeline, we're friends. Even though you're sometimes an annoying brat. I've gotten used to it. I know your sister, Ennea, too."

Tris's mouth fell open. For a moment, he said nothing. At last, he squared his shoulders, lifted his chin, and said, "What the hell. I'll power up the vortex for ya, but I need copper."

How on earth was I going to get that? The rock shop no longer existed.

"Lucky for you," Tris said, "I got a stash at home. Gimme a minute."

The leprechaun poofed away.

I set Max on the grass, suddenly too exhausted to hold him any longer. Seconds ticked by in my mind, loud as hammer blows, timed with my slowing heartbeat. I'd grown numb too, and a strange floaty feeling enveloped me. Part of me recognized this was a bad sign, but the numbness kept spreading, infecting my mind. I fell back onto the ground.

Tris blipped back into view at my feet. Copper dust crusted his lips and chin. He swiped at his mouth with the sleeve of his flannel shirt. "You ready? Considering your injuries, this is gonna hurt like a son of a bitch."

"Do it," I mumbled.

Warmth poured over my skin, seeping under the surface, blossoming through my whole body. I relaxed into the sensation, sighing with relief. The warmth transformed into a sizzling energy that tingled inside me, faintly at first, intensifying into a harder and hotter tingle with every second that elapsed. I gasped. The energy crackled and bit into my flesh from the inside, a million tiny teeth burrowing down to the source of the damage.

Bones cracked, resetting themselves.

A strangled scream burst out of me as my body convulsed.

Crack. Snap. Rip.

The scorching heat of the healing energies set my body on fire. I clawed at the weeds, sank my nails into the earth, clenched my teeth so hard I heard enamel breaking, but the vortex healed those wounds too with a ferocity that transformed my entire skull into a mass of misery. Desperate, agonized noises echoed around me, and with a jolt, I realized I was making those sounds.

The energy dwindled, sluicing out of me, washing away the pain along with it.

"It's done," Tris said, and vanished.

I lay sprawled on the grass for a moment, not because of exhaustion or pain, but because of a shock that paralyzed my every muscle. I was healed. I knew this without so much as glancing at my body. Tris had cooperated, and the vortex had worked. I lifted my left leg, bent the knee, swung my foot side to side.

No pain. No shattered bones. Even my torn shirt had been repaired.

Sitting up, I hauled in a deep breath and let it out little by little. The vortex had done more than heal my injuries. It had reinvigorated me. I glanced down at my hands, turning them upside down, revealing my empty palms.

Max.

I jumped to my knees and scanned the area.

A tiny red form lay in the weeds a few feet away, one leg missing.

"That lousy leprechaun," I growled. "He didn't heal Max."

I screamed Tris's name until he showed up.

"What's your problem, lady?" he asked. "I got other things to do besides help you."

"Max is not healed." I pointed at the salamander. "His leg is still gone."

"Can't do nothing about that. The vortex can't regrow parts that got lopped off." The leprechaun peered over my shoulder at Max. "He'll be fine. Those weirdos can regrow anything."

Tris winked out.

I touched Max with my fingertip, wiggling him slightly in an attempt to rouse him. "Wake up, Max. Come on, wake up."

His tiny eyelids fluttered open. He raised one itty-bitty hand—or foot, or whatever—and motioned for me to move away. It was the cutest thing I'd ever seen, but I couldn't appreciate the adorableness at the moment. I scuffled backward in a crouch.

With a burst of flames, Max shifted into human form. He remained prone on the ground, missing one leg.

"Are you okay?" I asked. "Aside from the, uh, missing limb."

He yawned loudly and sat up, propped up with both hands on the ground. "Feel better, but regrowing the leg will take time."

"Don't worry. I'll deal with Aello on my own."

"The hell you will." He fixed me with a mulish look. "I am your familiar, Lindsey, and I won't abandon you."

"No offense, sweetie, but you've only got one leg. Speed tends to be important in confrontations with crazy elementals."

Max frowned at me.

I gave him my best stubborn look.

He grumbled and raised one hand. A thick branch, stripped of its bark, appeared in his grasp. Next, he conjured some leather strips and strapped the branch to the stump where his leg had been, creating a kind of peg leg and securing it with another strap around his hip. With a self-satisfied smile, he poofed himself into a standing position. His peg leg wobbled a bit, but he found his equilibrium. Taking cautious steps, he figured out how to walk with his new appendage.

Max stopped in front of me, where I was kneeling, and spread his arms wide. "See? Good to go."

"Uh-huh," I said, dubious to say the least.

He rubbed his hands together. "What's the plan this time?"

Janus made a dismissive noise. "There is no plan unless we discern what Aello wants. We have no conception of her final goal or her true motivations."

"Maybe you have no clue," I said, "but I get it. She thinks I took someone from her, so she wants to take away the people I care about." My near-death experience and the excruciating pain of the healing had granted me a crystal clarity about a few things. "Why would she care about messing with Calder's fate? In the first shift, she stopped his forging. After Max and I undid that, she tried again, with a slightly different outcome. In both cases, if I weren't immune to the shifts, I would've wound up with someone other than Nevan. Aello wanted to keep me from ever meeting him."

Janus regarded me with an expression reminiscent of appreciation. "When the second shift did not take Nevan away from you, she resorted to a direct assault in addition to a third shift."

"Exactly."

Max cleared his throat. "Ah, Lindsey…"

"What is it, Max?"

"She won. Nevan is gone."

I rose, resisting the urge to fist my hands, resolved to stay calm and rational this time. "We are going to undo this shift too."

"That was a right mess when we tried it before."

"Are you suggesting I let her keep screwing with time? Maybe you'll disappear next."

"I'm not suggesting we give up." He hobbled toward me. "We need to defeat Aello on our own terms, here in the present, before we reverse the latest shift."

"We've had so much luck fighting her face to face."

Max touched my shoulder. "You're feeling hopeless because Nevan is gone, I understand that. You will get him back. If you think about what I've said, I know you'll realize I'm right."

"What if Aello creates another shift while we're plotting to take her down? I can't lose anyone else. All I've got is you and—" I flapped a hand in Janus's direction. "Him."

Janus flashed me an annoyed look.

I let my head fall back and gazed up at the blue sky. Max was right, of course. Running after Aello whenever she altered time had not worked. She seemed to get stronger while Max and I got weaker. Endued bullets couldn't kill her. How was I supposed to destroy her?

The answer hit me with the suddenness of a rock dropped on my head. *Duh*. How could I have forgotten?

I looked Max straight in the eyes. "I need to drag that whackjob across the nearest boundary."

"Yes, good luck with that," Max said, his voice dripping with sarcasm. "I'm sure she'll follow you to the boundary and happily traipse across it."

"Got a better idea? Endued weapons don't work on her."

Janus approached us. "Aello is immensely powerful, more powerful than any elemental should be. Until you discover the source of her power, you will have little chance of defeating her by any method."

I smacked his godly chest with the back of my hand. "Told you to shut up unless you've got something useful to say. 'She's unstoppable, oh shit, we're all going to die' is not constructive criticism."

The incubus and the god both watched me warily.

Had I cowed these two powerful beings?

Another idea struck me. "I need to go back in time to find out when and how Aello acquired so much power."

"Fabulous idea," Max said. He tried to bow from the waist, but the strap of his peg leg hindered him. "How may I serve you in this endeavor, my mistress?"

"Cut the sarcasm, that's how. I get that you think I've gone insane, but unless either of you two has a better idea, this is the plan."

Max and Janus exchanged a look, shrugged, and focused on me.

"We will follow you," Janus said.

"Thank you."

Both males winced at my use of the dreaded T-word.

I looked to Janus. "Since you can't go with us into the time stream, I need you to stay here and keep an eye out for Aello while we're gone. Don't want her sneaking up on us when we come back." I tapped a finger on Max's chest. "Could you conjure the endued shotgun shells for my derringer? And the barrel that fits them?"

"Well, I could try." He went motionless for a second, his gaze distant. Then he held out a hand, and the shotgun shells and barrel materialized in his palm. "There."

He offered the items to me.

I pulled out the derringer, dumped the spent .357 shells, and removed the barrel, replacing it with the one that fit the shotgun rounds. Plucking the rounds from Max's palm, I slid them into the barrel and snapped it shut.

"You'll have two shots," I told Janus, handing him the gun. "Endued ammo doesn't kill the Windy Witch, but shotgun shells ought to slow her down. Use them wisely. You've only got two."

"I could conjure more," Max said.

"But I would have to teach Janus how to reload. I've got an ooky feeling in my gut that tells me we don't have time for a lesson in loading ammo." I pointed at the derringer's trigger. "Aim at her forehead and pull that."

He took the gun in his hand, the grip firmly in his palm, and curled his finger over the trigger. The gun looked tiny in his big hand.

"Not yet," I warned. "Don't touch the trigger until you're ready to fire."

"I understand." He hefted the gun as if testing its weight and aimed the muzzle at the ground.

"You seem awfully comfortable with a firearm," I said. "Considering you've been locked up in limbo since the Stone Age."

He gave me a long-suffering look. "As I have said before, you and I are connected. I've sensed things about you over the years, particularly since you came into your powers." He glanced down at the pistol in his hand. "This gun is a vital appendage for you, as your arms and legs are. I've absorbed a bit of knowledge about it from you."

Yeah, I didn't know how to feel about a god having some kind of tele-pathic link to me. No time to worry about that, though.

"Remember," Janus said, "the time stream is your ally and your servant. Treat it with respect, and it will do as you command."

My ally and my servant. I would've thought that was dumb, because how could anything or anyone be both, but I knew better these days. Max had become my ally, my friend, and—thanks to the life debt—my servant, in a way. The contradictions felt strange but no longer impossible.

"Injure the timeline," Janus continued, "and it will defend itself."

"Yeah, I know." I gestured at Max's wooden appendage. "Will that shrink with you? Or are you going to be hopping around on one leg when we get to wherever we're going?"

He thumped a hand on his peg leg. "You can take me into the time stream as long as I'm on your person, and I can shapeshift this with me because it's attached to me."

To prove his point, he shifted into salamander form amid a burst of flames.

I couldn't help grinning at the sight of the small, red lizard with a tiny wooden leg fashioned from a minuscule twig. Tucking Max in my bra, I stifled a laugh when his peg leg tickled my skin.

"*Bonam fortunam*," Janus said. I must've looked confused, because he added, "It means good luck, Lindsey."

I nodded and jumped into the time stream.

Hovering above the twisting, diverging tributaries of the temporal river, I concentrated on the task I'd set for myself. Find the moment when Aello first acquired dark power. The river curved back in on itself, forming the same kind of loop I'd seen before. This time, I knew the loop would guide me to the critical moment.

Sailing down toward the intersection where the loop closed in on itself, I focused all my energy, boosted by Max's power, on diving into that single moment. Closer, closer. I sailed downward faster, plummeting toward my goal. Closer, closer.

An unseen force plowed into me.

I tumbled backward away from my destination, my mind spinning, dizziness whirling through me. I fumbled for a connection to the time stream, but something immensely powerful hurled me away from it. My mind slammed back into my body with so much force my feet flipped out from under me. Max flew out of my shirt to hit the ground with a sharp squeak. I shouted wordlessly, my head reeling, flat on my back in the grass. Above me, the sky seemed to twirl, dragging the treetops in its wake.

Max assumed human form with the usual burst of flames.

A gust of wind ripped through the clearing, dousing his fire.

I lay there dazed and motionless, observing events as if from a great distance, as if I peered through a spyglass.

Aello emerged out of a small tornado that snuffed out to reveal her. She aimed a taloned finger at me. "Foolish mortal. Did you not think I would learn your methods? I knew you would attempt to swim the waters of time once more, and I set a trap for you. My magics created a false beacon which you dutifully followed—to your destruction."

"Destruction?" Max said with a forced laugh. "We aren't destroyed."

The harpy grinned, her jagged yellow teeth exposed. "I have not finished yet."

She raised one hand, palm up, fingers writhing.

A gunshot detonated.

Blood spurted from a wound in Aello's forehead.

Another shot boomed, striking her forehead an inch to the left of the first round.

Janus held the derringer, aimed at her though he had no ammo left. The shotgun rounds had penetrated Aello's skull but caused far less damage than they should have. Yes, blood poured from the wounds. But her head should've exploded like a watermelon.

She swiped a hand across her forehead, and the wounds vanished.

I pushed up with my arms, but my head kept spinning. Christ, the force she'd used to kick me out of the time stream, it had been…something the likes of which none had seen.

Until today. Lucky us.

Aello lowered the hand she had swiped over her forehead. She fanned out her fingers to reveal the objects in her palm.

The shotgun shells. She had somehow reconstituted them.

Raising her hand, she blew a foggy breath at the shells.

One of them shot at me like an invisible gun had fired it.

Max dove toward me.

The shotgun round slammed into his side intact, a thick projectile punching straight into his flesh. He landed sideways across my lap, blood pouring from his wound.

Aello blew on the other shell.

Max bellowed and flung his hand up as if to catch the shell. It bored right through his hand, ripping it apart. He bellowed again, from pain instead of anger.

Aello curled her taloned fingers and snapped them straight.

The intact shotgun shell popped out of Max's side and flew back into Aello's hand like she'd reeled it in with a fishing pole. She raised it in her palm, her lips puckering in preparation for another wind-blown shot.

Aimed at Janus.

I howled with fury and swung my hand up. Blue energy burst forth from my palm, shooting across the distance to Aello in a concentrated stream that barreled into her chest at the instant she blew the shotgun shell at Janus. Her shot veered a hair off course and sideswiped Janus's shoulder. Aello was hurled backward a good thirty feet where she landed with a cracking thud.

Janus collapsed to his knees, one hand pressed to his shoulder, his face strained. Blood oozed out between his fingers.

Aello shrieked with the voice of an enraged tempest.

She vanished amid a gust that swept up earth and grass, flinging them in a spinning dervish.

Breathing hard, I glanced down at Max where he lay sprawled over my legs, bleeding but conscious. That bitch had shot him twice with endued shotgun shells. He couldn't heal from that on his own. He needed help, from a vortex or some other magical method.

I glared at the space where Aello had hunched seconds earlier.

She would pay for this. Whatever I had to do to stop her, I would do it.

Chapter Thirteen

Janus waddled toward us on his knees, clutching his injured shoulder as he made his way around the debris field Aello had left behind. His face had turned a touch ashen, most likely from shock rather than his not-life-threatening wound. "How is your familiar?"

"Not dead yet," Max muttered, "if that's what you were hoping for."

"Shush," I told Max, brushing hair from his eyes. "Janus is being nice for once. And I want to know the same thing. Those were endued shotgun shells, Max. You can't heal naturally from that."

"I know." He shifted position and winced, hissing in a breath. "Had to save you."

My throat went thick, my eyes burned, and my vision blurred. I brushed hair away from his eyes. "Don't you die on me, Max. I won't allow it."

"If the Janusite commands it, I have no choice, do I?"

"Better believe it."

When I sniffled, Max turned his head to gaze up at me with bleary eyes. "A healing vortex won't be enough this time, not with my leg working to regrow itself and the effects of an endued weapon on top of it."

"There has to be something. The Unseen is a world of magic, for heaven's sake."

He made a pained face, not entirely from physical discomfort. "There is one way."

Based on his expression and the resignation in his voice, I had a feeling I knew what way he meant. "The goddess."

Max nodded weakly.

"Well, go to her already."

He crimped his lips. "Lindsey, if I go to her, I may never get free of her influence. It was bloody difficult the first time round."

I swallowed, but the constriction in my throat wouldn't loosen. How could I ask him to go to an obsessed goddess who had the power to enthrall him? If he didn't go to her, he would die. If he did, I might never see him again.

At least he would be alive.

Our bond, cemented by his life debt to me, had kept him immune to the time shifts. Maybe it could give him the strength to resist the goddess's pull.

I bent closer to his face. "Listen to me. If you don't do this, you are going to die. You have something you didn't have the first time you went to this crazy goddess. You have me. Your life debt combined with the familiar's bond has made you immune to the time shifts. It will keep you free of her influence too."

"You can't know that."

"Maybe not logically, but Logical Lindsey gave up the ghost months ago." I laid a palm on his cheek and bored my gaze into his. "I trust my instincts these days and my intuition. Whatever that goddess does, you can always tap into our bond to break free of it. I believe it, and you need to believe it too."

I hadn't lied. I did believe it. Speaking the words had convinced me. But had I convinced him?

He said nothing for a moment, his face tight with pain. "All right."

"You'll do it?"

"I will."

Max slapped his hands on the ground and, with an agonized groan, heaved his body off of mine. Janus hopped up to assist Max in getting to his feet. Despite his peg leg and the bleeding wounds on his side and his hand, he stood up straight.

Janus stepped back.

I leaped up to grab Max's arm. "Wait. Before you go, at least tell me the goddess's name. If I need to go whup her ass to get you back, I will. It would help to know who she is."

Max's mouth ticked up at one corner. "Always the feisty heroine, eh?"

"Hiding under my bed got old pretty fast. It's dusty under there."

"I can't picture you hiding under anyone's bed." He sighed, then leaned in to whisper in my ear, "Hathor."

He poofed away.

Janus looked at me like he expected I'd share the information with him. Max had entrusted me with his secret, and I would not violate that trust merely to satisfy a prickly, powerless god's curiosity.

"Forget it," I said. "The goddess's identity is need to know, and you do not need to know it."

He harrumphed.

"Instead of being grumpy," I said, "you could try being helpful. With Max and Nevan gone, I have only one ally left. You." I eyed his wounded shoulder. "And you need a healing vortex."

"No. I will be fine. The endued ammunition seems not to affect me as badly as it would if I had powers. You should not waste energy on summoning a leprechaun." Janus scratched his head. "I have little to offer. This enemy, this harpy, I know nothing about her. My knowledge is limited to the time before I was destroyed and confined to the Temple of the Four Winds. You need someone who has a deep understanding of the Unseen realm as it is today, as it has been for the previous several millennia."

"Maybe I could get Tris to help."

"You need someone who will fight by your side, who will protect you, who will die for you if necessary."

I squeezed my eyes shut, clamping my lips between my teeth. I knew what he was getting at, and the idea tore a new gash in my heart. I pulled in a long breath and let it out slowly, opening my eyes. "I need Nevan."

"Precisely."

My surprise at Janus suggesting this without a hint of sarcasm evaporated in a heartbeat as the gravity of the situation settled on my shoulders, the weight of two worlds resting on me once again. I'd always had Nevan to shoulder the burden with me.

Aello had stolen him from me forever.

Or had she?

"Do you think," I said, voicing my thoughts without really expecting an answer, "that I could get Nevan back? He remembered me, on some level, even with the time shifts. What if I could bring him back from being erased?"

"You do have a powerful bond. I have never seen anything like it. Can you feel him?"

I hadn't tried to because the loss of him had shredded me inside. Our immediate connection might have been severed, but could a latent link persist?

"Try to sense him," Janus said, his tone gentle.

Even if I had to do this alone, I could. If Aello eradicated Janus, if she wiped away everyone else in both worlds, I would find a way to defeat her. With Nevan by my side, though, I'd have the shared power of our bond, of our love, to win the battle faster.

I closed my eyes and focused on the image of Nevan. His whirlpool eyes, the way they glowed and changed color with his emotions. Those lips, the ones that curved into a sensual smile whenever he wanted me. Nevan, the strong and virile warrior. Nevan, the sweet and generous lover. Nevan, my husband, my soul mate.

Something tickled at my ethereal senses.

Nevan, please, hold on to me. Come back to me.

The tickle intensified into a tingling shiver.

A thread whipped around me. I latched onto it, pulling with all my psychic strength, reeling it in closer, closer, closer. The connection strengthened, thickening into a rope instead of a slender thread. I dragged it toward me, feeling a physical sensation of muscles straining with the effort, though I knew this was a phantom sensation.

My eyes flew open.

Nevan stood in front of me, wearing only the loincloth. His gaze darted, his lips were parted, and his chest heaved as if he'd run a very long distance. Beads of sweat on his chest glistened in the sunshine.

That's when I realized sweat was trickling down my skin too, and I was breathing as hard he was. My body trembled a little. Nevan, on the other hand, appeared rock steady.

Christ, getting him back had taken a lot of energy.

"Are you okay?" I asked.

"Where have I been? It feels as if I went away for an eternity, which for an elemental is no mere figure of speech."

Eternity? I couldn't fathom how empty and frightening that must've been, and I realized I shouldn't try to understand it.

"Are you unwell, Lindsey?" Nevan asked.

Hearing him say my name, even just my first name, rushed a tide of relief through me. My knees buckled.

Nevan caught me in his brawny arms, hugging me to his body. "Lindsey?"

"I'm okay. Bringing you back took a lot out of me is all." I let my forehead fall against his chest, let his strong body support me. He'd called me Lindsey twice, which meant he remembered that much about me. Was it possible...I jerked my head up. "What do you remember?"

"About what?"

That idiotic hope sparked to life inside me. "About me. Us."

"You are Lindsey," he said, "I recall that much. But if you're hoping I've turned back into the man you married, I'm afraid you will be disappointed."

I couldn't move any part of myself, not even my eyelids.

He cupped my cheek and brushed his thumb over my lips. "I also recall wanting you, feeling connected to you in ways I cannot explain. And I remember growing quite jealous whenever another man touches you or approaches within ten feet of you."

At least he hadn't been altered any further. He seemed to have remained the version of Nevan he'd been before Aello expunged him from history, or at least from the version of it everyone else knew. Even the Windy Witch didn't have the power to erase him from my history.

Holy mackerel. I'd brought him back.

Movement to my left drew my attention to Janus. He looked shell-shocked, gaping at me like I'd turned into a unicorn. Did they have those in the Unseen? I'd never asked.

"What's wrong with you?" I said to the god.

He angled his head this way and that, his eyes unblinking. "You brought someone back from oblivion."

"Yeah, it was your idea. Did you think I couldn't really do it?"

"I believed you needed to, but…" He blinked once in slow motion. "Even I could never accomplish such a feat. I tried once, but I failed."

Wow. I had done something a god couldn't do.

His shocked expression softened into appreciation. "This is why the Four Winds chose you to wield my powers. They sensed your strength."

"I thought they chose me when I was born. I didn't have powers then."

"Not your magical strength." He rolled his shoulders back and lifted his chin, assuming his all-knowing-god pose. "Your strength of character, your determination, your unwillingness to accept defeat. Even when gifted with immense power, you refrain from abusing it. I suspect it has never occurred to you to misuse these gifts."

Did unleashing my magic during sex count as abusing my powers? I wouldn't ask Janus that. Frankly, I didn't care. He was right, though. Not once had I thought about using my magic to get what I wanted, like maybe conjuring a red Mustang convertible. My old Chevy Malibu did fine.

Since Janus had mentioned the possibility…

Oh no, I was not going there. Way too dangerous.

"He is right," Nevan said. "Even with my limited knowledge of you, I can tell you're the sort of woman who never misuses magic."

"Thank you, honey."

Neither man flinched, not even a teeny bit. They'd gotten used to my politeness.

Janus frowned. "You did not thank me."

"I appreciate your confidence in me too."

He actually seemed pleased that I'd thanked him. How strange.

A breeze tickled my skin, ushering in a chill that penetrated to the core of my being.

That was no mere breeze.

I grabbed Nevan's biceps. "She's coming."

"Who?" he asked.

Janus looked up to the sky. "Aello."

I tracked his gaze to the heavens, and my blood froze.

A storm cloud as black as the harpy's soul consumed the blue sky, roiling and spreading with unnatural speed. Part of the cloud stretched downward, a finger of black snaking toward the ground, writhing and expanding into a whirling funnel.

What was it with these wind gods and tornadoes? Skeiron had dispatched one to annihilate my family and friends during our final battle with the sylph king. Aello employed the same tactic.

A bell chimed inside me, an idea struggling to form, but I had no chance to examine it.

The tornado lunged downward. A huge pine tree was torn out of the earth and flung aside like a toy. One after another, trees were ripped free of the soil and cast aside as the funnel gouged its way through the woods toward us.

"We must go," Nevan shouted to be heard above the din.

Even while he kept his arm around me, he clamped a hand on Janus's uninjured shoulder.

The three of us stood there, exchanging confused looks.

"Whisk us away already," I shouted.

Lips parted, Nevan shook his head. "I cannot."

I tried to whisk us away. Nothing happened.

The tornado lifted into the sky, hovering a hair's breadth above the tops of the remaining trees. A shape emerged from the funnel, twirling on its way down to the ground.

Aello touched down with a nasty grin on her face.

I thrust up a hand, intending to hurl magic at her.

Nothing. I had nothing.

The harpy cackled. "I grow more powerful whilst you grow weaker. The Anemoi shall be avenged on you."

She stretched out one bony finger to waggle her talon at me.

"Are you done boasting?" I said. "We've got more important things to do than chat with a lonely old crone."

"Lonely?" She cackled again, the sound infused with the wind. "I have driven your familiar away from you, wounding him so grievously he shall not recover. And I—"

Aello froze, her black eyes swiveling to Nevan.

Had she really not noticed he was here until now? Maybe her thirst for vengeance left her vulnerable to tunnel vision. She saw only what she wanted to see.

Maybe I could exploit that weakness.

Her face seemed to grow even paler as she stared at Nevan.

"Yeah," I said, "Nevan's back. I plucked him out of wherever you sent him. Guess you thought you'd gotten rid of him for good, huh? Bad luck for you."

Aello spread her arms wide, and Janus flew forward into them. She locked an arm around Janus's neck and ground her elbow into his wounded shoulder. He cried out, gritting his teeth.

"You shall not win," the harpy snarled. "You may have saved your lover, but I have your mentor. Without this one—" She jabbed her elbow into his wound. "—you will have no one to advise you on how to manipulate time."

I started to move toward them, but Nevan clutched me tighter to his body. What could I do, anyway? Somehow, she had dampened our powers or canceled them out.

"Do not worry," Aello said with mock sympathy, "I will not harm your favorite god unless you attempt to enter the time stream again. Stay out, Janusite."

"You won't win. I will find another way to take you down."

"Oh, you will try." Aello smiled. "But you will fail. I have taken away another of your allies. What have you left? A sylph who does not know you and powers you cannot fully control." She tsked. "Poor little mortal, all alone with nowhere to hide."

She vanished, taking Janus with her.

Chapter Fourteen

A WEIGHT BORE DOWN ON MY CHEST, MAKING IT HARD TO BREATHE. I fought for air, my ears ringing, while I stared at the place where Janus and Aello had been seconds ago. She'd taken him, and I'd been helpless to stop her. How the hell had she gained the power to stifle ours? How was I supposed to fight that?

"Dammit!" I shouted, then I roared out my frustration.

Nevan enfolded me in his arms, my cheek to his chest. "I am sorry. You must've cared for Janus deeply."

"I barely knew him. But I'm sick of that witch winning every battle." I raised my head to meet his gaze. "How does she keep getting more powerful? I knock her down, and she rises up again stronger than ever. Endued weapons don't hurt her, and now she can cancel out our powers. How am I supposed to fight that?"

"Dark magics empower her. She must be ingesting a great deal of the blackest energies to accomplish these feats."

"Fantastic. I can't enter the time stream or she'll kill Janus. She took you away, and she nearly killed Max."

"Where is the incubus?"

"He had to go somewhere else to heal." I shut my eyes, doing my damnedest not to panic. "What if I don't have the power to stop her?"

"You brought me back, and you will find a way to defeat the harpy." He crooked a finger under my chin, rubbing his thumb over it until I looked at him. "We will find a way. Together."

He sounded so much like the old Nevan that it made my heart hurt. I may have returned him to the timeline, but I hadn't restored his memory.

My gaze wandered around the clearing. Trees lay uprooted and overturned, their roots dangling, the earth torn asunder with giant wounds from the harpy's rampage. Why had she summoned a tornado? I'd expected she might use it to mow us down, but she hadn't. Maybe she had simply wanted to make a big entrance. A voice in the back of my mind urged me to study her actions more closely, to figure out her motivations. It seemed vital, but I couldn't concentrate.

I buried my face in my hands.

Nevan peeled my hands away and kissed my forehead. "This place is rife with bad memories of losing your friends. I will take you somewhere less fraught with anguish."

He zipped us away.

We landed in a clearing beside a small stream. Its waters burbled softly, the sound calming me more than I would've imagined possible. Or maybe it was the hot sylph wrapped around me that made my muscles slacken and my thoughts spiral away into the ether.

I shuffled away from Nevan, leaning back against a tree. As much as I craved him and everything he made me feel, I couldn't take what I wanted, what I needed, from him. He was so much like my husband and yet he had no memories of our life together. How could I accept comfort from a man who viewed me as a virtual stranger? He knew my first name because I'd told him, and I doubted he would ever accept we were married.

Speaking more to myself than to him, I muttered, "Why can't you remember me? I rescued you from oblivion, but I couldn't save your memories of us. I'm your wife, but..."

My words died, because I had no clue what I'd been about to say. There was nothing more to say. I was powerless to restore his recollections of us.

"You claim to be my wife," he said, "and I wish it to be true. But it cannot be."

"Doesn't matter anymore."

"It matters to me." Nevan braced his hands on the tree's wide trunk at either side of my head. His eyes burned a brilliant bronze with ribbons of fiery red whipping through his swirling irises. His voice took on a darker, smokier tone when he leaned in close and said, "If we had been lovers, I would remember that. To have a woman like you beneath me, wet and wanting, begging for me to take ye...I'd remember."

"Aello messed with the timeline repeatedly. Everything is screwed up, and I can't fix it."

"Stop trying to." He brushed his nose against mine. "You're tense and frightened and weary. Everything seems hopeless when you feel this way."

"No kidding. Thanks for the revelation."

"Your sarcasm enchants me. I suppose that means we must've been lovers, otherwise I'd be irritated with you."

"Nice twisty logic, but it doesn't help either of us."

"You would feel better if I could remember you."

"Duh. If you're going to keep stating the obvious—"

"Hush, love." His breaths teased my skin, and the earthy scent of him surrounded me. He dipped his head to sniff my hair and inhaled a deep breath filled with the aroma of it. Groaning out a long sigh, he turned his head enough to bring his cheek into contact with mine. "Perhaps if ye stripped for me, the sight of your luscious, nude body would stir my memories."

Stir his memories? Well, this discussion was definitely stirring his penis to swell. I guessed my sarcasm really did enchant him, or least it enchanted his manly bits. As for me…My body had begun to ache and tingle in the most intimate ways. I wanted him. Of course I did. This version of Nevan possessed all the seductive allure of the man I'd married, and I couldn't stop my body from responding to his proximity, the radiant heat of him, and the sense memories of every time we'd made love. But he wasn't my husband. In his world, we had never met.

Whenever you are, it's always him.

Back when Bob had spoken those words to me, I hadn't understood what he meant. Part of me had figured he misspoke. He must've meant "wherever," not "whenever." That was before the timeline mutated. Post-shift, I had to wonder if Bob said exactly what he'd meant. And what was that, exactly?

Whenever you are, it's always him.

I gazed into the swirling eyes of the sylph penning me to the tree. Despite the fact he had no memories of me, despite the fact his past differed from what I knew of my husband's experiences, this man was Nevan. I felt it in ways I couldn't explain or quantify. I still shared his powers, and he still felt drawn to me. I'd been able to retrieve him even after Aello obliterated him. Our connection had weakened, but it had not disintegrated. A bond lingered between us, a connection even the shifting sands of time itself could not eradicate.

And that must've been what Bob had meant.

No matter what timeline or what time in the past I found myself in, Nevan would always be Nevan. The man I loved. My husband. Fragments of our life together must remain inside him, if only I knew how to revive them.

I'd shied away from intimacy with him because it seemed like cheating. I'd sworn to this Nevan I wouldn't have sex with him until he could speak my full name. Yet if he was *my* Nevan, dressed up in different memories but him at the core…

He rocked his hips forward, rubbing his erection against my belly. "What shall we do, darlin'?"

I longed to kiss him, touch him, beg him to vanish my clothes and ravish me all night long. I couldn't. I mean, he didn't know me. Maybe I was misinterpreting what Bob had said. The oracle did have a tendency toward vagueness.

Clearing my throat, I said, "We should keep this professional. You're helping me search for the crazy woman who wants revenge on me. That's all."

"Professional?" Nevan chuckled darkly. "When I first saw ye, darlin', ye threw yourself at me and kissed me like a wanton."

"I thought you were the same Nevan I married. I was wrong." Despite the fluttering in my tummy, I added, "We should brainstorm a plan to stop Aello."

"Mm, we could do that." He nuzzled my throat and dragged his tongue up to my jaw near my ear, flicking it out to tease my lobe. "But I can think of other, more interesting things we might do together."

Every hair on my body, from my scalp down to my nape and through my arms straight down to my toes, shivered and stiffened. Nevan had spoken those exact words to me months ago, not long after we'd met. I had been asking him questions he didn't want to answer, so he'd made an alternate suggestion: *Let's not start with the questions again. I can think of other, more interesting things we might do together.* The sylph currently licking my earlobe seemed to have no memories of me, but he had spoken the precise phrase the original Nevan had said to me.

Oh God, could it be true? Was this man really my Nevan?

Nevan had always trusted my instincts and my intuition. I trusted my gut because he believed in me. The changes to the timeline, and the changes they brought about in Nevan, had thrown me for a loop. Maybe that's what Bob had been trying to tell me, that I needed to trust my instincts no matter what things seemed to be on the surface.

This was Nevan. My husband. If he remembered one thing about us, he could remember the rest.

With a little jump start.

Max had half-jokingly suggested I have sex with Nevan to trigger his memories because it had worked before when I restored his soul. I'd assured Max the soul stone had done it, not my kiss or my body. Maybe I'd been too quick to dismiss the idea. Our deep, immutable bond had begun as an instant attraction beyond anything I'd ever experienced with another man. Maybe the physical connection could serve as a catalyst.

Then again, maybe I'd lost all my wits because I was insanely horny thanks to the hot, seductive sylph rubbing himself all over me.

Stop doubting yourself. Go for it.

What was the worst that could happen? I'd have awesome sex with Nevan, and he wouldn't regain his memories of me. Nothing gained, but nothing lost either. It wasn't like I'd never done the deed with him before.

He raised his head in front of mine, his eyes blazing with need. And that was no metaphor. "I want ye more than seems rational."

"Screw rational." I grasped his face, my pulse quickening and my breaths shortening. "Nothing about us has ever been rational."

I crushed my mouth to his.

He went stiff, in the sense of his body tensing. Another part of him had gone stiff several minutes ago. He sucked in a breath through his nostrils.

My pulse thundered in my ears.

Nevan shoved an arm behind me, fastening it around my back, and hauled me against him, our bodies plastered together.

I opened my mouth, doing exactly what he'd said—begging him to take me.

He thrust his tongue into my mouth, possessing and devouring me with every lash of his tongue. I coiled mine around his, moaning with intense pleasure, reveling in the flavor and feel of him, hungry for so much more than a kiss, more than his lips and tongue. I hungered for his body merging with mine. He plunged deeper into my mouth, groaning and whisking his hand down to my ass to clutch it with his strong fingers, kneading fiercely.

A desperate noise escaped me, part moan, part whimper. My body pulsated with a need so powerful it consumed my thoughts and my inhibitions, like I'd ever had any of those with Nevan, while he consumed my mouth.

He tore his lips away from mine, breathing hard, and latched both hands onto my bottom. "You are the most desirable woman in any realm."

Despite the fire raging inside me, the start of tears stung my eyes. He had spoken those words to me once before, on the night when I gave myself to him for the first time.

I hooked one ankle around his, flung my arms around his neck, and spoke the same words I'd said to him that night. "Take me, Nevan."

He stared at me, eyes aflame, chest heaving.

After a heart-stopping moment of frozen anticipation, he slid his hand down to clasp my thigh, the one raised slightly so I could lock my ankle around his. "I hope ye mean that, love."

"I do. My body is yours, I'm yours. In every way."

He hoisted me up, and with his hands, he encouraged me to lock my ankles behind his ass. His palms cupped my bottom, and his erection was nestled against my cleft with only my jeans and his loincloth separating our flesh.

Nevan kissed me like he'd never kissed me before, wild and demanding, almost brutal in his need. I met him thrust for thrust, lash for lash, our teeth clashing and our lips glued to each other, the lust inside us seeming to erupt from our pores in a spray of sparkling blue light.

No, that blue glow beyond my eyelids wasn't my imagination.

I opened my eyes even while we kept kissing. The sparkling energy of my powers activating enveloped us in a cloud of blue. It clung to our bodies, drizzling down our skin like droplets of water.

Nevan pulled his head back and glanced around the clearing. "This won't do at all."

We rocketed through the tunnel so fast I had no time to process the journey. Before I realized what he'd done, we rematerialized inside a house.

I blinked several times, struggling to catch my breath. No, we weren't inside a house. Nevan had brought me to a place I knew well, a place where we had spent countless hours together.

"This is my old apartment," I said. "Why did you bring us here?"

"I…don't know. I wanted to take you somewhere private."

"I used to live here, but I gave up this apartment when I moved in with you a couple months ago. You remembered my old apartment."

"No, I—" He glanced around, seeming panicked. "I must've chosen this location at random, unconsciously, because I sought a vacant premises."

A quick survey of the living room around us proved to me someone lived here. Personal items and furniture occupied the space, and the occupant had left a floor lamp on.

"Nevan, we need to talk about this," I said, "but I think we'd better go somewhere else first."

He didn't move, didn't even blink, his hands trembling the tiniest bit against my bottom.

Someone screamed.

Nevan and I jerked at the same instant. He yanked his hands away and sent me tumbling to the floor. I landed with a squeak, my feet in the air and my hair in my face. I blew the hair away from my eyes.

The young woman who had just stepped out of the bedroom screamed again.

I opened my mouth to speak but realized I had no frigging clue what to say. *Gee, sorry we scared the bejesus out of you, please don't call the cops on us. This home invasion was an accident, I swear.*

Footsteps thudded on the concrete walkway outside the front door.

A fist pounded on the door, and a male voice shouted, "Shelly, what's going on? You okay?"

Shelly screamed.

Nevan scooped me up and whisked us away.

Chapter Fifteen

W E EMERGED IN A CLEARING ALONGSIDE A TWENTY-FOOT-HIGH WA-
terfall. Though the wooden railing that used to protect the falls and
the pool below was no longer there and the path was gone, I recognized this
place. I would've known that waterfall blindfolded. The sound of it, the
scent of damp earth, the sensation of cool water misting over my skin. This
was the falls behind the shop, if the shop had existed in this reality. The
cascade tumbled down the cliff, pummeling the pool below and churning
up foam.

Nevan kept his arms around me, though his face had paled beneath its
bronzed surface. His gaze flitted everywhere. He licked his lips, though not
in a sexy way, more in the manner of someone struggling to comprehend
the incomprehensible.

He'd brought us to the spot where we had first met.

Nevan let go of me, stumbled backward a few steps, and shoved a hand
into his hair. "What the bloody hell is happening?"

I held up my hands in a conciliatory gesture. "Take it easy. I know this
is confusing, but you need to listen to me. You took me to my old apartment, and now you've brought us to the place where we first met." I dared
to move one step closer. "Like I told you before, the timeline has been
altered. Someone is messing with it, with you, with everyone except me
and Janus and Max. What you're feeling, it's your real memories trying to
come out. You need to stop fighting it."

"Why?" He squinted at me, streaks of ice blue unfurling in his irises. His
tone turned darker, almost angry. "Perhaps you are the one attempting to
rewrite my memories, to make me believe we have a relationship."

"No, Nevan." I lowered my hands and walked up to him, tilting my
head back to meet his gaze head-on. A few minutes ago, he'd said he
wished we really were married, but popping up inside my old apartment

had freaked him out. Maybe his memories struggling to resurface had knocked him off kilter too. "I have no reason to trick you. Trust your instincts, trust what you feel, and stop trying to make sense out of something that's not logical. It's emotion and magic and destiny."

He made a derisive noise.

"You're the one who taught me," I said, "how to trust in things I couldn't quantify, to trust my gut and believe in the magic all around us. Most of my life I refused to believe in things I couldn't see and touch and explain. Until I met you."

I rested my palms on his chest, praying he would believe me. How could the man who'd introduced me to a world of magic doubt what I'd told him was possible? I believed because of him, yet I couldn't make him believe what I'd told him, what he'd experienced himself. Maybe I was expecting too much. After all, his memories had been wiped away and rewritten. How could he accept what I claimed to be true? He might've brought me to the place where I'd met him three months ago by coincidence, since he was the guardian of the falls here.

No, his memories weren't rewritten. He'd taken me to my former apartment. Why would he do that if he had zero knowledge of me? The timeline had shifted, but rather than wiping out his memories, it must have overwritten them. Remnants lingered. Did all of his recollections of me, of us, hide somewhere inside him?

One way to find out.

I glided my hands up to his neck, around to his nape where I linked them. Leaning in, I pressed my body against his. "Whether you believe me or not, I know you want me. You could've run off to find any number of attractive elemental women to satisfy your urges, but you didn't. You came back to me. You got jealous of other men talking to me. Why is that?"

The colors in his whirlpool eyes morphed from white and ice blue, the colors of fear, into shades of fiery red and molten bronze. His lips parted slightly. His breaths quickened.

"Go on," I said, toying with the hair that fell over his nape. "Tell me why your attention has been focused exclusively on me. Say it, Nevan."

I shimmied my hips, rubbing myself on him.

His hands came around my waist, though he seemed to do it unconsciously, and his head tipped toward mine.

"I want you," I told him. "It's okay. Say it, Nevan."

The molten colors in his eyes sparked with bright gold, and he grasped my hips to tug me into his rejuvenated erection. "I want you, Lindsey, only you. Got no bloody idea why, but I cannot resist you one moment longer."

He slung his arms around me, pulling me into him and devouring my mouth in a kiss of raw, primal possession. I moaned into his mouth, sagging against him, lost to the thrill of his tongue ravaging me and the heat of his body soaking into my skin. He kissed me like he'd spent a thousand years in the desert and I was the only oasis.

Take me home, I wanted to say, but I couldn't speak, couldn't tear myself away from him.

I felt the world melt away, sensed we rocketed through the abysmal tunnel, but we traveled so fast I had no time to think about it. If I'd been able to think. Nevan's tongue scraped over mine, hot and demanding, obliterating thought and reason and intention. I clutched my arms tighter around his neck and flung my legs up to latch them around his hips. Oh God, the hunger, the heat, the desperate need to forget everything and succumb to the bliss of our bodies entangled...

Light glowed beyond my closed lids.

The air temperature had changed, becoming a perfect balance between warm and cool. With an enormous effort, I detached my mouth from Nevan's. My lids fluttered open, and the space around us came into focus. Smooth rock walls. Light that emanated from everywhere and nowhere. Chairs. A table. And a sylph-size bed covered with a fur blanket. All my stuff had vanished, of course, but I recognized this place.

We had come home.

"How did you do this?" Nevan asked, eying me with a cross between suspicion and wonder. "A mortal cannot cross the veil without assistance. Crossing it without opening a portal...It's impossible."

Yeah, that was weird. I couldn't explain it, but in this moment, I didn't care about anything except getting naked with Nevan.

"I'm the Janusite," I said. "I can open portals all by my itty-bitty self."

"You're the what?"

Maybe there was no Janusite, no destruction of the god and no prophecy, in this version of the two worlds. I didn't care about that either. Not now. Not until after I'd felt him inside me.

"But you did not open a portal," he insisted. "I would have sensed it opening for us, but I did not. And we aren't wet from piercing the falls."

I glanced down at my dry clothes and fingered my dry hair. How...

Nevan answered the question I could not voice. "You transported us here without the use of a portal."

Expanding powers? *Think about it later*, my aroused body urged.

I raked my lips across his, sneaking my tongue out to sample his skin.

Though his breath hitched, and he took hold of my bottom with both his hands, his expression blanked. "How could we cross the veil without a portal?"

His hands supported me, but I adjusted my hold on him to make sure I wouldn't tumble out of his embrace. "I don't know how I did it. All that matters is I did. I've given up trying to understand this stuff. What is, is."

If he'd retained all his memories, he would've found that statement highly amusing. I, the once pragmatic mortal who got into heaps of trouble on a regular basis, had given in to the mysteries of magic and the supernatural. He would never understand unless he *remembered*.

"Nevan," I said, tunneling my fingers into his silky hair, "let's not talk anymore. I need to be naked with you. I need to feel you inside me, and I can't wait another second."

I didn't even have to ask him to vanish our clothes. They disappeared the instant I said I needed him inside me.

Faster than I could process the change, we lay on the bed—me on my back, Nevan lying on top with his body covering mine. He pushed a hand between our bodies to palm my mound, then dived his fingers between my folds, already slick and swollen with desire. I moaned at his touch. He slithered down my body, kissing and licking and nibbling my flesh as he moved. When he reached my breasts, he skated his tongue around one taut peak, teasing me until I gripped his shoulders and made an impatient noise. His mouth sealed around my nipple, suckling with fervid hunger, his tongue raking over the tip.

"Oh Nevan," I breathed, and spread my thighs, my movement and my words pleading with him to take me.

A growl resonated low in his throat. He released my nipple only to catch the other one in his teeth and tug it. When I gasped, he released the stiff peak. "The scent of your lust is maddening. It fills my senses and makes me want to fuck ye like a wild thing."

"Yes, do it." I dug my nails into his shoulders. "Please."

That word invoked a slender tether of magic, creating a minor debt between us, snapping taut and binding us. I knew better than to speak the P-word in the Unseen, but I was beyond caring. Owing Nevan could not be dangerous, not ever, not if we both lived to the see the universe collapse in on itself and explode in a new Big Bang.

He slithered further down my body, between my legs, until his face hovered above my groin.

"Nevan," I moaned. "Do it. Hurry."

With a growl, he ducked his head between my thighs and latched his mouth onto my rigid nub, suckling and nipping and licking it until I was thrashing under him. The pleasure mounted with such force and speed that I felt sure I'd explode like a star going supernova. He shoved a finger inside me, thrusting it wildly even as his mouth tormented my bud with the same reckless ferocity. My release struck with the suddenness of a star detonating, convulsing my entire body, the ecstasy so intense it was almost unbearable, and I screamed.

Before I could come down from the climax, Nevan rose to his knees, hoisted my knees up onto his shoulders, and plunged inside me. He thrust hard and deep and fast, grunting every time he plowed inside me, blustering in a breath with every withdrawal. My body bounced on the bed, and I fisted my hands in the fur blanket. The decadence of its silken texture rubbing on my skin heightened my arousal. I whimpered and cried out, certain of one fact.

I would come again, and the orgasm would devastate me with its power.

Nevan slapped his hands onto the bed at either side of my head, his arms straight and rigid, punching into me again and again, the bed creaking and thumping on the floor, my breasts bouncing. His face had pinched into a pained expression, but he never took his gaze off of mine. Our gazed were riveted to each other even while our bodies merged with a frantic, almost crazed intensity. With my legs over his shoulders, bent close to my body, his every thrust drove him deeper than ever before.

Blue sparks erupted on my skin, dribbling down like water. While Nevan kept up his brutal pace and energy, the sparks crackled and expanded. I couldn't concentrate on them or what their presence meant, too consumed by the outrageous passion of our love-making. As our need escalated, so did the blue energy. It blanketed us in a cloud of sparkling, topaz-blue light, and it danced over our skin eliciting tiny shocks of electrical magic that only enhanced the intensity of our joining.

Our climaxes seized us at the same instant.

I screamed again, my cries echoing off the stone walls. He threw his head back and bellowed as the scorching jet of his release pulsed deep inside me.

Nevan collapsed onto the bed beside me, breathing hard, almost gasping for air.

Limp as a wet noodle, I lay there with my legs splayed where they'd fallen off his shoulders. Stunned, I could do nothing more than gape at the ceiling and wait for my breathing to return to normal. Even then, I couldn't speak. Nevan and I always had sizzling-hot sex, but this...

He rolled onto his side to peer down at me, his cheeks ruddy and his eyes ablaze. "That was like nothing I've ever experienced before."

"Likewise."

"Was that your magic?" He fanned a palm over my belly. "The energy that surrounded us, it came from you, did it not?"

"It did." I shivered at his touch, my skin sensitized by our passion. "We always have great sex, but this was a whole new level of wow."

"Mm, indeed." He swirled his palm over my belly, focused on the task with an adorable concentration. He froze, his hand over my womb. "I released my seed. If you become pregnant—"

"Relax, an oracle gave me a supernatural prophylactic." Our wedding gift from Bob, a spell to prevent pregnancy. It was the magical equivalent of handing us a box of condoms.

"I see," Nevan said, sounding like he didn't get it at all. He stared into my eyes for a long moment, so long I was about to say something when he finally spoke. "Lindsey."

"Yep, that's me." I smiled and tapped his nose. "And you are Nevan, the sexiest sylph in any realm."

He rose to hands and knees, swinging his right arm and leg over my body to straddle me. Poised over me, he held completely motionless and studied me with an unnerving intensity, not blinking, not breathing.

At last, he sucked in a shaky breath and fixed his tender gaze on me. "Lindsey Astrid Porter."

It was my turn to freeze, unable to move or speak or breathe. Though I'd told him my first name, I had never said my last name and definitely not my middle name. This version of him had no way of knowing my full name. Unless…I didn't dare think it.

Tears shimmered in his eyes. He choked on a breath, almost a sob.

I pushed up onto my elbows. "Nevan? What's wrong?"

He swiped a hand across his mouth. "I remember."

CHAPTER SIXTEEN

M Y HEART THUDDED SO HARD MY HEAD SPUN FOR A SECOND. "WHAT do you remember?"

"You." He hauled in a long breath that seemed to steady him. "We met near the falls when you were kneeling beside a dead man. You tripped, and I caught you before you cracked your lovely head on a large rock."

The entire room spun. My pulse raced, and I made a choked noise.

Nevan lowered his body onto mine, our faces aligned. He stroked my cheek with his fingers, his gaze so tender it made my chest ache. "We made love for the first time in this bed when you gave me your virginity. We married by the falls earlier today. You are my wife, my sweet Lindsey, the half of my soul I cannot live without. How could I have forgotten you?"

The question rang with anguish and guilt.

I bit my lip, tears blurring my vision. "Time was altered. The whole world, two worlds, changed fundamentally. Only Janus, Max, and I weren't affected by it. For you to remember me at all proves we have a connection nothing can erase. Nothing." I grasped his face and touched my lips to his. "This is a miracle, Nevan. Don't feel guilty, be grateful."

He claimed my mouth in a sweet, slow kiss that dissolved all my worries. Nevan was back. My Nevan. My husband, my lover, my best friend, my soul mate.

When we broke the kiss, he smirked at me. "This time, I needed less than a day to get you in my bed, in spite of your vow you wouldn't have sex with me until I spoke your full name."

"I was predisposed to give in." I swept my thumb over his kiss-swollen lips. "But in point of fact, I seduced you this time. Which means you're the one who's easy."

He sucked my thumb into his mouth, releasing it slowly. "For you, always."

"Even without your memories of me, you had no interest in other women."

"What we have transcends magic and time itself. How could I want anyone else? You own my heart and soul, Lindsey."

"Goes both ways."

He rolled off of me to lie on his back, and his expression turned serious. "What will we do about Aello?"

"I haven't got a clue."

"You are the Janusite, which means you have the power to stop her." He clasped my hand, holding it to his heart where his scar had once been before the time shifts. "You were able to cross the veil without opening a portal. I believe you can do anything you set your mind to."

"I appreciate the vote of confidence, but every time I've gone up against Aello, I have failed spectacularly." I made an explosion noise accompanied by a matching hand gesture. "Whatever I try, it explodes in my face. Max nearly died. You were obliterated from the timeline. Janus got kidnapped, for heaven's sake."

"You now have something you did not have during your previous attempts."

"What's that? A ticking time bomb strapped to my chest?"

"No." He flipped onto his side to face me, holding on to my hand. "You have me. My powers combined with your expanding magics may prove more powerful than the time-traveling harpy."

"May prove more powerful? I need something more than maybe." Despite my dismissal, his words had sent a surge of hope through me. Could he be right? I longed to believe it, but I'd gotten smacked down too many times today.

Nevan rose up on one elbow to gaze down on me, the force of his focus like a palpable energy between us. "We can do this together, Lindsey. If you can't trust yourself, trust me."

"I always trust you, Nevan. But this catastrophe is epically worse than the other times we've almost died and almost lost two worlds." I swallowed, my throat and mouth suddenly dry. "Aello can manipulate time, and I can't even try to undo the shifts. If I go into the time stream, she will kill Janus. He might be annoying on occasion, but he doesn't deserve to die."

"You always want to save everyone, even a sorcerer who tried to destroy you."

"The sorcerer had a piece of Calder inside him. That's who I had to save."

"But you also asked the Four Winds to spare Notus and Skeiron, despite all their depraved acts."

"I'm a sap. A weak, foolish sap."

"No." He draped an arm across my waist to grasp my hip. "You are a kind and compassionate woman. It's one of the many qualities I admire and adore in you."

"That's really sweet, honey, but it doesn't tell me how to destroy Aello." I scratched my arms, recalling my encounters with the Windy Witch. "Next time, she could kill me. I'm not immortal like Max and Janus. And you."

"I will be by your side to protect you."

"And possibly die doing it, like Travis did." I hugged myself as goosebumps cropped up on my arms thanks to a sudden chill. "If I were an elemental, that harpy would have a much harder time trying to off me. And maybe I'd have enough power to take her down."

Nevan pulled the fur blanket over me. "We will find a way, and I will not allow anything to happen to you."

"I know you mean that, but I don't want anyone else getting critically injured or dying while trying to protect me." Even with the blanket over me, the cold penetrated my skin. "You have to forge me."

"No." He glowered at me, but his eyes churned with the colors of fear. "I will never forge you or anyone."

"Max swore he'd never do it, but he forged Travis."

"Because you were distraught over losing your friend. Max forged him to spare you pain." Nevan sat up and rubbed his neck. "You're asking me to do this simply to give you more power."

"Not only that." I sneaked a hand out from under the blanket to touch his arm. "If you do this, we could have children. We could be together forever. Do you really want to watch me get old and die?"

"We've had this discussion before. I will love you no matter what, even when you grow old."

"I know, but this way—"

"No, Lindsey."

Shoving off the blanket, I sat up to confront him. "You'd rather let Aello murder me."

"Of course not." He flashed me an irritated look, but it quickly softened even has he rapped his knuckles on the fur blanket. "We don't know if you can be forged. Your Janusite powers cause magic to work differently around you. I could not enchant you to determine if you had a touch of the Unseen realm. You have acquired the ability to cross the veil without a portal, and you restored me to the timeline from which I had been erased."

"I'll take the chance. Forge me, please."

Another slender thread of magic snapped taut between us.

Nevan winced. "Cease using that word."

"Forge me."

He dropped his face into his hands, exhaled a long sigh, and raised his face to me. "If you can't be forged, you will die."

"I'm willing to risk it."

"But I am not." He clutched both my hands between his. "You've seen what the forging does to a mortal. How can you ask me to do that to you, not knowing if it will work?"

My mind flashed back to Calder and the cougar and the elemental monkey-thing. Calder had screamed with a soul-crushing agony.

A shiver raced through me. Did I really want that? Could I survive it?

"If I ever lost you," Nevan murmured, "I would pray to be destroyed."

"Don't say that. If anything happens to me, you have to go on living." I wriggled my hands free of his. "Okay, no forging. But promise me you will not destroy yourself or purposely let anyone else destroy you after I'm gone. Promise me, Nevan."

He flattened his lips.

"Promise," I insisted.

With a growl, he sighed and slumped his shoulders. "I vow to do as you ask."

A thicker thread of magic sealed the vow, shivering through me.

I kissed him. "Good."

"Never again ask me to forge you."

Drawing a cross over my heart, I said, "You have my word. No more forging talk."

He nodded wearily.

I kissed him again. "Somehow, arguing with you gave me the boost I needed to stop feeling powerless. I've got a plan."

"Do I want to know?"

"Would you rather I blip away and do this on my own?"

"Absolutely not."

I couldn't help laughing softly at his indignation. "You don't really think I'd go fight a crazy harpy by myself, do you?"

Nevan pulled his knees up in front of him and rubbed his eyes. "I know you would not do that, but our previous conversation disturbed me."

"I promise I will never ask you to forge me again, and I will never try to get anyone else to forge me." The newest magical tether canceled out the ones Nevan had sealed with me, our debts equal to each other. I patted his knee. "Let's talk about my plan."

He made a go-on gesture.

"Actually, it's the plan I already had but couldn't implement. I need your help figuring out how to do this without Aello noticing."

"You will need to tell me your plan before I can assist."

"Right." I squared my shoulders, planted my hands on my thighs, and told him. "I am going into the time stream to find the moment when Aello first tapped into dark magics. And I'm going to destroy her."

"First, you must devise a plan for doing that without the harpy noticing."

"I already said I need your help with that part. You're the king of the sylphs, a smart and determined man, surely you can come up with an idea."

He gave me an exasperated look. "Flattery won't make the answer appear to us. Besides, I am not the king in this version of reality. Notus is."

"Don't confuse me with facts. Especially when the facts keep shifting."

Nevan reached out to touch the corner of my mouth. "You're frowning, love."

"It's called hopelessness."

He pulled me into his embrace, combing his fingers through my hair. "Think back on what Aello has said to you in your previous encounters with her. She may have given you clues to her true motivations."

I ransacked my memories, squinting my eyes and my mouth in the effort.

Nevan began to paint circles on my back with one hand while the other combed through my hair. The soothing sensations relaxed me, and I let my mind drift.

Aello. The earthquake. The tornadoes. She was, according to mythology, a wind goddess. Wind. It meant something. She'd spoken of vengeance, how I'd taken "them" from her, and how she would avenge herself on me by taking what I loved. Aello had announced the Anemoi would be avenged. Whoever or whatever the Anemoi were, they must be the ones she believed I'd taken from her.

Something else she'd said surfaced in my mind, and I recited it to Nevan, doing my best to pronounce it the way Aello had. "*Daimones. Anemoi Thuellai.* Do you know what that means?"

His brows lifted as his eyes widened a fraction. "Are you certain that's what she said?"

"Positive."

"It's ancient Greek. *Daimones* means spirits or ghosts." Nevan hesitated. "*Anemoi Thuellai* means the storm winds. In mortal mythology, the Anemoi were the wind gods and the Anemoi Theullai were the *daimones* of the storm winds."

"Wind gods?" My thoughts reeled back to a couple months ago when another villain had tried to take Nevan away from me with the help of his formerly dead wife. "The sorcerer who worked with Ceara called himself the storm-bringer because he was predominantly the essence of Notus and 'storm-bringer' was Notus's moniker. He also had Skeiron's essence in him, and Skeiron was another wind god in Greek mythology."

"Indeed."

"But in the Unseen, Notus and Skeiron were sylphs. Elemental spirits forged from the earth and the air."

"I believe you're working it all out in that lovely head of yours." He gestured with one hand. "Please continue."

"Are you humoring me? You've probably figured out the answers."

"I haven't, and I enjoy listening to my clever love sort out mysteries."

"Aw, honey, you always say the nicest things." I went back to rifling through the clues. "Skeiron attacked me with wind, making the roof of my apartment collapse on top of me. And he summoned a tornado during our battle with the sylph army. Aello summoned tornadoes twice, but not to attack me. I couldn't figure out why she bothered orchestrating a grand entrance with a twister ripping up trees or why she stepped out of a small tornado the next time I saw her."

"You have developed a theory."

I tapped my lips, concentrating on everything I'd learned from Aello. My dreams. They involved Notus and Skeiron, and in those nightmares, I'd heard Aello's voice. The former sylph kings could not have been resurrected, not after the Four Winds took care of them. What if my dream hadn't been literal? Notus and Skeiron had not returned to take revenge on me, but maybe someone else had taken up the vengeance mission on their behalf.

The truth smacked me like a wet towel to the face. "Aello must've known Skeiron and Notus. She knows I'm the Janusite and knows my full name. Skeiron knew all of that. He and Notus must be the ones Aello thinks I took from her, which I did. I tricked Skeiron into crossing the boundary, destroying him. When he and Notus got resurrected by the sorcerer, becoming a part of him, I took out the sorcerer which means I took out Skeiron and Notus too."

"Aello seeks revenge for this."

"That's not all. I thought she was trying to get rid of me with these time shifts." I twisted in his arms to face Nevan. "Now I think she wants to resurrect Skeiron and Notus. The time shifts are her attempts to alter the past so the former sylph kings will be alive again. She must've thought keeping you and me apart would do the trick, so she stopped Calder from being forged. This changed my past, but she didn't count on me being immune to the shifts."

"So the harpy tried again."

"But she'd wounded time, and it defended itself. Again, she changed my past but not me. I'm still the Janusite, and we still belong together. On her next attempt, she wiped you away but again couldn't achieve her goal."

"You restored me to the timeline and restored my memories of you."

"Aello is seriously miffed about it."

Nevan scratched his jaw. "She took Janus to prevent you from attempting to unravel her time shifts. This harpy has the power to stifle our magics. I do not know how you might enter the time stream without alerting her."

"Yeah, I haven't got that figured out either."

We lapsed into silence, each gazing out into space, searching for an answer in the air or in the recesses of our minds.

I perked up first. "I may have an idea, but you won't like it."

"Your schemes are always certain to unnerve me."

"Ha-ha. Where do harpies live?"

"I haven't a clue."

"We're going to find out." I looped my arms around his neck. "Bob is hiding out from the time shifts, but we know where he lives. He'll give us Aello's home address."

"And then what?"

"You and Max will distract Aello by assaulting her home."

Nevan snorted. "Ridiculous. Besides, Max is recovering from his injuries."

"He's all better, I can feel it."

"Wonderful. And what will you do while he and I distract Aello?"

"I'll jump into the time stream and stop her from ever acquiring dark magics."

Chapter Seventeen

As it turned out, we didn't need to make the creepy journey through the dark, green-tinged woods and across the acid river to reach Bob's lair. All I had to do was call for him. Nevan and I had poofed into the clearing at the base of the mountain that contained our home when I realized this. Throwing my head back, I hollered for the oracle.

He appeared a few seconds later looking haggard. "What is it?"

And sounding grumpy.

"You okay?" I asked.

"These time shifts are giving me a migraine that won't end." He managed a wan smile. "Other than that, I'm terrific."

"I hate to bother you, but we have an emergency. Do you know where the harpy Aello lives?"

"Harpies migrate with the winds, but they usually have a permanent nest they go back to once in a while."

"Where is Aello's nest?"

Bob rubbed his temples and grimaced, then rubbed his eyes with the heels of his hands. After a moment, his face fell and his shoulders slumped. "I'm sorry. My foresight's blocked by the time shifts. Reality keeps realigning to adjust to the changes your harpy friend is causing. If this doesn't stop soon, she could break the timeline."

"Break the timeline?" I said. "What does that mean?"

"Chaos." He raised a hand to shield his eyes from the glaring light of the sun. "Trust me, you do not want to find out what true chaos looks like. I've seen it once, longer ago than any human ever born could re-member. When time breaks, the threads of reality become untethered and everything that might have been is. The strands become intertwined, overlapping and converging, often with grotesque results. Pray you never experience it."

A broken timeline? Grotesque results? A chill shimmied down my spine. It sounded like doomsday.

"How did time get broken before?" I asked.

"Same old story. An evil being bent on revenge for who-knows-what gathered enough dark magics to manipulate the time stream." Bob rubbed his eyes again. "This was eons ago, back before the elementals existed. It took all of the primordial gods to set things right."

"We better stop Aello before the problem gets that bad."

Bob flourished a hand, and a piece of parchment appeared in his palm. He offered it to me. "A map to Aello's nest. Be careful, Janusite."

I took the parchment, and he assumed the *I'm-about-to-disappear* posture.

He stopped blinking, his gaze unfocused, and intoned, "Blood for blood, life for life, the scales must be balanced. Sacrifice the past for the sake of the future."

Bob shook off whatever it was, cringed, and vanished.

The word sacrifice rang in my soul, but I had no idea what he'd meant and no time to figure it out.

"Max!" I hollered.

Nevan and I both glanced around the clearing, but the incubus did not appear.

I sucked in a deep breath and bellowed, "Max! Get your flaming red butt over here right this instant!"

My familiar materialized beside me, wobbling a little. His leg had regenerated, and the wounds from the endued shotgun shells had healed too. His pupils were dilated, though, and he gazed dreamily into empty space.

"Here I am, my mistress," he said with a slur and a clumsy attempt at a bow.

Max stumbled into me, grabbing my breasts while trying to steady himself.

I let out an annoyed sigh and batted his hands away. "What is wrong with you?"

Nevan chuckled. "He's inebriated."

"Have you been drinking?" I asked Max. "Doing drugs? High on magic or something?"

Max held up his thumb and forefinger, holding them an inch apart. "A tad of wine."

"Looks to me," I said, "like you've had more than a tad."

Nevan touched my arm. "Where did he go for healing?"

I opened my mouth to answer, but Max beat me to it. He thrust an arm into the air, wavering a bit. "The palace of Hathor, as my mistress commanded."

"Hathor?" Nevan said, his lip curling. "She is a goddess of the old order. It is said Hathor ensorcells everyone who enters her palace, essentially hypnotizing them into becoming her devotees. The details are secret, but she and her followers engage in orgies of drink and sex."

"Orgies?" I lodged my hands on my hips. "How do you know what goes on in Hathor's palace if it's a big secret? Have you been there?"

"I visited once, but I wasn't privy to the most secret rituals. Hathor found me displeasing."

"Why is that?"

He gave me a roguish grin. "I seduced her female devotees. Hathor doesn't like to share."

I eyed him with a squinty gaze. "You were ensorcelled, eh? A slave to the goddess's desires?"

"For a time, but even her magic couldn't stop me from…enjoying what other women had to offer."

"Uh-huh." I tried not to smile but succeeded only in making my lips twitch. "You really were a hound, weren't you?"

"If I'd known I would find you, I would have waited eternity without touching another female."

"I believe you. I waited all my life for you." A single word he'd spoken had gotten trapped in my brain, so I had to ask. "Is there a difference between enchantment and ensorcellment?"

"Does it matter?"

"I don't know unless you answer my question."

"As you wish." He rubbed my arms while he explained, "Enchantment is a milder form of ensorcellment. To ensorcell another being requires dark magics, which is why most elementals stay away from it and employ enchantment instead. Ensorcellment can cause undesirable side effects, mainly affecting the mind."

Max chose that moment to sway and grin like a drunken fool. "May I go back to Hathor?"

"No, you may not." I slapped his chest. "Snap out of it, Max."

"I'm afraid," Nevan said, "you'll have to wait until he comes out of the trance."

"Don't have time for that." I studied Max, weighing my options, then took hold of his face and shook it. "Time to sober up."

I tapped into my magic, summoning swirling strands of glittering blue. The strands snaked around Max's head, down his shoulders and arms, winding their way to his toes. Max's eyelids fluttered shut. My magic encased him, and I willed it to clear his mind, to free him of Hathor's ensorcellment and to sweep away any actual inebriation.

The blue tendrils dissipated with a snap and a sizzle.

I stepped back.

Max opened his eyes. He blinked swiftly, then mopped his hands over his face. Yawning, he stretched his entire body.

"Feeling better?" I asked.

"Enormously." He threw his arms out and inhaled a deep breath, expelling it in a rush. Thumping his chest, he said, "Healed and ready for duty."

I considered asking what had gone on in Hathor's palace but decided I had no need to know those details. What Nevan had said gave me all the clues I cared to have.

Max looked from me to Nevan and back again, a question in his eyes.

"This is the real Nevan," I said. "His memory has been restored."

"Ah, good." Max rubbed his hands together. "Now what?"

"Lindsey wants us," Nevan said, "to distract Aello while she attempts to enter the time stream."

"She's sticking to the plan where she goes back in time to stop Aello from acquiring dark magics."

"Indeed she is."

"You tried to talk her out of it, I'm sure."

Nevan made an exasperated noise. "Talking Lindsey out of anything is nearly impossible, as I'm sure you know."

"Hey!" I said, waving my arms between the two men. "Stop talking like I'm not here. Unless one of you has a better plan, zip it and get with the program."

Max bowed, elegantly this time but with a smirk. "Yes, mistress."

Nevan slipped his hand around mine. "I am always with your program."

"That makes one of us." I held the map to my chest. "What if I don't have enough power to stop Aello? She's been gathering more and more magic, I'd say, based on the way she keeps getting stronger while I get weaker."

"You are not weaker," Nevan said, moving to stand in front of me. "Sometimes I think you forget the prophecy Bob issued a century ago."

"I remember it."

"You've memorized the words, but you seem to forget the meaning." He grasped my shoulders, bending his head to level our gazes. "Say it, Lindsey. Say it and understand."

I flashed him a peeved look but recited the prophecy. "In the twentieth era of the mortal calendar, a girl child shall be born into an enlightened clan. She will possess the power of Janus, god of the doorways and of transitions, and like him she will face both ways, belonging to neither world but bound to everything. Boundaries fall in her presence. The veil shall open to her, she who holds the power to converge the worlds, she whose power is beyond any seen before in any realm. She is the bearer of the key and the staff, the child of the god, she is the Janusite."

"Do you recall what you inferred from the prophecy?" Nevan tightened his grip on me just enough to convey his resolve to convince me. "On the day you first manipulated time by freezing it. Do you recall?"

"Of course I do."

"Tell me."

"Ugh. I've told you before, and I don't see how—"

"Lindsey, tell me."

The intensity in his voice gave me pause, so I told him, "My family is the enlightened clan, a group of New Age believers. Facing both ways means both coming and going through the portals and moving through time. The part about boundaries means I can take elementals across the metaphysical borders in the mortal world and that I can cross the boundaries of time. I assume the veil that opens for me is the veil between realms, but I don't know what the part about converging worlds means."

"And the key and the staff?"

Despite knowing what he was doing, pushing me to accept I had the power to defeat Aello, his insistence I repeat things I'd told him several times before rankled.

Huffing, I said, "The Janus key indicates the bearer means no harm. The staff symbolizes Janus's dominion over pretty much everything—the worlds, the doorways between them, the boundaries, even time itself."

Nevan's lips ticked up at the corners. "Good, Lindsey. At last you see."

"You are so bossy." One of things I loved about him even when it annoyed me. He could be as stubborn as I was. Our mutual pigheadedness had saved us both in the past. "I get what you were trying to do, and I appreciate it."

That I could say without incurring a debt.

"Perhaps," he said, "you've overlooked the most important part of the prophecy. You wield powers beyond any seen before in any realm. Even Janus admits you have accomplished a feat he could not."

When I'd restored Nevan to the timeline. Janus had seemed shocked by that. The god had become so powerful in his own time that the other gods banded together to destroy him, fearing his powers. If I could do things he couldn't...

You are the most important being ever to be born in any realm, Bob had told me a couple months ago when I first met the oracle. *She whose power is beyond any seen before in any realm.*

Didn't that mean I had more magic than Janus himself back when he'd possessed all his powers?

A few minutes ago, Bob had pronounced the scales must be balanced and the past must be sacrificed for the sake of the future. Whose past? Mine? Maybe he'd been talking about Nevan and the way I kept bringing him back every time the past realigned to accommodate Aello's tinkering. Maybe I had to let him go to save everyone else.

No. That would mean Aello won.

I would never let her win.

Bob's prophecies could be averted. Wasn't that the point of foresight? Warn people so they could avoid catastrophe. Once, Bob had warned me Nevan would be my undoing, that he would destroy me. Well, he almost had after the sorcerer stripped his soul from his body. The Anti-Nevan, as I'd called the shell that had once been the man I loved, had tried to kill me. I'd summoned magics

I didn't know I had to bring Nevan's soul back from the void. He hadn't been my undoing. He would always be my salvation.

The prophecy had not come true. We fought together to ensure it never would.

If we could avert one prediction, we could do the same with another one. No sacrifice required.

The bullet points of the Janusite prophecy replayed in my mind, and suddenly, I understood.

"You're a genius," I told Nevan as I planted a firm kiss on his lips. "A total genius."

A wrinkle formed between his brows, above the bridge of his nose.

His adorable confusion spurred me to pepper his lips with quick little kisses. "Your bossiness paid off. I know what to do."

"Care to share?" Max asked.

"Yes." I gave Nevan one last kiss. Map in hand, I told the men, "The bearer of the key and the staff. It means I have the magic to sort of…soothe time. Show it I mean no harm. I have dominion over basically everything, so time will accept me and do as I ask. This gives me an advantage over Aello."

Nevan looked impressed, but he asked, "In what way?"

"The harpy has to jackhammer her way into the time stream and beat the past into submission to get her way. This explains the earthquakes, I think. It also explains the windstorms that accompany every single instance of her messing with time."

"Ahhhh, of course," Nevan said with appreciation. "You are one with time. She is an intruder."

"Exactly."

My husband grinned. "*You* are the genius, Lindsey."

"Couldn't have done it without you."

"If you two are planning to shag," Max said, "I'll go for a walk."

"Not having sex," I assured him. "Shouldn't you, as my familiar, be terribly impressed with what I've figured out?"

"I am impressed." Max's expression turned somber, almost regretful. "You two have a symbiotic relationship. You make each other stronger and understand each other completely. That's something most of us will never have."

"You'll find your girl someday."

He made a disgusted face. "Don't need a woman to make me happy. If Hathor couldn't convince me she's my fated mate, you can't convince me there's a bird waiting for me out there somewhere."

After more than two months with Max, I knew "bird" meant a woman.

"Fated mate?" I said. "Does your kind have those? For real?"

Max grumbled and ducked his head, kicking at the dirt. "Some say we do, but I don't believe in that bollocks."

As much as I itched to quiz him for more info, we had more important matters to discuss.

Nevan squeezed my hand. "Has your plan changed?"

"Uh-uh." I glanced from Nevan to Max and back again. "But I need both of you to make me a promise. Once you've gotten Aello's attention, you have to leave her nest before she gets there. Promise me."

"You would coerce us into incurring a debt?"

"I need to be sure you'll leave before she gets there. Aello can block your powers."

Nevan cupped my cheek in his warm hand. "I know you're afraid for us, but you do not need a magical promise. We will obey without needing a debt to enforce your request."

Max nodded. "It's true."

Of course they would. After everything that had gone down today—the worlds shifting, Max's injuries, losing Nevan, losing Janus—I'd gotten a touch paranoid.

"Forget the promise," I said. "Get the heck out of there before Aello blows in."

Nevan kissed me sweetly.

I gazed at him for a few seconds, transfixed by his swirling eyes and the love he imbued into every word, every touch, every look.

He backed up one step, squared his massive shoulders, and awaited my command.

The sylph king at my command. I always got a hot shiver when I thought about that.

I held up the map Bob had provided, studying the curving lines and strange symbols. "This doesn't make sense."

Leaning in to peer at the map, Nevan said, "If you were an elemental, it would make perfect sense. In the Unseen, maps are living things comprised of magic. Touch the paper and you'll see."

"A living thing? Is this map going to bite off my finger?"

"No, darlin', it won't."

His tone suggested I was being silly. What did he expect? Telling me a map was alive.

I clamped my lips between my teeth and touched the parchment.

A tiny green orb popped out of the parchment, hovering a hair above the page's surface. It pulsed twice.

"The starting point," Nevan said. "Follow where it leads."

"You mean we have to walk? No poofing?"

He threw an arm around my waist. "There will be poofing, love. Keep your finger on the map."

I pressed my fingertip to the parchment, and the green orb began to move.

So did we, whooshing through the deep, dark tunnel. As we moved, the little orb glided along the winding lines of the map. I assumed Nevan was somehow following those lines, following the map, though I had no idea how. I might be able to share his powers and teleport at will, but I had not passed Advanced Poofing class yet.

We touched down on top of a mountain with a three-sixty view of the neighboring peaks. Snow capped every single one of them, including the one on which we perched.

And did we ever perch.

Nevan balanced on the craggy tip of the mountain with me hugged to him. My feet dangled in empty space.

Max appeared beside us, his skin flaming, floating in midair.

"Where is it?" I asked, latching my arms around Nevan's neck. The map crinkled, partly crushed in my grip. "Where's Aello's nest?"

"There," Nevan replied, pointing straight up.

I craned my head back. *Way* back.

Above our heads floated a billowy cloud. Atop the cloud hunkered a building composed of what looked like twigs. Considering the distance between us and the cloud, I realized the twigs were actually massive trees stripped of their branches.

The harpy's nest.

"Okay," I said, folding the map and tucking it into my pocket, "it's go time. The second you guys get Aello's attention, you'll zip all of us out of here. Right?"

"All of us?" Nevan repeated. "Max and I can 'zip' ourselves. Who else are we to transport?"

"Me."

He got that adorable look of confusion again. "You will be in the time stream."

"Yeah, but I'd rather not have my physical form get ripped to shreds. I'm kinda fond of this body."

Nevan and Max both stared at me like I'd suggested we all wear pink tutus and prance around singing "tra-la-la."

"What is wrong with you two?" I demanded.

My husband answered. "Your body will not be here. You disappear when you enter the time stream. How can you not know this?"

It was my turn to stare at him dumbly. "My body goes with me? I assumed only my mind went into the time stream. When I'm in there, I feel incorporeal."

"Naturally," Max said. "You were incorporeal. We both were. Our bodies rematerialized once we exited the time stream. Why did you think you needed to have me on your person to take me with you?"

"I—" Slapping my hands on my cheeks, I groaned. "Never occurred to me I was teleporting us into the time stream. How was I supposed to know that? Nobody told me. It would've been useful to know."

Nevan peeled my hands away from my face. "You are correct. We failed to mention this, and you couldn't have known. Elementals tend to forget not everyone understands these matters as inherently as we do."

"I get that, but Janus could've told me. His mentoring sucks." Janus. Aello's prisoner. The mention of him yanked me back to the problem at hand. I took a calming breath. "Well, at least I know now. Let's get this show on the road."

Max glanced around—up, down, and sideways. "I thought we were enacting the plan here, not on a road."

"It's a figure of speech."

"Whose figure are you speaking of?" He smirked, eying me up and down. "Yours, I hope."

I lashed my arms around Nevan, suddenly aware of my feet dangling in the air, and mustered my sternest voice. "Are we ready to tick off the harpy and save the world?"

"Yes," both men said.

"Good."

I inhaled a deep breath and shut my eyes.

"Wait," Max said. "Shouldn't I go with you? What if you need a power boost?"

"I need you to stay with Nevan." I cracked one lid open. "Make sure he leaves before Aello gets here."

Nevan harrumphed. "I thought you trusted me."

"Oh, I do." I opened both eyes to meet his gaze. "But sometimes, in the thick of things, you decide protecting me is more important than your own safety. I recall a certain sword-through-the-chest incident."

"Shall I make it a promise?"

"Not necessary. But listen up. I will not pop out again right here once I'm done in the time stream. Wherever you go, I'll find you."

Max floated toward Nevan and slapped a hand on his shoulder. "Don't worry. I'll drag him away from here if he tries to stay behind."

One side of Nevan's mouth contorted in a cross between humor and annoyance. "I will flee and wait for you elsewhere."

I closed my eyes and aimed for the time stream.

The real world spiraled away from me as I soared into the ethereal home of time itself. I focused on the idea of the Janus key, willing time to understand I meant no harm and that I wanted to help it heal. The staff became my resolve to repair the damage Aello had caused and to discover the moment when she'd first absorbed dark magics. I willed time to understand my thoughts.

Please let me in, please help me. I can heal you, but only if you trust me. We are one.

The glowing river pulsed once, and I knew it had accepted me. I sensed it in my soul and in the way my powers pulsed in response.

Aello. Dark magics. The primary event that triggered the cascade of time shifts. *Take me there.*

The river shimmered and looped around to contact one moment in the past.

I dived toward it.

My body emerged in a small clearing in the woods. Disoriented by the journey through the time stream, I stood motionless for a moment, blinking repeatedly and taking slow breaths. Where was I? When was I? The surroundings gave me few clues. Trees. Whoopee, big frigging clue. At least I knew I was in the mortal world since trees in the Unseen had moss-like stuff instead of leaves or needles. I didn't know enough about trees to guess where in the world I'd ended up.

This location must have something to do with Aello. She must have acquired her first taste of dark magics here.

In the middle of nowhere? In the mortal realm?

Turning in a circle, I examined my surroundings for more clues but got nothing. Nobody in this world had enough power to jack up a harpy with dark magic. Besides, I could sense the boundaries, the ones that prevented elementals from traveling more than a mile from any portal. I sensed no boundaries nearby, which meant no natural water features within a mile in any direction. No portal. No way for Aello to get here.

I must've screwed up. Time had sent me to the wrong moment because I hadn't phrased my request correctly. What had I been thinking about in the time stream? The primary event that triggered the time shifts. The moment when something vital had changed, making it possible for Aello to devour dark power.

Maybe I hadn't screwed up. Maybe I was right where I needed to be.

Everything Aello had done became possible because of something that happened right here, right now.

A clue would've been helpful.

Reluctant to leave the spot where I'd materialized, I turned in a circle several more times, taking in as much detail as I could. Trees. Grass. Trees. Oh, there was a small bird. More trees. More grass.

"Gah!" I threw my head back to glare at the sky. "Time, what are you trying to tell me? You could be a teeny bit more specific. I'm no oracle."

A twig cracked. Leaves rustled.

I spun toward the sounds, my heart racing. On instinct, I reached for my derringer only to realize I didn't have it. I'd given the gun to Janus, and I had lost track of the weapon in the confusion following Aello's attack. *Should've brought a weapon, dummy.* Nevan's voice resounded in my mind like he was standing right beside me. *You have your weapons inside you.*

A figure traipsed out of the woods. The man halted, his surprised gaze swerving to me.

Dark-brown hair. Full lips. Striking, though completely human, hazel eyes. Muscular but not equipped with supernatural mass, and a few inches shorter than his elemental self, he may have looked less imposing. Despite his altered appearance, I would've recognized him if I'd been blindfolded. His presence tugged at something deep inside me, a connection stronger than time.

His sensual smile warmed me from my skin down to the region between my thighs. "Well, beauty, who might you be?"

That voice. That smile. I was face to face with the mortal man who would be forged and become…

Nevan.

Chapter Eighteen

Tuathal. That had been his name during his mortal life. I must've wound up on the island that would someday become known as Ireland, the land of Nevan's birth and first life, the land where he'd died and been forged. When I'd wound up was harder to determine. When I had asked Nevan how old he was, the only time I'd asked him, he had said, "Well now, I lost count after five thousand."

I'd landed somewhere in the Bronze Age.

"Are ye mute?" Tuathal inquired, sauntering closer.

Realization shivered through me. How could he speak English? This was the distant past, before the English language emerged. *Duh, Lindsey, it's magic.* Considering I could make myself invisible, auto-translating another language didn't seem so odd.

"What language are you speaking?" I asked.

He stopped ten feet from me, seeming nonplussed. "The tongue of the Parthalonians. You speak it as well, so why are ye asking me? Have ye hit your head, beauty? You seem confused."

Oh yeah, this whole situation confused the heck out of me.

Somehow, Nevan had played a vital role in the primary event. I needed to figure out what and how. What if I screwed up time worse than Aello already had? If I said the wrong thing, did the wrong thing…Then again, my very presence might have caused ripples already. Since I was one with time, I ought to sense any changes. Probably. Shutting my eyes, I let all thoughts drift away and focused on time itself. Traveling into the time stream wouldn't be necessary. I needed only to sense it, to feel if I had done any damage.

Everything felt fine. Or rather, the same as before I'd traveled back to this moment.

Time had sent me here for a reason. It must've known the answers began in this moment, which meant it must want me to intervene.

A hand touched my arm.

When I opened my eyes, Tuathal was standing inches away from me, his hand resting on my arm, concern in his eyes.

"Relax," I said. "I'm fine."

"Who are you? Why are you dressed so strangely?"

He wore a linen tunic with a hem just above the knees. A belt draped around his waist, not made of leather but of braided strands of thread or maybe animal hair. He wore sandals fashioned from a similar material with soles of leather.

I wore the outfit Max had conjured for me. Leather pants. Blouse. Boots. To an ancient Irishman, I must've looked very strange indeed.

He fingered a lock of my hair. "Soft as silk. Only wealthy women have hair as silken as yours. Are you of the nobility?"

"Not hardly." I did have the powers of a god but telling him that seemed like a bad idea. He already thought I was weird. Instead, I asked, "What were you doing right before you saw me?"

"Ahhh," he purred in that way future Nevan loved to do, "nothing before you matters."

Oh yeah, this was definitely Nevan.

Might his forging be the primary event?

I needed a straight answer from him, but I had a feeling this conversation would go much the way our very first conversation had—flirtation, evasion, and more flirtation.

"What were you doing," I repeated in a sterner tone, "right before you saw me? It's important I know."

He sighed with the same frustrated amusement as sylph Nevan. "If ye insist on knowing, I was scouting the area for enemy soldiers. The Fomorians have been conducting raids lately, and we fear they might stage an all-out assault soon."

The Fomorians. He'd told me about the enemy that had attacked his village. If the Fomorians were preparing to mount an assault, that must mean Tuathal was married to Ceara and they had a daughter, Daráine. That also made this, or a day very soon after, the day he died and became a sylph.

If time had sent me here, today must be the date of his forging.

What the hell did that have to do with Aello's vendetta? Sure, Nevan had been instrumental in taking down Skeiron, but Aello had already tried eradicating him from history. The tactic hadn't accomplished what she'd hoped. Notus was alive, but Skeiron was dead. If she wanted them both back, getting rid of Nevan clearly wouldn't do the job. The harpy also knew I could bring him back even if she annihilated him in the past.

I had no idea why I'd turned up here, in this moment.

Maybe I needed to watch events play out to understand.

Tuathal touched my cheek, skimming his fingertips down my skin, drawing me out of my thoughts with his sensual caress. "Would ye like to know anything else, beauty? I will gladly explain all the things I would love to do with you."

"Don't you have a wife?"

He compressed his lips, his jaw tightening, and retracted his hand. "I do."

"Then why are you trying to seduce me?"

"I—" Mouth open, he froze. After several seconds, he rubbed his forehead. "I have no idea. My wife and I are no longer intimate, but I should not behave this way with another woman. I never have before, but you…" He rubbed his forehead again as lines deepened across it. "I cannot explain my attraction to you. It is strong and nigh irresistible."

My throat went thick. Even in another lifetime, eons in the past from my perspective, he experienced our bond as strongly as I did. I wanted to throw my arms around him and kiss him, but I couldn't do it. He had a wife and a child. Though I knew his first marriage had not been a happy one, I also knew he would never cheat. Our bond had made him slip up for a moment. It confused him. Hell, it confused me to stand here with the human version of my husband, knowing he was married to someone else.

Tuathal stumbled backward a few steps. "I must go."

He turned to leave.

A horn blared in the distance.

Its long, low call resounded in my soul. This was it—the day Tuathal died and was reborn as Nevan. I sensed the truth, but I also remembered what he'd told me about the day the Fomorians attacked. The call had been sent out, and every able-bodied man had rallied to defend the Parthalonian village.

Tuathal stiffened. "The attack has come."

He sprinted into the woods.

I raced after him. We sped through the forest with him way ahead of me. I ran as fast as I could, but damn, he was faster. Dread coiled its icy fingers around my heart as I wondered what I would see once we arrived at the village. Had the carnage begun already? From what I knew about ancient warfare, it was brutal and gruesome, conducted with swords, spears, and bows and arrows.

Barreling out of the trees, I caught sight of the village up ahead. It occupied the center of an open plain surrounded by woods. Huts with thatched roofs comprised the village, with corrals for livestock and a larger structure that might've been a meeting hall. Along one side of the village, a small river snaked across the plain, disappearing into the trees where the landscape sloped downward.

Nevan had fallen in battle on the shores of a lake, at the base of a waterfall. He'd taken me to that same spot two months ago, though it looked much different in the twenty-first century. In that time, the ten-foot cascade emptied into a small pool, more like a big puddle. Nevan had assured me it had been bigger five thousand years earlier. The waterfall was where Notus had come to him with an offer to make him immortal. The falls and the lake must lie at the river's end or its headwaters. Which one, I had no clue.

I halted twenty feet or so past the tree line. No enemy soldiers were visible yet, but the alarm call must have signaled their approach.

Tuathal galloped toward the village.

Maybe I needed to observe this event, not participate. Less risk to the time stream.

I summoned my powers to cloak myself from view. Was I destined to watch all the men I cared about be ripped apart and reassembled? I'd witnessed Travis's forging, then Calder's, and now it seemed I must witness Nevan's forging too.

Uncertain if I could tap into Nevan's powers from this far in the past, I decided to try it anyway. I'd lost sight of Tuathal, so I willed myself to teleport to him. I popped up inside a small, thatched hut.

Tuathal crouched near the wall, murmuring words I couldn't make out to someone lying on a fur blanket. Edging closer, I peered over his shoulder.

A little girl, maybe seven or eight, lay on the blanket propped up with one arm. The graveness of her expression tugged at my heart. "I promise, Papa. I will stay here with Mama."

Movement drew my attention to the doorway as a woman entered the hut.

A chill slithered down my spine.

Ceara stomped toward her husband. "You cannot leave us, Tuathal. Your family needs you more than the village does. Protect us. Take us far away from here."

"The Fomorians have surrounded the village," he said, rising. "Soon, they will attack. There is nowhere to run, Ceara. You and Daráine will be safest here. Please do as I ask."

Ceara glared at him with a hint of the seething rage that would grow stronger after her resurrection at the sorcerer's hand. She really had hated Nevan from the start, blaming him for the fact her family forced her into an arranged marriage with him. She ought to have appreciated a good, brave man like Nevan. Instead, she loathed him for things beyond his control. After all, he'd been forced into marriage with her too, but he had made the best he could of it.

Tuathal bent to kiss his daughter's forehead. He reached for Ceara's hand.

She yanked it away. "Go, then. We do not need you."

He grabbed a sheathed sword, hooking it onto his belt, and walked out of the hut.

Into the fire, that's where he was going. Literally. He would be struck down by the enemy and reborn amid a bonfire of scalding magic. And I must bear witness to it, praying the solution to the Aello problem lay in what I would see.

Daráine sniffled.

Ceara huffed. "Crying is not permitted. You know this, but you are your father's child. Weak. Useless."

My fingers crooked into my palms, the nails scraping my skin. I wanted to smack Ceara so badly. What kind of woman belittled her daughter because she was unhappy in her marriage? The kind who would happily become the consort of an evil sorcerer. The narcissistic kind.

I wished I could spare Daráine the horrors of the battle, but at least I knew she would survive. Ceara claimed to have charged the enemy, sacrificing her own life to grant her daughter time to escape.

With one last glance at Daráine, I zipped to Tuathal.

He stood among a group of armed men arrayed in two staggered rows. They faced the woods, their weapons brandished, their expressions set in grim resolve.

The cacophony of an army's footfalls thundered ever nearer.

Within seconds, the battle commenced.

Chapter Nineteen

It went on and on and on. In the melee that ensued, I lost track of Tuathal. Every time I tried to whisk myself to him, I missed the mark. He must've been moving swiftly, dashing here and there to assist his fellow warriors or to take down one of the Fomorians. Despite my invisibility, I was not immune to the effects of the battle. The close quarters meant I had little space to sidestep the fray. The clashing of swords, the shouting voices, the thudding of sandal-clad feet, the *thwack* of each arrow finding its target—all of this created a din the likes of which I had never heard in my life.

Every time one soldier attacked another, blood sprayed from the brutal wounds.

My clothes had become damp with it. Damp with the blood of men. My stomach lurched, but I somehow managed not to throw up. Helpless to do anything except watch, I zipped to the edge of the woods. I needed to keep track of Tuathal, but he was somewhere in the thick of things. Even from here, the noise of the battle seemed loud, though not as deafening as when I'd been inside it.

Everywhere, soldiers fell. The Fomorians wore crimson tunics and armor with metal helmets, but the Parthalonians had nothing to protect them.

I squeezed my eyes shut, unable to watch any more of the carnage.

Tuathal would head down or up the river at some point during the battle. How was I to find him? The melee had screwed up my ability to track his movements with my magic. But I was the Janusite. Shouldn't I be able to block out the noise and find him?

Keeping my eyes shut, I willed the din to recede—and it worked. The terrible cacophony dwindled into silence. I commanded myself to stop smelling the stench of blood on my clothes, commanded my garments to cleanse themselves. Static electricity rushed over my skin, and though I dared not open my eyes yet, I understood my clothes had become pristine again.

Tuathal. Nevan. I sensed him, waging war but alive.

I opened my eyes.

The village was burning. The fire seemed to have started near the flank of where Nevan's people had met the enemy head-on, but the blaze was spreading.

I teleported back to the hut where Nevan had left Ceara and Daráine.

Ceara shoved Daráine out the door and stalked after her, forcing the girl to walk straight toward a group of Fomorian soldiers.

"Here is the child," Ceara said. "Do with her what you wish. She is her father's daughter, not mine."

One soldier, whose helmet was bronze-ish instead of silver, stepped forward to snare Daráine's wrist. He sneered at her, then at Ceara. "Females are of great value to our tribe, the younger the better. You have done well."

"You will keep your word?" Ceara said.

"Oh yes, our king will be well pleased to have another wife to service his needs, one as young and fresh as you. The others have grown old and tired."

Ceara sidled up to the soldier, rubbing her breasts against his bare arm. "I will happily service you first, General, as thanks for sparing my life." She wrapped her arms around his bicep. "You are certain I will be the favorite queen?"

He smiled with feral hunger. "You will be everyone's favorite, lavished with all the luxuries you desire."

Was she seriously handing her daughter over to savages so she could become queen of the enemy tribe? For wealth and status, she would sell her body and soul. I shouldn't have been surprised, given that she'd done the same thing with the sorcerer, but her actions stunned me anyway.

Her own daughter.

I stared numbly at the general and Ceara as they engaged in a sloppy kiss, and the general palmed her breast through her tunic. She made a hungry little noise as if she enjoyed the prospect of becoming the Fomorians' number-one whore.

My gaze flicked to Daráine.

Wait a minute. Nevan's daughter was supposed to have survived the battle and been taken in by a family from a neighboring clan. Of course, Ceara had lied about bravely sacrificing her life to save their daughter, so she might've lied about Daráine's fate too. I could not let this sweet-faced, innocent girl who looked so much like her father suffer the fate her mother had arranged for her. No way in hell. But if I helped her, I would be altering the past. My actions might rock the timeline to its core, setting off the apocalypse Bob had feared.

"Mama," Daráine said, choking back a sob. "I do not want to go with these men. I want Papa."

"Your papa is dead," Ceara snapped, "or he soon will be. Forget about him."

Tears poured down the girl's cheeks.

Screw the timeline. No child would be enslaved to a scumbag under my watch.

I clamped a hand on Daráine's shoulder and tugged her free of the general's grasp, then I whisked us away. We materialized deep inside the woods. The Fomorians hadn't penetrated this area, and somehow, I knew they never would. This forest lay inside the boundaries of Parthalonian territory, but it held no strategic value to the enemy. I could leave Daráine here while I checked on her parents—yes, both of them—and figured out what to do with the girl. She was supposed to end up with a good family from another clan of Parthalonians.

Had I been meant to find that family for her?

The idea rippled through me almost like a shiver, accompanied by a tingling certainty of the truth of it. I had no time to consider the ramifications of this revelation, though.

I knelt before Daráine, taking hold of her shoulders, knowing she could see me as long as I was touching her. "I'm a...friend of your parents. I'm going to make sure you're safe, okay? Do you understand?"

Her lips trembled. Her amber eyes, so like Nevan's, shimmered with tears. She kept her posture solid, though, and her voice amazingly steady. "I understand."

My auto-translate seemed to work with the girl too.

She had her father's strength and his determination. I saw it in her eyes and sensed it in her soul. Despite having a wacko for a mom, this girl would become a kind and loving woman. I knew this, and I didn't even try to comprehend how I knew it.

Maybe time had whispered it in my ear.

"I need you to stay right here," I said. "I'm going to see what happened to your mother and father. You'll be safe if you stay put. Got it?"

She sniffled and nodded.

My heart hurt for her, for what she had already endured and what she must endure next. At least she would have a good home after this and a good future.

"I'll be back," I said, and rushed toward the village.

Ceara was nowhere in sight. The general was gone too.

My aim had been off. I'd targeted the spot where I had left Ceara, not for the woman herself. I couldn't explain why I needed to witness her fate, but something drove me to do it. Nevan was alive and fighting, that much I sensed. So, I concentrated on Ceara.

And materialized in the woods.

The darkness under the canopy of trees blinded me for a moment, after the brightness of the sunlit battlefield in and around the village. While I waited for my vision to adjust, my ears picked up sounds. Grunting. Gasping. Wet, rhythmic slapping. I remained invisible as I tiptoed closer to the sound. By the time I reached the spot from which the noises emanated, I could see clearly in the gloom.

And I wished I couldn't.

The Fomorian general had Ceara pinned to a tree, her tunic hiked up around her waist and one leg hitched around his hip. He thrust into her again and again, grunting each time, pounding into her while she clutched at his shoulders, a look of pure ecstasy on her face.

Voyeurism was not my thing. I'd never watched a porno movie either. Yet I could not move or speak or tear my focus away from the scene before me, despite the nausea roiling in my stomach. Shock, probably. I hadn't expected to find Nevan's wife humping someone else while he was valiantly battling the enemy. Part of me could not accept she'd been as thoroughly rotten in her mortal life as she'd been after her resurrection.

Here was the proof. She'd always been rotten to the core.

The general thrust once more, let out a long groan, and slumped against Ceara. Breathing hard, he said, "You will be a splendid concubine for the king and for the Fomorian army."

She smacked his arm. "You have not finished."

He raised his head to give her a haughty look. "Yes, I have. If you are fortunate, my seed will take root in your womb."

"Fortunate?" she hissed. "I will never bear your spawn. And you have not finished because I am not finished."

The general pushed away from her, tugging her tunic down to cover her. "Why should I care about your pleasure, concubine? You are a tool, not a lover."

Ceara glowered at him. "That was not the agreement. I am to be the king's wife, not a concubine."

He chuckled with menacing humor. "You agreed to fucking all of us. What did you expect that meant?"

"It means that I—I will be the queen but have the freedom to choose whatever lovers I desire."

The general laughed again, this time with an undeniable disdain. "We will choose when to have you, not the other way round."

Ceara's eyes went wild, her breaths mutating into feral noises.

He shook his head. "Perhaps you are too base even for us. Fomorians have higher standards for our women than the low-born Parthalonians do."

She yanked his sword out of its sheath on his belt and drove it into his gut.

The general clamped one hand around the sword's blade and the other around Ceara's throat. He pinned her to the tree again, this time with a palpable rage. Gasping for breath, he eased the sword out of his body. The sword tumbled from his grasp, splashing blood over the grass.

"You," he growled at Ceara, "will pay for that."

She spat in his face.

He gritted his teeth, summoned all the energy he had left with a visible effort that contorted his features, and crushed her throat. Her windpipe shattered with a crunching sound.

Ceara's face went slack, her body too.

The general jerked his hand away, letting her dead body crumple to the ground. He staggered backward, clutching his belly. His body hit the ground with a thud. His eyes were vacant, the life gone from him.

I gaped at the pair of vile humans who had brought on their own demises. The general had been a thug with no morals as far as I could see. Ceara had wanted to become the queenly slut of the Fomorians though not a concubine passed around like a jug of wine, and she hadn't given a fig about what happened to her daughter or her husband. Though I couldn't muster empathy for Ceara or the Fomorian general, I wished they hadn't needed to die. I wished no one had died on this day, but their fates had been sealed before I arrived, before I was even born.

Once I'd eased their eyelids shut, I rushed to Nevan—to Tuathal.

He and a Fomorian soldier stood along the banks of the river near where its waters plummeted over a cliff into the lake below. Even from here, I could tell the precipice towered high above the lake, at least fifty feet by my estimation. Tuathal and the Fomorian had gone a good distance from the village, but I heard the noises of battle not far away. The melee had spread. Tuathal and the Fomorian brandished their swords, circling each other as if measuring up the enemy. Blood and dirt covered the bodies of both men, the whites of their eyes seeming to glow compared with their darkened flesh.

Neither man could see me. I didn't want to witness this, but I knew I must.

The Fomorian lunged at Tuathal but missed when his foe veered sideways. Tuathal slashed his sword at the Fomorian, scoring a glancing blow across the man's side. A new wound opened, expelling a thin stream of blood.

A victorious look brightened Tuathal's grim features, but the victory didn't last.

The Fomorian head-butted Tuathal in the stomach, hitting him so hard the breath exploded out of Tuathal and he stumbled backward, his sword hand popping open, the weapon striking the ground. The Fomorian roared and slammed his blade straight into Tuathal's stomach.

I cried out, but no one heard me. My pulse raced. The urge to intervene had my muscles tensing in preparation.

Sneering at his foe, the Fomorian jutted his chin and thrust out his chest. He wrenched the sword from Tuathal's body and kicked him in the gut so hard he staggered backward to the cliff's edge. Tuathal clamped both hands over his wound, but blood streamed from it around his hands and between his fingers. The Fomorian raised his sword above his head, and with a victorious cry, plunged the blade into Tuathal's heart.

I squeezed my eyes shut, then forced myself to open them. I would bear witness, for Tuathal, for Nevan. I owed him that much.

The Fomorian prized his sword free of Tuathal's body and jogged off into the woods, heading for the sounds of a fracas in the distance. His footsteps faded away.

Tuathal swayed, his knees giving out, and tumbled backward over the cliff.

My heart thrashed like it wanted to climb out of my chest. I zoomed down to the base of the falls, whipping my head left and right to search for Tuathal.

His body floated in the churning foam as the waters propelled him to the shore. He lay motionless on his back, eyes shut, half on the ground and half in the water.

Soon, he would be forged. I scuffled forward a few steps, compelled by the impulse to stop this, to save the man I loved, but I couldn't. This had to happen or else the future would be altered yet again. I'd come here to fix what Aello had done, not make things worse. I could not stop what came next.

Paralyzed, I watched the life drain out of Tuathal as the rise and fall of his chest diminished until I could barely detect it. His skin had gone pale, his lips were turning blue. A phantom hand clenched around my heart. I'd seen him like this once before, on the night Skeiron ran him through with an endued sword. Back then, I'd saved Nevan. Here and now, I had no choice but to let him die.

His body lay partially in the lake with one of his arms slung out to the side, his limp hand moving up and down with the gently lapping water. Fresh blood covered his palm from when he'd clasped both hands over his gut wound. The red liquid tainted the water.

The atmosphere shifted.

I couldn't describe the sensation. It seeped inside me with an unearthly feeling of wrongness. I hadn't experienced this when Calder was forged, but I'd had Aello to worry about then.

A figure rose up out of the lake, the figure of a man clad in a golden toga. Notus had arrived.

His eyes swirled with molten shades of metal.

I didn't dare move, though my magic should've shielded me from the view of anyone, mortal or elemental.

Notus crouched beside Tuathal. In a surprisingly gentle gesture, he swept a lock of bloody hair away from Tuathal's eyes. "Mortal, hear me."

Tuathal's eyes darted behind his closed lids.

"I have come to you," Notus said, "because I witnessed your bravery today. You will be an excellent warrior in my army, but before you may join the ranks, you must be forged."

Tuathal's lids parted a sliver.

"Do not attempt to speak," Notus told him. "You are far too weak. What I offer you is this—immortality and power beyond anything your mortal mind could possibly fathom. You will be as a god, immune to the weapons of this world. You will be strong and virile, more so than in your mortal life. I offer a new life, a new world, an eternity. Will you join me?"

Blood sputtered from Tuathal's lips, but he croaked, "Yes."

Sheesh, Notus had made forging sound awesome. If I'd lain dying, I would've said yes too. The first time I had asked Nevan about his forging, he'd told me elementals didn't mention the downside or the pain involved in the transformation when they recruited new members for their tribes. The creature that forged Calder hadn't even bothered with the glossed-over spiel. I guessed the kerkopes lacked the finesse of the other elementals.

Notus hovered his hands over Tuathal and began to chant in another language. My auto-translate magic seemed incapable of deciphering the words, or maybe they weren't words at all. The chant might consist of sounds without meaning rather than phrases.

Orbs of bluish-white light ignited around the two of them, swirling and blooming outward until they encompassed me as well. Their energy sizzled on my skin. While Notus chanted on, the orbs swelled and flared into a brilliance that blinded me.

Squinting, I flung my arms up to shield my face.

The forging had begun.

Chapter Twenty

Energy whirled around us, tingling stronger and stronger every second. Tuathal howled in agony, the sound like an animal rather than a man. I squeezed my eyes shut tighter, unable to breathe or move until the blinding brilliance winked out.

I cautiously opened my eyes and lowered my arms.

Once the monkey-thing had forged Calder, both of them had vanished. Tuathal lay where he'd fallen with Notus kneeling beside him. The king of the sylphs rose and gazed down at his newborn soldier.

Tuathal lay motionless but breathing evenly, no longer a bloodied mess. No, this was not Tuathal anymore. This was Nevan.

I absorbed the sight of the body I knew so well. Massive muscles. Bronzed skin. Black hair that shimmered in the sunlight. His tunic had disappeared along with his belt, sword, and sandals. Nevan lay completely nude. I'd witnessed his rebirth, the origins of the elemental warrior who had won my heart. Despite the thrill that knowledge shivered through me, I forced myself to focus on Notus. Why hadn't he whisked them both away to the Unseen?

Another figure materialized at Notus's side.

My brain struggled to comprehend what I saw. The female elemental alongside Notus was Aello. She looked different, no longer skeletal but fleshed out with curves and those perky breasts that had seemed incongruous with the body she'd sported last time I encountered her. Her hair was white as always, her eyes dark as pitch. A sprinkle of pinkness lent the pallor of her skin a life it lacked in the future.

She slid her fingers into the hair at Notus's nape. "My love, why have you done this? We agreed to have birth children, not these unseemly forged offspring."

Unseemly? I clenched my fists. Nothing about Nevan was unseemly.

"I sensed this battle," Notus said, "and came to witness it. You know how I relish a bloody fight. I thought I might glamour myself as one of the mortals waging this battle, but then I sensed this one." He waved a finger toward Nevan. "And I…wanted to forge him."

"Forge him?" Aello said with a derisive huff. "Why? He will require much work before he will be of any use."

"I know, but he evinced a courage and strength of will I've seen in few mortals. He deserves to become one of us."

Aello glanced at Nevan, and her lip curled. "Leave him here. We will return to him in a century or so, and if he has survived, we shall teach him our ways." She clenched Notus's hair, pulling his head back just enough to make him wince. "You agree, Notus. Do you not?"

"Yes, my love, I agree." He studied Nevan's unconscious form, something akin to regret flashing over his face. He shed the emotion with a gusty breath. "Of course you are right. Only those who survive the forging and learn to care for themselves on their own are worthy of joining the sylph army."

Aello threaded her fingers through his hair and feathered her lips over his cheek. "Let us go to the palace and see to making our own blood offspring."

"You know I cannot take you to my palace. We must go to your nest, as always."

Her mouth tightened. She flexed her fingers only to curl her talons into her palms. A bead of blood oozed down one razor-sharp claw, dripping onto the ground.

Notus seemed oblivious of his lover's anger, his attention swerving to Nevan.

"As you wish," Aello said, her voice tinged with the same fury evidenced by her demeanor. "Let us leave this place."

The duo vanished.

I stared at the spot where they had been. They were leaving Nevan here alone? A newly forged elemental? He needed help to get through the transition. It involved more than surviving the actual forging. I'd seen how hard the transition was for Travis. That Nevan got through it on his own for a century amazed me and made me love him even more.

Since I'd witnessed his forging, I needed to leave. Find Daráine. Take her to a good family.

How could I leave Nevan here to suffer alone? Somehow, he'd gotten through it. I had to believe he still would.

Nevan had mentioned someone nursed him through the transition. Notus had abandoned him. Who else would come to his aid? I had to assume his vaguely remembered savior would show up.

I zoomed back to Daráine, dropping my invisibility shield.

The girl sat huddled against a tree. When Daráine spotted me, she raced over to lock her arms around my waist. "You came back."

"Of course I did." I knelt to look her in the eye. "I'm sorry, sweetie. Your parents didn't make it."

Tears sprang forth anew, trickling down her cheeks, but she nodded with a solemn understanding beyond her age.

"I'm going to take you to a family," I said, "who will take care of you and love you like you're their own child. You will be safe, I promise."

Daráine gazed into my eyes for the longest moment, her eyes large and unblinking. She stretched out one hand to touch her fingertip to the skin beneath my eye. "You are an angel?"

"Uh, no."

"You must be. You come and go like a spirit, and you saved me." She clasped her hands over her heart, looking upon me with wonder. "You are an angel."

"No, I'm Lindsey."

"The angel Lindsey."

"Um…" I stood and grasped her hand, unnerved by her rapt gaze. Never had anyone called me an angel—except for Nevan. "I'll take you to your new family. Okay?"

She nodded.

I concentrated on the concept of a good, kind family of Parthalonians who would be willing to take in an orphan. Sounded like a tall order, but hey, I was the Janusite. Why couldn't I command the universe to find me the right folks?

We zipped to a thatched hut situated amid a gently sloping landscape hemmed in by woods. A village sprawled throughout the open area. The home in front of us resided on the outer fringes of the village.

I sensed Nevan remained unconscious. Our bond, diminished when he'd been a mortal, had surged in strength until it was nearly as strong as it would be in the future.

Since I'd conveniently brought us right to the hut's door, I knocked.

The door swung inward, revealing a round-faced young woman with pink cheeks and a welcoming smile. This was Daráine's new mother. I recognized, on a level too deep to explain, this woman would care for Nevan's daughter.

"Hi," I said like an idiot while I waved my hand like one too. "This is Daráine. Her parents were killed in the battle that's going on over in the next village. She needs a new home, and I know your family will be the right one for her."

"Battle?" The woman's face blanched.

"Oh, don't worry. The Parthalonians will defeat the Fomorians before the battle ever gets this far out. You'll be safe." I glanced down at Daráine, feeling a strange tightness in my throat, and asked the woman, "Will you look after Daráine?"

The woman's mouth opened, but Daráine spoke first.

"She's an angel," Daráine said. "Lindsey is her name."

"An angel," the woman said with true awe. She seized my hand, pancaking it between hers. "I am Brónach, wife of Marcán. We will gladly care for this poor child."

"Good," I said, though her awe had me cringing inside. Why did everyone think I was an angel?

"We will love her as our own," Brónach said, squeezing my hands as burgeoning tears glistened in her eyes. "You have my word. We are honored an angel has chosen us for this sacred duty."

Honored? Sacred? Sheesh, talk about overkill. Sure, my clothes must've seemed strange to these folks, but labeling me an angel seemed like a giant leap.

Daráine hopped on her toes. "Lindsey does not always glow. I think she hides her true nature so she might walk among us."

"Of course," Brónach said like that made total sense.

Glow? What on earth were they talking about? I glanced down at myself but saw no such thing.

"She stopped glowing again," Daráine said. She fixed her amber eyes on me. "Thank you for bringing me to my new family. Will Papa be allowed to watch over me?"

No, he wouldn't. Notus forbade him from taking a peek at his daughter's life or the lives of her descendants. Telling a lie seemed like the kindest thing to do.

"I'm sure he will," I said. "Your father loves you very much."

The girl hadn't asked about her mother. I couldn't blame her.

Brónach babbled some more craziness about Lindsey the angel. My skin itched the longer she insisted on calling me an angel. I retreated as quickly as politeness allowed, saying goodbye to Daráine. The two of them retreated into the hut. As the door swung shut, Daráine waved to me.

I waved back, suddenly choked up. She wasn't my daughter, but a sharp pang stabbed into my chest at the thought of leaving her. Later, after Aello was dealt with, maybe I could take Nevan back in time to see the life his daughter had led. He deserved to know she'd been happy.

And I knew she would be.

This trip through time had shown me one thing that must have been the reason I'd come here. Aello had been Notus's lover, and though she seemed determined to call the shots in the relationship, Notus refused to accept that. He'd let her talk him into abandoning Nevan, but he had dismissed her suggestion they go to his palace. The sylph king didn't view the harpy as his equal. Notus would eventually become depraved, but in this moment, he'd held on to a scrap of humanity. He hadn't wanted to leave Nevan, but Aello commanded him to do it and he gave in.

Nevan couldn't have known Aello. He would've told me. She had known of him, though.

I should leave. My mission was done.

But Nevan needed me.

I returned to the lake where Nevan lay unconscious. Tiptoeing closer, I peered down at him searching for signs of…I didn't know what. Signs of the man I knew. Signs he was okay. His entire body was slack, and his eyes did not move behind his closed lids. How long did it take after the forging for the former human to wake up? How would he behave when he did? With no answers to guide me, I gazed out across the lake. Coldness washed through me when I noticed my own image reflected on its surface.

A soft, blue glow surrounded me.

No wonder Daráine and Brónach had mistaken me for an angelic being.

I had stopped cloaking myself when I returned to Daráine. I'd had to, or else the girl's new mother would've thought she was a little off, the way she talked to an invisible angel. I hadn't realized I was glowing. Freaking glowing.

How had that happened?

My magic shimmered blue, but it always dissipated as soon as I stopped using my powers. It never created a full-body halo.

A soft moan drew my attention down to Nevan. Eyes half closed, he raised his gaze to me.

Crap. I was supposed to be gone before he woke up. Maybe I should've blipped away the instant he saw me, but I couldn't. He gaped at me like I really was an angel, the answer to his prayers for salvation.

If I had been meant to help his daughter, maybe I'd been meant to help him too. Nevan had mentioned hazy memories of an angelic being who took care of him immediately after his transformation. He hadn't recalled what the angel looked like, only that he owed his existence and everything he had with me to the mysterious being. Whenever he called me his sweet mortal angel, he used those words because he believed I had saved him much the same way his mystery angel had saved him after his forging.

What if I was that angel?

Maybe I was giving in to a delusion that suited my desires. I wanted to stay with him, to soothe him, to care for him during this arduous transition. I loved him. The man currently gaping at me didn't know me, much less love me.

Time, if I'm not meant to stay with him, whisk me back to my present right away.

Nothing happened. I waited, growing more uneasy with every passing second and with Nevan's awed gaze trained on me. Time did not yank me out of the past and back to my present day. Delusion or not, I took that as a sign I was meant to stay, at least for a while.

I crouched beside Nevan.

He jerked. His entire body convulsed, his face wrenching with agony. An anguished cry burst out of him.

"What's wrong?" I asked. "Are you okay?"

His eyes swirled wildly, the whites stained with red. When he tried to speak, he broke into a hacking fit. His body began to tremble.

I smoothed hair from his eyes and caressed his forehead with one palm. With my other hand, I clasped one of his. The heat of his skin scorched so hot it almost burned, but I held on anyway. Christ, I'd had no idea things got this bad after the forging. No wonder Nevan and Max hadn't wanted me to see Travis right after his change.

"Shh," I murmured, rubbing my thumb in circles on the back of his hand while I kept stroking his forehead. "It's all right. You don't need to speak, just try to relax."

He sucked in a ragged breath, exhaling it gradually. His gaze stayed glued to me.

"I will not leave you," I said, "until you're through the worst of it. I promise you that."

Another convulsion seized him.

"Easy," I said. "Take it easy. I know it's hard, Nevan, but please try."

Lips parted, he furrowed his brow. He tried to speak again but managed only a croak.

"Hush," I whispered. "You need rest."

Dimly, I recognized the sounds of the battle had receded a bit but not gone away, audible behind the rush of the falls. Nevan needed a quiet, soothing place to recover. A vicious battle was not the kind of background noise that would ease his transition.

Like I had any clue about how to ease him into a new life, a new world, a new body.

I had to try.

"Close your eyes," I said, "and sleep."

A shudder racked his body, though less fiercely than the seizures had. I spread one palm over his forehead and the other over his heart, praying for some guidance on how to help him. I shut my eyes, willing his pain to lessen, knowing I didn't have the power to heal.

He sighed, his whole body relaxing.

I opened my eyes. The glittering blue of my magics streamed out of my hands and into him.

Nevan seemed…peaceful.

The noises of the battle raged on.

I transported us away from the melee, straight into the Unseen.

Chapter Twenty-One

I LOST COUNT OF THE DAYS. AFTER TAKING US INTO THE UNSEEN REALM, I'd fervently wished we could hide out in a cave somewhere far away from other elementals, somewhere lovely and peaceful. My wish had been granted. Without realizing what I'd done, I had teleported us to the perfect place for Nevan's convalescence.

What on earth was I doing? I needed to go home to my own time and find a way to defeat Aello. Nursing Nevan had not been part of the plan. How could I abandon him? Notus had forged him and run away to get it on with Aello. Nevan needed someone to care for him.

Besides, time would wait for me.

And so, I spent day after day tending to him, often simply talking to him about nothing in particular, babbling away to let him know I was here. I discovered I could conjure the things I needed, like he could—or would be able to eventually—so I conjured cloths and blankets and basic implements for making food and gathering water from the stream outside the cave. He drifted in and out of consciousness, wrenched by the occasional seizure but more often shivering. I wrapped him in blankets and laid cool cloths over his forehead. Despite his chills, he was running far too hot even for a sylph.

When I was fifteen, my mom and Ash had gotten sick while my dad was away on business. They'd had simple colds, though. I made them chicken soup from a can and got them fresh boxes of tissues. Today, I was caring for someone whose body had been ripped apart molecule by molecule and reassembled into a different kind of being. Despite having zero experience with nursing newly forged elementals, I kept trying. I fed him soups I made from conjured ingredients, dribbling the liquid into his mouth a little at a time.

Gradually, Nevan stayed awake for longer periods. After several days by my guesstimate, he began to speak, though only to say simple things like yes or no. When I asked how he felt, he told me, "Better."

That was the biggest word he used for a long while.

Every evening, I sat beside him for hours stroking his forehead and face, running my hands over his chest while my magics danced over his skin. With rapt attention, he would watch me doing this. As soon as I stopped, he would drift into a deep and peaceful sleep.

I slept when he slept, though my slumber was haunted by nightmares of tornadoes and earthquakes and everyone I loved vanishing.

One morning, I woke to find Nevan sitting up, studying me.

"Are you okay?" I asked, pushing up onto my elbows.

"I am well," he said. "The pain has greatly subsided."

"Your speech is a lot better too." I sat up and laid my palm on his forehead. "You're back to your normal temperature."

"How do you know what is normal for me? I have been...changed."

"Yeah, but I'm familiar with your kind." *And with your body*, I thought but kept it to myself. Telling him we were lovers, much less husband and wife, would damage the time stream for sure.

Or so I assumed. Time didn't confide in me.

Maybe I should've worried that I'd started to think of time as a living thing, but I didn't care about anything right now except Nevan.

He sucked in a breath, his eyes widening a touch. "You are beautiful, transcendent, a being of light and kindness."

"I can't deny I love hearing you say that, but I'm not—"

Nevan touched his fingertips to my cheek. "You are a miraculous spirit. An angel."

"No, really, I'm not." I glanced at myself and, naturally, I was glowing again. "I can see why you'd think I'm an angel, but I'm a woman, plain and simple."

"Nothing about you is plain or simple. You shimmer with heavenly light."

The sensation of his fingertips on my skin awakened parts of me that ought to stay dormant. Lust was not helpful right now.

My body disagreed.

"Are you sure you feel better?" I asked. "I mean, how much better?"

He slapped his hands on his chest, smiling. "Fully better. You have healed me with your angelic powers."

Oh jeez. I ought to nip that idea in the bud, but the way he was gazing at me with adoration, I knew he would never accept I was not an angel. Couldn't blame him. I did have powers. The glowy, glittery kind.

"Listen," I said, "since you're feeling better, I should go."

His smile crumbled. "You cannot. Please, I—"

I clapped a hand over his mouth when the P-word triggered a zing of magic between us. "Careful there. The P-word is a big no-no here in the Unseen. So is gratitude. And whatever you do, never, never, never admit to owing anyone your life."

He peeled my hand away from his mouth, smirking. "I never realized how much I would enjoy a domineering woman until you entered my life, angel."

"Call me Lindsey." What the hell, he might as well know my name. I'd probably screwed the time stream anyway by staying with him.

"Of course, angel Lindsey."

"Not angel. Lindsey. Only Lindsey, no other words before or after."

His smirk deepened. "Whatever you wish, darlin'."

My heart stuttered. He'd called me *darlin'* like he so often did in the future. He had become my Nevan.

He cupped my face in one big, warm hand. "I am appreciative of your efforts to aid in my recovery."

"Nice job with expressing gratitude without actually expressing it." I resisted the urge to turn my face into his hand and kiss it. Resisted a lot. "You're a fast learner."

"I have an excellent tutor." He rubbed his thumb over my bottom lip. "A beautiful, sensual one."

The breath caught in my throat at the husky tone of his voice. I coughed and said, "Do you remember what happened? Do you remember being human? Being forged?"

"Yes, I recall everything after I fell in combat." He withdrew his hand, grasping the nape of his neck. "However, my former life grows dimmer every day. All I can remember of it is meeting you immediately before the battle and that there was a battle. The details elude me."

"And the forging."

He grimaced. "I recall those details rather more clearly than I would like."

The Nevan I'd married remembered quite a bit about his mortal life, but maybe temporary amnesia was a common side effect of the forging.

Nevan stopped blinking, his gaze locked on mine, his eyes aflame with whorls of bronze, silver, and gold. "You came to me before the battle. That proves you are an angel."

I didn't ask how he came to that conclusion because I really didn't want to know.

"Get up," I said, hopping up and gesturing for him to do the same. "You've been lying around for days. Exercise and fresh air will do you good."

He sprang to his feet. The blanket that had covered him from the waist down slid off, puddling on the floor.

Naked Nevan. Close enough to touch.

My breaths quickened, my pulse too. I clutched my hands over my belly, desperately fighting the need to run my hands over his velvety flesh.

He tugged one of my hands free and led me out of the cave into the golden sunshine. The stream burbled softly, its water oh-so-inviting. My scalp itched. I hadn't bathed since before my time-travel adventure began.

"I must really stink," I said, not realizing until it was too late I'd spoken the words aloud.

"Stink?" Nevan said.

"You know, smell bad. I haven't bathed in days, maybe longer. Didn't want to leave you alone for more than a few minutes in case you needed me."

He waved toward the stream. "Let's bathe together."

Oh, I knew how this would go. Bathing would become fondling and fondling would escalate into thrusting and moaning. Could he have sex yet? Was his body capable of it? I didn't want to damage his recovery simply because I had a serious case of lust.

Nevan moved closer, took hold of the top button of my blouse, and unhooked it. "I will not molest you, unless you want me to. You have my word."

"And yet you're undressing me."

One side of his mouth kicked up in a half smirk. "You cannot bathe in your clothing."

"Uh-huh." I batted his hand away. "I can do this myself much faster."

He looked dubious until I poofed my clothes away. His gaze raked over my body from my toes up to my face. His tongue slipped out to moisten his lower lip when he drank in the sight of my breasts.

I leaped into the deepest part of the stream where it flared out into a small pool before narrowing again.

"Come on in," I said. "The water feels incredible."

He stared at me, his chest heaving.

I dunked my head under the water, washing away days' worth of grime. When I surfaced again, I combed my fingers through my wet hair and sighed with contentment.

Nevan jumped into the pool, catching me around the waist before I'd recovered from the mini tsunami his body had created. Pressed against his hard, hot body, I suddenly forgot all about time travel and wounds to the time stream and everything else I should've been concerned with now that he had recovered from his forging.

He seemed a lot better off than Travis was even months after his transition.

Based on the erection blossoming between our bodies, Nevan was fully capable of doing anything he wanted.

Maybe I should've stopped this, but I'd lost the will to say no.

He touched his mouth to mine in a tentative kiss. Against my lips, he whispered, "I do not know—do not remember—"

"Sex?"

"Yes." He cleared his throat and wriggled against me. "Have you and I…"

"No." Not in this time, anyway. Nevan had introduced me to the joys of making love, so it seemed appropriate I should do the same for him. I linked my hands behind his nape. "Let me show you how it's done."

I covered his mouth with my own, my heartbeat accelerating when he grasped my ass in both his hands. His erection rubbed against my belly, my nipples scraped on his chest, and the lapping of the cool water intensified every sensation. I licked at the seam of his lips until he parted them for me, then plunged my tongue deep into the heat of his mouth.

He groaned, the sound resonating in his chest, vibrating into my breasts.

Lost to the feel of him, I teased the roof of his mouth with my tongue, swirled it around his, and moaned when he responded with greedy thrusts of his own tongue. We kissed forever it seemed, entranced by the flavor of each other, unwilling to sever the intimate contact even as his cock grew harder and my sex grew wetter.

I whisked us onto the grassy bank of the stream, a cushion of greenery beneath me and Nevan above me, his body molded to mine.

He broke the kiss, gazing down at me with burning eyes. "I want ye. Don't know how to—"

"Do what feels right."

"But I need ye to like it."

I dragged my tongue up his throat to coil it around his earlobe. "I'll love it, trust me."

He regarded me for a few more seconds. Exhaling a soft growl, he slithered down my body inch by inch, his hot skin gliding over mine, the sensation delicious and arousing. His lips tickled my skin as he moved, and when he sealed his mouth around one nipple, I gasped. He suckled the peak, swirling his tongue around the areola. I clutched at his head, holding him to me, writhing beneath him while he released my nipple only to latch onto the other one and lavish it with the same attention. I bucked my hips, arching my back, my mouth falling open.

When he moved lower, his head between my legs, and his mouth closed around my taut bud, I let out a strangled cry.

"Nevan," I gasped. "Oh yes, Nevan."

He nipped and licked and sucked on my clit until I was thrashing under him, moaning and whimpering, sinking my fingers into his hair and scratching his scalp with my nails. My release detonated like a bomb, an explosion of pleasure that seized my entire body. He kept tormenting my nub until the last spasm faded away.

Breathing hard, I said, "And you claim not to remember sex. That was...wow."

Nevan lifted his head to peek at me over the hairs of my mound. "Is that all we do?"

I laughed. "No, not by a long shot. Trust your instincts."

His lips stretched into a closed-mouth smile of pure, animal hunger. "I'm very glad to hear that is not all. I relished your pleasure, but..." He glanced away. "I am feeling a powerful need to claim your body."

"Do it."

Rising to his knees, he grasped my hips and lifted them off the ground. His mouth was open, his tongue slid across his lower lip. With his gaze hooded, he stared at my groin like he was a starving man and my body was a juicy steak.

"Lindsey," he growled. "Your pink flesh glistens, so wet and delicious."

I gasped when he plunged inside me with one swift, powerful thrust. He hesitated there, buried inside my body, his chest heaving and his eyes a tempest of churning colors. God, I loved the feel of his cock filling me up, the heat and hardness of it intoxicating. Just when I started to speak, to encourage him, he withdrew partway and plowed in deep again, pulling out and thrusting in over and over at a measured pace, his every muscle taut and his expression strained with concentration and need.

I grabbed his biceps, urging him to bend toward me.

He obeyed, his gaze never wavering from mine, and I clutched his biceps while he penetrated me again and again, his hips undulating.

"Oh Nevan," I moaned, and latched my legs around him. A faint voice in the back of my mind told me I shouldn't be doing this. What if by staying with him, by having sex with him, I'd irrevocably altered the future? Our future? I shouldn't have let this happen, but I didn't give a damn about the timeline anymore. I'd become an eyewitness to his courageous but tragic death and to the forging that had shaped him into the man I loved. How could I ever have left him to suffer alone?

He wasn't suffering anymore.

Nevan slanted toward me more, his thrusts quickening and becoming more ravenous. He grunted in rhythm with every plunge of his shaft into my wet, aching flesh. I grasped his shoulders, my nails digging in, and bucked my hips into his thrusts. His face captivated me, the hunger in his expression mixing with a mild confusion and rapt adoration. No man had ever looked at me the way he did, whether he was a mortal warrior, a newly forged elemental, or the sylph king.

Magic rose inside me as my need escalated toward climax. Blue energy shimmered on my skin, only a few sparkles at first, growing into a glittering sheen that formed a second skin over my entire body. Blue sparks leaped off my skin to crackle on Nevan's.

His eyes went wide, his gaze flicking to the magic sizzling between us.

Rather than stopping or even slowing down, he accelerated the pace of his thrusts, as desperate to find release as I was, slamming into me and bouncing my body. I clung to him, and my moans escalated into whimpers and sharp cries. While my body went rigid, and my sex milked him hard, he threw his head back and bellowed. The scorching jet of his release pulsed deep inside me.

I went limp on the cushy grass bed, moaning with satisfaction. This man knew how to make love to me, even when he had no idea who I was. I silently thanked Bob for his wedding gift because I had zero ability to resist Nevan anytime, anywhere. At least the magical prophylactic ensured I wouldn't get knocked up with a dangerous hybrid pregnancy.

But I wanted children with him. I wanted it so much.

We couldn't have that.

Nevan brushed his fingertips over my cheek. "What vexes you?"

"It's complicated." I took hold of his hand, pressing it to my face. "I love being with you, Nevan."

"Why do you keep calling me that?"

Chapter Twenty-Two

I PONDERED HOW TO EXPLAIN IT BUT GAVE UP AND TOLD THE TRUTH. "It's your new name. Every elemental picks a different name after the forging. Yours is Nevan."

"How do you know this?"

"Um…Let's just say it suits you."

He smiled. "You have named me, angel Lindsey. I am grate—"

I sealed his lips shut with two fingers. "No gratitude, remember?"

"Mm." He sucked my fingers into his mouth, releasing them slowly. "I will try to remember that."

His gaze fell to my hand, the one holding his to my cheek, and his brows knit together. He raised my hand between us, studying it intently.

Blue magic sparkled along my skin and dribbled onto his.

"You have great power," he murmured. "My angel Lindsey."

Every time he called me "angel," I melted inside.

He slid his hand down to my wrist, raising my palm to his mouth. The energy on my skin crackled, and he canted his head this way and that to examine it. He lifted my hand higher and dragged his tongue from my wrist up to my palm, swirling it around the sensitive center.

I sucked in a breath.

Topaz-blue energy glittered on his tongue as he raked it up my middle finger to the tip.

"Nevan," I breathed, excitement tingling between my thighs.

He suckled my fingertip, then glided his tongue down to lap at my palm.

"Oh God," I moaned, amazed at how easily he could turn me on. I'd never thought of my palm as an erogenous zone, but whoa mama, it was.

He groaned, licking his way down to my wrist. "I want to devour you, feast on your body from head to toe, make you moan and beg for more."

"I'd beg right now, but that's another no-no in the Unseen realm."

147

"You brought me here, and I know you can travel in the blink of an eye." He shoved both arms under my body and hoisted me up to sit on his lap. "Take us back to the mortal world so I might feast on you for hours and hear you beg me to give you pleasure."

Helpless to resist him, I whisked us to the other side. Making love over the blood stain that marked his death sounded not the least bit sexy, so I made sure we ended up on the other side of the lake in a secluded spot shaded by tall trees.

And we enjoyed each other.

For hours, maybe longer. Time meant nothing in the bubble of our desire. My magics awakened his and mingled with the newly born powers inside him, heightening every sensation and triggering some of the most intense orgasms I'd ever known. In between rounds of mind-blowing sex, we kissed and touched, exploring each other's bodies. By the time we finally lay exhausted and thoroughly sated in each other's arms, the sun had set in the mortal realm.

Christ, how long had I been here, in this time? Nevan and Max needed me to come home, but then again, I was in the past. Did it really matter how long I stayed? I would return to the moment right after I'd left. Nevan and Max would've done as I'd instructed, leaving Aello's nest before she arrived.

Excuses, I knew this. Something about this version of Nevan, the freshly born sylph learning about his new body and new powers, entranced me. The chance to see him in this time, to understand his past in a way I never could simply from hearing him talk about it, kept me here.

I conjured the blankets from the cave, and we wrapped them around ourselves, our bodies skin to skin inside our little cocoon.

He nuzzled my cheek. "You are a revelation."

My throat went thick. He'd spoken those words to me on the night we'd first made love, the night thousands of years from now when I'd given my virginity, my heart, and my soul to him.

No more excuses. As much as I longed to stay here with him, to understand his past, I needed to go home. I'd seen him through the worst days of his transformation. He could survive on his own.

For a century?

With all these vast and incredible powers, maybe I could summon Notus and shame the jerk into taking care of Nevan. Sure, no problem. I mean, it had taken me how long to get the hang of time travel? I suddenly thought I could wave my hand and summon the sylph king, not to mention convince him to do the right teing.

Nevan had told me once Notus started out as a good king, a good man, until he let dark magics take hold of him. The same fate had destroyed Skeiron. Had Aello been the driving force behind their downfalls?

I stroked Nevan's cheek. "You don't need me anymore. The worst is over."

"You cannot leave." He pushed up on one elbow, his eyes glinting with the cold shades of fear. "Stay with me. I need you, Lindsey."

My heart hurt for him, but I forced myself to say, "I have to go. People I love are waiting for me, and they need me more than you do right now. You are strong and smart, and I know you'll be okay."

He opened his mouth as if to speak but froze. His attention swerved to the other side of the lake.

A shiver of awareness rippled through me. Someone was coming.

Notus.

I knew this, though I had no idea how. I also knew, or sensed, Aello was not with him and that he meant no harm to Nevan. Jumping up, I conjured my clothes into a pile on the ground. I didn't have the finesse to make them appear on my body. Gesturing at Nevan, I said, "Get up and put something on. Notus is coming back for you."

While I pulled my clothes on, he got up and scowled. "I would prefer to stay with you."

"I'm sorry, that's not an option." I framed his face with my hands. "No one knows you better than I do, so believe it when I say you'll be fine. One day, we will see each other again, but not for a very, very long time."

"Why must we part ways?"

"Too complicated to explain." I slapped his behind. "Cover that fine ass and prepare to meet your king."

Nevan snatched up a blanket the same color as his skin. He held it up, examining the large sheet of fabric. Frowning, he tore off a wide strip and strapped it around his hips. The cloth covered his hips and his groin but little else.

I'd witnessed the birth of his signature loincloth.

"Let's go," I said, trying really hard not to think about how much I had influenced Nevan's past while I zipped us to the other side of the lake near the falls.

We stood mere feet from the spot where he had perished.

I pulled him into my arms and whispered into his ear, "No matter what happens, I will always be here for you, somewhere, sometime. Always. But you're about to start a new life, and you need to embrace it for better or worse." I kissed him softly. "You'll do fine. I believe in you, Nevan."

Though it physically pained me to do it, I backed away into the trees, out of sight.

Nevan stared after me, his longing a palpable force.

I willed myself invisible.

A figure emerged from the water. Notus sauntered up to Nevan and said, "It is time for you to begin your new life."

Nevan barred his arms over his chest. "Why did you leave me here alone? I might have died."

The sylph king chuckled. "You are immortal. Nothing can kill you."

Bullshit. Notus had no intention of telling his new soldier about endued weapons, magically enhanced poisons, or dark spells. Though I desperately wanted to warn Nevan, I had to let this play out the way it had been meant to before I intervened. He needed to get back on the path laid out for him.

"Come with me," Notus said, stretching out an arm to indicate the lake. "The waters will ferry us into your new world."

Water was the portal to the Unseen.

Nevan glanced back at the woods, at where I hid.

"We must go," Notus said.

They leaped into the lake and vanished.

I straightened, rolling my shoulders back, and realized I was assuming the same about-to-zip-away pose that Nevan and Max always assumed. The posture felt natural. How strange that I'd accepted my powers and grown comfortable with them right when an evil witch wanted to destroy me and Janus wanted his powers back.

Janus. Max. Nevan. I had to get back to them.

Something moved in the trees to my left.

Aello, the not-skeletal version of her, strode out of the screening foliage and stopped on the spot where Nevan and Notus had stood a moment earlier. She glared down at the dried blood stain, the evidence of Nevan's demise, and tilted her head left and right. She squatted to touch the stain, lifting her fingers to her face to sniff them. Her lip curled.

"Sylphs," she snarled. "They stink of the earth even as they command the air. Newborns are the worst."

The harpy rose, muttering under her breath.

She froze, only her eyes moving.

I didn't move, didn't breathe. She couldn't see me.

"Come out and show yourself," Aello said, turning in my direction. "I can feel the air disturbance from your breaths."

From this far away? She was a wind elemental, but I'd never heard of them feeling breaths from twenty feet away. Even if I believed she could feel my exhalations, I would not uncloak myself. I should've left right then, but an inkling of something important about to happen kept me rooted in place.

Aello's gaze flitted as if she struggled to pinpoint my location. "You are the one who nursed the newborn sylph through his transition. He is stronger than any bantling should be but not strong enough to thwart my plans. You may hide yourself from my sight but know this. I will have my way, and you will never again lure my lover into doing your bidding."

Notus was her lover. Had Skeiron haunted her bed too? Maybe she'd done three-ways with the two sylphs. *Yech.* I did not need that image burned into my brain.

"I saw you," she said, "moments ago with the newborn. I know your face, and one day, I will know your name and your weaknesses. Notus was to be mine and only mine, but like any foolish male, he had to procreate. His progeny is not even his blood child." She hissed like a steam vent suddenly blown open and slapped a hand on her chest. "I was to bear his blood progeny. He swore he would wait for our child, but the siren call of a pathetic mortal lured him to this place. You called him here, I know this. Do not deny it!"

Denials wouldn't help, I knew that. Aello might have gotten more depraved and insane over the eons, but she'd clearly veered down that path even before Nevan or I came into the picture. Crouched behind a tree, I was riveted to the bizarre monologue unfolding before me.

"He would not wait!" Aello shrieked. "Our firstborn was to be the child of my womb, not a bastardized sylph forged out of a pathetic mortal. You caused it, you must have." She shook her fists in the air. "Show yourself!"

The depth of her hatred made my skin crawl. She despised me because I'd taken care of Nevan and eased his transition from mortal to elemental. In some twisted way, she thought I had stolen her chance to have Notus's firstborn offspring and that I had hypnotized the sylph king into both forging Nevan and coming back for him.

And I understood what all of this meant. I was the trigger for the primary event.

What was to come had already unfolded long before I became the Janusite. How could I have triggered Aello's time-shifting revenge plot? I hadn't traveled back in time until now, after she absorbed untold dark magics and set in motion the shifts that had damaged the time stream. This couldn't have anything to do with me.

Except I'd known almost from the start Aello harbored a seething hatred for me. Her vengeance was aimed smack at me, beginning with the first time shift. She'd altered my past repeatedly in failed attempts to get rid of me. She had erased Nevan as a means of eradicating me, though it hadn't worked. I was one with time, and she could never divorce me from the time stream.

And yet, everything she'd done had been aimed at me. How was it possible I had triggered a millennia-long quest for retribution? The truth trickled through me, raising every fine hair on my body.

Nevan had told me someone nursed him through his transition. The first time he'd seen me in the rock shop, back when he'd been glamouring to disguise his appearance, he had felt he'd known me before. From the second I'd bumped into him in the woods near the falls, I had experienced a sense of connection and belonging I'd never known in my entire life before him. We fell in love so fast, so hard. No mere coincidence had brought us together. I, the Janusite, had not accidentally bumped into him, the one and only elemental charged with finding the one and only mortal gifted with the powers of a god. We were destined to find each other, to love each other, to make each other stronger.

Fate. Immutable, undeniable. It had brought me to this moment in the distant past. By the time I was born in the twentieth century AD, I had already traveled into the past. It seemed contradictory—how could I have been here in this moment before I was born—but I understood the truth of it.

I sagged against the tree, my vision blurry as I struggled to focus but failed. Did this mean I'd never had a choice? No free will? I could not, would not, believe that. I had chosen to be with Nevan, and he had chosen to be with me. Our bond transcended time, but it existed because we chose it.

Aello howled and shook her fists at the sky.

The harpy vanished.

I dived into the time stream and sprang out in the midst of a battle.

Chapter Twenty-Three

I SQUINTED INTO THE STORM OF COMBAT RAGING AROUND ME. I hovered at the periphery of a clearing, at the edge of the battle. Powerful gusts of wind ripped grass and dirt from the earth, whirling it around the sylph soldiers clad in obsidian armor who battled an army of bare-chested soldiers with impossibly thick torsos and long, filthy hair. I had not returned to my own time. I'd intuited this the instant I emerged from the time stream. Though I had intended to go home, time must have believed I needed to witness this moment.

Time believed? Sheesh, a few hours ago I would've laughed at the idea. Now, I realized it might be true. Since I was bound to time by my powers, it served as a conduit. Unconsciously, I had known I must come to this point in history, though I didn't understand why.

Swords clashed in a deafening cacophony of metal on metal. Sparks rained down from the gnashing blades. The enemy was unfamiliar to me. They had legs as thick as tree trunks and skin the color of wet sand. Their greasy hair hung around their faces, obscuring them, but I caught glimpses of features as gnarled as a knotty pine tree.

Hands grasped my upper arms and hauled me backward. I yelped, but no one could've heard me over the din.

"Quiet," a voice hissed into my ear even as I was towed further backward into the shelter of the trees.

Those hands spun me around to confront a body sheathed in silver armor shot through with gold and bronze. Dirt and blood stained the metal and the face of the man grinning at me.

"Nevan." I grinned too, despite the brutal fight going on behind us. The fact he had blood on his face at last sank in, and my grin waned. "Are you hurt?"

"The blood is not mine." He flourished his hand the way I'd seen him do countless times, and instantly we were inside a calm, quiet bubble. He flicked his wrist. His armor and body were washed clean in a heartbeat. "I had thought to never see you again, my angel Lindsey."

"Well—"

His mouth covered mine, silencing me. I wrapped my arms around him, marveling at the way his armor fit like a true second skin, soft and hard at the same time. I'd felt his armor before, but he had never kissed me while wearing it or kissed me while in the midst of a battle. I melted like I always did for him, relishing the slick glide of his tongue over mine, responding with a matching passion. After a few seconds that seemed like a blissful eternity, we separated our lips.

Nevan swept stray hairs from my face, tucking them behind my ear. "I'm pleased to see ye, darlin', but why have ye come? This is a dangerous moment for a visit."

"Not sure why I'm here." Something important must've been about to happen, something to do with Aello, but I couldn't explain all of that to this version of Nevan. I could ask a question, though. "Have you met Notus's queen?"

He pulled his head back, tipping it to the side. "You come to me during a battle to ask me that? Notus has no queen."

"A lover, maybe?"

"I am not privy to the king's dalliances," Nevan said curtly. He backed away from me, his lips tight. "Are you interested in becoming his angel lover?"

"Absolutely not." I moved toward him, laying my hands on his breastplate. "I have no interest in your king. Only you."

His stiff posture softened a bit, as did his voice. "I am pleased to hear that."

I glanced over my shoulder at the armies doing battle. "What's going on here?"

"The gnomes have undertaken a foolish mission to defeat the sylphs." Nevan's gaze hardened into steel when he looked toward the battlefield. "They will fail."

Yes, they would. Notus remained king of the sylphs until Skeiron defeated him. Another sylph took him down, not the gnomes.

Before I undertook my mission to the past, before the first time shift, Nevan had mentioned the sylphs once fought a battle with the gnomes. The reason for their attack was a mystery. Maybe I was here to find out why. Maybe the reason related to Aello.

The ground shuddered.

I clutched at Nevan. "What was that?"

"A gnome. They strike the earth to cause a tremor and unsettle the enemy." Nevan cocked his head, listening. "I must go. The king summons me."

"Be careful."

He pulled me into his arms and ravished me with a kiss that left me breathless, my heart racing.

Then he vanished.

I knew Nevan was not the reason I'd come here. I also knew he would survive this battle and serve Notus until the king became depraved and Skeiron deposed him. After that, Nevan would serve Skeiron willingly until the new king became as depraved as Notus had been, using a bargain to turn Nevan into his slave and the seeker of the Janusite. Nevan had forsaken his duty and refused to hand me over to Skeiron even after we both knew I was the prophesied mortal gifted with a god's powers.

Cloaking myself once again, I wandered the periphery of the battle in search of whatever had drawn me here. Aello, I assumed. Where was the harpy?

The better question was why should I wait for her to show up. I had all these freaking powers at my disposal, and ever since I'd first entered the time stream, those powers had become easier and easier to tap into at will. I closed my eyes and let my mind go blank.

There.

At the instant my eyes opened, I zipped to the location I sought, to the individual I sought. The harpy squatted behind a tree, watching the combat with a look of dark glee on her face. She held her palms together, her long nails tapping against each other. Her lips peeled back from her teeth in a creepy version of a smile.

I tiptoed closer to peer past her into the clearing.

Nevan swung his sword at his opponent, their blades striking with a sharp clang of metal on metal that reverberated through the clearing despite the racket around them.

"Ohhh," Aello murmured, her voice raspy. She clacked her talons. "Strike him down, gnome. Make it painful."

She imbued the last phrase with a disturbing intensity. Her eyes burned bright red. Tendrils of roiling black magic snaked out from her talons, wending their way through the smoky, fetid air toward the gnome soldier who grappled with Nevan. The tendrils spiraled around the gnome, and his eyes began to blaze red.

He stomped his foot. The earth quivered.

Magical energy shot out into his sword. The silver blade mutated into glistening black tinged with crimson.

An eerie certainty slithered down my spine. That blade was endued. It would destroy Nevan.

The gnome rammed his huge, booted foot into Nevan's gut, knocking him off balance. While Nevan struggled to stay upright, the gnome raised his sword above his head, grasped in both his gnarly hands. The creature sliced the blade down toward Nevan's chest.

I flung my hands out. Blue energy spurted out of my palms, a jet of magic aimed straight at Nevan. It blew him sideways, out of the sword's trajectory. Nevan caught himself before he fell to the ground, sprang upright, and barreled toward the gnome. His sword plunged into the enemy soldier's chest.

It wouldn't kill the gnome, but the wound would take him out of commission for a while.

Aello flapped her head in every direction, her sharp eyes searching for me.

Not that she could see me. Her frustration increased with every whip of her head, making her eyes glow like red coals about to erupt into flames. Mouth open, breaths hissing out of her, she sprang to her feet.

"I know you are here," she hissed. "You shall not save him today."

Aello thrust her arms out.

Black energy poured forth from her talons. It boiled in the air, writhing and seeking whatever it might latch onto amid the chaos. In fact, the chaos seemed to fuel it into greater and greater power. It coiled around the gnome soldiers, transmuting them into red-eyed demons intent on a single shared goal implanted in their minds by Aello.

Destroy Nevan.

Oh, like hell she would.

I roared and flung my arms out, unleashing twin torrents of blue energy. The black and the blue collided above the heads of the warring armies.

And exploded.

Chapter Twenty-Four

THE BLAST KNOCKED ME BACKWARD ONTO MY ASS. MY EARS RANG, and the supernova flash of the explosion had rendered me temporarily blind. At least I hoped it was temporary. I lay there for a moment, immobilized by the shock of the explosion and the knowledge of what I'd done. I had intervened in the battle. What if I'd altered history?

No, time had brought me here. I'd been meant to stop Aello from destroying Nevan. He was meant to live on and find me a long, long time from this day.

As I lay there waiting for my limbs to obey me again, I wondered about this turn of events. Nevan, the version of him in this time, remembered meeting me after his forging. Why did present-day Nevan have no memory of it? He would've told me if he remembered encountering me during a battle. He had mentioned other times in his life when his memories were hazy but dismissed it as unimportant, nothing more than a side effect of living forever. Was he right? Caught in the middle of a moment present-day Nevan clearly had forgotten, I had to wonder.

My vision cleared, and my ears stopped ringing. I sat up and surveyed my surroundings.

Aello lay sprawled on her back a few feet away. Her eyes, though open, stared vacantly at the treetops above us.

I clambered to my feet, brushing off my clothes. Dirt and debris from the explosion had covered me, but I managed to get rid of the worst of it.

Aello's head rolled to the side. She locked her black gaze on me, her irises as dark as the pupils, fathomless pools of evil.

My skin crawled. I staggered backward a step.

"You," she rasped, and pushed up onto her knees. "You destroyed the entire gnome army. It is not possible!" Spittle sprayed from her lips with those words. She pounded her fists on the ground. "I will avenge myself on you if it is the last act of my existence. More power, that is what I require. Blacker magic. Darker spells. Whatever it takes to rid the universe of you."

Her hand shot up, one talon aimed at me.

I summoned my magic, cloaking myself again. Whatever I'd done had left me a touch woozy, and I did not want to tangle with Aello in this condition.

The harpy pounded her fists on the earth. Clods of dirt shot up, splatting down around her.

I rushed to the clearing.

Every last gnome was gone.

The sylphs meandered through the clearing, expressions slack, exchanging head shakes and muttered words.

Nevan stood tall and proud at the periphery of the clearing, a small smile curving his lips as if he knew a secret no one else did. He believed I had gotten rid of the gnomes. Well, I had. I hadn't meant to eradicate them, scattering them to the Four Winds. Save Nevan, that had been my only thought. Something inside me warned the gnomes hadn't wanted to assault the sylphs. Aello's hand had moved them like marionettes.

Had I eradicated the gnomes? Aello told me so, but I shouldn't believe a thing that whackjob said.

I shut my eyes and concentrated on locating the gnome army. Relief weakened my knees, but I locked them to stay upright. The gnomes had been teleported back to their home territory, unharmed. Whether Aello retained her hold on them, I couldn't tell for sure.

Eyes open again, I resumed my visual survey of the area.

Notus loitered on the other side of the clearing, his obsidian armor and every patch of exposed skin splattered with blood. He jerked his head as if sensing something, his attention directed past me.

I half turned, noticing Aello not ten feet from me. Since I was invisible again, she had no idea we stood so close to each other.

Notus marched across the clearing toward Aello.

The other sylphs, even Nevan, failed to notice their king had left the battlefield. I let my ethereal senses unfurl a bit and realized she had used dark magics to cloak herself. How could I see her? The answer hit me the second I thought the question. My Janusite powers trumped hers, at least in this time and place. Aello might have acquired dark magic, but she hadn't amassed enough to beat me yet.

Notus reached his lover, pulling her into a passionate embrace.

I sensed he was now cloaked along with her. The other sylphs seemed not to notice the couple ravaging each other with a sloppy, icky kiss that involved plenty of groping and grunting.

They broke their kiss but stayed entangled.

Notus skimmed his hands up and down Aello's arms, his gaze bound to hers, his pupils large and dark. In a hushed tone, he said, "You did this, my love, did you not? You saved my army from annihilation."

I snorted, though neither of them heard me. *She* saved the day? The harpy had wanted to annihilate Nevan even if that meant destroying the sylph army and Notus too. She'd told me once she would exact her vengeance whatever the cost, and she'd meant it.

"Yes," Aello purred in that raspy voice, "I spared you, my love. Come with me and I will ensure neither of us is ever endangered again. We will share power the likes of which you cannot imagine."

"My army needs me to command them."

"And you shall return to them forthwith." She clenched her fingers in his hair, making him wince. "Introduce me to your precious army, my love, as you promised to do long ago."

Something in her voice told me she wasn't asking.

Notus caressed her long white hair. "I promised one day to bring you into the fold. You said you understood why I cannot do so yet. My people are sylphs, you are a harpy. They will not accept you as my queen. I could introduce you as my adviser and ally."

"Adviser?" She bared her teeth, clenching his hair so hard I swore I could feel the pain. "I am your lover, the woman you vowed you wanted to bear your offspring. You dare suggest I should accept being your adviser instead of your queen?"

He shook his head, blinking several times, seeming to break free of whatever spell she'd cast over him. Notus tore her hands away from his head and took one big step backward. "You will not bear my offspring. I will procreate only via the forging. It is cleaner and simpler, my love, surely you must realize this. Children require time to raise and nurture into soldiers, but a forged being is reborn as an adult who is easily molded to suit my needs."

She flinched like he'd backhanded her across the face. "You deceived me? Swore we would have our own blood offspring when you had no intention of doing so?"

"You deceived yourself, Aello. I enjoy sharing my bed with you, but that is all. The king of the sylphs cannot take a harpy for his queen. If you wish to be introduced as my adviser—"

Aello shrieked.

The ear-splitting sound reverberated off the perimeter of the magic bubble around the three of us, though they had no clue I was within it. As Nevan had done with me earlier, Notus or Aello had ensured privacy via magical means.

Aello stomped her foot. A flush speckled her pale skin, and muscles in her neck and shoulders strained beneath her flesh. "I shall not be an adviser to you. For centuries, since you ascended the throne, I supported and bolstered you with my body, my mind, my magic. When you needed a hand during battle, I provided it. How else would you have defeated the titanium fae, the strongest fae tribe in existence?" She stomped her foot again. Clods of earth sprayed up around her sole, and the earth trembled. "I ensorcelled the gnomes so that they would gift me with their earth powers. I did this to destroy the traitor amidst your army, the one you refuse to see. He will be your undoing."

Notus went stone-still, his eyes wide.

Aello glared at him, her chest heaving with each breath, her white face now crimson. Spittle trickled down her chin. "You would not be king without me!"

While her face burned red, his coppery skin had turned faintly ashen.

He was afraid of her. An instinct told me that fact explained their entire relationship.

"You," he said, keeping his tone mild, "coerced the gnomes into attacking the sylph kingdom."

"Of course I did." She slapped a hand on his chest and dragged her talons down his skin, drawing a slender trail of blood. "To protect you."

"From what?"

Her hand shot out, one talon aimed straight at Nevan. "From him."

"Nevan is a fine soldier."

"He will be your undoing and yet you refuse to see it."

The sylph king lifted his heel, clearly intending to take a step backward, but stopped. "I might have been destroyed during the battle."

"I would have spared you." She peeled her lips back, exposing her teeth. "No longer shall I protect you."

Notus held up his hands. "Allow me to make amends, my love. I did not realize how much you desired blood offspring."

Her entire body quivered with fury. "You did not realize?"

She bellowed the words loud enough to rattle the trees in the immediate vicinity.

My ears rang in the aftermath of her outburst. That woman could holler like nobody else in the universe.

Notus stared at his wild-eyed lover with her hair whipping around her face in the breeze that seemed to emanate from her body. He took one step backward.

"I did not intend to mislead you," he said, his tone cautious. "You suggested blood children, and I neglected to inform you of my plans. That was…an unkind oversight."

"Oversight?" Her voice shrieked like an eagle's cry, only louder and far more piercing. She raised her arms, and the air around us came alive, writhing in wild currents. "You betrayed me, *my love.*"

She grated out the last two words between her locked jaws. No doubt about it, she did not consider him her love anymore.

The wind condensed into a dust devil.

Aello moved her fingers, and the dust devil inched toward Notus. "I saved your life this day. Express your appreciation to me." She twitched her fingers, and the mini tornado surged to within a few feet of Notus, who cringed but did not move. "Express it now and express it fully."

He started to speak but seemed to choke on the words. "Aello, I beg of you—"

"Do not beg." She wriggled her fingers, spurring the dust devil to spew debris at Notus and forcing him to raise his arms to protect himself. "Acknowledge the debt."

The way Notus cringed at her threats suggested to me the harpy had wielded her windy powers at him on previous occasions. An abusive girlfriend who beat her lover with tornadoes? Hell, it wouldn't be the strangest thing I'd seen. For the strong, virile king of the sylphs to be bullied by a female…I couldn't imagine what horrors she must've inflicted on him to get him so firmly under her thumb. He had tried to reassert himself, proclaiming she would never be his queen, but Aello knew she held all the power in this perverse relationship.

I ought to do something, to stop him from incurring a life debt. What, exactly? Pop my head out and inform the king I'd saved his army? I doubted he would believe me. Ah, but I did have an advantage. This was Aello of the past, before she'd absorbed immense amounts of dark magic. She seemed to command a lot of dark mojo, but nowhere near what she had in the twenty-first century. Maybe I could take her out and end the madness in this moment and in the future.

I squeezed my eyes shut and conjured an endued sword.

When I looked at the weapon, I realized I'd summoned Nevan's endued sword—his sword from the future. *Powers growing, Miss Janusite?* I didn't have total mastery of my Janusite magics, but I was getting better with it.

The invisibility cloak around me fell as I lunged toward Aello, the sword aimed at her back. The blade would pierce straight through to her heart.

Notus shoved Aello out of the way.

The sword plunged into his gut.

Chapter Twenty-Five

I STOOD FROZEN, MY HAND ON THE SWORD'S HILT AND ITS BLADE BUR-
ied in his abdomen, blood oozing from the wound. A wicked zing of
adrenaline electrified my veins, shortening my breaths. I could not look away
from the point where the sword entered his flesh. Why had my invisibility
spell failed? I sensed the answer. After sparing Nevan during the gnome
battle, compounded with time travel and magically easing his transition, I
had used up too much energy. I needed to rest my powers, but I didn't dare
take a break.

The sword in my hand poofed away.

Aello flung out a hand, hurling me away with a gust of wind. She
crouched beside Notus, assessing him with her gaze, seeming unaffected by
his dire situation.

She grabbed his chin. "Acknowledge the debt, and I will see you are
healed."

Blood dribbled from his mouth, but he said nothing.

"Do it," she said, "or you shall die."

He inhaled a wet, ragged breath. "I owe you my life, Aello. Thank you."

"At last you make an intelligent choice." She mashed her mouth to his. "I
shall take you to a vortex where you may be healed."

They were about to leave. I had to follow them, but I needed to give my
powers time to recuperate. Hell, *I* needed time to recuperate.

I tried to freeze time. The attempt made my head throb and white lights
spark in my vision.

A rest, that's what I needed. Somewhere safe.

Notus and Aello disappeared.

I would find them again, but right now, I had to take refuge in a safe
time and place. I sat back on my heels, my shoulders slumping. What if I
couldn't do this? Save time, save the worlds, save everyone I loved.

Footsteps drew my attention to the figure approaching me from the direction of the battleground.

Nevan knelt in front of me. "Are you unwell, Lindsey?"

"Exhausted, that's all." I rubbed my neck, and a question occurred to me. "How long has it been since you saw me?"

"A few moments."

"No, how long since the first time you saw me?"

"Since my forging, three hundred twenty-eight years have elapsed."

I straightened, hands on my thighs. "That long? And you haven't forgotten me?"

"Centuries to an immortal are like hours to a human."

Why did past Nevan retain his memories of our first meeting? If my theory was right, I had always been meant to travel back in time, and everything I'd done in the past had already occurred before Nevan and I met in the twenty-first century. The Nevan of that time had no memories of meeting me in the distant past.

The headache from my failed time freeze was getting worse the more I tried to think about anything, especially the vagaries of time travel. I needed a nap. Badly. My whole body sagged, and I swayed a little.

Nevan grasped my shoulders. "You are unwell. What is wrong?"

"Magic drain." I scrubbed my hands over my face. "I need a place to rest, a safe place. A nasty piece of work is ticked at me and—"

"I know of a place." He frowned. "Have you seen Notus? No one can find the king."

"He got stabbed with an endued sword and left to find a healing vortex."

Nevan hooked a finger under my chin. "Wait here. I will inform Skeiron of what has transpired with the king, then I shall return to you. Who wounded Notus?"

I shrugged, feigning ignorance. Better not to tell him about the whole Aello thing and that I'd accidentally stabbed Notus. Way too complicated.

Nevan poofed away.

My head pulsed with pain.

He reappeared, scooped me up in his arms, and took us away. We emerged inside his underground lair. It looked a little different, but I knew it was the same place I shared with him in the future. A pallet topped with a thick padding of furs took the place of the bed I knew from my time. A plain sheet lay over the furs, thrown back like he'd just climbed out of bed. Nevan laid me down on the pallet and settled in beside me, pulling me close and tugging the sheet over us.

His armor was gone, leaving only the loincloth.

My sleepy brain lost its verbal filter, and I mumbled things I shouldn't have, things he wouldn't understand, anyway. "I don't know if I can do this, stop a crazy woman who hates me and I don't know why, not completely. God, I want a normal life. Boring, normal, safe. Oh, that sounds so good. Why do I have to save the frigging world again? Thought I could follow her into the past and keep her from getting so much dark magic, but I failed. I suck."

Nevan stroked my hair. "You are brave and clever and very, very powerful. Whatever troubles you speak of, I am certain you shall prevail."

"I used to think that. Not so sure anymore."

"Accept my word on this. You will prevail." He kissed the top of my head. "Rest, angel Lindsey. All will seem better once you are rested."

Unable to keep my eyes open any longer, I let them flutter shut. As I drifted off to sleep, a tingling sensation swept through my body, a soothing indication my powers were recovering.

It felt like I slept for days.

When I woke, I lay in Nevan's arms as before. His eyes were closed, his breathing regular and shallow. He'd fallen asleep too. Stretching as much as I could with his body cradling mine, I yawned loudly.

Nevan roused and yawned too. "How do you feel?"

"Much better. How long was I out?"

"Several hours."

I sat up and stretched some more. "Gotta get moving."

Though I felt reinvigorated in body and in powers, I suffered from a niggling doubt about my ability to defeat Aello. It seemed no matter what I did, she was two steps ahead. Maybe if I had full control of my powers...

But I didn't. Aello had abducted the one being who could teach me how to use these magics that simmered inside me.

Nevan sat up and bracketed my face with his hands. "Your doubts are plain to see on your angelic face, love. Whoever this enemy is that you must defeat, you must believe you can do it. Otherwise, you will fail."

"I know. Not as easy as it sounds to regain my self-confidence. Regenerating my powers is a piece of cake in comparison."

"While I do not understand how a slice of cake relates to your powers, I gather the phrase indicates one thing is simpler than the other."

"Yes." I ran my hands through my hair, doing my best to comb out the bed-head look with my fingers. "Maybe too much time travel has knocked me off kilter."

"Whatever it is you need to accomplish, you will succeed."

"Your confidence in me is sweet, but I have no clue how to do what needs to be done."

He thrust his hands into my hair, hauling me in for a kiss. The merging of our lips and our tongues enlivened my body, awakening parts of me that never failed to perk up whenever he touched me. As much as I would've loved to indulge in another steamy encounter with him, I really needed to move ahead with the Aello hunt.

But oh, his kiss made me long to forget everything, to drown in him.

When he pulled away, he kept his hands in my hair, his fingers massaging my scalp. "You are a miracle, Lindsey, and you have the power to succeed."

His words penetrated to the deepest parts of my soul. His belief in me gave me hope and strength, no matter which version of him spoke those words. I wanted to thank him for that so badly but knew I couldn't.

Instead, I told him, "You are the miracle, Nevan. Whenever I need a boost to keep going, you give it to me. Even in this time, when we barely know each other, you understand what I need better than I do."

Nevan skated his hands down my arms. "You were glowing while you slept."

"What?" I looked at my body but saw no such glow. "I couldn't have been."

"You were." He slid his hand down past my wrist to lace his fingers with mine. "Even while you sleep, you rejuvenate your powers."

Daráine had mentioned I glowed, and I'd seen it in my reflection in the water. I had no doubt the Nevan in my century would've mentioned it if I gave off an ethereal light while I snoozed. Only since I'd traveled back in time had my magic changed, seeming to grow from the contact with the time stream. I had no idea why that would be or what it meant.

My questions concerning Aello's motives and plans seemed more pressing. If she wanted me gone, why did she keep attacking Nevan? She tried to get gnomes to murder him, and she'd manipulated time itself in her attempts to get rid of him. My encounters with her in the past made it clear she despised me and blamed me for something. It seemed to involve her desire to have "blood offspring" with Notus, but he preferred ready-made soldiers.

Nevan had once told me elementals considered pregnancy to be unseemly and that they preferred to connive to increase their numbers via the forging. He'd also said the forging demanded a hefty price in suffering. I had witnessed that aspect. Nevan suffered for days after his transformation.

"I am glad to have seen you again," he said, lifting my hand to kiss each knuckle, "even if only for a short while. All these years, I have wondered what became of you. I have missed your light and your sweet presence."

His words set off a warmth that bloomed out through my chest, but they left me with an uneasy feeling in my gut. Nevan of the future had confessed to me he'd slept around for a long time before he became the guardian of the falls. After that, his search for the Janusite made elemental females turn their snooty little noses up at him. He had to kiss mortal woman as part of the test to determine which one might be the Janusite, and those elemental women thought his duty tainted him. Before that, he'd been a player.

And he knew nothing about me until the day we met.

Yet Nevan of this time had thought about me for over three hundred years.

I chewed the inside of my cheek for a moment. "During all this time I was away, did you…um…fool around with other women?"

His lips curved into a tender smile, and he traced a fingertip down my cheek. "In all my existence, I have been with but two women—my wife and you. Since the day I first saw you, I have wanted no one else."

Okay, that begged another question. If he'd wanted only me, why did he fool around in the future? He'd kept it up until the day Skeiron enslaved him, commanding him to search for the Janusite. It made no sense. How had Nevan forgotten me after retaining the memory of our first meeting for more than three centuries? Why would he forget?

Someone must have forced him to forget.

I considered the idea Aello might have messed with his memories, but that didn't jibe with what I knew about her. She wanted to take Nevan away from me for good, not fiddle with his recollections.

As much as I longed to linger here, ensconced in Nevan's arms, I had to track down Aello.

"Wish I could stay," I said, "but I have problems of world-shattering importance to deal with."

"I understand. Any chance I could be of assistance?"

Oh, I would've loved some backup, especially of the Nevan variety, but I wouldn't risk Aello getting her bony fingers on him or anywhere in the vicinity of him.

"You are so sweet," I said, and kissed him. "But I have to do this alone."

He nodded his understanding, though he looked bummed about it. Really bummed.

An impulse overpowered my good sense, and I kissed him again, hard. "I love you, Nevan. I always have and I always will. No matter what time or place we find ourselves in, you are the only man who will ever lay claim to a piece of my soul."

"I love you too, Lindsey. It's inexplicable but undeniable. I will wait until the end of eternity for you."

The end of eternity. I would live a finite mortal life while he would live forever. Since the moment I'd realized I loved him, I had worried what might happen to him after I died. Knowing our bond transcended time, I feared even more for his future after me. Eternity alone.

If he'd forgotten about me once, he might do it again. I prayed he would. Never would I wish for him to suffer.

Throwing my arms around him, I hugged him so tight he choked back a gasp. "We'll see each other again, I promise."

I let go of him and zipped away, rendering myself invisible at the instant the time stream spit me out inside a gloomy cave. Nevan lived underground, but not in a cave. His home, our home, was carved out of the guts of a mountain by magic rather than by natural processes. The fae witch Ennea did her work inside a cave, but it had a homey feel thanks to the golden light of oil lamps and the scents of various potions and magical ingredients. Sometimes her laboratory smelled like a kitchen.

This place stank of damp, rotting earth and decomposing flesh with a hint of an unspecific fetid stench. *Lovely.*

As my vision adjusted to the gloom, I realized the only light came from an open fire burning on the other side of the space. A pile of wood, everything from twigs and leaves to rough-cut logs, blazed with yellowish-orange flames. The smoke spiraled up toward the ceiling and snaked out through a dark hole in the cave's roof.

In front of the fire hunched a wizened old man dressed in filthy robes. His long gray hair was too dingy to be called silver, and his scruffy beard seemed in need of grooming.

Before him stood Aello and Notus.

The sylph king stared straight ahead with bleary eyes, his jaw slack, and swayed ever so slightly.

The harpy had done more than force him into a life debt. She seemed to have enchanted him too, or more likely, ensorcelled him. Once, I'd watched Nevan enchant a girl as part of the test to determine if she had a touch of the Unseen realm in her, a prerequisite for being the Janusite, or so Skeiron had believed. That girl, Sandy, had seemed dazed. Notus behaved like he had no mind of his own.

What on earth did Aello have planned for him?

"Sorcerer," Aello said, lifting her chin, "how dare you leave me to wait outside your lair."

The old man squinted at Aello. "Why have you returned? The magic infusion I provided to you three days agone is all I can give. You know this."

His voice was reedy but clear, unlike his cloudy eyes.

"I need more," Aello said. She pointed a talon at Notus. "This one must be made to do my will."

"Control spells are dangerous." The sorcerer eyed Notus. "As is prolonged ensorcellment. If you leave him in this state, he will become mindless but not in the way you wish."

"Infuse me with more dark magic, so I might handle him myself."

The sorcerer tipped his head back, aiming a cold glare at Aello. "Infusions are not gifts, harpy. They come at a price."

"Name it."

He scratched his chin, toying with his long beard. "Bring me a fae child. Male, preferably. Only then will I consider providing another infusion."

Aello's lips peeled back in the closest approximation of a smile she seemed able to pull off. "I anticipated your request. Since last time you desired a fae girl, I knew you would ask for a male this time."

She had given this creep a little girl? What the hell had he done with the child?

The harpy waved her hand.

A boy of seven or eight appeared beside her, his hands and feet bound with rope and a gag in his mouth.

The sorcerer reached for the boy.

Aello smacked his hand away. "After the infusion."

I needed to stop this, all of it. Her infusion, whatever the hell that meant, and the payment in the form of a child.

The sorcerer gestured for Aello to kneel.

She sank to her knees, tilting her head back and opening her mouth.

He held a hand in front of her mouth, bending his fingers as if he held an invisible ball.

I summoned all the power inside me and hurled an orb of blue energy at the sorcerer. It slammed into his chest, reeling him backward. I lobbed another orb at him. He staggered backward, gurgling and clawing at his singed chest. Tendrils of glittering blue energy crawled over his skin, spreading outward from his chest into his arms and legs and up his throat. Soon, the magic engulfed him.

He stumbled into the fire.

And his body splintered.

Chapter Twenty-Six

No blood or guts spewed forth from the sorcerer. He broke apart into black-and-purple shards, and his disassembled body melted into a seething cloud of the same colors. The robes he'd worn crumpled into the flames of the burning fire, igniting and disintegrating within seconds. The dark magics his death had unleashed spread outward in a mass of roiling, screaming energy that sought a new host.

A tongue of dark magic licked at me, then recoiled.

I grabbed the fae boy and sent him home. How I did it, I had no clue. I wanted him to go back to his family, and he went. I sensed he was safe and where he belonged.

Notus remained dazed and seemingly unaware of everything unfolding around him.

Aello, still on her knees, opened her mouth wider and flung her arms out. "Take me, I welcome you into my body."

Oh hell no. This was my chance to prevent her from becoming unstoppable. I hurled orb after orb at the mass of black energy, but every one of them ricocheted and hit the wall, the ceiling, the floor. One orb nicked Notus, who gave no reaction. I kept firing off balls of blue power, funneling more and more of myself into the effort.

The dark magics flooded into Aello through her mouth.

Her body convulsed. She screamed, but the power burrowing into her muffled the sound.

Gasping for breath, I stopped throwing orbs. It was too late.

The last wisp of darkness rushed inside Aello. She dragged in a deep, rasping breath and gusted it out. A sick kind of glee overtook her features, and she let out an ear-splitting cackle. Why couldn't I stop this? No matter what I did, she won. The Janusite was supposed to be the most powerful being ever to have lived. How could I not defeat one crazy creature?

Because I had not yet embraced the full spectrum of my powers. Deep inside, I feared what might happen to me if I did. Oh, I told everyone I was cool with these powers. I'd even convinced myself of that. Here in this terrible place, confronted with another resounding failure, I at last faced up to the truth.

I was too damn scared to accept all the gifts the Four Winds had infused into me.

Aello got to her feet haltingly and turned toward Notus. She took his face in her hands. Her talons scratched his skin, drawing beads of blood. "Henceforth, you shall worship me as if I were your queen. You are correct, however, that I should not become your queen in fact. I will rule your kingdom through you. The power I have acquired will ensure this."

She sank her talons into his flesh. Crimson rivulets dribbled down his face. Black-and-purple strands of dark magics seeped out of her talons into his blood and slithered up the rivulets into his veins. He twitched and gurgled, his eyes rolling back into his head.

Aello released him. "Look at me."

Notus obeyed.

"What are you?" she asked.

"I am yours, my beloved." He smiled, slung an arm around her waist, and hauled her into his body. "We shall rule the worlds together. The dark magics we share grant us all the power we need."

Aello's gaze zeroed in on me. "You have lost your cloak, Janusite. And you have lost yet another battle with me."

I hadn't quite regained my breath from my magical exertions. Perspiration ran down my temples and into my eyes. It mutated into a cold sweat that chilled me to the core. Even if I'd had a clue what to say, my voice would've refused to work.

"Do not despair," Aello said in a sickly sweet tone, "I shall not kill your beloved sylph—not yet. He will serve Notus, and by extension me, obeying our commands without realizing his king has become a servant of the darkness. I shall enjoy deceiving the poor fool and keeping him from you." She raised one taloned finger. "The longings of his heart will pain him far more than any physical distress."

She flicked her finger.

A force like an invisible maelstrom sucked me into the time stream, propelling me forward and out into the world again.

I struck the ground face first, the breath knocked out of me, stars bursting in my vision. For the longest moment of my life, I lay there unable to move. Every bone in my body ached. Slowly, I pushed myself up onto all fours. Then, I sat back on my haunches to study my surroundings. I'd landed in a cemetery of all places, one I did not recognize. The landscape looked different too, and I knew I wasn't in Michigan anymore. Broken headstones were scattered around me. This place seemed familiar, but I couldn't quite place it. I'd returned to the present, but where in the world was I?

"Nevan!" I shouted. "Max!"

They materialized in front of me.

Nevan dropped to his knees before me and clutched my upper arms. "Why did you not come to us? What is wrong?"

"Aello clobbered me again." I shut my eyes for a moment, then met Nevan's worried gaze. "She tossed me back to the present. No, that's not right. The present-day Aello dragged me back here at the same instant the past Aello evicted me. I can feel that's what happened. I couldn't stop her, I couldn't change anything, I—"

He pulled me into his arms, my face buried against his neck. "You are exhausted, love. How much power did you employ to fight Aello?"

"Too much, twice." I raised my head. "Do you remember when we first met?"

"Of course. Slightly more than three months ago, by the waterfall."

"Nothing before that?"

"Should I recall an earlier event?"

"No, never mind." I let my forehead drop onto his shoulder. "Nothing makes sense anymore."

Nevan murmured soothing sounds and caressed my back, but even that could not expunge the guilt of my latest failure.

I curled my fingers into his chest. "Did you at least succeed in your part of the plan?"

"We ransacked Aello's nest, yes. She did not come, however, and so we left."

Another plan gone kablooey.

"Just wondering," Max said, "why are we in a cemetery? And where are we? This doesn't look like Mandan County."

"It's not," I said, raising my head again. I glanced around and suddenly realized why the landscape seemed familiar. "We're in Kentucky. This looks like the area where my parents live."

"Why would Aello dump you here?"

"Beats me." I rifled through my memories of everything I'd seen and learned during my trip into the past. "Aello put some kind of spell on Notus to make him do what she wanted. She must've ensorcelled him, and maybe that's why Notus turned into a sleaze. Aello's voodoo wrung his brain dry."

One corner of Nevan's mouth lifted. "I do adore your colorful descriptions."

I started to reply but didn't get the chance.

The earth trembled beneath us, vibrating into our bodies. The shaking escalated into rocking and rolling so fast none of us had time to react. The ground heaved upward and split apart. Headstones tumbled into the newly created chasm even as the earth continued to rumble and rock beneath us. At the instant the earthquake unleashed its final shiver and settled into an eerie calm, a shock of paranormal origins walloped me. I spluttered and twitched, struggling for breath.

Nevan held me until the effect waned.

"What was that?" he asked.

"Another time shift." I swallowed, my throat tight and dry. "A much bigger one."

Max took a step toward us and vanished.

I jerked, stunned by a realization I could not deny or explain. He was gone. Dead. Erased.

"No!" I shouted. I tried to stand, but Nevan held me fast.

"Lindsey, look." With one finger, he rotated my face toward a headstone a few feet away. "The time shift, it has…"

He trailed off, shaking his head in disbelief.

The headstone read, "Lindsey Astrid Porter, beloved daughter."

I leaned closer, staring at the date of death. I had died on the day I was born.

"That's impossible," I said. "Aello couldn't have murdered me. I'm right here."

"You are one with time," Nevan said calmly, despite the fear in his eyes. "She cannot remove you from it."

"But she took away my life." My gaze bounced here and there, a frantic search for something I prayed not to find—until I found it. "No."

The syllable came out as a gasp.

Nevan followed my line of sight, and his arms clinched me harder.

Two more headstones accompanied mine. The names on them identified the deceased as Kenneth Porter and Lucinda Porter. They'd died the same day I had.

My brother had never been born.

I scrambled to my feet, kicking Nevan in the stomach in my haste to get up. He paid no attention to the kick and sprang to his feet. We faced each other, bound by our bewilderment and fear.

Aello blinked into view right behind Nevan.

Before I could shout a warning or shove him out of the way, she rammed a sword straight through his body. Its tip protruded from his chest, blood dripping from it.

"No!" I screamed.

The harpy ripped the sword out of his body.

Nevan slumped to his knees, hands clutching his gut, blood dribbling from his lips and between his fingers.

"I have won again," Aello boasted. "Pitiful Janusite, you will never defeat me."

Roaring with an unholy rage, I ran straight at her.

She vanished.

I stumbled and fell to my knees. Scrambling around, I got in front of Nevan again.

He slumped against me and mumbled, "Endued sword."

"Shit." With one arm, I held him against me. My free hand trembled as I touched the gaping wound. *Not again, no not again.* Memories of the last time he'd been skewered by an endued sword replayed in my mind. Tears flowed down my cheeks. I cupped his face, not giving a damn that I was smearing his own blood on his cheek. "You can't leave me like this. Hold on, Nevan, please."

He tried to speak but managed only to cough up more blood.

I threw my head back and screamed, "Tris!"

Nothing.

"Triskaideka!" I bellowed. "Get out here this minute!"

A frigid certainty echoed inside me. Tris wouldn't come. He couldn't hear my call because Aello had destroyed him and Ennea too. Every ally, every friend, I'd ever had was gone. I was alone. While tears poured down my face, hot and bitter, I crushed Nevan to my chest. Sobbing, I begged for a miracle. None came.

He sucked in a wet, rattling breath. The swirling colors in his eyes went dark. His chest no longer rose and fell, and the sizzling heat of his skin cooled.

I shrieked wordlessly, mindless with a grief I'd never believed I would know. He was immortal. I'd worried about how he would feel when I died, but not...not this.

For a long, long time I stayed there with him clasped to my breast. Eventually, the tears dried up. I laid Nevan on the ground, kissed him one last time, and got to my feet, staggering slightly.

"Ah!" I screamed at the heavens. "Why do I have these powers if I can't stop a harpy from destroying the world? What good is being the Janusite?" I shook my fists in the air. "Why did you do this to me? I never wanted these powers. I can't even use them to keep an evil bitch from killing everyone I love. What's the point?"

When no one and nothing responded, I closed my eyes. Freaking out wouldn't fix anything. I needed to suck it up, get hold of myself, and think. Aello might have eradicated everyone I loved, but nothing that happened was unfixable. Whatever she could do, I could undo if only I summoned the willpower and magic to do it.

Seconds ticked by, maybe minutes, maybe longer. I concentrated on my breathing. In, out. In, out. Let my mind empty, thoughts and worries gone. In, out. In, out.

An idea hit me like a bolt of lightning. If I needed to stop a wind goddess, I should talk to the ultimate wind deities. The Four Winds.

I had no idea exactly where their temple was. Nevan had taken us there last time. These frigging powers of mine had to be good for something. They would get me there, they had to. Without conscious thought to do it, I whisked myself to the wind-swept mountaintop where the Temple of the Four Winds resided.

Chapter Twenty-Seven

THE FIRST TIME I'D VISITED THIS PLACE, WITH NEVAN AND MAX, WE had touched down on the side of the mountain and awaited permission to enter the fog-shrouded temple. Today, I popped out on the mountaintop at the base of the long series of steps that led up to the temple. A light fog surrounded the huge structure, with its Corinthian columns and massive wooden doors. The temple was composed of white stones that shined with an ethereal glow thanks to the sunlight filtering through the fog. The place seemed like a mirage or a dream, but I knew it was real. Where in the world it was located, I couldn't say. The location hardly mattered.

Steep steps embedded in the mountain stretched up the long rise to the portico where a shallower series of steps led up to the doors. The temple boasted powerful wards that prevented anyone from teleporting in its vicinity or inside its walls. So, I trudged up the steps the old-fashioned way. My legs ached by the time I reached the portico. There, I paused to catch my breath, from the hike and from the thinner air up here.

My chest ached too, though not from the altitude. Last time, Nevan had stopped several times on our journey up the mountain to literally breathe fresh air into my lungs. Today, I had to endure the journey on my own. Even with Nevan gone, I managed to tap into his air powers and refresh myself.

Did that mean he wasn't completely gone? *No wishful thinking, it's bad for you.*

With a thunderous grinding noise, the doors crept inward.

Oh yeah, I remembered the racket those doors made. My bones vibrated from it.

This was all the invitation I would receive. I rolled my shoulders back and slogged up the remaining steps and through the doors. A breeze, tepid and gentle, investigated me like phantom fingertips. My hair ruffled, and goosebumps cropped up on my skin. Yes, I recalled this too. The arduous hike up the steps was a test of my commitment to meeting the Four Winds. The breeze feeling me up was their way of determining whether I belonged here.

The breeze faded away, but no one appeared.

"Hello?" I called out. "Please, I need to talk to you. Something terrible has happened."

A female figure winked into view an arm's length in front of me.

Her white robes dragged on the polished stone floor but left her arms and head exposed. The paleness of her skin matched the white of her hair, but her eyes were a pure, glossy black and seemed to lead down into an abyss from which no mere mortal would return. A chill whispered through me, stiffening the hairs at my nape.

"Thank you," I said.

My admission of gratitude, and my previous use of the P-word, failed to cause even a whiff of a debt. This place, I sensed, had its own rules.

The wind-being canted her head, her expression curious and yet remote. The female Wind looked every bit like an avatar of power and a guardian of magical energies.

"Lindsey Astrid Porter," she said in a voice both alien and ethereal, like a mystical breeze wafting around me. "You seek our assistance. For what purpose?"

"Don't you know what's going on out there? Aello—"

"Has disrupted and contaminated the proper flow of time." The wind-being rose to hover a few inches above the floor, her robes dangling. "We are aware of this. It is your duty to repair the damage."

"I've tried, honestly I have. Nothing works." Snapshots of memory flashed in my mind. The gravestones. Max vanishing. Nevan…I sucked in a breath, tears stinging in my eyes. "I don't have the power to stop her, much less reverse what she's done."

"You are incorrect." She floated back down to the floor, her black gaze sharpening on me. "The Janusite was created for this purpose. It is your destiny."

"Aello has so much dark magic, I can't—"

"Silence!" The wind-being's voice ricocheted off the walls. She seized my chin between her thumb and forefinger, the frigidness of her flesh infecting mine. Her tone became stern, almost like a parent chastising a child. "You are the Janusite, the one being in all of eternity imbued with the essence of the god Janus, but you are much more than a vessel. You have accomplished feats Janus never achieved. Your power grows, even as you deny it. Nothing holds you back except your fears."

Hot tears trickled down my face. "I don't know how to stop Aello. I went back in time to keep her from getting all that power, but I failed. Again."

The wind-being's gaze bored into mine for a long, agonizing moment. The darkness of her eyes captured my focus, and the intensity of her gaze drilled straight down into my soul. Finally, she released my chin and said, "You work toward the wrong goal."

I flapped my arms and my head. "Then tell me what the hell I'm supposed to be doing. Please."

"We cannot. You must arrive at the proper conclusion of your own volition."

"Just what do you think I've been doing?" A single sob burst out of me, and my knees buckled. I hit the floor hard, pain arcing through my legs. "I tried. I can't do this alone. You need to stop Aello, you're the only ones who can."

The wind-being watched me, her mood unreadable, her air of remoteness becoming more pronounced. A faint breeze tousled her white hair.

My head fell forward, my shoulders caved in, and I wept.

She touched my shoulder.

I lifted my head to find her kneeling before me, her black eyes softened to a silvery gray with distinct dark pupils.

"Lindsey," she said, her voice softer too, like a warm summer breeze. "Perhaps we have asked too much of you. Pouring these powers into your mortal mind and body without a thought for how you would assimilate them, it was an oversight on our part."

My jaw went slack. Had a mystical avatar of power admitted to screwing up? Yeah, she had. Not for the first time either. Two months ago, she'd admitted she and her three windy friends had messed up when they failed to stop the sorcerer from absorbing the essences of Notus, Skeiron, and Calder.

Miraculously, I summoned my voice. "Why did you release Janus? He wants his powers back, you know."

"We are aware, and in time, you shall understand the reasons."

"Am I supposed to give him back these powers?"

"Only you may decide." The wind-being rose, her eyes turning black again. "To defeat Aello, you must answer one question. What are you willing to sacrifice to heal the time stream?"

"You mean what else. I've sacrificed everyone I love and still can't win."

"What you have lost thus far is not gone. You continue to limit your thoughts to a mortal perspective." She leaned in, her hair billowing in a wind I did not feel. "You are the Janusite."

This being expected me to understand her meaning. I didn't. My brain and body were exhausted, my powers were dwindling again, and I couldn't puzzle out any of this.

I'd worked toward the wrong goal, she had said a minute ago. *Duh.* Every plan I'd come up with had cratered, even when I managed to reverse one of her time shifts. Going back in time hadn't worked either. How could I beat the harpy when she wielded so much dark magic? Max had been erased, which meant somehow Aello had circumvented his life debt to me and rendered him no longer immune to the shifts.

So much power.

Was Janus no longer immune too? And what had Aello done with him?

I retained my powers, meaning Janus did not have them. Aello couldn't strip away my immunity to the timeline changes. Not yet. Back in the cemetery, I'd experienced an epiphany of the sucky kind, realizing the root of my problems. Now, I raised my eyes to the enigmatic being who hovered before me.

"Nothing I do works," I said, "because I'm afraid of my powers. You said as much a minute ago."

She nodded.

"If my fears are holding me back, how do I get over them?" I flattened my palms on my thighs, and my fingers bent of their own accord, scratching on my leather pants. "Aello has taken everything. I don't have the luxury of figuring out why I'm afraid. She will keep screwing with the timeline until she breaks it, won't she?"

The wind-being nodded again.

"What do I do?" I spread my hands, palms up. "Please, give me a hint."

"All that you require is inside you. Look to your natural power for the answer."

I felt my brows squish together, tightening my forehead. "I don't understand."

"Your natural power is what you have always possessed." The wind-being bent from the waist to level our gazes. "Harness your spirit and your strength of will, the only powers that will never desert you. If you require more strength, seek it from your heart, not your magic."

She straightened and began to float backward.

"Wait," I said. "May I ask one more question?"

The being stopped moving. "You may."

"Why did Nevan not remember meeting me in the past?"

"You know the answer."

I started to protest but clapped my jaw shut. Did I know? How could I? Nevan seemed to remember everything else about his past but not the time we'd spent together after his forging and, three centuries later, after the gnome battle.

My spine snapped straight as a realization zapped through me. Oh, it couldn't be.

"You understand," the wind-being said.

The weird part was, I did get it. "I'm going to ask you to make him forget, so he won't spend thousands of years longing for me but not knowing when or if he'll see me again."

She gazed at me from so nearby yet remained as remote as a distant galaxy. Her lips twitched the tiniest bit. Almost a smile? Nah, it couldn't have been.

But maybe it was.

I scrambled to my feet. "Please make sure Nevan forgets having met me in the past when I time-traveled to him. You can do that, right?"

"We can, and we will. The sylph will lose all memory of those visitations." The wind-being swept closer and leaned in low, her face inches from mine. Her eyes turned a very human shade of gray-blue. "He will forget until the present and the past become one."

Sure, whatever that meant.

"I don't suppose," I said, "you have any advice for me? About what to do next? I appreciate your advice about how to get past my fears, but I don't know how to beat Aello."

Her humanlike eyes reverted to pure black. "I have told you all I can. You must speak with the oracle." She opened her palm, revealing sprigs of a leafy green plant. "And feed him this."

Warily, I plucked the sprigs from her hand. "The oracle. You mean Bob, right?"

She vanished in a burst of wind.

Chat over. Elementals really knew nothing about politeness.

Nevan did. He was chivalrous and brave and—

I squeezed my eyes shut, determined not to cry again. Whatever lay ahead of me, I needed all my faculties and powers intact for it. I could not afford to be saddled with grief and guilt. Nevan would want me to stay strong. I would do it for him.

After one last glance around the Temple of the Four Winds, I hurried out the doors. They shut behind me with an earsplitting grinding noise. Fog enshrouded the temple as I trudged down the long, long series of steps until I'd moved outside the wards. I blinked myself into the Unseen, to the edge of the dark and slimy forest that concealed Bob's lair.

If a single one of the kerkopes attacked me this time, I'd slice the creature in half with a bolt of pure magic. No more polite Lindsey. Nobody murdered everyone I loved, murdered me, and got away with it. The wind-being had sent me here, so Bob must have some answers.

Awareness prickled my skin, lifting the hairs on my arms. I didn't need to trek through the creepy forest like I had before, I realized. I could teleport myself directly into Bob's lair because his wards were down.

Not good, not good at all.

I zipped myself into the chamber hidden within, or perhaps beneath, a gigantic boulder. I'd never quite understood the geography of this place. A semi-translucent coating of pale gold gave the dark, rock-hewn walls an otherworldly quality appropriate for the den of an oracle. A fire burned within a five-foot-wide bronze bowl perched atop legs with cat-like feet. The flames writhed and licked at the air as if they were alive, their amber color evoking Nevan's eyes.

My throat constricted, my chest too. I would get him back, somehow, some way.

What are you willing to sacrifice to heal the time stream?

The wind-being's words echoed in my brain, but I refused to answer that question. Soon I might have to, but not yet.

I squinted into the firelit gloom of the cavern, searching for a sign of the oracle. "Bob? Are you here?"

A groan drew my attention to the shadows beyond the living flames. I trotted around the bronze bowl, spotted a figure slumped against the wall, and veered toward it. Bob aimed bleary, bloodshot eyes at me as I dropped to my knees in front of him. He sat propped against the wall, his legs splayed wide. His navy-blue suit was rumpled, and his skin had turned a grayish green.

"Here," I said, thrusting the leafy sprigs the wind-being had given me at him. "You're supposed to eat this."

Bob tried to lift a hand, but it fell back down to his lap.

Holding the sprigs near his mouth, I made a train-like chugging sound. "Open up, let the choo choo in."

Despite his obvious distress, he pulled off an irritated look even as he opened his mouth.

I stuffed the sprigs in there.

He chewed hesitantly at first, then began to chomp with vigor. The sprigs sticking out of his mouth got pulled in, masticated, and swallowed within seconds. The grayish-green tone of his skin warmed into a healthier shade. His eyes ignited with green fire.

Bob sighed, his lips curving into a relaxed smile. "I needed that."

"What was that stuff?"

"Medicinal herbs." He raised his brows. "They're hard to come by. How did you get them?"

"One of the Four Winds told me to give them to you."

"Miriella," he said with a wistful tone and a smile to match. "She still cares, even though we broke up when I became an oracle."

"You had a thing with one of the Four Winds?"

"A long time ago." He pushed up with his hands, straightening his posture. "Never mind that. You want to know how to defeat Aello."

"Are you saying you know how I can do that?"

"I'm not a vending machine for answers. Stuff a little medicine in my mouth and I spit out a plan? That's not how this works."

Folding my arms over my chest, I said, "You're grumpy from your time-shift migraine. Do you have any insight or not?"

"Sure, I've got insight." He closed his eyes, and the flames behind me flared high and bright. "You cannot divest Aello of the dark magics. Only by finding a way around them can you bring an end to her reign of terror."

"The harpy has too much power."

Bob let out a frustrated sigh. "I know you're upset about Nevan, but you need to focus. The answers await if only you open your third eye to see them. You are the Janusite, Lindsey. Remember the prophecy."

"That's all you've got."

"Yes, but it's more than enough."

I bowed my head and grasped the back of my neck. More than enough? I understood Bob was not a vending machine for answers and that even an oracle had limitations, but I'd hoped for a less-fuzzy insight from him. Riddles made my head hurt.

Bob settled a hand on my shoulder. "What you've lost is not gone for good. Not this time."

Miriella had made a similar proclamation.

I dropped my hands and lifted my head. "Are you saying I can get Nevan back?"

"You can do whatever you need to do." He got to his feet, stretched, and yawned. Then, he offered me his hand and helped me up. "Look to your lineage and you will find the answer to a question you've asked since the day you opened your eyes and your mind to your destiny."

My destiny seemed to be to watch everyone I loved die. Repeatedly.

Cut the self-pity, woman. It won't get them back.

Bob took hold of my hands, his fiery green gaze locked onto me. "Here's the only piece of concrete advice I can give you. Pay one last visit to the past and you will understand Aello's true motivations."

"Any particular time in the past?"

He touched one glowing fingertip to my forehead.

Energy zapped me, firing straight into my brain.

"There," Bob said, stepping back. "That will get you where you need to go. Good luck, Lindsey."

"Isn't wishing me luck a no-no in the Unseen?"

"No, luck is not a debt. Not even a tiny one."

"Glad to hear it."

His gaze zeroed in on mine again, his eyes aflame with that preternatural green glow. "Do you remember what I said about true chaos?"

"It will happen if Aello breaks the timeline."

Bob slanted closer, and his voice grew softer, deeper, darker, infused with the weight of wisdom and certainty. "Chaos is coming."

He tapped my forehead, and I tumbled into the time stream.

Chapter Twenty-Eight

I MATERIALIZED INSIDE A CLEARING IN THE WOODS IN THE UNSEEN, based on the mossy foliage on the trees and the unnaturally azure color of the sky. My invisibility spell activated the second I touched down, shielding me from the view of the two men half a dozen feet away.

Not mere men. Sylphs. They both wore obsidian armor that glinted in shades of forest green in the sunlight. Each sylph brandished a sword, his posture battle ready. One sylph had platinum-blond hair, the other black.

Skeiron and Notus.

I hung back at the edge of the clearing, knowing I needed to observe whatever was about to go down here. This must've been the moment when Skeiron defeated Notus using the dark magics he had acquired. The dark magics Aello had invested him with.

Notus chuckled darkly. "You lack the strength to overthrow me, Skeiron. I, however, lay claim to more than enough power to smite you for this blatant attempt to usurp the throne."

Skeiron twirled his sword, aiming the point at Notus. "You, my king, have become a monster. I will end your reign this day. For the good of the kingdom."

Wow, Skeiron sounded like he meant it. Nevan had told me Skeiron used to be a decent guy and that he'd been a good king at first. The dark magics he'd absorbed to win his battle with Notus hadn't consumed him until later. I sensed the power within him, but it paled compared to the seething energies within Notus.

The king raised his sword upright, sunlight glancing off its tip. "This is your last chance to end this blasphemy."

"Blasphemy?" Skeiron sneered. "You are no god."

"Are you certain of that?" Notus spread his arms, unleashing green currents of magic that spun around him. "With power such as this, I may as well be a god."

"Never will I bow down to you."

"Do you believe you have a choice?"

Notus thrust out a hand, unfurling serpents of dark energy from his palm. The magic lashed out at Skeiron, whipping around his body and descending on him with such force his knees bent and pain contorted his features. Skeiron roared and punched his sword through the blanket of dark magic.

The energy shattered. Glistening particles rained down.

Notus thrust out his palm again.

Skeiron charged his king, plunging his sword into Notus's heart.

The king froze, his eyes wide. His sword slipped from his grasp.

"I have a choice," Skeiron growled as he ripped the sword from his king's chest.

Notus fell to his knees, gurgling, blood dribbling from his mouth. He collapsed to the ground face-first.

Despite Notus's greater magics, he had fallen. Skeiron must have acquired an endued sword. Notus had arrogantly assumed his underling could not best him, what with the boiling, vile crap Aello had funneled into him. But Skeiron, invested with dark magics he'd somehow obtained and armed with an endued weapon, had amassed just enough power to oust his king.

Skeiron snatched up Notus's sword, turning it in his hand, studying it with a strange expression.

He vanished.

I was about to leave, wondering why the hell I'd needed to witness this, when Aello appeared beside Notus.

The harpy knelt and laid a hand on his head, her eyes churning with ice blue amid the pure black of her irises. She clenched her jaw and hissed through her teeth, "He will pay for this, my love. You served me well, and no one takes away what is mine."

She hovered her palms over his body. The dark magics contained within Notus flowed out of him and into her hands. The king's flesh dissolved, and the bones disintegrated. Nothing remained except a coating of pale dust.

Aello poofed away.

I followed. Not sure how I did it, but I'd stopped trying to figure out everything. The wind-being, Miriella, had said it was my duty and my destiny to repair the damage to the time stream. Bob had told me I must take one more trip to the past so I could understand Aello's true motivations. Both of those tasks revolved around the harpy. I had to follow her.

We emerged simultaneously, the harpy and I, inside an underground space that had no exterior door, like Nevan's lair. Unlike his home, which felt comfortable and welcoming, this space seemed utilitarian. A straw mat served as a bed with only a roll of fabric as a pillow.

Skeiron hunkered in the center of the room, naked, holding a white toga in front of his body as if about to cover himself with it.

Aello tilted her head left and right, her eyes sparking with fiery red. She skimmed her gaze up and down his muscular body and ran her tongue over her bottom lip. Her hand seemed to move unconsciously to her throat, and her fingers petted her skin. She was attracted to Skeiron.

Why oh why, Bob, do I need to see this? If these two made out, I'd lose my lunch.

Not that I'd eaten lunch. When had I last consumed food of any kind? Breakfast this morning. God, I could hardly believe everything I'd experienced, including the days I'd spent with Nevan after his forging, had taken up less than one day in the present. Or the future. Whatever. In my time, the place where I belonged, it must've been afternoon in the mortal world.

Aello slunk out from behind Skeiron, circling around to his front.

Skeiron went rigid, his gaze glued to the harpy. "How have you entered my home? It is protected by powerful wards."

"None as powerful as my magics."

Or mine, you whacked-out windbag.

"What does a harpy want with me?" Notus asked.

Aello slunk closer, rested a hand on his thick bicep, and tipped her head back to flutter her eyelashes at him. "You are strong and virile, an excellent candidate to be my lover and the father of my children. You defeated Notus in spite of the potent dark magics he carried. Yes, you would make an excellent slave."

Skeiron chuckled. "Slave? Harpies are as mad as the stories claim. I am to be king of the sylphs, not the slave of an unhinged creature."

"You will change your mind."

Aello's robes disappeared, revealing her perfect body with perky breasts neither too big nor too small, a flat stomach, and a narrow waist that flared into womanly hips. Her creamy skin accentuated the dusky pink of her nipples.

Red-hot fire ignited in Skeiron's eyes, his black pupils dilating.

The harpy glided her hand up and down his arm. "You may enjoy my body for the rest of eternity, so long as you do my bidding."

"I can have your body," he said, his voice husky, "with or without your permission. A female, even one as fetching as you, lacks the power to command a king."

"You are wrong." She flung a hand up in his face. "Heed my commands."

His features went slack, his gaze blank.

She wiggled her fingers, and slender threads of dark magic snaked up his nostrils. "Henceforth, you belong to me. I had thought to kill you for taking Notus from me, but you may prove a much better instrument than he ever was. You disobeyed your king, committed treason to depose him, and acquired dark power to do it. Nothing compared to my power, but impressive nonetheless."

Maybe this was what Bob had thought I needed to see. I inched forward, tiptoeing despite knowing she couldn't see me. My human brain didn't quite believe I was invisible.

Aello placed her hand on Skeiron's face. "Eventually, I will gift you with the dark magics I gave to Notus. First, you must prove yourself to be worthy. I will observe you for a time to determine your weaknesses and make certain you are the slave I have sought. Notus thought himself above such things, and it took centuries to make him ready for the power I had to offer, but my intuition suggests you will be more amenable to serving me."

She slid both palms down his bare chest.

The toga tumbled from his hands.

Aello explored his manly parts.

Fortunately, I couldn't see those parts of him from this angle. I didn't need to watch her molest him.

"You may wonder," she said, "why I do this."

I shuffled forward half a step, not wanting to miss a word. Her true motivations, revealed at last. I knew she wanted revenge on me for taking out Skeiron, and in a way, Notus too. I hadn't killed him, but I had destroyed the sorcerer who had ingested the essences of both sylph kings.

Aello stepped back from Skeiron, who remained ensorcelled. "I had sisters. Did you know that? We ruled the skies together and chose our mates from the Anemoi, the most powerful *daimones* of the cardinal winds, who possessed powers second only to the gods themselves. I was to become the mate of Zephyrus. I would have been a supreme queen among elementals."

She began to pace in front of Skeiron, her robes materializing around her body, the long hem dragging on the stone floor.

The soon-to-be king stood as motionless as a statue, which was what she had made him into with her magic. He would not move or speak or think until she released him from whatever ensorcellment she'd woven around him.

"My sister Celaeno became jealous," Aello said. "She seduced Zephyrus and became with child by him. I was handed over to Boreas as if I were a slave to be passed from male to male. But my sister Podarge had already installed herself as Boreas's favorite bedmate. Though he would wed me, he warned me he would continue to bed my sister as well. I refused the arrangement, so Boreas married Podarge instead." Aello gritted her teeth, her shoulders bunched and her talons flicking. "I will spare you the sordid details. My other sisters became involved as well, seducing whichever Anemoi would bed them, and soon we were all fighting each other. It was a stormy period in both realms, the skies and seas whipped into a frenzy by our fury with each other."

She whirled in a circle, growling like a rabid animal.

The details of this elemental soap opera were bizarre, but I didn't get how this triggered a plot to avenge her lost lovers on me.

Aello shut her eyes, seeming to exhale out the worst of her anger. Relatively calm again, she approached Skeiron. "My sisters banded together against me. I was banished from the palace of the Harpyiai, from my home. I wandered alone for centuries until I came upon a lonely sylph who had recently ascended the throne. Notus became my lover, promising to give me the blood children I longed for. But he betrayed me."

Here it comes, a voice inside me whispered, and I leaned forward in anticipation.

"'Everyone betrays me," Aello growled, spittle spraying from her lips. "Notus forged a mortal into a sylph warrior instead of giving me a child. I imbued him with the most fearsome power imaginable. Did he employ it to elevate me? Of course not. The treacherous toad fought my ensorcellment, regaining a sliver of free will. He used the magics I granted him to subjugate his people. You will serve me better, Skeiron, shan't you?"

She trailed the tip of one talon along his jaw.

A muscle ticked there as if deep inside he fought her ensorcellment. One day he would become as warped as Notus had thanks to the nasty side effects of the voodoo Aello had woven around him.

"Yes," she purred, "you will obey me. For I will not grant you these magics until you prove yourself a loyal thrall. No more treating a lover as my equal. You are mine to command and control. To achieve the ultimate power, I require a steadfast warrior by my side." She pressed her lips to his. "I consumed the magic of a dark soothsayer, did you know? I have seen the future, one that no wise and good oracle will envision for thousands of years to come."

The harpy waved her hand.

Skeiron's toga materialized around his body.

"You shall not know of that future yet," she said, "not until the prophecy is issued. But you, my pet sylph, shall fight for me during the battle to destroy the enemy I have seen so I might appropriate her power. Once, I was to have been a queen of the Anemoi. Then, I thought to become queen of the sylphs. I no longer care to reign over the pathetic kingdom of the sylphs or that of the Anemoi. I am destined to reign over two worlds, and every being within them shall fall to their knees at my feet."

She was insane. Totally, irretrievably insane. The soothsayer's magic had given her the ability to glimpse the future, and clearly, she had foreseen the rise of the Janusite. Despite her wackadoodle obsession with revenge, she would wait thousands of years for the chance to annihilate me. She would have no choice but to wait since she seemed not to have gained the ability to screw with time until my wedding day.

Lucky me.

"Unfortunately," Aello said, "the soothsayer's magic was swiftly depleted once I ingested it. But I learned all that I needed to know."

It was clear she hadn't foreseen Skeiron's demise before she depleted her stolen magic. Aello had waited eons for Bob to issue the Janusite prophecy and for Skeiron to begin the hunt for the Janusite, all the while amassing greater and greater dark magics. Her true motivation? To avenge herself on everyone. Her sisters' betrayal had warped her mind, or maybe she'd always been warped, and Notus's betrayal had cemented that twisted outlook. Aello blamed everyone but herself for her unhappiness. Once she'd foreseen the arrival of the Janusite, of me, she'd set her sights on obtaining the power I guarded.

Suddenly, I understood. Every time she'd said "you" when speaking to me, she had meant it in the collective sense. I was not the sole object of her rage. She used me as a conduit for it. Maybe she wanted Skeiron and Notus back strictly so she could mete out her own vengeance on them, or maybe she wanted her playthings back.

My thoughts spiraled back to the moments after I'd witnessed Calder's forging. What had Aello said? *Never again shall I suffer betrayal. You took them from me, and I will have them back whatever the cost. I shall avenge what you have done before it was done.* Betrayal. That was the key to her motives. She cared little about the individual she aimed her fury at, only that she had the opportunity to spew all that hatred at someone. "You" referred to everyone who had turned on her, or in my case, possessed power she coveted.

The power to control time, drop the mystical boundaries, open the veil between realms, and converge the worlds.

Aello already controlled time without my powers. Or did she? The magics she'd consumed seemed less than reliable. I could travel through time without injuring the time stream. She did damage with every attempt. I felt the disruptions she'd caused, and the upheaval of the earth that accompanied her attempts spoke to the violence of her manipulations. With my magics, she would have the ultimate power she craved.

The bitch would never get my powers.

At last, I knew the answer to Miriella's question. What would I sacrifice to heal the time stream? To fix the damage Aello had wrought, I would give my life.

"You will forget what I have told you," Aello told Skeiron, "and remember only that you desire me above all others and wish to serve my will and mine alone."

She waved her hand in his face.

He blinked furiously and focused on her. His mouth twisted into a lustful smile. "My love, how may I serve you?"

I'd seen enough, so I returned to the present day, to the spot where Nevan lay dead. Blood stained his torso crimson, and his vacant eyes stared into nothingness.

Nevan. A weight bore down on my chest, squeezing my heart. I fell to my knees beside him, stroking my fingers through his hair, and bit down on my lip so fiercely I tasted the metallic tang of blood. Nevan's skin chilled mine.

Aello had taken too much from me. She would take no more.

I sat back on my heels and shut my eyes, replaying everything Bob and Miriella had told me. They'd wanted to help me, I sensed that much. Both had tried to advise me, each in their own way with the limitations of their positions. If oracles could provide explicit instructions for how to accomplish goals, nobody would need to make decisions on their own. I finally understood this and accepted it. To maintain free will, the powers that be—God, the Oversoul, whatever you called it—had instituted limits on what anyone gifted with foresight could see and reveal.

Bob had told me what I'd lost was not gone for good. Did that mean I could get Nevan back? And Max and my family and everyone else?

Miriella assured me nothing held me back except my fears. To let them go, I had to trust in my ability to control these powers. Nevan had always trusted me, in every way. Max believed in me too and never feared my magics. Every good elemental being who knew I was the Janusite trusted me to use the power wisely. How could I doubt myself when so many powerful beings believed in me?

No more doubt. No more fear.

I knew it wouldn't be that easy—say I was over it, and poof, I was—but I had to keep moving, keep striving for answers. One question rang like a giant bell in my mind. What on earth was I supposed to do about Aello?

I cradled my forehead in my palms, rocking in place. What else had Bob said? *Blood for blood, life for life, the scales must be balanced.* Yes, Aello would balance out the scales with her own death. The answers, Bob told me, awaited if only I could open my third eye and see them. I came from a family of New Age devotees, so I understood the concept of the third eye. It granted insight beyond what normal perception allowed. Tapping into the third eye required meditation and focus.

Which I had none of at the moment. Relax? Focus? I was sitting next to the body of the man I loved. All my friends and loved ones had been murdered.

Rein it in, Lindsey. Suck it up and do what must be done.

I looked down at Nevan, and my heart clenched. My fingers trembled as I eased his eyelids shut. I bent to touch my lips to his. "I'll fix this, I promise. We haven't come this far for one whacked-out harpy to destroy our happiness. This is not how it ends for us."

Tears threatened, but I reined it in like never before. The steel vaults in my mind, where I'd once locked up my strongest emotions, slammed shut around the anguish and the fear. I must banish all of it or I would never get through the next part.

"Not saying goodbye," I said to Nevan. "Just sending you to a safe place for a while."

I flicked my wrist Nevan-style, and his body vanished.

He lay in state inside our underground lair, but he was not gone for good.

Bob had explained that I could not divest Aello of the dark magics. I needed to find a way around them. She had circumvented Max's life debt to me, rendering him no longer immune to the time shifts, which allowed her to kill him. She'd killed Nevan too, despite our transcendent bond. If that raging nutjob could sidestep the rules, so could I.

Miriella had told me I was more than a vessel for Janus's powers and that I'd been working toward the wrong goal. I now understood she meant my attempts to undo Aello's time shifts and to prevent her from acquiring dark magics in the first place.

No more running after Aello. Ditch the wrong goal? Check.

I was created for this purpose, Miriella said. It was my destiny to repair the time stream, but I had to stop limiting my thinking to a mortal perspective. Only by embracing the full experience of being the Janusite could I see the answers. I would open my third eye to the possibilities. Expand my horizons? Check.

Nevan had always kept me centered, and I'd done the same for him. Though his heart no longer beat, he could still guide me.

I assumed the lotus position, like I'd watched my parents do so many times, and rested my hands palms up on my knees with the thumb and forefinger of each hand touching. Eyes closed, I emptied my thoughts, letting my consciousness float on a serene sea, opening up to the possibilities beyond my normal perception. Floating, floating. Sensations rushed through me, indescribable, beautiful, suffused with a purpose I could not deny. My third eye was activated. Seeing. Sensing. A wider world, a wider universe, lay open before me.

My lids flew open.

I comprehended at last, absorbing everything Bob and Miriella had told me, assimilating my new insight with their advice and my experiences. Ah yes, there it was. The right goal. To get around Aello's dark magics, I needed to do the unthinkable.

Converge the worlds.

The idea had unnerved me before. I hadn't comprehended what it actually meant. Converging the Unseen and the mortal realms did not mean the worlds would become one gruesome hodgepodge. Convergence would free up all the magics of the Unseen and pull them into the mortal world. I would have access to untold power, enough to circumvent Aello's dark magics.

Okay, awesome, I had a plan. How exactly did I enact it? My fingers drummed on my knees. Sitting here in the middle of a cemetery, in front of my own gravestone, I realized I had no clue how to converge two worlds or what chaos that might wreak in its aftermath. To unleash the Unseen would mean disrupting the veil between the worlds and dropping every boundary in the mortal realm. Elementals would have free rein.

That did not sound like a good thing.

Come on, girl, stop limiting your perspective.

Right, no limitations. I seized the sliver of doubt that had crept around my heart and stuffed it into that blasted steel vault. No more fear, no more doubts. I could—I would—do this.

Do it already, I commanded myself.

Jumping to my feet, I gazed out across the cemetery but let my vision recede until the world around me seemed like a faded photograph. And I summoned my powers.

Energy flowed into me. Blue, sparkling energy. It filled me, empowered me, gave me—

The earth heaved up beneath me.

I tumbled down the slope created by the upheaval, spinning toward a yawning chasm.

The blue sky mutated into a churning mass of purple and sapphire, clouds of pure black laced with steel gray writhed across the heavens like airborne serpents, and the trees at the periphery of the cemetery morphed into black things alive with squirming foliage composed of half green leaves and half mossy stuff.

A pair of suns burned in the sky.

I caught the edge of the chasm before I tumbled into it, dangling there with my feet swinging. The strain on my arms lanced pain through them. I scrambled to pull myself up, grunting and shouting from the effort, until I fell flat on my back on the quivering ground.

A bird swooped across the sky at the level of the treetops.

Not a bird. I squinted, struggling to see despite the tremors reverberating through me.

The pterodactyl screamed and flapped its huge wings as it soared up and out of sight.

A gushing noise issued from somewhere beyond the trees.

I scrambled to my feet and struggled to stay upright. The earth rattled like a bass drum pounded on by King Kong. More chasms split open, trees plummeted into the voids while alien voices bellowed and shrieked.

Animals? Humans? Something else?

The gushing noise swelled closer, grew louder, until I recognized the sound. *Heaven help us all.*

A tidal wave at least a hundred feet high barreled toward me. The wall of water tore trees from the earth and flung them into a maelstrom within its ever-advancing mass.

Creatures fled the woods, stampeding past me. Dinosaurs. Woolly mammoths. Saber-tooth tigers. Odd-looking horses. Cows. Emus. A blue whale was spewed out of the tidal wave. It thwacked into the ground at the other side of the cemetery, flopping in terror.

I whisked myself away with only one thought for my destination—a safe place.

My body materialized atop a craggy, windswept mountain shrouded in fog. The earth shivered here, though faintly, not with the mad chaos I'd just fled. I turned around and spied the steep white steps I'd mounted earlier. Only the last dozen or so of the steps was visible through the fog. Dread iced through my veins as I hurried up the steps, taking them two at a time, oblivious of the pain in my chest and my legs, ignoring the fact I'd become breathless from the altitude. I summoned fresh air to rejuvenate myself.

I reached the portico, my legs burning and shaking, gasping for air even as I summoned more fresh, clean air to revitalize me. The fog, though thinner here, made the giant doors seem like a monster waiting to swallow me. The thunderous grinding noise kicked up, and the doors inched apart.

Beneath my feet, the white stone of the portico floor trembled.

I sprinted into the Temple of the Four Winds.

All four of the Winds hovered midway inside the building, their stark gazes swerving to me.

"She's done it," I said, "hasn't she? Aello has broken time."

Miriella nodded solemnly.

Chapter Twenty-Nine

"I WAS ABOUT TO CONVERGE THE WORLDS," I SAID, "AS A WAY TO GET around Aello's dark magics. Not sure if that would've worked, but it felt like a good plan and I've learned to trust my intuition. I can't do that now, can I? She's messed up the entire universe."

Miriella spoke, though her floaty friends watched me. "You are correct. You cannot converge the worlds until you repair the damage to the time stream."

The Four Winds all seemed shaken. For beings as powerful as they were to fear what had happened…*Bad, bad, bad.*

"How can I repair the time stream," I asked, "when everything is in chaos?"

"You must," Miriella said, her voice no longer serene and detached as it had been the other times I'd seen her. She sounded frightened. "If the damage is not repaired, everything will end."

Terrific. The end of days had come, and I was the only one who could stop it.

One of the male winds came forward, wringing his hands. "Entering the time stream amid the chaos poses a grave danger to you, but there is no alternative."

Miriella grabbed my hand, hers cool but not cold, her skin so soft I had no words to describe it. "We will gather all our powers to protect you, but only the Janusite possesses the power to save all of creation. Trust in yourself, Lindsey."

I cleared my throat. "Just to make sure I've got this straight, with time broken everything that was, is, or could have been has become a reality."

"Yes." She grasped my hand tighter. "You must exercise extreme care. With the threads of time untethered, you may encounter perversions of the world you knew, of the humans and elementals you knew. Trust no one and nothing except for yourself."

"Um, that sounds like you expect me to go back out into the chaos. I was thinking I'd jump into the time stream right here."

"No," the male wind-being said, almost shouting it. "You must locate the physical place where the break occurred and enter the time stream there. If you enter it anywhere else…"

I would die. He didn't need to finish his sentence for me to get the gist. The stark expressions and worried voices of these beings told me as much.

Miriella released my hand. "Our prayers go with you, Lindsey Astrid Porter."

"Good to know." If I needed prayers, things were even worse than I'd imagined. "I will save time, save the worlds, save everything." I shrugged, lifting my arms. "It's my destiny, right?"

Four heads nodded.

"Can I zip myself out of here? Or do I need to go outside first?"

Miriella almost smiled. "You may 'zip' from inside the temple."

"Good." I assumed the posture. "Wish me luck."

I teleported away, not really sure where I was going. I'd meant to head straight for Aello, but the turmoil consuming both worlds must've knocked me off course. I emerged alongside the falls behind where the rock shop should've been but hadn't been all day. A false night had descended on the world during the few minutes I was gone, the result of a sky overwhelmed by churning black storm clouds. A profound darkness enveloped me, rife with strange sounds. Though the trees and grass looked different, like a twisted combination of the Unseen and the mortal world, it was the creepy noises of creatures I'd never heard before that raised every hair on my body.

Everything had changed, possibly with grotesque results.

That did not make me feel better.

Aello, where was Aello?

Not here, that was for sure. I took a deep breath, exhaled it slowly, and willed my body to relax. My third eye activated. I channeled its insight into my powers, funneling glittering blue power into my body. *Aello, Aello, Aello, take me to where Aello shattered time.*

I shot through the abysmal tunnel with energies pricking at my skin, an experience I hadn't endured in a long time, not since before I discovered I was the Janusite. The broken time stream must've affected even the way teleportation worked. I tumbled head over heels through the tunnel and exploded out into the woods in the Unseen. Here, as in the mortal realm, everything had become an amalgamation of both worlds, but I sensed I was in the elemental world.

No Aello.

Gah. Chasing her through the broken timeline was like chasing a wisp of smoke. I needed to find a way to zero in on the place where she'd wrecked the worlds, the place where she had barged into the time stream and pulverized it.

A figure appeared in front of me.

I smiled. "Max!"

My heart lifted at the sight of him, until I noticed his demeanor. His eyes were wild, his hair too, and his taut muscles strained from the tension in his bunched shoulders and his fisted hands. He breathed hard, his teeth bared.

His erection stood at attention.

Max lunged for me.

I lurched backward.

He snared my arms, his fingers squeezing so tight I winced. "I haven't fed in ages. Thanks be to the Oversoul for dropping a scrumptious female in my path."

"Oh no, I am not—"

He ducked his head to sniff my neck, then raked his hot tongue up my throat and shivered with a lustful gleam in his eyes. "You taste so fucking good."

I tried to wrest free of his grasp, but he had the advantage of elemental strength. "Let me go. I do not want to have sex with you."

"Who gives a bloody damn?" He growled again, with ravenous hunger. "I must feed, and you are the meal I've been searching for."

He hauled me into his body, his stiff shaft caught between us and throbbing against my belly.

"Don't do this," I said. "Please, Max, this isn't you. It's the hunger talking, but you can fight it. You're a good man."

His laughter was harsh and dark. "I am an incubus, darling. I take what I need from whoever I can find." He bit my bottom lip. "You'll enjoy it, trust me."

I rammed my knee into his groin.

He grunted—and grinned.

"Seriously?" I said. "You think it's fun when I crush your manly parts?"

"Violence can be arousing."

Max froze with his mouth open as if he'd been about to say more. He blinked rapidly, his eyes swirling with silver and copper, and ducked his head. His body swayed a touch, just enough to make it clear something was going on inside him.

When his hands fell away from me, I shuffled backward.

He groaned miserably and lifted his head. "Lindsey?"

"Uh-huh," I said, edging backward some more. "Who are you?"

If the past and the present had become one, and if the broken time stream led to grotesque results, then I needed to be extra careful. Maybe Max looked and sounded like himself again, but how could I know he'd stay this way?

"What happened?" he asked, glancing around like he had no idea how he'd gotten here. "I remember the cemetery and..." He grimaced, peeked down at his waning erection, and grimaced again. "Oh, I remember. But it wasn't me. Was it? I would never—It felt like I was myself, but a different version of me."

He gripped the back of his head, frisking his hands up and down as if brushing away the confusion.

"Yeah, it was clearly a different you," I said, taking a cautious step toward him. "Aello has broken the time stream. Past and present are intertwined. Everything is very, very screwed up."

"That's no excuse for my behavior." He scrunched up his face. "I am so sorry, Lindsey."

"We'll chalk it up to timeline insanity."

If Max had come back from the dead, what about Nevan? I didn't have time to search for him, and if I called for him, he might show up as Nevan's evil twin. Having met an evil version of him once before, when Ceara and the sorcerer stripped his soul from his body, I had no desire to meet the Anti-Nevan again. I would find him after I healed the time stream.

"Perhaps I can help you," Max said. "I am your familiar after—"

He froze again. Something rippled through him, like a hard shiver or a jolt of magic. Whatever it was, his entire demeanor shifted.

And yeah, his dick got interested again.

Except this time, he seemed way more crazed. He breathed hard, his chest heaving, and veins stood out on his neck. He snarled and growled like an animal.

Before I could process the change, he leaped at me, whomping down inches away. "Hungry. Feed. On you."

He grabbed for me.

I slapped my hands on his chest. Blue energy surged out of me and into him, hurling him backward. He smacked down a good twenty feet away, dazed, and lifted his head to gaze at me.

He licked at the air as if sampling it. "Your magic tastes good. Ravage you. Now."

"Go hump a tree, caveman."

I zipped away.

Whirling through the tunnel, I commanded it to drop me off in the precise spot where Aello had mangled the universe. I called on all my willpower, all my magic, to issue the command.

The tunnel spit me out inside the rock shop.

Aello stood atop the sales counter, her hair billowing around her in the eerily warm and slippery wind that whipped inside the corrugated-metal building. The rows of wooden bins, each filled with different kinds of rocks, seemed to have been thrown around by an angry creature.

Yeah, like the one standing on the counter.

The harpy bellowed, throwing her hands up.

I hurled a glowing orb at her.

The orb struck her in the chest. She stumbled backward and fell off the counter.

I summoned another orb.

Aello sprang up from behind the counter, vaulted over it, and puckered her lips to blow a gale-force wind at me.

The orb snuffed out, and I flew backward straight into the wall.

Aello shrieked. "I destroyed time, and yet you exist. You retain the powers of Janus."

Her wind pinned me to the wall.

She had lost her power-dampening ability. I sensed it. Shattering the time stream had consumed too much magic, forcing her to give up at least one of her dark spells. Despite the loss, she'd held on to enough magics to remain formidable.

She sprang across the shop to me. "Give me the power."

The powers she coveted rose inside me, stronger than ever, and I understood what I must do. Destroying her was the wrong goal. I needed to stick to the new plan.

I shot out a bolt of power, enough to shatter the wind pinning me to the wall. "Sorry, Wackadoodle Dandy, I've got more important things to do."

Aello thrust her talons at my throat.

I leaped into the time stream and shut the metaphysical door behind me, sealing it with strong magics. No one else would get inside unless I allowed it. Oh yeah, I could imagine the earsplitting shriek Aello must've let out when she realized I'd locked her out.

I glanced around, chilled by the sight before me.

The river of time had splintered into countless streams. They coiled and writhed and lashed out at each other. Sparks cleaved the darkness around the rivers, crackling with enough energy to singe my skin.

How was I supposed to tame this chaos?

I didn't have time to figure that out.

A snapping, gnashing river of time energy lashed out at me.

CHAPTER THIRTY

I COLLARED THE STREAM AND TRIED TO TAME IT, BUT THE THING whipped and gnashed its energy like teeth. Arcs of electricity shot through my entire body, piercing me with sharp pains. How was I supposed to repair this? Angry snakes of energy lashing out every which way, every which time. The energy scorched my skin, and I had no choice but to let go of the stream.

What would I do if I'd injured myself? I would disinfect the wound and bandage it up. Great, all I had to do was figure out how to disinfect the time stream.

Bob had urged me to remember the prophecy.

Like Janus, I held dominion over doorways, transitions, boundaries, the veil between worlds, and time itself. I also wielded the power to converge the worlds.

A branch of the time stream lashed out at me, but I dodged it. More serpents of energy snarled at me, whipping their glowing streams at me. Time was pissed.

The wound needed to be repaired ASAP.

Only the Janusite had the power to fix this. *Think, Lindsey.* Two months ago, I'd used my blue magics to reinvigorate Nevan when the sorcerer had been slowly draining his soul and then I had employed the same energies to restore his soul. Just today, I'd brought Nevan back after Aello expunged him from the timeline, and later, I had revived his memories of me. Why couldn't I do the same for the time stream? Cleanse and heal it with my Janusite magics.

Repairing time wasn't quite the same thing as reinvigorating my lover, but I understood what I needed to do to make this happen even if I could not describe it. I needed to fully embrace my powers with no fear of potential consequences. After that, I would converge the worlds.

I pictured Nevan making that affectionately harried face. He would say, "Lindsey, darlin', you do come up with the most unusual ideas."

My chest ached.

Once I did this, everything would go back to the way it had been, the way it should be. Nevan would be alive. Everyone I loved would come back.

I stopped trying to dodge the serpents of energy. Let them whip me. Let them snarl and hiss at me. I gritted my teeth against another crack of time-stream energy. I closed my eyes, shutting out the chaos around me, and breathed deeply. Once. Twice. Three, four, five times until my body slackened and my mind went blank. No holding back. I threw open the gates of my mind, of my powers, and let everything pour into me.

Blue, shimmering light erupted around me, visible as ghosts behind my eyelids.

The energy kept gushing into me, warm and cool at the same time, sharp and soft, enlivening and calming. This power didn't belong to me. It *was* me. Bared to the universe, to the unknowable and unseeable source of all magical power, I absorbed all that it could give me, all that I had a right to claim. The energy bonded to me, suffused me, set my body and my soul to tingling.

When I opened my eyes, the blue magics swirled around me in a semi-transparent cloud. Beyond the encompassing cloud, the time stream curved and looped in a placid river of intersecting and diverging streams. A current of gentle warmth lapped at my skin, almost as if the time stream were thanking me.

You're welcome.

Power coursed through my veins, as natural as blood. I commanded the full potency of my magics—no fear, no reservations, no inhibitions. *I am the Janusite.* The recognition of that fact shuddered a thrill through me, because for the first time in my life, I was completely liberated. Nevan had freed my heart and soul, but today, I had unbound my full potential and embraced the power within me.

With phase one accomplished, I headed back into the world.

I surfaced in the cemetery. The three new gravestones had vanished, so at least my family and I were no longer dead.

"Lindsey."

That familiar voice made me wheel around and fling myself at the speaker. Nevan caught me, holding me up with my boots a good foot above the ground. I kissed him like I hadn't seen him in centuries, and he kissed me back with an equal passion, our lips glued together and our tongues devouring each other. I clung to him, reveling in the feel of his body, warm and alive and strong, unwilling to relinquish this moment one second sooner than necessary.

He set me down, though his hands lingered on my hips. "Is the timeline repaired? I sensed...something, and it felt like you."

"Yes, I healed the time stream." I glanced around, biting my lip. "No idea if that reversed all the shifts Aello created."

"It did," Nevan said with a certainty that stopped me.

"How can you know that?"

"Because I remember." He frisked his hands up and down my arms. "Everything. I have memories of events that did not occur in this timeline, of things Aello expunged that have not been restored, and things that cannot be but are."

Everything that could be would be. That's what true chaos meant.

"Please don't tell me," I said, "all those freaky creatures are hanging around. I repaired the damage to the time stream, so the chaos should've been undone."

"It was." Nevan grasped my upper arms and kissed my forehead. "I meant that I recall events concerning you that I had no memory of before Aello interfered with time. These events could not be, but I know they are."

"Cut out the cryptic talk and tell me what the heck you mean."

He scrubbed a hand over his mouth. "Before the first time shift, I told you about my dreams of an angel who came to me after my forging and cared for me while I adjusted. I believed those were mere dreams, but now I realize those events occurred." He smiled sweetly, cupping my face with his hands. "The angel was you, Lindsey. You stayed with me after Notus abandoned me. You cared for me. I would not have survived the transition without you by my side, without the magics that enabled you to alleviate my suffering. But it was your love that truly saved me, the warmth and sweetness of your heart."

I laid my hands over his. "Time sent me there, to witness your forging and learn about the part Aello played in your fate. She convinced Notus to leave you there. I couldn't walk away, not knowing how hard it's been for Travis—and he has lots of people who care about him and help him. You had no one. At first, I thought I was messing up the timeline by staying, but since then I've realized the truth."

"What truth is that?"

"You and I have always been meant for each other." I peeled his hands away from my face and clasped them to my heart. "I was meant to take care of you in the aftermath of your forging. That's how it always happened, even though neither of us knew it until today."

"I believe that." His lips kinked upward, and his eyes swirled with warm shades. "We made love alongside a stream in the Unseen, thousands of years ago."

"Um...yeah."

"You appeared to me again centuries later, after the gnome battle. I took you to my home, but you were far too exhausted for sex. We slept in each other's arms."

I hunched my shoulders. "Bob told me whenever I am, it's always you. And you always will be the only one I have ever had sex with in any time and in any world."

He pulled me into his arms. "Not complaining, love. I enjoyed reacquiring the memory of that day by the stream. You gave me my first sexual experience as an elemental. It seems appropriate since you are the only one I have ever loved." He winced a little. "I can't claim to have been as steadfast in my fidelity to you as you've been to me. How I could forget about you, I cannot comprehend."

"I made sure you would forget."

Nevan froze. "What?"

"When I said goodbye to you after your forging, you didn't see me again for over three hundred years. You spent all that time wondering about me, wishing you could see me."

"I don't recall telling you that."

"Not those exact words, but you did say you wondered what became of me and you missed my light and my presence."

He kissed the tip of my nose. "I said I missed your light and your *sweet* presence."

"That distinction is really important." I gazed into his eyes, determined to make him understand why I'd done this to him. "You would've spent thousands of years wondering about me, dreaming about me. Our connection transcends time, Nevan. If I'd left you with those memories of us, you would've suffered for nearly five thousand years without knowing what became of me or when you might see me again. I couldn't leave you that way."

Nevan linked his hands behind the small of my back. "What did you do?"

"I asked the Four Winds to make you forget."

He tipped his head to the side, his eyes narrowing slightly. "And they did this? Because the Janusite asked?"

"Because *I* asked. They're not as cold and remote as they seem, especially Miriella."

"Miriella? You know the name of one of the Four Winds?"

"Turns out she used to be Bob's girlfriend. Miriella said you would remember those prehistoric events when the past and the present became one. That happened a few minutes ago when Aello broke the time stream." I glanced around the cemetery. "Did everything go back to the way it was?"

"I imagine so." He whisked us to the parking lot of the rock shop. "But you'll want to see for yourself."

He knew me so well.

"Thank you, honey," I said, giving him a quick kiss.

I rushed into the shop and found Stan behind the counter. When I hugged him, he reacted like I'd shoved a gun in his mouth but quickly regained his grumpy composure. He had vague memories of something bad going down. I decided to leave him with his ignorance and hoped it gave him peace, if not bliss. We zipped to my parents' house, finding them in the midst of a game of Monopoly, unaware anything had happened. My extreme relief at seeing them alive and well clued them in to the fact something went on, and I vowed to explain everything later.

Nevan informed me of several important facts. Skeiron was dead. Notus was dead. Calder had been forged and destroyed. Travis remained a newly forged elemental struggling with his transition. Everything had gone back to the way it should have been, the way it had to be.

Aello was on the loose. Nevan hadn't needed to tell me that. I sensed her, like a storm just over the horizon.

We returned to the chasm where Janus had appeared this morning. Christ, had it only been a day? The storm clouds that had swallowed the sky earlier were gone. The sun was setting, but I had one task left to accomplish.

"Janus is Aello's hostage," I said.

Nevan nodded. "It would seem so. Unless she has destroyed him."

"She hasn't. He's alive, I can feel it."

"How?"

"I got my powers from him. It gave us a connection." When he looked an eensy bit wounded, I patted his chest and added, "Nothing like what you and I have. But I can feel he's alive and kicking."

Nevan harrumphed. "I suppose that's a good thing."

"It is." With no more time to waste, I shouted, "Max!"

He blinked into view ten feet away, wearing gray slacks and refusing to look at me.

"What's with the pants?" I asked. "Suddenly shy?"

Face pinched, Max stared at the ground with his shoulders slumped. "I had to come when you called because of the debt. You should ask for help from someone else."

"You are my familiar." I took two steps toward him, but he scuffled backward. "What is wrong with you?"

He hunched his shoulders and bowed his head. "I remember the previous timelines."

For a couple seconds, I had no idea what he meant by that. Then it hit me. He had retained his memories of the chaos after Aello broke the time stream. He remembered trying to assault me.

"Oh Max," I said, "that wasn't you."

"If I have the memory, it must've been me." He gripped his head with both hands. "I tried to—to harm you. To slake my hunger with you even though you told me you didn't want it."

Nevan stomped up beside me and hissed under his breath, "He did what?"

Slapping a hand on his chest, I gave him my sternest look. "Let me handle this. Can't you see he's beating himself up enough for the both of you?"

Nevan stepped back, though he strapped his arms over his chest and fixed his hottest glare on Max.

Well, I couldn't expect him not to be upset about this.

I inched toward Max, halting an arm's length away. "The world had descended into temporal chaos. Everything that is, was, or could be turned into reality. One version of you hadn't fed in way too long and got a little… overly frisky. That was not the real you."

He shoved his hands into his hair, rocking on his heels.

"The Max I know," I said, edging closer, "is good and kind and strong. You have fought alongside me to stop some of the worst villains in the universe. You wouldn't betray me even when the sorcerer had a hold over you. I trust you." I tugged his hands away from his head and covered them with mine. "You are my friend, Max, and I love you. No time-shifting chaos or crazy, vengeful harpies will ever change that because I know who you really are. If you can't trust yourself, then trust me."

Although I kept my focus on Max, on the top of his bowed head, I sensed Nevan had relaxed. If I could convince Max to do the same…

I threw Nevan a look that I hoped said "don't freak out about this" and then I pulled Max in for a hug. He remained stiff at first, his head down and angled away from mine. Little by little, he began to unwind that coil of tension inside himself, his body slackening. Though he did not put his arms around me, I held him until he finally grumbled out a sigh and pulled away.

With a long-suffering expression, he said, "I haven't been hugged in almost two thousand years. Naturally, it's a married woman who gives me my first cuddle in eons."

His lips twitched upward. His eyes gleamed with humor.

Thank goodness. I had my friend back.

I eyed him with mock suspicion. "How could you not have been hugged for two thousand years? You're an incubus. You've had lots and lots of sex."

"But no real intimacy." He glanced at Nevan and quickly averted his gaze, scratching behind his ear. "Must we discuss this in front of your husband?"

Nevan blustered out a sigh. "You bloody well are not discussing sex with my wife in private."

"I've never had sex with your wife, in private or in public."

"You know what I meant." Nevan clenched his fists.

I shook my head, trying not very hard to repress a smile. "Nevan, chill out. Max is teasing you." I jabbed a finger into Max's chest. "And you, stop harassing Nevan."

Despite my stern words, I was happy. Everything had gone back to the way it should've been.

But one big problem loomed ahead of us.

"We don't have time for this nonsense anyway," I said. "It's time for me to converge the worlds."

Nevan arched one brow.

Max arched both of his.

"Yes, yes," I said, holding up my hands in a staying gesture, "I know what you're both thinking, and I admit it's a stark-raving insane plan. Unless either of you has a better idea, this is what's happening. Since I can't divest Aello of her dark magics, I need to get around them."

"How does converging the worlds accomplish this?" Nevan asked.

"It's hard to explain. I feel this will work." Hooking my thumbs in the pockets of my leather pants, I thought hard about how to convince them this plan would work. "Right now, there are limitations in effect for both worlds, a kind of legal code governing the actions of elementals. Max told me about all that back when we first met." I shot Nevan a sidelong glance. "Somebody was too busy arguing with the sylph tribunal to explain the Great Bargain to me."

"Such a discussion seemed unimportant. The Great Bargain was struck long, long ago." Nevan gave me a sly smile. "If the elders who struck the Great Bargain had ever met you, my mortal love, they would have banned all debts and bargains out of sheer frustration."

"Pardon me for being polite."

His gaze swung heavenward. "Lindsey, will ye never stop saying such things?"

"We're in the mortal realm at the moment, Mr. Prickly Pants."

"You are considering merging the worlds." He moved closer to take my hands in his. "If you do this, the mortal realm will become infused with the magics of the Unseen. Debts and bargains will have real power here."

"Relax, honey, I don't plan on thanking anyone while I'm beating the crap out of Aello."

"How comforting." He bent his head to fix his intent gaze on me. "Do you have any conception of what converging the worlds will do? I have no bloody idea, but I cannot imagine it will be pleasant."

"Saving the world never is—until the saving is done." I took a breath and let it out slowly. "Listen, I know this is super-crazy dangerous. But even the Four Winds and Bob agreed this is the way to go. I have to do a lot of third-eye opening and magic gathering to get powered up. Unleashing the Unseen will give me unfettered access to all the magics I need to get around Aello's dark powers."

"I don't like this. You will be in grave danger." He nodded toward Max. "Your familiar and I are immortal and thus difficult to kill, but you are a human being. No magic is required to end your life. A rock to the head will suffice."

He was worried. I'd known he would be, and I didn't blame him. How many times had we watched each other almost die? Today, I'd seen him actually die. More than ever, I understood the risks. My knowledge of the Great Bargain made this plan even scarier, because the ancient elders of the elemental races had enacted the Bargain for a good reason. Before they instituted the rules, elementals ran wild in both realms. They rampaged through the mortal world without any limitations, taking whatever they wanted and tricking humans into making bad deals, enslaving them with the magic of debts and bargains.

Things had gotten so bad the elementals themselves realized the need for rules.

And I was about to strip away all those rules and the protections they afforded to mortals. The chaos of a broken time stream no longer seemed like the worst that could happen.

"We need lots of help," I said. "And more space. Let's blip over to the parking lot again."

Max and Nevan followed me to the gravel parking lot beside the rock shop.

"It's time to call in the cavalry," I said.

Nevan backed up, sensing what I was about to do.

I hollered as loud as I could. "Triskaideka! Ennea! Get your leprechaun asses over here and bring as many of your friends as you can. All hands on deck!"

When I glanced at Nevan, he flourished his hand in a circular gesture.

An entire garrison of sylph soldiers materialized behind him, clad in gleaming bronze armor with matching helmets, their face shields down, and tough-looking boots. Nevan had donned his armor too, though it gleamed silver with streaks of gold and bronze. The face shield of his helmet was raised so I could see his expression of grim determination.

Max had shed his slacks, now completely nude.

I gestured at his body. "Don't you want some armor or at least a shield?"

"No need." Flames burst from his skin, swathing him in fire from head to toe. "I have a different sort of armor."

He snuffed out the flames.

I wasn't convinced fire would be enough to protect him, but I had to trust his judgment on this.

"What about a weapon?" I asked him.

Max bent the fingers of one hand. A sword materialized in his grasp, its blade a shimmering crimson.

"Cool," I said. "Where are—"

Ennea and Tris appeared before I could speak their names, accompanied by a small army of their fellow leprechauns. Every one of the copper fae wielded a weapon, everything from clubs to swords. They wore no armor, only regular clothes that looked like it had come from a shopping mall. These folks had probably conjured their clothing, which meant it came from who-knew-where.

"Looks like everyone's here," I said.

"Not quite," Max said, pointing to the empty space at my left.

I opened my mouth to ask what on earth he meant but clapped it shut when Travis materialized ten feet away from me. He wore the same outfit as this morning—faded jeans and a cotton shirt that hung open, exposing his outrageously muscular chest.

Nevan's mouth crimped at one corner. "He could have the decency to button up."

"At least he wears clothing," I said. "Max is naked."

"I am well aware of that fact, but I've given up trying to convince your familiar to cover himself." Nevan aimed his sharp gaze at Travis. "Are you well enough to be here? We are about to do battle with the most powerful elemental in history."

Travis straightened and squared his shoulders. "I can do this, and I want to help."

Nevan looked to me for confirmation.

"He stays," I said. "We need all the help we can get."

"Then he needs a weapon." Nevan flicked his wrist, and a gleaming black sword appeared in Travis's hand. "That will do."

I squinted at the sword he'd conjured for Travis. "Is that Skeiron's endued sword?"

"Yes."

Travis raised and lowered the sword as if testing its weight. His lips curved into a smile of feral appreciation. "Yeah, this'll do just fine."

My husband moved to stand beside me. "May I speak to your army?"

"Don't need my permission. Most of them are your soldiers, King Nevan."

His lips twitched in an almost smile. "I thought we agreed you would call me that only when we're in bed."

"You said only when we're naked, but I couldn't resist. You are glorious in your armor."

"Our fearless leader needs a weapon." He held out both hands, palms up, and a weapon appeared in each. His left hand held my derringer in its holster, while his right held a shiny silver sword in a leather scabbard, the blade smaller than the one he usually employed in battle. "Choose one or take both."

I took both.

When I tried to clip the derringer's holster onto my waistband, I realized I needed both hands for that. I gave Nevan the sword. "Hold this for a sec." Once I'd secured the handgun, I reclaimed the sword, attached its scabbard to my waistband opposite the derringer, and whipped the sword out to flourish it in the air. "Nice. It's lighter than your usual weapon of choice."

"This one was crafted specially for you by the chief armorer of the sylph kingdom. It is endued, naturally, as is the ammunition for your little firearm." He tapped the holster on my hip. "I took the liberty of choosing the smaller ammunition."

My wonderful husband had armed me with .357 rounds and an awesome, me-size sword.

I had no choice. I had to smack a big one on his mouth. "You're the best husband ever."

"The sword is your wedding gift. I did not have an opportunity to present you with it this morning."

I turned the sword in my hand, admiring the artistry of the sylph who had created it and testing its weight to get a feel for my new weapon. "Oh honey, I love it. I would give you my wedding gift for you, but it's not appropriate for public viewing. And honestly, sexy lingerie seems pathetically inadequate compared to what you gave me."

"Any gift from you is a treasure to me. Especially if it's sexy."

Tris flapped his arms in the air. "Hey, are we gonna fight or what? Your tender moment is making me nauseous."

"Yes," I said, "we're about to fight. Nevan, make your speech."

"For everyone to understand what is at stake, they must know the truth."

About me, he meant.

I scanned my gaze over the crowd. "Do it."

My husband lifted his chin, surveying our ragtag army with a regal air. His voice boomed, echoing off the shop building. "We are about to do battle with an enemy of immense power who has a vendetta against the Janusite."

Suddenly, he had the undivided attention of every being gathered in this parking lot.

Nevan waved toward me. "My wife, Lindsey, is the Janusite."

Gasps and surprised exclamations ensued.

"Defending Lindsey," he said, "is the most important task for all of us. She is the only one who holds the power to defeat our enemy, the harpy Aello. To accomplish this feat, Lindsey must drop all the barriers between the worlds. Whatever the cost, we must prevent Aello and any minions she brings with her from leaving this location."

Max raised his hand but didn't wait for permission to speak. "What about all the elementals who will be racing over here to pillage the mortal world?"

"Leave them until after Aello is dealt with." Nevan swept his steely gaze over the crowd. "Protecting Lindsey is our primary mission. Without her, we are all doomed."

We were doomed unless I saved everyone? Jeez, no pressure there.

"Raise your hands," Nevan said, "and repeat after me."

Each of the gathered beings raised one hand—except for Max, who raised both.

"One hand," Nevan said to Max.

The incubus shrugged and smirked. "You said hands, plural."

I threw Max a chastising look.

He lowered one hand, keeping the other raised.

Satisfied, Nevan continued. "Repeat after me. I vow on my immortal existence to defend Lindsey Astrid Porter above all else until Aello is defeated."

A deafening chorus of voices repeated the statement.

Promises held no power in this world, not yet, but Nevan knew what he was doing. Nobody would dare cross the king of the sylphs who also happened to be married to the Janusite.

One mortal with the powers of a god and an army of elementals. I prayed it was enough.

Nevan grasped my hand. "It's time."

I rolled my shoulders back. "Here goes nothing."

A gust of hurricane-force wind blasted through the parking lot. Leprechauns and sylph soldiers struggled to stay on their feet as the wind spun around them, whipping up a cloud of dirt and gravel that pelted everyone in its path.

The sky turned an eerie shade of greenish black that infected the air around us. A rumbling racket, like a runaway freight train in the sky, erupted overhead.

Oh no. I knew that sound.

The blackest part of the clouds gyrated like a whirlpool, tightening into a gigantic funnel wider than the parking lot and the building combined.

And the tornado descended on us.

Chapter Thirty-One

I HAD NO TIME TO ENACT MY PLAN AND CONVERGE THE WORLDS. I HAD no time to do anything except run to get out of the path of the tornado. The winds ripped through the parking lot and the woods in a rotating mass of air that pummeled everything in its path. Trees uprooted and flew past us, raining dirt on our heads. Gravel pummeled us. A thorny bush went airborne and scraped against my arm on its way past me. Nevan kept his hand clamped around my upper arm like he thought he could anchor me to the ground, but the tempest around us had other ideas.

Yes, the storm had a mind—not of its own, but of Aello. An inhuman scream wailed behind the cacophony, evidence the harpy lurked within the tempest.

The screech of metal rending itself apart broke through the chaos.

I risked a backward glance. The roof of the shop building peeled away from the structure. The corrugated metal panels split apart, sailing through the air.

One huge chunk headed straight for me and Nevan.

He saw it too and seized me with both arms, whisking us away. We came out at the edge of the woods where giant holes scarred the earth, evidence of the uprooted trees that had taken flight. The chunk of the shop roof that had been flying toward us impacted the ground twenty feet away. Its leading edge pierced the earth even as the bulk of it crumpled from the force of the wind.

We couldn't fight a freaking tornado.

I glanced at Nevan. Maybe we could.

His gaze intersected with mine, and I knew he understood.

Nevan grasped my hand and nodded.

We faced the tornado. Our powers merged, flowing between and through us as if we had become one being. His elemental powers, his dominion over the atmosphere, joined with my Janusite magic in a mighty combination that provided all the energy we needed to do this.

Our arms raised at the same instant, and we launched a rocket of power.

It struck the twister.

The spinning mass of air and debris shattered.

Aello tumbled out of the sky amid the last wisps of the dying tornado and smacked onto the ground face-first. She didn't move, not even a little. Not so much as a finger twitched. She was not dead. Hitting the ground might've stunned her, possibly injured her, but not even an endued weapon could take her down.

Our army of allies stood shell-shocked, unable to move or do more than gape at the creature lying prone on the ground.

"Seize her!" Nevan shouted.

Max and Travis reacted first, zipping to the harpy and clamping their hands around her arms to heft her off the ground. Dazed, she swung her gaze left and right, her head lolling.

"It's time," I said to Nevan.

He grasped my meaning without further explanation. "Proceed."

Aello shrieked. The sound pierced my eardrums and lanced straight into my brain, making me wince and clap my hands over my ears.

Travis and Max took the brunt of the sonic force. They let go of Aello to shield their own ears and doubled over, their faces contorted with agony.

Creatures winked into view all around the harpy.

No, not mere creatures. I blinked swiftly, sure I must have hallucinated, but no. An army of gnomes gathered around Aello, every one of them bearing a wickedly sharp, serrated sword in one hand and a nasty, barbed club in the other. Aello had retained her hold over the gnomes after all these thousands of years.

The gnomes' weapons were endued. I felt the magic emanating from them.

Nevan and I exchanged a glance. This was it, and we both knew it.

The largest gnome, positioned in front of the small army, stamped his foot.

And the ground shuddered. Waves rippled out through the earth, knocking down anyone in its path.

Screw this. I grabbed Nevan's hand and willed time to stop. The world screeched to a halt, everything and everyone frozen in a single moment. Some of the fae hung suspended in the air, mouths agape, arms thrown out as if to break their falls.

Nevan and I alone remained unaffected by the time freeze.

"Watch her," I told Nevan, nodding toward Aello. "She's full of wicked-nasty dark magics and might be able to shake off the freeze."

"The harpy will not touch you. No one will harm you as long as I live."

A chill shivered through me. As long as he lived.

Gravestones. Nevan bleeding.

I shook off the memory and focused on my task. Power surged through me, hot and tingling, a torrent of magic so intense I gritted my teeth against the onslaught. I let every iota of it gush into me. Blue energy danced on my skin and on Nevan's, a sprinkle at first, then a downpour. When it became a torrent more powerful than Niagara Falls, more powerful than anything in the mortal world, I knew I had all that I needed.

No turning back.

I threw open the gates.

The veil between worlds disintegrated with a palpable sensation of pressure that built in a heartbeat and released with explosive force. My ears popped. I tottered but stayed upright, thanks to Nevan's solid body beside me and his hand anchoring me. He stayed grimly focused on Aello, the sword raised in his other hand.

The magic of the Unseen streamed into the mortal realm, and the indefinable essence of this world streamed into the elemental realm in a continuous, two-way flow. The worlds had converged.

When the barriers in the mortal world fell, my knees buckled. The power inside me had mushroomed, so vast and intense I could hardly breathe.

Nevan slung his arm around my waist, his attention on me for one second too long.

Aello broke free of the time freeze.

I spotted her a millisecond before she vaulted into the air headed straight for me. I released the frozen world, and everyone came alive again.

Nevan whisked me away.

When we popped out on the other side of the parking lot, beside the torn-apart shop, I punched his chest. "I have to fight her. You can't poof me away every time she makes a move."

"I will not let her harm you."

On the other side of the parking lot, Aello screamed. Her hoarse and infuriated cry echoed off the trees.

"Please, Nevan," I said, feeling the zing of a small debt about to be formed. "You have to let me do this. Trust me."

He flinched, no doubt feeling the same zing. "I will not interfere again unless you are in imminent danger of death."

"Thank you."

My gratitude sealed a debt between us, albeit a small one. To hell with magical debts. The Great Bargain had been obliterated when I brought the worlds together, but we had way more important problems.

The gnomes had sprung into action. They clashed swords with the sylphs and battered the physically smaller fae. A gnome jabbed his blade at Tris, but the leprechaun dodged it and sank his dagger into the other creature's side.

Nevan gave me a pained look. He wanted to stay here to protect me, but he also wanted to help our friends and his soldiers.

"Go," I said. "I've got this."

He raised his sword and charged into the fray.

My husband, my friends, and my allies could handle themselves, so I had to focus on my mission.

Destroy Aello.

The magic of the Unseen whirled around me, coursed through me, filled me with more power than any single being should ever have. But I owned it. The energy of two worlds converged within me.

Aello soared across the parking lot, the battlefield, toward me.

I held my ground, touching the derringer's holster with one hand while raising the sword with the other. My gun held two rounds of endued .357 ammo. Neither the sword nor the bullets would kill her unless I got around her impenetrable wall of dark magics.

The harpy whumped down inches from me, teeth gnashing, snarling like a wild beast. She thrust out her talons to nab me.

Without thinking about it, I raised a shield around my body, one so close-fitting it might as well have become part of my skin.

Aello's talons struck the barrier. Sparks flashed, firing energy down her fingers. She lurched backward half a step and snarled again.

"Give it up, windbag," I said. "You will never get my powers."

"I am owed," she said. "You do not deserve what you have been given, and I am owed this much and more."

Though I couldn't explain how, I sensed her anger was my way around her magic. Bringing the worlds together had weakened her and strengthened me. The vile magics she commanded thrived on the separation between the worlds. The convergence had diluted her power. That's why she couldn't get past my shield. Once, her dark power had been the strongest thing in either realm. Now, it paled next to the power of two worlds that simmered inside me.

Getting her royally pissed off would give me the opening I needed for the final blow.

"You remember," I said, "meeting me way back when, on the day Nevan was forged. I saw how Notus treated you. He liked screwing you, but he never intended to make you his queen. Know what? Nevan married me. I'll be his queen soon. A mere mortal will have the throne you coveted but could never get."

Aello hissed like a freaking snake and jabbed a talon at my shield. It spat energy at her, crackling it down her finger into her arm, the blue magic sparkling all the way.

She snatched her hand away and cradled it to her chest. "You shall never claim any throne. A mortal body cannot contain this much power for long."

"I'm tougher than I look." And she refused to understand, unable to accept the truth. I was not a vessel. The power belonged to me and had become a part of my essential being.

She proved my point with her next words.

"You are mortal, inherently weak in body and mind. Magic is not your destiny. Only gods and elementals have magic infused in the very essence of their being." She raised a talon but kept it clear of my shield, using motions of its razor-sharp tip to emphasize her words. "You were never meant to have this power. The Four Winds selected you at random, or perhaps they released Janus's essence and let it fall where it may. You are a worthless specimen of humanity, a pitiful creature who has no conception of what to do with real power. Your weak body will succumb to the stress of all the magics you have ingested this day, and you will die."

Her statement, meant to unnerve me, had the opposite effect. It empowered me, and words Bob had spoken resurfaced in my mind. *Look to your lineage and you will find the answer to a question you've asked since the day you opened your eyes and your mind to your destiny.*

Understanding zinged through me. Every puzzle piece clicked into position.

Janus and I were connected, not strongly, but enough we could sense things about each other. He had no interest in me as a woman, but from the start he had seemed determined to work with me, even after stating he wanted his powers back. Maybe he hadn't realized the truth at first, but I suspected he'd figured it out long before I had.

The prophecy said it all. *She is the bearer of the key and the staff, the child of the god, she is the Janusite.*

Child of the god. I'd dismissed it as a metaphor, but it was a literal statement. My lineage. I was a direct descendant of the god Janus.

Squaring my shoulders, I looked Aello straight in the eye. "You are the pathetic and weak one. How many kings have you chased and tried to ensorcell into loving you? Even under the influence of magic, Notus didn't want you. He did what you ordered him to do, but he would never make you his queen. Notus betrayed you. I bet Skeiron betrayed you too, didn't he? In fact, I'd bet no king in the whole elemental world would take you for his queen or give you the blood children you wanted. You're a nutjob, Aello. A sad, lonely old creature who can't get what she wants no matter how much power she swallows."

The harpy bared her gritted teeth, her nostrils flaring.

"Know who has the real power?" I asked, then I leaned in a touch. "Me. I am the direct descendant of the god Janus, a being so powerful the other gods destroyed him because they feared what he might do. I am the Janusite because I was born to save both worlds."

Aello's body began to tremble from the rage building inside her. I'd pushed every one of her buttons, and she was about to blow.

Black smoke wisped from her skin and her ears and churned in the spinning colors of her irises. Her body shook harder, her teeth grinding with an audible noise.

I tightened my grip on the sword and got my other hand in position to pull out the derringer if necessary. "This is my destiny, not yours."

Chapter Thirty-Two

THE BLACK SMOKE THICKENED, ROILING AROUND US BOTH, BUT IT COULD not penetrate my shield. Aello screamed like no creature I had ever heard. Even the unearthly bellows of Skeiron couldn't compare to the racket bursting out of the harpy.

I rammed my sword into the weak spot in her magics, guided by my intuition and the certainty of my purpose. The power of two worlds bore down on me, on her, and my blade pierced her magics just below her navel. I turned the blade upright, slicing open the energy that protected her.

The black smoke splintered into a million tiny, knife-like shards that rained down around us both, bouncing off my shield. The darkest magics ever conceived evacuated Aello's body and littered the ground.

I wanted to kill her so badly, but I needed one last thing from her.

Summoning the power of the worlds again, I hurled my body at hers and tackled her to the ground. I had to take care. Even without her dark magics, she had a lot of elemental energy inside her—the energy she'd been born with, the magic that belonged to her, not like the stolen power she'd amassed. She clawed at my shield but couldn't get to my skin.

All around us, the battle raged. Nevan skewered a gnome with his endued sword. The beast toppled to the ground, hitting like a car-size boulder dropped from the sky. The ground shuddered.

I rammed the tip of my sword into the soft underside of Aello's chin. "Where is Janus?"

"You will never find him." She smiled with malevolent arrogance. "You may have stripped away the dark magics, but I retain great power. If I do not return to Janus within the hour, by the mortal clock, your forefather will die."

"Bullshit."

"You may believe what you like, but the truth remains immutable."

Why was I arguing with this witch? I had more power than any being in the history of either world. If I wanted answers from the harpy, I could take them from her mind.

Keeping the sword at her throat, I flattened my other palm on her forehead. Blue energy crackled around us, glowed in my hand, and seeped into her skull. Her eyes bulged. She thrashed beneath me, but I used the strength of my shield to pin her in place.

The answer I'd sought sprang into my mind. *Janus, there you are.*

I pulled my hand away from her forehead and patted her cheek. "You are no longer necessary."

Aello shrieked in another language.

Every gnome jumped into the air and whammed back down onto the ground.

Waves, like giant swells on the sea, upraised the earth and rippled outward, each swell higher than the tallest beings in the vicinity. Fae were launched into the air by the uplift. Sylphs tumbled down the backsides of the swells.

Max and Travis rolled up and over each wave, rolling and rolling until they hit the remnants of the shop building. Three gnomes swarmed around them, their serrated swords at the ready.

Nevan landed on his back with a gnome looming over him.

The gnome raised his giant, barbed club in preparation for a killing blow.

Aello cackled.

I raised my sword, gripping it with both hands, and plunged it into Aello's chest. Blood stained her white robes, spreading outward and soaking through the fabric. She gurgled and choked, spitting blood. I ripped the blade from her chest and slashed it down toward her throat. The sword separated her head from her body.

For a frozen moment, I knelt over the dead harpy and stared into her vacant eyes. I had destroyed her. I felt the essence of Aello oozing out of her body, spiraling up toward the heavens.

A wind whipped around us. It scooped up her essence and carried it away.

The Four Winds had claimed her essence and her powers. They would lock it all away in a vault nothing and no one could breach. After their mistakes with Skeiron and Notus, the Winds would never repeat those oversights. Aello was gone, forever.

A sensation of impending doom crawled over my skin and sank its teeth into my flesh. I had thrown open the gates of both worlds, knocked down the barriers and stripped away the protection of the Great Bargain. One with both realms, I experienced the effects of the change as physical pains that stabbed into my body.

The battle in this parking lot was not the only problem. Elementals throughout the Unseen had detected the fall of the barriers and were pouring across the unprotected entryways into the mortal world, an invading horde of powerful creatures intent on storming over the now-gone boundaries to ravage my world.

A masculine cry made my attention swerve to Nevan.

The gnome had struck out with his club, but Nevan had rolled to the side just in time. With his club embedded in the dirt, the gnome abandoned it and brought out his serrated sword. He stomped his foot.

Nevan bounced off the ground. The second he hit the earth, the gnome slashed his sword downward.

I tore the derringer out of its holster, swung it up, and fired twice.

My first shot slammed into the gnome's back. He jerked, and the sword slipped out of his grasp. The second shot penetrated the back of his skull.

The gnome collapsed.

I teleported myself to Nevan, who had scrambled to his feet again. "Are you okay?"

"Yes." His gaze darted toward the shop building. "Travis and Max appear in need of assistance, though."

"Go help them."

"What will you do?"

I swallowed hard. "I have to bring the barriers back up. Elementals are going crazy with their new freedom. Anyone who's already crossed the boundaries will be destroyed, but I can't do anything about that."

"Only the worst sorts will have stampeded into the mortal world."

That made me feel a little better. I waved for him to move. "Go. Max and Travis need you."

Nevan stayed put, but his focus wavered between me and our friends. He didn't want to leave me alone, but only I could spare this world from untold carnage.

Finally, he zipped to Max and Travis.

I spread my arms wide, tilting my head back, and compelled the boundaries to re-form. They shot up like invisible walls that sprouted from the earth. Every natural body of water in the world regained its boundary protection, limiting every elemental to a one-mile radius of the water feature.

Pains lanced my body as if thousands of knives had been driven into me.

I gasped for breath, stunned by the pain. I was feeling the death of every elemental that had rampaged past the boundaries while they were down. The essences of a multitude of elemental beings were scattered to the Four Winds. I wondered briefly how that would affect the wind-beings, but they had known I would need to drop the boundaries and recreate them. I hoped they were prepared for the deluge of orphaned powers.

They could handle it. Somehow I knew this.

With the barriers up, I needed to reinstate the Great Bargain and close the veil between the worlds. I sealed the portals with a burst of magic. The fabric of both worlds shivered as the rules instituted by the Great Bargain took force once again. From here on, only mortals with a touch of the Unseen in them could cross the veil, and elementals could not travel more than one mile from any water features and the portals they concealed.

I dropped my arms and confronted the battle raging around me.

While I'd been hip-deep in magic, the noises of the battle had receded from my perception. The instant I released the supernatural energies, the melee assaulted my senses.

Max and Travis stood over the bodies of two gnomes.

Nevan was backed up to the remains of the shop building. A gnome had him pinned there with the creature's sword millimeters from his throat. Blood seeped from a wound in Nevan's side. His sword lay on the ground a few feet away.

I tried to zip to him.

A split second before I could teleport, a blade sank into the back of my shoulder. The magic of the endued sword scorched through me even as the jagged blade punched out the front of my shoulder. I cried out. The sword was yanked free of my body, and my legs crumpled. I hit the ground on my rump, slumping sideways onto the ground.

The gnome who had sneaked up behind me towered over me, my blood dripping from his sword. He hoisted the blade up over his head, preparing to plunge it into my chest.

Nevan bellowed.

Gasping for air, unable to get enough, I glanced in Nevan's direction. The grief on his face wrenched my heart and snapped me back to reality.

He zipped to my side and tackled the gnome before the beast could do me in. Nevan wrestled with the creature, struggling to get hold of the sword.

Max and Travis appeared beside me.

"Help him," I croaked, pushing up on one arm.

I sensed the gnome was about to teleport away with Nevan. The creature wanted to get him out of the way so he could return and kill me.

Max and Travis couldn't get there in time.

I flung my body at the wrestling duo.

The three of us blipped to the mile marker on US Highway 41, the edge of the boundary around the falls. A chill rushed through me, raising the hairs on my arms. This was where I had destroyed Skeiron.

My shoulder throbbed and blood ran down my arm and chest, but my wound wasn't fatal. I scrambled to my feet and fired an orb of blue energy at the gnome, since I didn't dare fire off a fatal blast that might catch Nevan too. The orb stunned the gnome enough to let Nevan get the upper hand. He snagged the sword, sprang to his knees, and raised the blade.

The gnome shook off his shock and swung his leg out to the side. He kicked it into Nevan and sent him tumbling sideways across the boundary.

"No!" I screamed.

He screamed too, in abject agony. His entire face contorted into the most horrific expression of pain I'd ever witnessed, worse than when I'd watched Skeiron being destroyed. Nevan's body shuddered with such force his back bowed up off the asphalt and his limbs convulsed. Sparks of white-hot energy tore at his flesh, rending it apart piece by piece, molecule by molecule.

I tried to grab his feet to haul him back across the boundary, but I couldn't get hold of him. The forces ripping him to shreds bit back when I touched him. Despite the protection of being the Janusite, I sensed the violent magics of the boundary would consume me too if I got caught up in them.

And I didn't give a damn.

Dimly, I realized Max and Travis had materialized behind me.

Max grabbed me around the waist and dragged me away from Nevan. I kicked and scratched at him, but he would not let go.

"I have to save him," I shouted. "Let me save him."

"No, Lindsey, it's too late." Max wrapped me in his arms, his cheek against mine. "You cannot stop the process once it's begun. If you try, you will die too. Nevan wouldn't want that."

A curtain of pure white magic enshrouded Nevan. The cloud obscured my view of him, though I knew his body was being deconstructed. Torn asunder. Destroyed.

Sobs racked my body. Tears streamed down my face, and without Max holding me up, I would've fallen into a heap on the ground. At last, I understood the truth. Nothing, not even the power of the Janusite, could stop the destruction process.

The cloud disintegrated.

Nevan was gone.

Chapter Thirty-Three

I SCREAMED SO LOUD MY THROAT BURNED AND CLOSED UP. COUGHING, sobbing, I sagged into Max. He turned me around to hold me, my face buried against his chest. Words I did not want to recall flared in my mind. *Blood for blood, life for life, the scales must be balanced. Sacrifice the past for the sake of the future.* Bob had said that. *What are you willing to sacrifice to heal the time stream?* Miriella had spoken those words. I finally understood she hadn't meant it as a choice, the way I'd taken it at the time. Powers beyond my comprehension had made the decision for me, and at last I realized why.

I had continually chosen Nevan over everything else. Maybe I could've stopped Aello sooner and avoided the chaos brought on by the time stream breaking apart. Instead of focusing on my duty as the Janusite, I had expended too much energy on bringing Nevan back every time Aello screwed with the timeline.

This was the lesson I'd needed to learn.

"It's my fault," I said, my face buried against Max's chest. "Nevan died because I wouldn't do what I was supposed to do, what I was destined to do. I put him before everything else. He died because the universe needed to teach me a lesson."

"No," Max said with fervent certainty. "That's bollocks, Lindsey. As long as I've known you, you have risked your life and the lives of everyone you love in order to protect two worlds. None of us has sacrificed as much as you have."

"Then why is he gone? It has to be my punishment."

Max took my face in his hands and forced me to look at him. "Nevan gave his life to save you. Honor that sacrifice by not blaming yourself for it."

Sacrifice. I was so sick of watching people die because of me.

I blundered backward away from Max. "This isn't over."

Max studied me for a moment until comprehension dawned on his face. "No, Lindsey."

"Yes," I snapped. "Nevan died once today. I will not let it happen again."

"If you go into the time stream again, you might damage it. You are in no condition to manipulate those sorts of magics or to manipulate time itself."

He aimed a pointed glance at my shoulder, where blood trickled from my wound.

But God, he was right. I knew it, and I hated it. Hated him for making me see it. Hated the Four Winds for putting these powers inside me.

"Think about it," Max said. "If you abuse your powers to save Nevan, you will become like Aello. She was willing to do anything to get what she wanted and ripped apart the time stream in the process. You are nothing like her, Lindsey. Don't let grief warp who you are."

My stomach hurt. My chest hurt. Something deep inside me hurt with an ache like nothing I'd ever experienced before. Max was right. If I gave in to this pain and altered the past to spare myself from the grief I had to feel, I would become exactly like Aello. She had done it to fulfill her selfish desires. Was I any different? I would risk fracturing the time stream simply to have Nevan back.

He wouldn't want that. I didn't want that.

I covered my face with my hands, silent tears streaming between my fingers. A numbness crept into me, drying up the tears, and I lowered my hands. "I have to rescue Janus. I know where he is."

"Let me do it," Max said. "You need to rest."

A wet iron blanket seemed to have dropped on top of me, so I couldn't argue with his assessment. I didn't want to go anywhere or do anything.

My gaze fell on the gnome, who lay dead with his own sword rammed through his chest.

"Travis did that," Max said. "I went for you, and he went for the gnome."

"Oh. Good." Nothing seemed anywhere close to good, but I spoke the words without really knowing or caring what I'd said.

"Tell me where Janus is," Max said, "and I will retrieve him. Travis, take Lindsey somewhere else, away from all of this."

I didn't need to speak. I simply willed Max to go to the place where Aello had hidden Janus, which turned out to be a second nest she had built in the Unseen.

Travis took my hand, about to poof us both away.

"Wait," I said. "The battle."

"You don't need to be there. Aello's gone, so is her dark magic. The fae and the sylphs can handle a passel of gnomes."

My jaw tightened. I all but growled, "No one else will die today because of me."

He studied me for a few interminable seconds, his expression unreadable. At last, he sighed and whisked us to the battlefield. The noise assaulted my ears. The metallic clashing of swords. The whumping of clubs and other blunt weapons. The grunts and shouts of warriors from three species of elementals as they attacked each other relentlessly.

"Stop!" I hollered.

Everyone froze.

Literally. I had inadvertently frozen time. Only Travis and I remained unaffected.

"Damn," Travis said in a hushed voice full of awe and a hint of fear. "You did that just by saying the word."

"I stopped time."

"Yeah, I can see that."

"Don't worry, I haven't broken the time stream. Didn't mean to freeze the world, but this'll do."

"What do you mean it'll do?" He sounded baffled, and I couldn't blame him.

"No one else is dying today," I said, gesturing toward the nearest gnome. "Not even the ones trying to kill my friends."

Travis puckered his mouth, his forehead crinkling. "You want to save the gnomes too?"

"Yes. They were ensorcelled by Aello, forced to do her bidding. It's no different from when Brennus was forced into a bad bargain with Skeiron and became his unwilling henchman." I took three steps forward, closer to the battle. "Maybe I can't bring Nevan back, but I can stop anyone else from dying because of what Aello did."

"Do what you need to do. I got your back."

He did, always. Even when he'd been jealous of Nevan, Travis had fought for me and with me, ultimately dying because he'd wanted to protect me from Ceara.

I stretched my arms out in front of me, holding my hands palms out, and released a pulse of blue energy that engulfed the battlefield.

The gnomes vanished.

Done, I lowered my hands.

"Uh," Travis began, "what'd you do with the gnomes?"

"Sent them home. I also removed the leftover effects of Aello's ensorcellment, freeing them to do what they want instead of what a dead harpy bitch wanted."

Bitterness had infected my voice, but I didn't care. I had a right to my anger and pain. After everything that had happened, I'd earned it.

The fae started clapping and cheering, but the sylph army milled around looking confused.

I called out to them, "The battle is over. Go home."

One sylph soldier stepped forward, his attention landing on me. "What of the king?"

"Go home." My throat thickened, and tears stung my eyes. I couldn't explain it to them. Not now. Not like this. Standing on a blood-spattered battlefield with my shoulder wound oozing. "Please, just go."

Maybe something in my voice clued him in, or maybe it was my expression, but the sylph nodded sharply and turned around to wave to his troops. They disappeared.

Travis laid a hand on my good shoulder. "You need a doctor, Lindsey, or at least a healing vortex."

"Not yet."

I marched straight across the parking lot to Tris and Ennea.

They were smiling and laughing, slapping their fellow fae on their backs. When they caught sight of me, Tris and Ennea fell silent, their smiles wilting.

"Did you lose anyone?" I asked.

"Nah," Tris said, "we're all good. The sylphs didn't lose nobody either."

Ennea studied me with concern in her eyes. "What is it, Lindsey? What's happened?"

"She's injured," Tris said.

"It's more than that." Ennea moved closer, searching my face. Tears burgeoned in her eyes. "Oh no, Lindsey. Tell me it's not—"

"Nevan is dead." My voice was dead too, like everything inside me. "Destroyed."

Tris was blinking furiously as if fighting back tears. "Get him to a vortex. I can power it—"

"It's too late for that. A gnome pushed him over the boundary." I sucked in a breath, or tried to, but I couldn't pull in enough oxygen. Every ragged breath only made me feel worse, made my chest tighter, made my eyes burn hotter. "I restored the boundaries. Had to do it. Elementals were flooding through the open portals and straight into the mortal world at large. I had to do it. Nevan…"

"He died protecting her," Travis said. "He died protecting all of us."

Ennea threw her arms around me, hugging me fiercely. "I'm so sorry, Lindsey."

"It ain't fair," Tris said, his voice cracking. "Nev belongs with you. He can't be gone."

Travis pulled me away from Ennea. "I know you guys loved him too, but Lindsey needs some space."

"Of course," Ennea said. She swiped at her eyes and straightened. "Anything you need, hon, you let us know. Anything."

"She needs healing," Tris said, getting hold of himself again, though his eyes glistened with a hint of moisture. "Let's get her to the vortex. I'll grab some copper from the shop." He peered over his shoulder at the roofless building with warped wall panels. "Might take me a minute to dig around and find it."

"Meet ya there," Travis said.

He grasped my good shoulder and rushed me to the vortex. I could've gotten there myself if I'd been able to think. With the battle over, the last of the adrenaline that had fueled me sluiced out of my body. I sank onto one of the stone benches that surrounded the vortex.

Travis loitered an arm's length away like a soldier guarding a queen.

I would've been a queen. If Nevan…

Ennea and Tris materialized. Tris was in the midst of wolfing down two big handfuls of raw float copper. After finishing off the lot, he dusted off his hands.

"Ready," he said.

Travis scowled at him. "Do it already."

As the vortex powered up around me, I sat there slumped on the bench, not moving, not thinking, not feeling. Though the wound healed in a matter of seconds, I barely noticed the tingling sensation of the magical energies washing through me.

Does it spin you? Sandy, a goofy blonde, had asked me that question on the day I'd met Nevan. She had thought the vortex must spin like a whirlpool. But no, it wasn't the vortex that spun. It was Nevan's eyes, those bottomless pools of swirling bronze and silver and gold.

Max and Janus turned up right as the healing energies wound down. By the look on Janus's face, I knew Max had told him about Nevan.

Janus glanced at each of my friends in turn. "May I have a moment alone with Lindsey?"

When Max looked to me for the answer, I said, "It's okay."

"Travis and I will not go far," Max said.

Both incubuses poofed away.

Ennea and Tris lingered until I waved for them to go. Once they had left, Janus sat down on the stone bench across from me. He watched me without speaking, the silence between us stretching on for a minute or more until I spoke.

"I figured it out," I said. "Why we're connected. I'm your direct descendant."

"Yes."

"Why didn't you tell me?"

He rested his elbows on his thighs, head down. "At first, I was not certain you could handle the powers you had received. My powers. After thousands of years in a kind of purgatory, I believed I was owed something." He raised his head to look at me. "I was wrong about you and about these powers. They belong to you now. You have made better use of them than I ever did, accomplished feats I would never have attempted. And you succeeded."

"I failed. Spectacularly."

"No, Lindsey, you did not. Not every battle can be won or should be won." He exhaled a long, weary breath. "You healed the time stream. You saved two worlds. In the final battle, when it counted the most, you sacrificed everything for the greater good."

"Having trouble feeling triumphant about it." Tears trickled down my cheeks. "Not sure any of this was worth it. Since I became the Janusite, I've watched people I cared about suffer and die. Today, I got to witness Calder's forging and Nevan's forging. Not experiences I ever wanted to have. I couldn't save either of them in the end. What was it all for? Why was I the special one chosen to suffer this pain? You must have loads of other descendants who would've done a better job than I have."

"You are wrong." Janus crossed the vortex to kneel in front of me. "You were not chosen at random. No one else could have borne this burden."

"Oh come on. Any of your other descendants could've done it."

He watched me, his mouth crimped and his gaze searching mine. When my skin started to itch from the intensity of his focus on me, Janus finally spoke. "I understand your pain, Lindsey. I loved a mortal once and lost her."

I couldn't speak. Had no clue what to say to that.

"She did not die," he said. "Her name was Vita. I had never loved anyone until her, but she taught me how to care for someone other than myself, showed me that even a god has much to learn about living. The other gods grew jealous of my powers and resented me for refusing to misuse my dominion over time to aid them in their petty quests. Only for Jupiter would I enter the time stream. He was—is still, I presume—a wise and good leader. The others gave in to their baser instincts far too often."

"Can you get to the point, please?"

"Of course." He rested his hands on my knees. "The other gods banded together to destroy me. I did not know it at the time, but Vita was with child. She did not know either until after I was gone. For a virtual eternity, I languished in limbo but endured visions of the woman I loved and our child. Even after she died, having lived a full and happy life, I remained connected to our lineage. To our descendants. In each generation, only one child was born."

"But I have a brother."

"The Four Winds knew the Janusite had arrived when your brother was born. After countless millennia of one child per generation, fate had given us two of you. The Winds waited until you were ready and then they gifted you with my powers."

"Why me? Why not my brother?"

"The prophecy, Lindsey. It states the Janusite will be a female."

I didn't want to be talking about this, didn't want to talk at all, but I had to ask the questions. Maybe by understanding this one thing, I would understand why I'd lost Nevan. "Bob didn't issue the prophecy until a hundred years ago. Why did the Four Winds sit around twiddling their thumbs for all those thousands of years before that?"

"No one twiddled anything. The Winds knew of the prophecy before the oracle became aware of it. They crafted the prophecy for him. You were always destined for this purpose."

"Destiny. Fabulous." I dug my nails into my thighs. "I was fated to lose the only man I've ever loved. What was the point? Making me suffer through all of this so I could watch Nevan die over and over until it stuck."

Janus pried my hands away from my thighs and closed his hands around them. "Why did you remain a virgin for so long?"

"What?" I tried to wrest my hands free, but he held fast. "Even if it was any of your business, you've got a hell of a nerve asking me now."

Tears spilled down my cheeks faster, dribbling between my lips, the saltiness mutating into a sour taste in my mouth.

"Perhaps you are correct," Janus said, "but the answer is important."

When he asks, tell him, Bob had said.

I squeezed my eyes shut, inhaling through my nostrils several times until I felt able to respond. I met Janus's gaze when I said, "Calder asked me that once. I told him I couldn't be with anyone unless it felt right. Even when I decided to sleep with Calder, I knew deep down it didn't feel quite right, but we were engaged. Then he got himself forged, and after I shot him, he disappeared. When I met Nevan—"

Janus held my hands but said nothing, though the sympathy in his eyes nearly broke me. I took several seconds to steady myself with deep breaths.

"When I met Nevan," I continued, "everything with him felt right and easy and…like it was meant to be. I fought it at first because I was afraid he'd turn out to be like Calder, but I gave myself to Nevan after four days. I'd been with Calder for six months. I've thought about it a lot since the day I found out Calder had become a monkey-thing and Nevan had to kill him. I can't deny it anymore. I never wanted anyone else, not really, because I was always meant to be with Nevan. My trip into the past proved that to me."

Janus cleared his throat and fidgeted, though he kept hold of my hands. "I had sensed you traveled into the past and experienced something profound. I was not privy to the details."

"I witnessed Nevan's forging. Turns out the angel he vaguely remembered, the one who took care of him afterward, was me. I saw him again three hundred years later. After that, I asked the Four Winds to make him forget those two times we met in the past. I didn't want Nevan to spend thousands of years pining for me, never knowing when or if we might meet again."

"That was a truly selfless act." Janus let go of my hands and moved to sit beside me on the bench. "Perhaps your story is not over yet."

"Nevan is gone forever. The last page has been written, and the book's been slammed shut."

"Perhaps. Or perhaps not." He rubbed his jaw, his gaze going distant. "I believed my story with Vita was over, but I was wrong. It will never end as long as our descendants walk the earth. We live on through them."

"Better hope my brother has kids, then. I won't be perpetuating the lineage." I stared down at my hands and suffered the disconcerting sensation they weren't mine. "I love Nevan. No one else will ever come close to him. I will never be with another man."

"I have a feeling," Janus said, "love will find you again."

"Are you an oracle all of a sudden?"

"No, I do not have prescient insight. It is my belief, or perhaps my hope for you."

We lapsed into an oddly comfortable silence. I'd known Janus for one day, the longest day of my entire life, but I felt a kinship with him that stemmed from more than having his powers or being his descendant. We had both suffered losses, endured the jealousy of other powerful beings, and survived to fight another day.

I couldn't fight anymore. This had been my last battle.

"Listen," I said. "I want to give you back your powers."

"They belong to you."

"I did what I was destined to do. I'm done." I shimmied around to face him. "This is how it's supposed to end. I finally get that. Besides, the first thing you said when you appeared in that hole in the ground was 'I want my powers back.' It's time I returned them to their rightful owner."

He hunched his shoulders, his lips twisting into an uncomfortable expression. "When I declared I wanted my powers back, I did not know you. I believed no mere mortal could harness my powers properly, and I also believed you were a foolish and frivolous creature. I was wrong about you. No one else, not even I, could have accomplished the feats you have. Not in a thousand years, much less one day."

"But—"

"It is true." Janus turned his face to me, his lips forming a small smile. "I am proud of you, Lindsey Astrid Porter."

"Thanks." It sounded lame, but I couldn't think of anything else to say.

"Do not thank me. I owe you a debt of gratitude I shall never be able to repay." He groaned, rose, and stretched. "I am alive again because you demonstrated that my powers are not tools for evil. They are tools for good. The Four Winds worried the other gods were right about me, but you proved them wrong. Thank you."

"Once you have your powers back, what will you do?"

He canted his head as if thinking hard. "I have no idea."

"You'll figure it out." I levered my body, which seemed to have morphed into solid iron, off the bench and let my shoulders sag. "How do I give you back your powers?"

"We will figure that out later." He touched my arm. "You must go home to your family. You have suffered a grievous loss only time and the support of your loved ones will heal."

Max and Travis showed up then, almost as if they'd been eavesdropping. They wouldn't do that, though. Max had likely sensed I was ready to go.

I said goodbye to Travis and Janus, and Max took me home. To my parents' house. Not to the underground lair I'd shared with Nevan. I couldn't go there yet, maybe never. To save the worlds, I'd sacrificed my past—my life with the only man I had ever loved. Whatever future lay ahead for me, I would deal with the best I could.

Alone.

Chapter Thirty-Four

I TRUDGED THROUGH THE FOOT-DEEP SNOW TOWARD A DESTINATION I knew so well, but in these conditions, I had to consult the GPS on my phone for assistance. Behind me lay the rock garden with its whimsical statuary and the shop, shuttered and vacant for the winter. In the three weeks since I had converged the worlds to stop an apocalypse, two feet of snow had fallen, shrouding the familiar landscape. I made my way down the trail to the falls in slow motion, the snow like a river of mud bogging me down with every step. I should've worn snowshoes, but I'd never been good with those.

The only sound was the crunching of my footsteps and the rushing of my breaths.

Sweat dribbled down my temples. I paused for a rest, shoving the hood of my parka off my head, inhaling the cold air and exhaling it in a cloud of condensation.

Familiar shapes stuck out of the snow.

I pushed toward them and sidestepped the drift that had covered the three stone benches. The vague outlines of the seat-shaped boulders assured me I'd found the right spot. Bending down, I brushed the snow off the nearest bench.

Further down the snow-covered path, the falls rumbled.

A sharp pang stabbed into my chest. The falls. Where I'd met Nevan.

I bit down on my bottom lip and flumped onto the stone bench. How many times had I sat here with Nevan? Before him, I'd refused to believe in the supernatural because I had allowed the taunts of other school kids to humiliate me into giving up the beliefs my family had instilled in me. Nevan showed me the truth, gently, sweetly. He'd coaxed me into believing in more than magic and other realms of reality. He had shown me a kind of love I never imagined could exist, the soul-deep kind that changed a person. And oh, he'd introduced me to sex—making love, that's what it had always been with us. However hot and fevered it might be, sex for us always began with love. Even that first time, when I'd known him for four days. I had fallen for him so fast…

My mind rewound to that night. Despite the bad guys pursuing us, we had taken one night for ourselves, one night ensconced in Nevan's underground lair protected by magical wards. He gave me pleasure, yes, but he gifted me with something far more significant.

Unbreakable, undying love.

Tears filled my eyes, blurring my vision. I sniffled, dug a tissue out of my pocket, and tore off my mittens to blow my nose and dab at my eyes. Nevan. Three weeks without him had been empty, like a yawning cavern of loneliness. Only my voice echoed back to me in the void every time I called out his name in the dark of night, certain I felt him near me.

"What are you doing here?"

I jumped at the sound of Max's voice.

My friend stood five feet in front of me, wearing only black pants. The snow around his feet and calves had already begun to melt from the inhuman heat of his body.

The tissue clutched in my fist, I gazed up at him with bleary eyes. "Hi."

He lifted one brow. "Hi? Lindsey, it's bloody freezing out here. What are you doing?"

Waiting. Praying. Dying a little more every day.

Max spanned the distance between us in two steps, wading through the snow like it was a mud puddle. He knelt in front of me, laying his hands on my knees. "You can't keep doing this. It's the dead of winter, and you could get lost or injured coming out here every day."

I hunched my shoulders. "Have to be here, just in case."

His expression softened into…not pity. Empathy. A deep and sorrowful empathy. Max understood how I felt more than anyone—except for Janus. Both of them had lost their loves a long, long time ago, and I knew the losses pained them to this day.

But the look on Max's face broke me.

A sob wrenched my body. Tears flowed down my cheeks. My eyes burned, and the salty taste of liquid pain seeped into my mouth.

Max perched on the bench's edge beside me, wrapped his arms around me, and held me until the sobs ended. Even then, he kept one arm around me.

I blew my nose, loudly, and swiped my face dry with one mitten. "Sorry."

"Don't be. You've held it all in for weeks, about time you let it out."

My gaze wandered around the snowy clearing. "I have to be here, every day. What if Nevan comes back and—"

A small, hiccuping sob cut off my words.

"Christ, Lindsey." He moved his free hand to clasp both of mine, the heat of him thawing my cold skin. "Your hands are half frozen. Put your mittens on."

I pulled my thick mittens on, but the chill would not relent. Part of it stemmed from the wintry weather. A larger part was borne out of grief.

Max squeezed me gently. "Nevan wouldn't want you to freeze to death out here waiting for him."

"Have to be here in case—"

"No, Lindsey. You need to leave this place. Go back to your family, start living again." He moved to kneel before me, his big hands around my mitten-covered ones. Even through the down-filled layers of my mittens, his radiant skin warmed mine. "You can't stay in this limbo. It's not healthy."

Yeah, I knew that. Everyone kept telling me. Stan let me bunk in the shop only because I'd sworn I wouldn't stay here for too long. We hadn't specified a length of time, though. Stan called me at the shop two or three times a week to encourage me to leave. I couldn't. I broke down in tears every time he, or anyone, suggested it. My parents several times a day. They even threatened to fly up here and drag me home with them.

I could not leave.

Bob checked in on me once or twice a week. The first time, he'd come up with an excuse to stop by, saying he really ought to remove the magical prophylactic he'd given me on the day I married Nevan and lost everything. After that, Bob didn't bother with excuses. Even Janus had checked on me periodically, despite being busy with the duties he'd regained when I returned his powers to him. The Four Winds had helped with the transfer of magics, and now the god was powerless no more. He controlled the portals, the boundaries, everything I'd had dominion over during my tenure as the Janusite.

A god had been destroyed and resurrected.

"Janus came back," I said. "He was destroyed, his essence and his powers scattered to the Four Winds. They brought him back. A frigging sorcerer resurrected Skeiron and Notus and Calder. If they could come back, Nevan might too. Skeiron and Notus were evil. Nevan's good, and he deserves to be saved, they have to see that. If those fucking wind people can't see—"

"Hush, Lindsey."

Tears streamed down my face, hot but swiftly chilled by the air. "He risked everything so many times to save worlds that don't want him. How can they leave him—" I couldn't speak the word. Dead. After all the good he'd done, selflessly and bravely, why did he have to die? "It's not fair."

"I know, I know." Max brushed his fingers over my cheeks, drying my tears. "You can't stop living because Nevan might come back someday. Go home. Let your family help you."

"But it's my fault." I sucked in a ragged breath. "If he'd never met me, he would've been safe. Nevan betrayed his king for me, protected me without a thought for the cost to himself. He fought shapeshifters and kerkopes and sorcerers and harpies for me." I covered my mouth with my hand, squeezing my eyes shut against the threatening sob. "He died *for me*."

Max slung his arms around me and hoisted me to my feet. "I'm taking you home, Lindsey. It's time."

"Not until you let me absolve you of the life debt."

Lips scrunched, he shook his head. "You want to force me into agreeing, using your grief as the tool."

"No. I don't want to have this hanging between us anymore." I bit down on my bottom lip to stop its quivering. Didn't work. "After everything that's happened, the time has come to give up the debt. You need to face up to your past and stop letting it control you. Letting me do this will be a first step."

Max sighed and rubbed his eyes. "All right."

"Janus!" I hollered.

I'd expected the god to poof into view. Instead, he ambled out of the woods dressed in a cream-colored toga, like he'd been hanging around among the trees.

"What were you doing in there?" I asked.

Janus stopped a few feet away and scratched his cheek. "I, ah…"

Max chuckled. "The almighty god has been keeping an eye on you wherever you go."

I studied Janus, sure Max must've been exaggerating. "Is that true?"

Janus crossed his arms over his chest, averted his eyes, and let his arms drop to his sides. "Yes, it's true."

"Why have you been stalking me?"

He squished his lips into a slash and locked his arms over his chest again. "Someone needed to ensure you took no rash actions."

It took a moment for the meaning of his statement to hit me. When it finally sank in, I grinned. "You were worried about me. That's so sweet."

Janus rolled his eyes and glanced at Max. "How do you endure this child's incessant use of humiliating terms?"

"You don't like being called sweet?" Max asked. With a dismissive shrug of one shoulder, he added, "Doesn't bother me at all."

Janus scowled at Max but aimed a neutral look at me. "Why have you summoned me?"

"I need you to pull a bit of the Unseen through to this side of the falls so I can absolve Max's debt to me."

The god flourished one hand the way Nevan had always done when using his magic.

My throat constricted, but I swallowed hard and asked, "Is it done?"

Janus nodded and disappeared.

I turned to my onetime familiar. "I hereby absolve you, Max, of any and all debts and obligations to me."

The magical tether between us snapped. He was free.

"Satisfied?" Max said. "May I take you away from here now?"

"Yes and yes."

He whisked me away.

Boundaries no longer restricted him or Travis, Ennea, and Tris. One of my final acts as Janusite had been to gift them with unfettered access to the mortal world so they could visit me anytime, anywhere or travel anyplace else they wanted. After everything we'd gone through together, I trusted them without reservation. None of my friends would abuse the privilege I'd granted them.

Max and I landed in my parents' living room.

The picture window revealed a vastly different tableau from the one Max had torn me out of in Michigan. Here in Kentucky, the grass was brown and the trees leafless, but no snow had fallen. Sunshine streamed in through every window.

My parents sat on the sofa, Dad's arm around Mom. Ash occupied the recliner kitty-corner to the sofa. All their gazes veered to me and Max.

"Lindsey needs you," Max said, taking one wide step backward.

I couldn't stop it. Sobs erupted out of me, and tears blurred my vision.

"Oh sweetie," Mom said, leaping off the sofa to encompass me in a bear hug. She stroked my hair and murmured soothing sounds.

By the time the worst of it ended and I could see again, Max was gone.

No longer the Janusite, I could never enter the Unseen realm again without the help of an elemental. No longer a wife, I'd become a widow. But this world wouldn't recognize my union with a supernatural being. Most of my friends were elementals. I had become nothing. An unemployed, powerless, thirty-two-year-old human being living with her parents.

Without Nevan...

I dropped my butt onto the coffee table, my shoulders caving in. Tears trickled down my cheeks.

My brother slid forward in his chair, no more than three feet from me. "Don't cry, Zee. Nevan will come back, I know he will."

Oh God, how I prayed my ten-year-old brother was right. But I'd lost my faith in happy endings the day I had watched Nevan disintegrate.

Chapter Thirty-Five

BEFORE I REALIZED IT, FIVE MONTHS HAD GONE BY. I GOT A JOB. AFter brushing up my paralegal skills for a couple months, I landed a position at a small law firm in a nearby town. Though this kind of work had never been my passion, it paid the bills. I could've rented an apartment, but for the time being, I preferred to stay with my family rather than living alone. For the first three months, we did not talk about Nevan or the Unseen or any of the supernatural events we'd all participated in or witnessed. When spring came, I could talk about Nevan without bursting into tears or feeling like I might throw up.

Max visited me often. So did Tris and Ennea, though naturally, Tris had to act like he didn't give a hoot about anything. Whenever someone mentioned Nevan, Tris would get a funny look on his face, and I knew he gave more than a hoot. He missed Nevan. We all did.

No one more than me.

Every night, I dreamed of him. Sometimes we were doing ordinary things like holding hands and talking about the weather. Other times, I dreamed of Nevan making love to me, whispering to me in that ancient language, and I would wake up aroused and crying. Once in a while, I dreamed of the day he had died. Always, I tried to save him. And always, I failed.

Today, on this lovely May afternoon, I reclined on a beach towel with my feet outstretched, held up by my elbows braced on the towel behind me. I gazed at the waterfall in front of me, surrounded by woods. Though this waterfall featured a wide cascade no more than ten feet high, somehow it reminded me of the falls behind the rock shop. Once a week, I visited this place, always in the morning before anyone else bothered to come here. Peace and quiet, that's what I craved.

My family and friends understood this. They let me have this one potentially unhealthy habit because I'd convinced them I was not wallowing in my grief. Admiring this waterfall reminded me of Nevan, but not in a bad way. I felt closer to him here.

"Am I bothering you?"

"No, it's fine." I smiled at Max, who wore a pair of dark-green shorts in deference to the mortal realm's laws about indecent exposure, and patted the ground beside me. "Have a seat."

Yes, Max was the only one allowed to come here with me. I'd thought my parents or Ash might be offended by this, but they didn't mind at all. They understood Max and I had a special bond, a friendship with a deeper meaning. I couldn't explain what Max meant to me, except that I didn't want to think about my life without my second-best friend.

The top spot would always belong to Nevan.

Max settled on the grass beside me. "It's a lovely day."

"Uh-huh." I waved a hand. "Go on and say it."

He bent his knees to rest his arms on them. "Maybe I should stop saying it. You ignore my advice every time."

"Come on. I got a job, I hang out with my friends and family, and I haven't had a sobbing fit in months. What more do you want?"

"Stop coming here."

I shook my head. "Not an option."

He compressed his lips and hissed a breath out his nostrils. "Lindsey, it's not good for you. If you brought your family, it might be different. But you sit here for hours by yourself, daydreaming about your deceased husband. You haven't said it, but I know you're waiting for him to come back."

"Thinking about Nevan is not unhealthy."

"I know you better than that." Max twisted his torso to face me. "I wouldn't be surprised if you're thinking about going back to Michigan. To the rock shop. And the falls."

He really did know me too well. I'd thought about it ever since spring arrived and I realized the snow must've melted back home. Yeah, I supposed it wasn't a good sign that I thought of Mandan County, Michigan, as my home. That wasn't quite right, though. Nevan was my home.

"Speaking of unhealthy habits," I said, "are you still refusing to feed?"

Max turned his face away from me. "That is not the same thing."

"But it is harmful to you, way more than my fascination with waterfalls is to me."

"Your obsession with waterfalls, you mean."

I gave his thigh a light slap. "You will die if you don't have sex very soon."

His skin had developed that same faint pallor I'd noticed months ago when he had refrained from feeding. He must not have long now before he'd get sick again.

The incubus beside me threw me a mockingly suggestive glance. "Are you offering to ease my suffering?"

"Cut it out, Max. I know you are not interested in having sex with me."

He let out a pitiful sigh. "Wish I were. It might be easier."

"Sorry I can't help you." I considered his profile for a moment, then said, "Are you holding out for that special someone?"

He scoffed. "Special someone? You and Nevan might've had a spiritual connection, but an incubus is not meant for that sort of relationship. I consume sexual energy. Only a nutter would want to sign on for an eternity of that."

"I thought the women enjoyed it."

"Yes, but—" He contorted his features in frustration. "Leave it alone, Lindsey. Please."

Being me, I couldn't do that. "I know there's a girl out there for you. When you meet her, suddenly everything will make sense."

He twisted his mouth into an irritated expression. "Bollocks. There is no fated mate for me."

"You said your kind do have them, though."

"It's probably a myth." He scrubbed a hand over his eyes. "Even if it's true, I don't deserve that kind of love."

His eyes widened for a second as if he couldn't believe he'd admitted that to me.

I bumped my shoulder against his. "You deserve love, Max, and you will find it. I believe that with all my heart."

He grumbled.

"Don't be such a grump," I said. "You're a sweetie, and you will find your mate."

"I am not a sweetie."

"Yes you are." I pinched his cheeks. "Face it, Maxie, you are a sweet, sweet salamander."

He rolled his eyes. "I'm beginning to agree with Janus about your incessant need to label us with bloody ridiculous adjectives."

"Come off it," I said, bumping shoulders with him again. "You like it when I call you sweet and adorable. Even Janus has given up grumbling when I call him things like that. You badass elemental males aren't so tough after all."

"That's because you turn us all barking mad. If I develop a sudden urge to take up knitting, it will be a direct result of you telling me I'm sweet so many bloody times."

"I love you too, Max."

He tried not to smile but lost the battle.

"So," I said, "when was the last time you fed? You said the longest you went without sex was six months, and it's been that long this time."

"Bleeding hell, Lindsey." He twisted his mouth into a half scowl, but quickly ironed it out. "Since I know you won't give up asking until I answer, I suppose I have to tell you. Being with Hathor provides a much larger energy boost than any other female could give me. I can last another few months."

I started to speak, but something made me stop. A sensation shimmered inside me, like an inner tingle spiked with electricity. Every hair on my body went stiff. Goosebumps popped up all along my arms.

My gaze swerved past Max to the woods beside the waterfall.

"What is it?" Max asked, squinting in the direction where I stared.

"Not sure…"

A figure ambled out of the trees, a man, his face cloaked in shadows.

I bounded to my feet, kicking Max in the process.

The figure moseyed out of the shadows into the bright sunshine.

My hand flew to my mouth. I couldn't breathe, couldn't move, my pulse thundering in my ears and adrenaline ripping through my veins. My head grew light, my ears rang.

Nevan strolled toward us, his gaze fixed on me, his mouth curving into the most loving and beautiful smile I had ever seen.

"Bugger me," Max exclaimed, leaping to his feet.

I bolted for Nevan and hurled my body at him.

My husband caught me and spun us around and around and around. I threw my head back, laughing like a crazy person. Nevan set me down on my feet, his arms fastened around me, pressing our bodies together.

He swept hair away from my eyes. "Hello, darlin'. Did ye miss me?"

Sobs exploded out of me, this time spurred by pure joy.

He held me until I stopped crying, caressing my hair and murmuring to me. "Shh, love, it's all right. I've told you before, I will always come back to you, whatever the cost, however long it takes. Nothing will keep me from you."

"What took you so long? It's been almost six months."

"The Four Winds had to contend with a deluge of scattered powers. Elementals flooded over the boundaries once they fell. It took this long for them to sort through it all and decide what to do with me."

"I don't care why they sent you back as long as you're back for good."

He tucked an errant lock of hair behind my ear. "I am here for good, forever. The Winds know how much you have sacrificed to save the worlds. They appreciate it, and this is how they express their gratitude."

By sending him back to me.

My eyes blurred with tears, I kissed him with all the passion and devotion and longing I'd stored up inside me during these agonizing months without him. I moaned with the deepest pleasure I'd ever known, spurred by an overwhelming relief and a soul-deep satisfaction. My breasts pushed against his hard chest, but as my mind surfaced from the spell cast by our joy, I noted one important fact.

His skin did not burn with supernatural heat.

I pulled away, backing up a few steps to get the full picture of him. My mouth fell open, but I couldn't make any sounds come out of it. I gaped at him, taking in the totality of the changes.

Nevan's skin had lost its glistening bronze sheen. He sported a tan of the normal, human variety caused by moderate sun exposure. And his eyes…Once molten whirlpools of color, they had become human too, a beautiful shade of deep honey brown. His hair was black as before, and it framed his face in luxurious waves. His build had transformed from supernaturally ripped to a body stacked with muscles that would impress any mortal female but would not arouse suspicion about his origins.

The scent of him had changed too. No more thunderstorms and earth. When I'd been plastered to his new body, he had smelled of sweat and man—mortal man.

My husband had transformed into a human. A really hot human. Even his polo shirt, khaki pants, and brown loafers couldn't dim the smokin' hot appeal of my man.

I held a hand to my chest, absorbing the sight of the new Nevan one more time before I met his gaze. "Am I crazy, or are you human?"

He smiled and laughed softly. "I should've known you would figure it out quickly. My wife is intelligent and perceptive. Yes, I am human." His features tightened, and he watched me with wary eyes. "Do you mind being with a normal, puny mortal?"

Puny? Nevan? Not a chance in hell of that.

I bridged the distance between us, splaying my hands on his chest. "I love *you*, Nevan. Don't care what you look like or if you've lost all your powers. None of that defines you. The man I married is good and strong and smart, with or without supernatural mojo." I ran my hands over his chest, loving the feel of his muscles beneath his shirt. "And for the record, you could never be puny. Even as a lowly human, you are one hot guy."

"But I cannot whisk you anywhere." He looked miserable, like he expected me to dump him because he couldn't teleport anymore. His expression turned even more morose when he added, "Sex with me will not be as it was before. You may be…disappointed."

He worried I wouldn't like having sex with him when he had no powers. Was that adorable or what?

I caught his face in my hands. "It was never your powers that made the sex life-altering. It was love. Maybe you can't float us on a cloud while we do it, but trust me, we will have amazing sex."

"Ye can't know that."

"I can, and I do." I touched my lips to his, letting the contact linger for several seconds. "Was sex with me crummy because I'm not an elemental?"

"Of course not."

"Then I will love being with the new you."

Someone cleared his throat behind me.

I glanced over my shoulder at Max.

He waved toward the woods. "I should go. You two need time alone."

"Okay," I said, "but don't be a stranger."

Max nodded and vanished.

Nevan made a wistful noise. "I used to be able to do that."

"Oh honey," I said, looping my arms around his neck, "you'll get used to being a powerless mortal. It's not so bad, you know. No more worrying about boundaries, no more fighting with the tribunal, no more—"

"I can no longer protect you. What if an elemental attempts to harm you?"

"Nobody knows I used to be the Janusite."

He pulled his head back. "Used to be?"

"Yeah, I gave Janus back his powers. It's a long story that I will tell you later. The point is you should chill out, Nevan. There's a huge upside to you becoming human."

"Which is?"

"It's safe to get me knocked up."

He stared at me, not blinking, for a very long moment.

"You awake?" I said, waving a hand in his face.

"Oh yes, love, I am awake. Perhaps for the first time in my entire existence." He hugged me to his firm body. "You're right, there are significant benefits to becoming human. I can't wait to start a family with you."

"I'm excited about it too." I wound a lock of his hair around my finger. "You were a mortal once before. Do you remember what sex was like back then?"

"Vaguely." He screwed up his face. "The only woman I bedded as a mortal was my wife, Ceara. She disliked me and disliked sex. It was not a pleasurable experience."

Oh right, Ceara. The bitch who'd been resurrected by a sorcerer. She had informed Nevan that having sex with him had been horrible and that she'd wanted to murder him in his sleep, but only if she could've gotten away with it. No wonder he worried about what mortal sex would be like with me.

"You've got a new wife," I said, "one who adores you and can't get enough of your body. It will be different this time around. You're with the right woman now."

"That I am." He slid his hands up my back. "I wish I could whisk you away to your home, but alas, we will have to rely on mortal transportation."

"I have a car, but, um…" I made a sheepish face. "I'm living with my parents at the moment."

He groaned, his head drooping.

Chewing on my lip, I chewed on the problem too.

I raised one finger. "I've got it. There's a motel five miles from here."

Nevan's head sprang up, and his lips curved into the sensual smirk I knew so well. "You, my love, are a genius."

I laughed. "You're just incredibly horny and wouldn't care if I suggested we do it in the grass right here."

"A bed would be preferable. There may be creatures lurking in the grass, and I have no power to save you from them."

"Creatures?" I tried to suppress my laugh, but it snorted out of me anyway. "I assume you mean snakes and bugs."

"Yes." He swept me up in his arms. "Where is your vehicle?"

I pointed to his left. "Follow the trail."

Chapter Thirty-Six

THE MOTEL ROOM FEATURED WORN FURNITURE AND WORN BEDDING, but the proprietors kept it clean and tidy. We didn't care about the furnishings. After so long apart, with Nevan in limbo and me grieving for him, we both would've settled for the backseat of my Malibu—if my still-very-large husband could've fit in the backseat. Since he didn't, I floored the Malibu to get us to the nearest motel as fast as possible, speed limits be damned.

We stood beside the bed facing each other. Nevan had already swept the covers aside, but he'd hesitated after that, which explained why we were gazing into each other's eyes in silence instead of getting it on.

"Are you worrying," I said, "the new you will disappoint me?"

"No," he replied, settling his hands on my hips. "But I may have…ah…forgotten how to do this the mortal way."

"Relax, it's like riding a bike."

"I have never ridden a bicycle. Or driven a car. Or earned a paycheck or—"

I silenced him with one finger on his lips. "Chill out, honey. You'll adjust to the mortal way of life. It'll take time, but you will get used to it. I can teach you all about being human, you know, since I'm kind of an expert on that. Been doing it all my life."

Rather than comforting him, my statement seemed to make him miserable. "I was a sylph for longer than any civilization on earth has existed. My mortal life was a drop of water compared to the vast ocean of my immortal life. Being a sylph is essentially all I've ever known."

"Stop fretting, would you? Everything will work out, trust me." I slipped my arms around his waist, molding my body to his. "And stop thinking of this as an obstacle. You've been given a brand-new chance at life. Don't waste it."

"How do you suggest I begin this new life?"

"By making love with your wife." I stepped back and patted the bed. "Sit down and let me show you how it's done."

He gave me a dubious look. "I am the only man of any species you have ever been with. You know as little as I do about mortal sex."

"Shush." I patted the bed again. "Sit. That's an order."

A smirk tugged at his lips as he obeyed. "My, but you are fetching when you're domineering."

"Thought I was fetching when I'm vexed."

He had told me that not long after we met, when I'd gotten frustrated with his refusal to answer my questions.

Seated on the bed's edge with his feet on the floor, Nevan ran a hand up and down my thigh. "That too, darlin'. Everything about you is fetching and irresistible."

"Keep saying things like that."

He paused in running his hand along my thigh and scraped one fingernail on the denim of my jeans. "I can no longer vanish our clothes."

"Oh, that's a good thing." I moved backward out of his reach. "You're going to like the way I get my clothes off."

Nevan braced his palms on the bed behind his hips, leaning back into them. "Proceed, my sweet mortal morsel."

I pointed a finger at him. "You're a sweet mortal morsel too."

"Are ye planning to disrobe sometime this century? I don't have eternity anymore."

"Disrobing in progress."

I frisked my hands up and down my body, shimmying my hips in a sexy little dance that ensured I had Nevan's full and undivided attention. His gaze tracked the movements of my hands, and when I slipped them beneath my shirt, his tongue flicked out to moisten his lips. A soft growl resonated deep in his throat.

Pulling my hands out from under my shirt, I took hold of the top button and toyed with it. "How bad do you want to see me naked?"

"I'm beginning to feel like an incubus who hasn't fed in a century."

"Mmm, that sounds intriguing." I unhooked the top button, then the one below it, and the one below that. Nevan's hooded gaze snapped to each button in turn as I undid them. When I'd freed the last one and my blouse hung open, revealing my lacy red bra, I glided my fingers along the lapels. "Maybe I should go slower."

He dug his fingers into the bed as a breath blustered out of his nostrils. "If ye go any slower, I'll be forced to tear your clothing to shreds."

I whipped off my shirt and let it flutter down to the worn brown carpeting. "See? I was right. You love watching me undress."

"Ye aren't naked yet," he hissed through clenched teeth. "And I am not accustomed to waiting so bloody long for it."

"Guess I should take pity on you," I said, unhooking the button of my jeans, "considering you're new to the human existence and all."

"Yes, take pity on me. Immediately."

I laughed. "You are so cute when you're sexually frustrated."

Then I took pity on him. I shucked my jeans in two seconds flat, removed my bra in about three seconds, and shed my lacy red panties so fast I stumbled trying to kick them off. Nevan half rose off the bed to catch my hips and steady me, right before he sat back down and dragged me into his hard body, wedged between his thighs.

"Your turn," I purred, resting my hands on his broad, muscular shoulders. "Shall I disrobe you? Or would you rather do it yourself?"

One side of his mouth kicked up in a lopsided smirk. "I am unskilled in disrobing, since I haven't needed to do it in five thousand years. You'd best take care of the task for me, darlin', to make certain it's done right."

I grabbed his polo shirt, yanked it out of his waistband, and tore it off over his head. He lifted his arms to help me out, smiling when I tossed his shirt over my shoulder. I knelt between his legs and undid the button on his pants so fast I almost ripped it off and then jerked the zipper down, revealing a salient and salacious fact.

"You don't have any underwear on," I said, rolling my gaze up to his though my head stayed bowed. "I should've known you'd be a naughty mortal. Unless the Four Winds picked your clothes for you."

"They did, but I suspect they are not aware that most humans wear undergarments."

"Goodie for me."

I pulled his pants down, and he hoisted his hips up to let me haul them down to his ankles. My pulse accelerated the second I glimpsed his erection waving in the air between us. Removing his shoes and finally getting those pants off of him took me longer than my lust could endure, but my hands had started shaking with anticipation. At last, I had him naked.

Sitting back on my heels, I roved my gaze over his entire body. "Wow, you are no less sizzling-hot as a mere mortal. I may need to carry my derringer with me everywhere we go to keep other women from swarming over you."

He chuckled and plowed his hand into my hair, cupping my nape. "What will you do with me now?"

"You asked me that question the first time we got it on. But this time, I know exactly what I want to do with you."

I grasped his shaft in one hand and bent to close my mouth over its head. When I began to stroke and lick him, his eyes drifted shut and his head fell back. Braced with his arms, he let me do whatever I wanted with him. I feasted on him, on the flavor and feel of his cock, and relished his every response. He groaned and rocked his hips into my ministrations. His expression turned pained the longer I worked on him, and his chest heaved with each breath.

He sprang forward to grasp my head, staying my actions. Breathless, he told me, "Best stop. I have a feeling I won't be able to get in the right state again soon enough if you finish this. I need to be inside ye, love. Right away."

I relinquished his shaft. "But you taste so good."

He picked me up and tossed me onto the bed.

My body bounced, my breasts bounced, and I squeaked.

Nevan pounced on me, straddling my body on all fours. He shoved a hand between my thighs, and a delighted sort of surprise lit up his face. "Ready then, are ye?"

"For you, always." I grasped his arms. "Since it's been such a long, long time, let's skip the foreplay and get right to it."

"You know I will do anything for you."

He nudged my legs apart with one of his knees and plunged inside me.

I gasped, gripping his arms so tight my nails must've dug into his skin.

"Ahhh, Lindsey." He threw his head back as if lost in ecstasy. "This is even better than before."

"Get moving, please, before I lose my mind."

He looked down at me, poised on his straight arms. "I want ye to lose yer mind. And feel free to beg as much as ye want."

I wrapped my legs around his hips, loving the fullness of him inside me. "Please, Nevan, please make me come."

He thrust again and again, his eyes rolling back in his head like he'd never felt anything as good as this. I clung to him, lost to the bliss of making love with my husband—my very human husband who drove me wild with need for him. No need for magic. Our bodies meshed to perfection, fitting like they'd been designed for each other. We had been made for each other, for sure.

"Oh yes," I moaned as he quickened the pace, plowing into me so forcefully I bounced with each thrust. "I love you, Nevan, I love you so much."

He dropped his body onto mine, mashing me to the mattress even while his hips pumped faster and harder. I flung my arms around him and sank my teeth into his shoulder, desperate to prolong this moment but needing a release so badly I whimpered.

My body went rigid, and a climax of stunning power ripped through me.

Nevan cried out, his body rigid too as he reached his own release.

I felt him come apart inside me, and I came harder.

He went limp atop me, gasping for breath.

We lay there for a while—how long, I had no idea—enjoying the sweet pleasure generated by our unabashed lust for each other and our unbreakable bond even time could not destroy. Even death could never untie the knot that sealed our love.

Nevan rolled off of my body, lying on his side next to me. "Thank you, Lindsey."

"Thank you? For what, exactly?"

He picked up my hand and kissed the knuckles one by one. "For proving to me life as a mortal will never be less than what I had as an elemental. It is, in fact, much more."

"Sex isn't the only benefit." I flipped onto my side to face him. "No more worries about a dangerous hybrid pregnancy. We can have a baby anytime we want. If you want that."

"Of course I want children with you." He brushed his fingers through my hair. "And I would love to have a baby as soon as possible."

"Glad to hear it." I tickled his chest with my fingertips. "Because we may have just made one."

He sprang up, braced on one elbow, eyes wide. "How?"

I laughed softly. "Sometimes I forget you never lived in the age of safe sex. We didn't use a condom, and I am not on birth control pills. This means there's a chance we made a baby today."

"A chance?" His shocked expression melted into something more suggestive. He closed a hand over my breast. "We should keep trying, to make certain we're successful."

"I'm all for that."

We kept trying for three hours. Sometimes we loved each other tenderly, and sometimes we made the bed thump. By the time we checked out of the motel, the sun was sinking below the horizon and I felt sure we had made that baby we'd both wanted since the day Nevan asked me to marry him.

On the drive to my parents' house, we couldn't stop grinning at each other. Nevan had to remind me to pay attention to the road. I promised to teach him how to drive soon, and he vowed he would never get distracted while behind the wheel.

"We'll see about that," I said, winking at him. "I've got skills in distracting you."

He rested a hand on my thigh, squeezing lightly. "You have skills in everything to do with me."

"Same goes for you." Since we were waiting at a stoplight, I took the opportunity to kiss my husband. "And we have the rest of our lives to explore all the ways to drive each other crazy."

"It may take a lifetime for me to adjust to this world." He frowned. "I must find employment, correct? I have no skills in regard to that."

"Oh, you've got skills. You were king of the sylphs, which means you've got leadership down pat." I kissed his cheek. "We'll find a job that suits you. Don't worry. I have tons of experience in massaging resumes."

"As long as I have you, I believe anything is possible."

"Don't worry," said a male voice from the backseat, "everything will work out."

Nevan and I both jumped, though I yelped and he grunted. We twisted around to aim dual scowls at Bob.

He reclined across the width of the backseat, his feet propped on the armrest behind Nevan's seat and his back against the door behind my seat. The oracle had his hands linked behind his head.

I smacked his knee. "Are you trying to kill us? What if I'd been driving down the road?"

"Your car is not moving. No danger involved." He sighed and scratched his nose. "Do you want to know why I'm here, or should I go away?"

"Why are you here, Bob?"

"To give you a glimpse of your future." He swung his feet off the backseat and sat up to face us. "You've got nine months to sort out your lives."

Nevan squinted at the oracle. "Is that a threat?"

Bob shut his eyes, letting out a long sigh. "No, it's a statement of fact. Sort things out and get ready. Your lives are about to change again."

He glanced at my abdomen, and his lips formed a knowing smile.

Bob vanished.

Nevan harrumphed. "What the bloody hell was that about?"

The oracle never issued a prediction without a good reason. Nine months, he'd said. Nine months to sort out our lives.

"Oh God," I said, one hand on my belly. "I'm pregnant."

Nevan's expression blanked. "What?"

"That's what Bob meant. Right after we got engaged, he told us a way would present itself. You became a mortal, that's the way he meant." I grinned so wide I thought my jaw might dislocate. "You got me knocked up today. We're having a baby in nine months."

Nevan grinned and laughed, pulled me in for a steamy lip-lock, and showered kisses over my face and my neck and my arms. When he got to my hands, he held them to his face. "I have everything I've ever wanted."

"Me too."

"But I must find a means of earning a living."

"You will. We've got nine months to get ready."

The oracle popped in again, his head and shoulders wedged between our seats.

I jumped, again, and smacked his arm. "Quit doing that."

"Sorry, but I forgot your present." He held out a plain brown envelope big enough to hold letter-size sheets. "I conspired with the leprechauns on this. Tris and Ennea needed a little foresight to guide their magics."

Nevan plucked the envelope from Bob's hand. "Magics? Is it safe for my wife?"

"Yes." Bob winked. "And you're welcome."

He disappeared.

My husband stared at the envelope, holding it between his thumb and forefinger. He rotated it left and right while he tilted his head to study the packet.

I snatched it away from him. "You're being overly cautious, and I'm impatient."

With two fingers, I pried open the metal clasp. I tipped the envelope, letting the contents slide out onto my palm. A paperclip secured the sheaf of papers.

"What is it?" Nevan asked, leaning over to peer at the pages.

"Not sure." I removed the paperclip and flipped through the sheets. My jaw slackened. "It looks like they gave you everything a mortal man needs to blend in. Birth certificate, social security card, driver's license, college transcripts, bank accounts, even a magically manufactured life and work history." I angled the papers toward Nevan and pointed at a handwritten note as I read it aloud. "It says, 'Study hard, Nev, you're a new man with a new story.' Tris signed it himself."

"I can read, Lindsey."

"Well, you were born before the age of written language. I've never seen you read, so for all I knew, you didn't."

"That does make a Lindsey kind of sense."

I slipped the papers back inside the envelope and handed it to him. "Get to know the modern mortal version of you. His name is Nevan Liam O'Rourke. And there's a marriage license too, so I am now Lindsey O'Rourke."

"The name suits you."

A thought sprang into my mind like a firework bursting in the sky. "I've got it."

"Do I want to know what?"

I slapped the back of my hand on his chest. "Behave. I figured out what you can do to earn a living. We should buy the shop from Stan."

Nevan eyed me sideways. "How are we to afford it?"

Snatching the envelope from him, I dumped out the contents and found the page listing bank account information. Every hair on my arms and my scalp prickled and stiffened. "Holy shit. Look at the present our elemental friends gave us." I flapped the paper in his face. "They've made us well off but not so wealthy it'll raise eyebrows. We have enough money to buy the shop and a house with plenty leftover to keep us comfortable."

He gingerly took the paper I held. His brows rose. "You are correct."

"Told you."

"Are you certain you want to go back to Mandan County? Many terrible events occurred there."

"It wasn't all bad. Besides, we can make new, better memories." I kissed his cheek. "With our children. I want them to know all about you and me and the magical things we did together. But if you'd rather not buy the shop, that's okay."

Nevan grinned. "Let's do it."

We had the rest of our lives to do anything we wanted. And whatever lay beyond this world, I knew we would always be together. If time itself couldn't separate us, life after death wouldn't either. We would have a full and beautiful life on this earth with our children and grandchildren.

And we would discover the next world together.

If you loved

Visit

AnnaDurand.com

to subscribe to her newsletter
for updates on forthcoming books in this series
&
to receive free gifts for signing up!

ANNA DURAND IS A BESTSELLING, MULTI-AWARD-WINNING AUTHOR OF contemporary and paranormal romance. Her books have earned bestseller status on every major retailer and wonderful reviews from readers around the world. But that's the boring spiel. Here are the really cool things you want to know about Anna!

Born on Lackland Air Force Base in Texas, Anna grew up moving here, there, and everywhere thanks to her dad's job as an instructor pilot. She's lived in Texas (twice), Mississippi, California (twice), Michigan (twice), and Alaska—and now Ohio.

As for her writing, Anna has always made up stories in her head, but she didn't write them down until her teen years. Those first awful books went into the trash can a few years later, though she learned a lot from those stories. Eventually, she would pen her first romance novel, the paranormal romance *Willpower*, and she's never looked back since.

Want even more details about Anna? Get access to her extended bio when you subscribe to her newsletter and download the free bonus ebook, *Hot Scots Confidential*. You'll also get hot deleted scenes, character interviews, fun facts, and more! Plus you'll receive the short story *Tempted by a Kiss* and mutliple bonus chapters in both ebook and audiobook formats.

VISIT ANNADURAND.COM TO SIGN UP.

www.ingramcontent.com/pod-product-compliance
Lightning Source LLC
Chambersburg PA
CBHW060928190726

48286CB00002B/679